DOES YOUR MOTHER KNOW?

DOES YOUR MOTHER KNOW?

Maureen Jennings

A Castle Street Mystery

THE DUNDURN GROUP
TORONTO

Editor: Barry Jowett
Copy-editor: Patricia Kennedy
Design: Jennifer Scott
Printer: Friesens

Library and Archives Canada Cataloguing in Publication

Jennings, Maureen

Does your mother know? / Maureen Jennings.

ISBN-10: 1-55002-639-9
ISBN-13: 978-1-55002-639-9

I. Title.

PS8569.E562D63 2006   C813'.54   C2006-903855-4

2   3   4   5   10   09   08   07

We acknowledge the support of the **Canada Council for the Arts** and the **Ontario Arts Council** for our publishing program. We also acknowledge the financial support of the **Government of Canada** through the **Book Publishing Industry Development Program** and **The Association for the Export of Canadian Books**, and the **Government of Ontario** through the **Ontario Book Publishers Tax Credit program**, and the **Ontario Media Development Corporation**.

Printed and bound in Canada.
Printed on recycled paper.

www.dundurn.com

Dundurn Press
3 Church Street, Suite 500
Toronto, Ontario, Canada
M5E 1M2

Gazelle Book Services Limited
White Cross Mills
High Town, Lancaster, England
LA1 4XS

Dundurn Press
2250 Military Road
Tonawanda, NY
U.S.A. 14150

To Iden, as always

CHAPTER ONE

The Balmoral was an elegant, old-fashioned hotel, and the conference rooms had the high ceilings and deep windows that spoke of a more generous age. I had a good view of the park below, swathes of lush green lawn and full-leaved trees bathed in the spring sunshine. I'd been in Edinburgh all week and the weather had been, as they say, "unsettled." To tell the truth, that rather suited me. You might say I was unsettled too, and dull, cloudy days were easier to take than blue skies and everybody rushing outside to take advantage of the sun. I rather liked being shut up with the other conference attendees, with no choices to make except from the lunch menu. The police shrink had assured me this state of mind would pass soon. I knew the language: post-traumatic stress syndrome. I'd seen other cops go through it, but now it was happening to me and all I felt was weirdly numb and listless. Fortunately, the conference concerning the latest developments in the field of forensic behavioural sciences was interesting. *Just what the doctor ordered, Christine,* although it wasn't Dr. Quealey who'd suggested it, but my new boss, Jim Henderson. *Perfect timing. Get away on our nickel and come back full of valuable information, which we will expect you to share.* All sessions with the shrinks were supposed to be strictly confidential, even if they were mandatory after a death, but the way he'd looked at me I was suspicious that word had got out. I was appalled at the idea that people might be going around pitying me, so I put on my happiest face, expressed my gratitude, and packed my bags.

The sun played coy and vanished behind a cloud. I shifted in the stiff-backed, Regency-style chair and tried to concentrate. My attention was impaired not only by the lack of oxygen and too many deep-fried scampi at lunch, but also by the absence of any sound system. The presenter was a petite woman with a matching voice. She also had a Scottish accent, which meant I couldn't understand a lot of what she said. To my ears, the native Scots sounded as if they had folded their tongues, stuck them to the top of their palates, and were chewing on them. As they also disdained to pronounce final consonants, everything melted together into one long dancing word.

"Fuss, tacka pea sov clinpepper and writ doon t' following tittle."

After momentary bewilderment and an exchange of glances, the group, about thirty of us, mostly male, and as far as I could tell, non-Scots, turned the pages of our notebooks and waited, pens at the ready.

The speaker, who had introduced herself as Sergeant Pamela Rowan, now said (in translation): "I'm going to give you half an hour for this next exercise. Don't rush. It's not a competition. Think about what you write and be as honest as you can be. Here's the subject: What would you say has defined you? By that I mean is it your nationality? Your size? A birth defect? Your position in the family? That sort of thing. In what way has this had an impact on your life? I'm sure you see the point. In our work we want to know what fantasy our rapist is acting out. Is he too short? From a minority culture? An orphan? A single child? This last is very common as you know. All these yobbos play out some private fantasy that's consistent from crime to crime. He makes his victims lie face-down; wear granny knickers; say naughty words; swallow his semen; and so on. I realize this is probably not new to you, but I want to get across to you that, to some extent, we can work backwards as it were. The patterns can give us insight into what kind of life the yobbo had growing up." She grinned. "No, I'm not going to ask you about your particular fantasies, so don't worry. All I want you to do is think about your own life in the way I just said. What has defined you? Why are you police officers, for instance? It can't be the wages. Unless you're from America, that is."

Groans and hisses from some Yankee members of the group.

"For example," she continued. "I meself was the wee gal in a family of five galumphing boys."

There was an appreciative chuckle from the audience. She didn't have to say more than that.

"You laughed because you're thinking, ah, ah, she was a tomboy. True, I was for a while. But early on I realized I wasn't going to win in that arena. All of my brothers could outrun, outshout, outpunch me, and believe me, they did all of the above. The one place we were equal was in the mind, the intellect." She tapped herself on the side of her head. "Here, in here, I was not only as good, I was often better." She put her hands on her hips and raised her voice. "I might not have been able to out-hit my brothers, but I could outwit the fuckers."

The unexpected F-word dropping out of the mouth of this proper-seeming woman incited a roar of laughter. I laughed too. Not that I had brothers as such to compete with, but it was still more difficult for a woman to make headway in the Canadian police force, no matter what was said officially. I understood what Sergeant Rowan meant about the levelling effect of the intellect, and I liked that.

"Now get to work. You have half an hour. No more dilly-dallying."

Somebody behind me coughed, the lung-congested cough of a heavy smoker, there was the scratch of pen on paper. I glanced around. I wasn't the only one dilly-dallying. More than one pair of eyes were focussed out the window. With few exceptions, the men, all of them in the field of crime prevention, had what I'd come to think of as a typical "cop" look. A mask of politeness covered any errant emotions, but couldn't quite hide the perpetual wariness behind the eyes of everybody I'd ever known on the police force. I wore the mask too.

I brought myself back to the assigned task. It was edging a bit too close to the personal for my liking, and I was procrastinating. I

wondered idly what the guy in front of me was writing so earnest-
ly. He was big, with wide shoulders and hips, and he was spilling
over the sides of the chair. I think his name was Phil or Pete. A fellow Canuck, I knew that much. A boy who grows up quickly is
often picked on, unless he discovers he can intimidate if he needs to.
Had Phil/Pete always been forced to prove himself? As for me, I was
slightly above average height, at the moment slightly below normal
weight, attractive enough not to obsess about it, not so pretty that
it became a crutch. How's that for non-revealing information?

The earnestness in the room was infectious. All right, what *did*
define me? First thing, of course, unquestionably, was being the only
child of a single mother. No, to be more precise, being the daughter
of Joan Morris, itinerant hairdresser, part-time short-order cook,
occasional whore.

Whoa. That came out with a little spurt of acid. Joan would
never acknowledge the whore part, of course. But in my book, an
endless parade of boyfriends, many unnamed, who stayed for a
night or two, then departed, occasionally leaving money or booze
on the kitchen table, qualified her for the label.

I stopped writing. I had thought I was long over being angry.
And I was — most of the time. But if you wanted something that
defined me, that was it. The impact that situation had had on my
life made far too long a story to write in half an hour, but I know
it influenced my choice of a career. If your childhood is in perpetual chaos, you can grow up craving order and believing in it. And
according to Dr. Q., my past had affected my judgement in the
case of Ms. Sondra DeLuca. *It's only human, you were tired, over-
worked, and you identified with the child.* I didn't buy that.
Anybody with any sensation in their body would have reacted
when they saw Sunrise, which was the ridiculous name her mother had saddled her with. My childhood had been one long tea in
the royal nursery in comparison to that little being's.

My best friend is Paula Jackson, and her dad is an ex-cop. Old
school. *Sure you meet the scum of the earth in this job. Ignorant
at best. At worst, plain evil. But it isn't your job to judge them. It's
your job to enforce the law, end of story.*

I glanced up and met the eyes of Sergeant Rowan, who smiled at me reassuringly. I must have been scowling. I reassured her back and returned to the exercise. Then, the door at the front of the room opened and a disembodied hand beckoned. Pamela walked over; there was a brief whispered conversation. She accepted a piece of paper and returned to the centre of the room.

"Sorry to interrupt, but can I have your attention for a moment. . . . Would Detective Sergeant Christine Morris please identify herself?"

A jolt of adrenaline shot through my body, a long-conditioned response to such public inquiries.

I raised my hand. "Yes? "

Ms. Rowan came toward me. "A message for you."

I unfolded the paper she handed me. "*Urgent. Please telephone Inspector Harris, Northern Constabulary.*"

Ms. Rowan was waiting, sympathy and curiosity in her eyes.

"Do you know what it's about?" I asked.

"They didna say, except to ask if you would ring as soon as possible. Come back later and I'll give you the handouts."

I nodded thanks, gathered up my things — briefcase, jacket, purse — and eased myself along the row of chairs.

I couldn't stop my pulse from beating faster. An urgent call could mean anything, of course — more fallout from the DeLuca situation, for instance — but I realized my thoughts had zipped straight back to my mother. That track was the oldest and deepest. I expected this message would concern Joan. They always did. What was that question again? What was the thing that defined me and what impact had it had on my life?

CHAPTER TWO

I decided to follow up on the call from the privacy of my room and as I left, I could sense the curious eyes following me. And how familiar was that?

"*Will Christine Morris please come to the office immediately?*" Occasionally this meant my mother wanted me to call her because she'd got locked out, the most frequent reason, or she needed some cash, or she was going on a short trip with her latest boyfriend and could I go stay with Paula, etc. These calls were always of the utmost urgency. Sometimes she showed up at school. She was usually rude, on her way to being drunk, or briefly recovering from being drunk. During my university years the phone calls were less frequent, probably because I'd travelled to the other side of the country, but after I graduated and joined the Toronto police force, she seemed to think she now had an extended family, and I received calls on a regular basis from various police departments. *Did I know my mother was homeless? Drunk and disorderly? Looking for me?* When the latest in the succession of boyfriends absorbed her, I'd have a reprieve until the inevitable happened and she was dumped. Then there would be a deluge of calls, to her "only child and blood." This meant she needed money. And I always sent it, in spite of excellent advice to the contrary from well-meaning friends.

However, over the past few years the contacts had become fewer and fewer, probably because of my undisguised hostility. For the past two years I had had almost nothing to do with her, didn't even know where she was. Then, about a month ago, I received a phone call.

"Can we get together, Chris? There is so much to talk about. I've joined AA. I'm up for a special award."

"Let's see, that's the revolving-door record isn't it?"

There was silence at the other end of the line. "I know I haven't been that reliable in the past. But this time it's really going to work. I've been seeing a wonderful therapist for almost a year now . . . "

"I thought you had no time for shrinks."

"Oh, she's not one of those. She's a psychodrummer . . . "

"Surely that isn't what it sounds like?" A little sigh but exasperation under control.

"Charlene is a student of ancient Native healing rituals. The people of the First Nations understood the primitive power of the drum. Our first sound was a heartbeat."

"And as I understand it, so was the gurgle and swoosh of the intestines. Do you fill bottles and shake them to get that sound?"

That drew blood, and her voice lost its conciliatory tone.

"Why are you always so sarcastic, Chris? I can't do anything right. Mothers are human beings too, you know. If you had children of your own, you'd be more forgiving."

Touché and blood.

Then she said, "Charlene and me are working on a plan of healing. She says I have to exorcise some ghosts. Send me good energy, Chris. I'll call you when things are clearer. I know I have a lot of bridges to repair."

She hung up. Perhaps this latest summons was to mark her celebration of successful engineering.

I slipped the plastic card in the door lock, got the green go-ahead, and entered my room. The message light on the telephone was flashing red. I dropped my briefcase by the bed, took a drink of water from one of the bottles provided by the hotel, then sat down at the table.

The message wasn't from the police department but from Paula, a colleague now, but chiefly friend and soul sister since we were seven years old.

"Chris. I just wanted to tell you there's a Scottish police officer trying to get hold of you. He called the department and they forwarded it to me. I gave him your hotel number, so by now you may have heard from him. If not, expect to. I'm afraid it's Joan again. He wouldn't say what it was about, except that it concerned your mother. I hope it's not too bad. Please call me as soon as you can. It's nine o'clock here and I'll be in the office till six. The Brampton case is still a bitch. Why people who should know better blab nonsense on national television is beyond me. Ugh. Call. Hope the con is going well. Love ya."

I decided to get some concrete information before I called her back, and dialled the number on the piece of paper. The phone was answered immediately. A male voice, deep and impatient, as if the last thing he wanted to do was answer the bloody phone.

"Harris here."

"This is Christine Morris. I have a message to call you."

A pause and the sound of paper being shuffled.

"Name again?"

"Morris. Christine Morris. I received a—"

"Och, ay. Got it here. Miss Morris, I understand you are the daughter of Joan Morris of 202 Penryth Avenue in Toronto, Canada."

I actually hadn't known that was my mother's latest address, but I said, "Yes."

"We are anxious to get in touch with Miss Morris, and I wonder if you know of her current whereabouts?"

That was a surprise. "No, I don't. As far as I know she can be located at the address you have just given. But why, may I ask, do you want to talk to her?" I made a clumsy joke. "Is she in trouble of the criminal nature?"

That remark crashed like a glass on cement. I could practically see the fragments flying.

"I am not at liberty to disclose the circumstances of the case, Ma'am."

Whoa. What case?

"Inspector Harris, I realize we have never met but I am a police officer myself. I've heard the word 'case' before. What are you referring to?"

He cleared his throat. It was hard to tell his age, but he certainly sounded old school. I was already carrying two strikes against me. I was female and a foreigner.

"There has been a car accident. According to witnesses, Miss Morris was the driver of the car, but she left the scene."

I could feel the familiar clenching in the intestinal area. "Where was the accident and how much damage was there?"

"The accident took place on the west side of the island."

"Sorry, Inspector, I don't wish to sound obtuse, but what island are you referring to?"

"Here. The island of Lewis."

I started to ransack my sketchy geography file. "That's in the Hebrides?"

"It is. Sometimes referred to as the Western Isles."

I got the tone but ignored it. "Hold on a minute. You're saying that Joan Morris was in an accident here in Scotland?"

"Yes, it occurred on Friday night but was not discovered until early this morning." I heard a beep on his phone that indicated another call had come in. "Excuse me a moment, Ma'am."

He put me on hold and I waited, drumming my fingers. The telephone table was underneath the window, and I could see out onto Princes Street, where the double-decker buses were plying up and down and normal people went about their normal business.

"Back. Sorry about that, we're awful busy just now." He didn't explain why, but he was obviously in a hurry to get off the phone.

"How did you get my name?"

"The car was hired and she had left a next-of-kin name and phone number on the waiver. I telephoned and was told you could be reached at the hotel."

"So you already know I'm with the Canadian police?"

"Yes, Ma'am, I did know that."

But you weren't going to give me the time of day, were you?

"Was anybody injured in the accident?"

"Yes, as a matter of fact, there was a fatality. The passenger."

"Good Lord! What passenger?"

"The person's name was Sarah MacDonald."

"Who was she?"

There was another beep.

"Just a minute." He put me on hold before I could protest. He was longer this time getting back and my annoyance was mounting. I reached for one of the tourist brochures on the desk to see if there was a map of the Western Isles.

"Sorry, Ma'am. You were saying?"

"I asked who was Sarah MacDonald, the woman who was killed."

"I don't know the point of that question, Ma'am."

"Surely my point is obvious. Was she a hitchhiker? A Canadian?"

"Och no, she is a resident of Lewis, Ma'am. Lived here all her life."

"And she was a passenger in a car that supposedly my mother was driving?"

"No supposed about it, Ma'am. We have witnesses who saw Mrs. MacDonald get into the car and Miss Morris was the driver."

I took a deep breath. "Are you at liberty to give me more details?"

More sound of papers shuffling, or maybe he was just turning the pages of the *Scotsman*.

"It appears that the driver lost control of the vehicle at a sharp curve in the road and the vehicle went over the side. The passenger was thrown out and killed. The drop is quite steep."

"And now Joan Morris has left the scene and you can't find her?"

"That is so, Ma'am. Have you been in contact with her?"

"I didn't even know she was in Scotland. It's bizarre."

"She did no tell you she was taking a trip?"

"No."

"Would she be visiting relatives or friends here?"

"No. She has no family that I know of. "

He didn't say anything, but even over the silence I could tell he didn't believe me. How could anybody not know such basic facts about their own mother? But it was true. Joan had insisted her family was dead, and even though as I grew older I begged her to tell me about her past, she refused. *Let sleeping dogs lie with their own bones.* Joan had a quaint way of turning a saying, but it was clear what she meant and she had never broken down, even when mired deep in the maudlin molasses of booze.

"Well, if she does get in touch with you, Ma'am, please have her call me at the number I gave you. Do you still have it written down?"

"Yes. But Inspector Harris, one question: was there alcohol involved?"

"We will be getting a report from the coroner, but the two women were together in a local hotel and, according to the bar-keepers, they were both drinking substantially."

I wasn't surprised, of course, but even so, a stab of disappointment hit me in the gut. So much for building bridges.

"Right! Did you search the area? Perhaps . . . is it possible she's injured and unconscious somewhere in the vicinity?"

"The car came to rest partway down the hill. Mrs. MacDonald was flung out, which was why she died. She wasna wearing a seat belt. Of course, we've done a search, but so far there is no sign of a body. We have to assume Miss Morris has gone somewhere under her own steam."

"If she does contact me, of course I'll have her call you. And perhaps likewise you will let me know further developments. I'm here at the conference until Monday."

"One of my lads asked about going on that one. I told him there were better ways to spend our money. Higher wages, for instance." The beep came again and I beat him to it.

"You have another call."

He said goodbye and we hung up. So she had finally done it, the ultimate self-destructive act. She'd come close many times before, but this was without a doubt the worst. The least charge that would be brought against her would be vehicular homicide. Add drunk driving and leaving the scene, and she could be facing some serious incarceration time. For a moment I felt like a kid again, not knowing what to do or how this latest escapade was going to affect my life. I went back to the telephone to call Paula, which is what I always did, but the phone rang first, and I picked up the receiver at once.

A woman with an English accent said, "May I speak with Miss Christine Morris, please? It's concerning Mrs. Joan Morris."

CHAPTER THREE

"Speaking," I said to the caller.

"Miss Morris, my name is Emily Waring. I have a bed-and-breakfast establishment here in Portree on the Isle of Skye. One of our guests is Mrs. Joan Morris, who is, I believe, your mother."

She had an arch British way of speaking that sounded artificial to my ears, as if it were lately acquired. But then, what did I know? She could be a duchess who found running a B&B more lucrative than keeping up the manor.

"Yes, Joan Morris is my mother."

"I do hope you won't think my call an impertinence, Miss Morris, but I was rather anxious to speak to her."

"Has she left without paying the bill?"

I was too abrupt.

"Oh my goodness gracious, no. Nothing like that. She has rented the room until next Saturday and has paid in advance. It's just that I had asked her if she would move to the room I have at the front of the house, the Rose room. It's a very nice room but a little smaller. I have guests coming in from America to whom I had promised the Garden room some time ago. I did apprise Mrs. Morris of this fact and she was quite agreeable."

"Yes?" I said, wishing the hell she would get on with it.

"She told me she was going on an excursion and would be back in plenty of time to move her things. However, she has not yet returned. I was frankly becoming a little concerned."

"And you do want the Americans to have the room they asked for?"

Her voice became frosty. "That is only part of my concern, Miss Morris. If one of my guests says she is returning on a certain day and has not done so, I do begin to worry. Your mother is a visitor here. Anything could have happened."

And it has.

"Of course. I appreciate your calling me. How did you get my number, by the way?"

"I always take the precaution of asking for a next-of-kin reference. I telephoned the number in Canada that Mrs. Morris had given me and they directed me to your hotel."

Cindy, our receptionist, was going to be wondering what the hell was happening with all these people trying to reach me.

"Did Mrs. Morris say where she was going on her excursion, by any chance?"

"No, she did not. She said there was a possibility she wouldn't return the same day, but gave no indication it would be longer than that. I assumed she was touring."

"So she didn't take any luggage with her?"

"Well, I noticed she did take an overnight bag, but her large suitcase is here."

"Mrs. Waring, I should tell you that I have heard from the police, and it seems my mother has been involved in a car accident."

I heard her gasp on the other end of the line. "Dearie me. Where did it happen? Is she injured?"

In the stress of the moment, I thought Mrs. Waring's posh accent shifted down a little to Coronation Street.

"The accident occurred on the Isle of Lewis, in the Hebrides. The police don't know if she was injured, because unfortunately she has disappeared. It's possible she is in a state of shock."

A euphemism for running like a scared fox from the consequences of her action.

I swallowed a gulp of the Evian water, although I was starting to wish I could down the famous single malt the Scots loved so much.

"I will have to give the police your address, Mrs. Waring. They might want to come and go through my mother's luggage."

"Gracious me, that's rather excessive isn't it?"

I thought she might as well know now as when the constable showed up. "Apparently, there was a passenger, a local woman. She was thrown from the car and killed. Leaving the scene of an accident when there is a fatality is a criminal offence."

"Oh dear."

"I'm going to give you the telephone number of the inspector in charge of the case. If Mrs. Morris does show up will you call him or persuade her to do so? And I would appreciate it if you would let me know as well."

"Yes, of course. You must be positively ill with worry."

I didn't answer. She gave a deprecatory cough.

"Miss Morris, may I have your permission to move your mother's things out of the Garden room and put them into the Rose room?"

"Of course. And will you give me your telephone number?"

I didn't say, "If my mother is dead I'll have to come and get her luggage," but the statement hovered in the air like a miasma.

I wrote down the number and address she gave me and we hung up.

The management had thoughtfully left several pamphlets on the table for the benefit of the guests. I hadn't felt much like looking at them earlier, but now I quickly sorted through until I found one that said *The Hebrides* on it. Good, there was a map nestled in the middle of all the advertisements. On an angled line north from Edinburgh, I located Skye. The town of Portree where Mrs. Waring had her B&B was on the east coast. Continuing in a northerly direction, I found the string of islands labelled Outer Hebrides. Lewis was the northernmost and largest of those islands and the west side, where the accident had occurred, faced the Atlantic.

Dotted lines indicated you could get from Skye to Lewis by ferry or plane.

I studied the map. Where was Joan going? Why was she driving on a dangerous, unfamiliar road so late at night?"

Then I saw it. The Standing Stones of Callanish. A note said the megaliths rivalled the splendour of Stonehenge and were probably built about five thousand years ago. Although nobody knew for certain, it was likely the stones were erected as lunar or solar calendars.

Well, that went along with psychodrumming and therapies that believed in "energies." Is that where she was going? Would she be doing it at night? I shrugged to myself. All the better to commune with the spirits — both kinds, knowing Joan. It had been at least a month since I had talked to her. She might have been travelling all around Europe for all I knew, getting good energy from all the stone circles she could visit.

However, the puzzling thing at the moment was her passenger. Why was this woman with her? Harris said she was a resident of Lewis. Was she a tour guide, or even another psychodrummer showing Joan the way? Poor woman. I'm sure somebody was grieving.

I dialled Paula's number. I needed to talk to her.

CHAPTER FOUR

"Paula, it's me."

"Chris!! What the hell's happening? Is Joan in trouble again?"

"Deep, deep doo-doo."

I ran through what I'd learned from Inspector Harris.

"Are you going to the scene yourself?" she asked.

"No way. The department paid for this conference, I'm enjoying it, and I don't feel like bending my life out of shape again because of Joan. I'm sure she's going to show up at the nearest bar."

"Will you be able to concentrate?"

"Come on, Paula. You know me. Concentration is my middle name."

"Oops, sorry I asked."

I heard somebody in the background calling Paula's name.

"Coming," she called. "God, Chris, I'm sorry. I've got to go. We have a planning meeting ten minutes ago. Yet another new piece of software they want us to try."

"How's work?"

"Okay, good, busy. Everybody's looking forward to you getting started."

I doubted that, but even her saying so gave me a pinch of homesickness. Paula was the one who'd talked me into applying for the job as a criminal profiler at the OPP centre in Orillia. I did get the position, more correctly called a Behavioural Science Analyst, but I'd been there only a week when Jim suggested I attend the Edinburgh conference. Somebody else had been slated to go but had come down with a pregnancy. I was really the only one who could take her place.

"Say hello to all those eager folks then. Give Big Al a hug. Tell him I'm better."

"Are you?"

"Of course. The Scottish air is bracing. Just what the doctor ordered."

"Chris, don't bullshit me. How're you doing?"

"Better, truly I am. I'm only thinking about Sondra once every hour instead of every two minutes."

"Good. There's been no new news on that front. The press have gone scragging after some other target." Another call in the background. "Shit. I've got to go. Call me immediately with the latest, do you hear?"

We hung up and I went back to gazing out of the window, which I seemed to be doing a lot lately. The famous castle loomed over the city from its black crags, and even from here I could see it was speckled with tourists. I'd done a quick skim of the guidebook on the flight over, and I knew this castle wasn't quite as bloodstained as most. Nevertheless, the sombre grey walls and protective battlements were reminders of a much grimmer past, when life was cheap and destiny was determined by the reigning powers. Usually, I find history keeps our petty pace of daily living in perspective, but this afternoon I wasn't comforted. In spite of my defiant words to Paula, I was a tad preoccupied. Frankly, I didn't really believe Joan was dead. There had been too many times before when she'd vanished from sight only to surface with a new boyfriend in a new town. When I was quite young, these disappearances threw me into hysteria, although then the absence might last only a night or two. Since we had no family to turn to, I was usually left with a neighbour (resentful/judgemental, kind to me/indifferent to me). By the time I was fifteen, I'd become inured to these separations, and I moved in with Paula's family, the Jacksons. It was Joan's turn to have hysterics. She accused Alice Jackson of trying to replace her in my affections. Too late for that. I refused to talk to her or come home, and after weeks of drink-induced maudlin tears, Joan finally gave up and left me in peace. I pretended the Jackson family was my own flesh and blood, and they were generous enough not to make an issue of it.

As if on cue, a shadow had drifted across the sun and the sky was quickly looking overcast, threatening rain. I went back to the telephone and called Inspector Harris, who answered right away.

Something of what I was feeling (righteously pissed off) must have come through in my voice, because he wasn't as supercilious as before. On occasion, it helps to have attitude. I told him about the call from the B&B lady and gave him the address and phone number.

"As a matter of fact, I was about to telephone you meself. We have found a small suitcase and a handbag that must belong to Miss Morris. Her passport is inside, along with her driver's licence and Visa card."

"Was there any money?"

"Forty pounds sterling and some loose change. Some Scottish coins and a Canadian dollar coin."

"A loonie."

"Beg pardon?"

"That's what we call them. From the moment they were minted they've been called loonies. It's from the loon on the reverse side. It's a national bird."

"Ay. Well I should say then, we found one loonie in the change purse and the rest were of Scottish denomination, not called anything other than pees."

I could tell he was trying to make nice.

"We missed both the handbag and the suitcase at first because the boot, as we call it, was quite crushed into the back seat. We had a hard time prising it open."

"I wanted to ask you something, Inspector. You said the road drops off at the crash site. Is it near the sea? Could she have drowned?"

A call came through and beeped him, but this time he ignored it.

"Ay. I'm afraid we canna rule that out. She would have to walk off a wee space, but it isn't totally out of the question. If that's the case, given the tide, it will take a while for a body to be delivered up."

Another beep summoned him. A busy man indeed.

I sighed and made my decision. "Inspector Harris, do you have any objection if I come to see you in person?"

"Och, no. Not at all. You're in the business as it were, and obviously you know your mother better than we do. You might be able to shed some light on where she's got to."

"How do I get there?"

"The fastest way is to fly into Stornoway. Unfortunately, there isna a flight now until tomorrow. But one comes over at four o'clock. They're running planes on Sunday these days, God forbid. Do you want the telephone number for the airport?"

"That's okay. I can look it up. You've got a call waiting."

"I'm afraid we can't bear the cost of your flight, Miss Morris. It will have to be on your shilling, or should I say, your loonie?" The man was positively morphing into a comedian by the minute. "I can arrange to have somebody pick you up at the airport."

"Thanks."

After he hung up I phoned the airport and booked on the only flight that left for the island, four-ten the next afternoon.

I picked up my briefcase and headed out of the door. I refused to totally waste the afternoon, and I wanted to hear what defined some of my colleagues. And hey, I had a good excuse not to have done the exercise myself.

CHAPTER FIVE

At conferences like this, meant for homicide investigators, people tended to hang around with those who did the same kind of work. The two young female front-line officers from Vancouver had glommed onto the Scottish drug-control guys. I had gravitated to an international group of criminal profilers from the States, England, and even Australia. That evening, there were six of us, gathered around a table in the hotel restaurant, exchanging work-related gossip. I loved this scene. Two years ago, I'd passed the big four-O birthday, and although I kept myself in good shape, it was inevitable that I'd attract fewer of the ocular goings-over that guys do no matter how married, liberated, and pro-feminist they think they are. Once in a while, I missed the sexual *frisson*, fearing I was becoming an invisible "older woman." Mostly, though, it was a relief. I was with men all the time, and we were all more relaxed if we didn't have to worry about figuring out the silent language of the sexual dance.

None of this group at the table had been in the same class that day, so I was spared having to give an explanation of my summons.

The restaurant was classy and, in a small balcony at one end of the room, a young woman played the harp. Perhaps the subtle angelic insinuation got to the guys, because after dinner they all decided to go off in search of a livelier scene. I begged off and went back to my room early. There was no flashing red light on the phone to indicate a message, but I checked with the front desk anyway. Nothing, Madam. After that I went to bed.

Fat chance of getting any sleep.

It was insomnia time, my nervous system flooded with adrenaline. At 1 a.m. I got out of bed, put a pillow next to the wall, and lay down on my back, my hips on the pillow, my legs straight up against the wall. A friend, Jayne, who was a Yoga enthusiast, had shown me this position, and it never failed to calm me down. I started to breathe again and all the tension I'd been holding in my gut began to let go. I stayed in that position for about ten minutes, getting up close and personal with the hotel carpet, which smelled like cleaning fluid. Finally, the pose had done its magic. I got back into bed and switched off the light. The street was surprisingly quiet considering we were in the centre of a large city. Maybe the Scots were better behaved than Canadians at night.

Was Joan dead? Like probing a sore tooth, I tried to determine my state of mind on that question, but other than some anxiety, I didn't really feel anything. It had been so long since I'd actually seen her face to face — at least two years — and even before that there were long stretches when I heard nothing from her. But you can't really ever forget you have a mother, nor can you help but grieve when she dies. Or so I've been told.

The next morning, in spite of the late night, I was awake early. As my flight wasn't until the afternoon, I did what I've always done in times of stress: I plunged into my job. The session I'd signed up for was called "Forensic Psycholinguistics: Using Language Analysis for Identifying and Assessing Offenders." It was a subject I was particularly interested in, and after a quick breakfast at the lavish buffet where I sampled home-cooked porridge, I went to the classroom. Looking around, I had the feeling I was as hung-over as some of my pals from the night before, but for different reasons.

The presenter arrived punctually and set up his papers at the podium. He was middle-aged, tall and skinny, and grey-haired. He looked like my idea of an English gentleman: dry as dust in his tweed jacket and plain green tie. He just needed a briar pipe to complete the image.

"Good morning, ladies and gentlemen. I am Clive Nicholls. Please take your seats as quickly as possible because we have a lot of material to cover this morning." His accent was crisply British and sounded much more authentic than that of Mrs. Waring.

A couple of stragglers came into the room and suddenly, Nicholls raised his voice.

"Move your bloody arses in here."

There was a moment of shocked silence, and Nicolls smiled. "I do apologize for those remarks, but I wished to make a point. In moments of stress, people will revert to the language of their childhood, as Eliza Doolittle did when faced with the potential loss of her wager at the horse race." He smiled again reassuringly. "An American might revert to 'Move your ass' or 'Move your butt'; a Canadian might say 'Get a move on, eh.'"

I was getting a bit sick of that joke. Besides, it's a rural expression rather than an urban one.

"George Bernard Shaw brilliantly devised the first psycholinguist in the character of Henry Higgins. 'I can place a woman within a mile of the place of her birth,' he claimed. And we as psycholinguists, by analysing speech patterns, can provide invaluable help to officers in the field when they need to locate the identity of an anonymous caller, for instance, who claims he has placed a bomb in a local filling station, then hangs up. Similarly with victim statements."

He glanced around the room. "We've all no doubt had the difficult experience of questioning a suspect who will look us in the eye and swear to his innocence in such a convincing manner that we doubt ourselves, even though he may have been caught on videotape and his guilt is incontrovertible. Some of these suspects even pass the so-called lie-detector test. As we know, that is a popular and misleading term for the polygraph, which registers only changes in pulse, skin temperature, and so on." Another pause. Like every good performer, Professor Nicholls knew the importance of timing. "A sixteen-year-old virgin male will send the stylus off the edge of the paper if asked 'Have you ever had sex?' He might answer 'No' with absolute honesty, but his embarrassment at the question makes him appear to be lying."

There were chuckles among the members of the audience. Most of us had gone through that little demonstration when we were being shown how the polygraph machine worked. Each of us had been wired up, while the others watched the zigzags moving across the paper.

First we'd been asked basic questions, like name, address, age, and so on. The stylus made normal zigzags on the moving piece of paper. Then the questioner would throw in a question like, "Are you sexually active?" and, without exception, the stylus would do a big jump. Who wants to talk about that in front of your new buddies? For the men, it was, "What if you aren't getting any?" For the women, "What if you're getting too much?" Yes, folks, there is still a double standard. Interestingly, another question that evoked a bit of a zig was "Do you believe in God?" Not as much as the sex question I admit, but still, some people were embarrassed to be asked that.

Nicholls took a sheaf of papers from the podium and started to hand them out.

"I am going to give you a victim statement. It is a real one from a previously solved case. The woman said she was sexually assaulted under the circumstances she describes. I will read it through, then we will go over the things a linguistic analyst looks for: balance before, during, and after the description of the crime; syntax; prepositions, additions, and omissions. Then I will ask you to decide if you think she was telling the truth or not — and why you think that."

We spent the next hour and a half going over the statement. At the end, we were divided fifty-fifty as to whether or not the woman was telling the whole truth. I thought she wasn't, and was gratified to find out I was right. Hey, I had a very good nose for a lie. Even though by now, my eyeballs felt as if they were resting on my cheekbones, I was totally absorbed.

After this session, I took off. I turned down a couple of invitations to go exploring but I didn't go into explanations about where I was going. Too complicated, and to be honest, embarrassing. I wanted to take things a step at a time. We weren't due to meet again until Monday, and I hoped to be back by then, or at least miss only one session.

I grabbed a cab to the airport, the cabbie telling me unasked the entire story of his troubled marriage. I half-thought he'd follow me on board, as he wasn't close to being talked out.

The plane to Stornoway was one of those small-prop kind that you have to walk out to and that tall people can't stand upright in. I had a single seat by the window, which I was glad about, but I was even happier to be told by the cheery voice of the captain that our flight would be only forty-five minutes. I tried to concentrate on the view, but there was nothing to see but clouds until finally the island came into sight. It was flat and resembled a sawed-off stump of tree.

We landed with an alarming sheer, but safely.

Because I had only carry-on luggage, I exited directly into the main lounge of the airport, which was small and brightly modern. It could have been an airport anywhere in the world. A few people were grouped together waiting for the new arrivals. One was a stocky man with a bushy, rust-coloured beard. He was dressed in full regalia: Scots bonnet, glorious tartan kilt, and khaki jacket. When he saw me, he waved and headed towards me. Wrong. He walked straight past me to greet the group of Americans following. I heard him say, "Welcome to Lewis," and I gathered he was a tour guide.

As I stood hesitating for a moment, the outside door opened and a man hurried in. He was fortyish, with salt-and-pepper curly hair, wearing a blue windbreaker and black pants. He was also sporting a colourful shiner and a cut lip, which gave him a distinct tough-guy look. He came over to me.

"Hello, are you Miss Morris?"

"I am. And you must be my welcome welcoming committee."

"Sergeant Gordon Gillies. Sorry I'm late."

"Traffic?"

He laughed. "No, we don't have traffic here. It was a wee demonstration. You'll see when we go out."

"Nasty?"

"No, nothing like that. They're very polite. I just had to chat with them for a minute or two." He reached for my bag, not waiting to see if I was a militant independent. "Here let me carry that. The car's just outside."

He took me by the elbow, an old-fashioned gesture I hadn't even seen for years let alone experienced. It seemed churlish to jerk my arm away, so I walked awkwardly beside him. Outside the airport, the surrounding area was as quiet and barren as an Arizona desert, with scrubby bushes scattered around the fields, and a sizeable parking lot with a few parked cars, the tiny English kind.

The demonstration he'd referred to was happening just across from the airport lobby doors. There were probably twenty or so men and women holding placards, all neatly printed with declarative statements: DON'T FLY SUNDAYS. HONOUR THE SABBATH. THE DEVIL AND MAMMON ARE ONE AND THE SAME.

Even though the group wasn't shouting at us or yelling obscenities, they had situated themselves on each side of the entrance to the parking lot, so that we had to walk the gauntlet to reach the car. I'd encountered many demonstrations and picket lines when I was on the beat, and believe me, the face of violence is ugly and frightening. This wasn't like that at all. They really could have been a welcoming committee. All were smiling cheerily, dipping their placards up and down like fans at a hockey game.

At the closest end of the row stood a young woman dressed in a white blazer and a pink-striped dress. A matching pink-straw hat sat rather too squarely on her straight blond hair. She was so candy-coloured that she made me feel positively dull and mannish. I'd put on my long navy London Fog raincoat for warmth over a brown turtleneck sweater and brown cotton-knit pants. I glanced down, and yes, the woman was wearing white nurse shoes. Her particular placard read: LISTEN TO THE LORD. She stepped into our path, blocking the way, and smiled at me with what I could only call a professional smile. She didn't mean it.

"*Failte*. Welcome. Perhaps we could have a few words with you." Her accent wasn't British, but I couldn't place it.

"Sorry, Miss Pitchers," said Gillies. "We don't have time. The lady has an appointment."

The young woman didn't budge. "She is a visitor here and she needs to be apprised of the situation."

"I'll tell her myself. Now, if you wouldn't mind . . . "

For a moment, I thought the woman wasn't going to step aside, but a young man standing next to her stepped closer and touched her arm. He looked anxious. The other demonstrators watched us quietly.

"We should let them go, Coral-Lyn."

The woman hesitated, and her eyes met mine. Hers were blue and, in spite of the intensity of her words and the broad smile, her expression was cold. "Enjoy your stay with us, Madam." She moved aside, and Gillies led me towards a car at the rear of the lot.

"Who are they?"

"Sabbatarians. Members of the Lord's Day Observance Society. They're against Sunday flights."

"They were very civil about it."

"That's because you're an incomer. There have been some angry exchanges between their group and those who want to bring Lewis into the twenty-first century. Sunday flights only started up last October. This is a conservative island with a deeply rooted history. Most people want to observe the Sabbath by having no commerce going on at all, but there's a lot of pressure to accommodate tourists. We need the income they generate. It's an age-old struggle. Conservation versus innovation."

I wondered about his personal convictions, but by then we were at the car. Besides, I was shy about asking him. It might have been a throwback to the demure female role, but I was aware I didn't want to disturb the rather pleasant feelings I'd had towards him so far.

CHAPTER SIX

Given the romantic-sounding name, I had expected Stornoway to be picturesque in an Old English sort of way — but it wasn't. The houses were in a no-nonsense style with buff-coloured stuccoed facings and no frontage for the pretty gardens the English loved. However, they all looked neat and well-kept; there wasn't a high-rise in sight, nor anything remotely resembling a seedy area.

"Stornoway has been a working harbour for decades," said Gillies. "Less so nowadays, more's the pity. Thank god for the tourists who want to come and cluck sympathetically at all the hardship people endured. It always looks prettier from a distance."

"Was it? Hard I mean?"

"Yes, but it wasn't soul-destroying work like the British working classes had to endure. The Hebrideans fished and worked their crofts, which can be hard physically but is healthy. And people helped each other. There's a stereotype of the Hebrideans as a bunch of religious old-fashioned bigots, but they're not. Conservative? Yes, for the most part. Most of them can trace their ancestors to the beginning of civilization as it is known on the islands. That makes you want to preserve your own traditions." He grinned. "Mind you, they can get very stubborn and argumentative about what those traditions are, which is why we have such a splintered church. But you'll be hard put to find a more welcoming people. So, to go back to your question, yes, life was hard and made worse by the absentee landlords, who sucked the crofters' sweat, like fat leeches."

I didn't correct him, point out that leeches sucked blood. There was an edge to his voice that suggested this was a sensitive issue.

"Were the landlords English?"

"Most of them, but there were some unscrupulous clan chiefs who were just as greedy. Power corrupts. These days the only people who can really afford to own vast tracts of land to play in are rock stars. The good thing is they tend not to be as stuck in the old traditions, because most of them have come from the lower classes themselves. Besides, a lot of the crofters are joining together and buying the land that their families have worked for generations. Community ownership is thriving." He smiled over at me. "Perhaps there is justice in the world after all."

We turned down another street and I saw an unobtrusive sign that read simply, POLICE, hanging outside a plain brick building, with no fuss or grandeur to it. Certainly no controversial and peculiar sculptures graced the outside entrance the way they did at the main police headquarters in Toronto. Police woman with trowel; a child pulling some kind of monolith on a cart. What did that mean? Nobody knew any more, and we ignored the strangeness of these sculptures until some puzzled tourist inquired. "They're symbols, huh?"

The street was devoid of cars and there were few pedestrians. All the stores were closed. It was Sunday observance indeed. We parked in one of the reserved places in the side parking lot, and Gillies directed me through a door and down a narrow hallway. The glassed-in front lobby was manned by a young uniformed officer, who waved a greeting.

Inspector Harris's office was at the end of the hall and the door was closed. Gillies knocked and received an immediate, "Yes?" barked out in an irritated tone of voice.

He opened the door.

"Miss Morris is here, sir."

"Who?"

"Miss Morris. It's her mother who . . . "

He was interrupted by the unseen man.

"Och, ay. Bring her in."

Gillies ushered me into the office. It was a small room dominated by a desk, which was lined up across the end by the window. The inspector was in the chair behind the desk, which meant his back was to the window and his face in shadow. He was holding a telephone receiver to his ear, his hand covering the mouthpiece. He was obviously in mid-call.

"I'll call you back," he said into the phone and hung up. He heaved himself to his feet and reached across the desk.

"Miss Morris, I'm Jock Harris."

We shook hands briefly. He wasn't a bone crusher, which was a relief, but he seemed uncomfortable, as if men and women shaking hands was new to him. He was younger than I had expected, with reddish hair, cropped close to his head, Scottish style. His face was puffy around the eyes and he seemed fatigued.

"Please have a seat. Would you like a cup of tea, or coffee? I warn you, it's from a machine."

"No, thanks. I'm fine."

I took the chair, and Gillies leaned against the wall behind me.

"We haven't had any more news," said Harris. "I've got one of the constables going house to house in the area of the accident, but we've had no joy so far." He rubbed his hand over his face, wearily. "We're a bit short of men at the moment. A couple of days ago we were told one of the Royals wants to come over and play a few rounds of golf in the fresh air of Lewis. Nothing official you understand, but it's a security nightmare for us. Rumour has it he's bringing a companion, a lass, and if that gets out, we'll have every media shark in the world on our doorstep." He paused. "Was your mother pro-royal or anti?"

"I'm not sure. Pro, probably. She did get up in the middle of the night to watch Princess Diana marry Charles."

"Ach. That doesn't count. Bloody fairy tale come true, wasn't it?"

He didn't seem to want me to answer that, which was good because I didn't know what he meant. He dropped back in the chair.

"Gill, will you take Miss Morris to the incident room and show her the suitcase?" He did the face-rubbing gesture again. "Where are you staying?"

Gillies answered for me. "I'm going to book her into Duke's."

"Ha. Make sure they give her the discount on us. Police work."

"Aye. I'll do that."

"I'm sorry I can't spend more time with you Miss Morris but . . . "

I stood up and his voice tailed off. I was hardly out of the door when he was reaching for his telephone.

I followed Gillies out of the room and across the hall to the incident room.

From its appearance, I gathered there weren't many incidents in Stornoway, or at least ones that required much discussion. There was an old-fashioned chalkboard on the wall, but it was wiped clean of any previous notes. About a dozen chairs were lined up in front.

"I have to ask. Which Royal was he referring to?"

"I'm not supposed to say. But this particular young man likes to do things on the spur of the moment. Poor laddie, he must feel planned to death most of the time."

"Good grief, you're not talking about one of the princes are you? The secret is safe with me, I'm just a colonial."

He grinned. "Och, you're the worst."

For a moment, I burned with curiosity, but felt badly about it. Poor laddie, indeed, never to be free from that kind of relentless attention.

A female constable came in carrying a wire basket.

"Thanks, Rosie," said Gillies, and he took it from her and placed it on the front table.

She gave me a quick, curious glance tinged with sympathy and left.

A new-looking, red-leather overnight suitcase and a brown purse were in the basket.

"It's all yours," said Gillies.

I took out the purse. As Harris had said, there wasn't much in it. A passport, a leather credit-card case that contained a Visa card, social security and health cards, and a driver's licence. All the essential documents of contemporary life. I opened the passport. The expiry date was a year from now, which meant the photograph had been taken about four years ago. Joan had the typical stunned expression that passport photos seem to necessitate. Her hair was dyed dark, well-cut as befitted a hairstylist. Her chin was full, her lips on the thin side. She looked older than she was.

I unzipped the suitcase next. "I'll take out each item and put it on the table."

I was taking refuge in the old routines.

"One nightdress, red silk with lace trim at the neck, size medium, label HOLT RENFREW." I spoke out loud. "That's an upscale department store in Toronto. Next item. A matching dressing gown, same label, same size. Two pairs of underwear, white, medium, both new, also silk. A short-sleeved, crew-necked sweater, yellow cashmere, size medium. The label on that is LEONE'S."

I must say I was surprised. Not at the new clothes, I'd bought new undies for my own trip. (Who wants a customs official searching through shabby panties?) What surprised me was the quality of the clothes. Silk and cashmere? Wow. Joan had never been fussy about what she wore. She regularly shopped at places like Second Time Around or Goodwill. She must have come into some money, or maxed out her credit card. Besides, she swore she *liked* synthetics. Easier to care for.

I continued with the rest of the contents.

"A bag of toiletries, blue toothbrush, toothpaste brand Crest, deodorant brand Lady Eve, a tube of Nivea face cream, a package of DuMaurier cigarettes, unopened."

"Is she a smoker?" Gillies asked.

"Supposedly not. She stopped a couple of years ago."

"Was that her brand?"

"Yes."

I turned back to the suitcase. "Last item. A package of Ramses condoms. That's it."

"Do you think it is your mother's suitcase?"

I was sharp with him because I was embarrassed.

"If you mean would she be carrying condoms, why not? She's just turned sixty. Why shouldn't she be sexually active if she wants to be?"

"Sorry. I wasn't being some sexist clod, I was just wondering if these belongings are consistent with her lifestyle."

"The cigarettes and condoms are, the fancy clothes aren't."

I could tell he wanted me to expound on that, but I didn't. Nothing against him, it was far too long and complicated a story to go into at the moment.

I fished inside the inner soft pocket of the case. There was something there. I took out a small photo album. I'd never seen it before, but in the window on the cover was a photograph of me taken at my graduation from the police academy. I had no idea Joan possessed such a thing. I opened the album and started to flip the pages. All were photographs of me from infancy to about my early teens, when she seemed to have stopped documenting my development. Underneath each picture was a note of my age when it was taken. There was a picture of her holding me in her arms when I was six months old. I was truly surprised at how young and pretty she was. And that she looked proud and happy.

I handed the album over to Gillies, who went through it carefully, pausing at this photograph of the two of us.

"You take after your mother."

"Same colouring, but I'm taller."

"An attractive picture if I may say so," he said, indicating the police graduation photo.

"Thank you. Our hats aren't as smart as the Brits', but they're better than they used to be."

He replaced the album in the basket. "Any conclusions?"

"You tell me. I'm far too subjective on the question of my mother's behaviour. As a police officer, what do you think?"

He tapped the suitcase lightly to emphasize his words. "New case, new fancy clothes, prophylactics. I'd think she was planning a lovers' tryst, except you said she didn't know anybody here."

"She never mentioned she did, but you have to understand, she never confided in me nor I in her. I haven't actually seen her in person for two years. We spoke on the phone a month ago, that's all."

"And she never said anything about a trip, or a new boyfriend?"

"Nothing. Hey, maybe she was just hoping. Be prepared for anything. Always take your shopping bag, like the Soviets did when they went out in the morning. You never know when there's going to be a run of carrots in the shops. Mrs. Waring, the B & B lady, said Joan had planned to return the next day."

"It could be just what you said then: being prepared."

He glanced away. I knew what he was thinking. Casual sex is the norm these days, but surely a woman of sixty wasn't going to jump into bed with a stranger. But I thought, why should she change her habits now?

"She's gone to some trouble to show you off. There aren't any other pictures in the album."

I was mystified at that. If you didn't know, you'd think this was a proud mother.

"Would it be possible for me to take a look at the scene of the accident?"

"It would. Of course. We can go now."

"No Royals to attend to?"

"Not at the moment. Let's repack this and I'll put it in the evidence locker."

I did so, and closed up the case.

"Be right back," he said as he left me. I was glad to have a few moments to myself. I knew I'd come across as Miss Calm and Professional, but that's not what I felt inside.

I sat down in one of the chairs and stared at the blank chalkboard. *I have to exorcise some ghosts. A path of healing,* she'd called it. It was true what Gillies had observed. Joan had taken care with the album. People did carry around photographs of their children. Of course they did. I had two or three pictures in my wallet of me and the Jackson family and Paula's youngest, Chelsea — my godchild — but I didn't carry an album like that with careful notations.

I should explain something. Until I was well into my twenties, I had what you might call a father complex. I walked around with yearnings in my chest that were so constant, it was like living with shortness of breath. I got huge crushes on older male teachers and kind neighbours. I adored Paula's father from the get-go. Fortunately, maturity cooled down both that yearning and my curiosity about the past. Joan made it clear she wasn't going to tell me who my father really was. She slipped up on the name a couple of times, when she was plastered. At first he was John, then Paul, but when she called him George, I realized that she'd been inspired by the Beatles, and I stopped asking before going through the trauma of hearing I had a father named Ringo. Finally, I concluded that all of it was lies and she didn't even know who had been the sperm donor. My conception had been the result of some meaningless coupling.

Or had it? To tell the truth, I never totally gave up wondering, watching her for some clue that she might let slip. Who did she want to show me off to? Were the photographs intended for *him*, the man who had fathered me? Not a dead hero, but a live man. If this was the case, given her behaviour so far, it was possible this man lived here and she'd come to meet him.

Looking at that possibility was rather like staring down a well. I couldn't see the bottom but I could hear the bucket being winched up and I had no idea what it was going to contain.

Gillies came back into the room.

"All right?" he asked.

"Let's go," I said.

CHAPTER SEVEN

I was automatically walking to the right side of the car before I realized my error and headed for the left. The Scots followed the perverse English way of driving, and the steering wheel was on that side, passenger seat on the left.

"Allow me," said Gillies and he opened the car door for me. I clambered in rather awkwardly. The car seemed like a toy to me.

"How did you come by your black eye?" I asked him as we drove off.

He laughed. "Playing shinty." Glancing over at me, he grinned again. "It's not what you think. Shinty is one of the island's favourite sports. Sort of a mixture of field hockey and lacrosse. I got caught with my opponent's stick." Gingerly, he touched his cheekbone. "At least I got a penalty shot out of it."

"Did you win the game?"

"No."

He moved out to pass a slow car in front of us, and involuntarily I flinched as we seemed to come too close.

"This driving on the left takes some getting used to."

We were soon out of the town and on a two-lane road that wound across what he told me was Barvas Moor. Houses became few and far between. I put down the window and stuck my face into the rushing air.

"Oh, what is that wonderful tangy smell?"

"I don't know what you're smelling. You never know with visitors. It could be sheep; the sea; the peat."

"Hey, I know sea and I doubt sheep smell this good. This is sort of smoky."

"Then it's the peat. It's still used for fuel by the crofters. It was an old tradition for the villagers to band together to 'bring in the peat' as they called it. You'll see the stacks near the cottages."

"Did you do that?"

He shook his head. "I'm an incomer. I grew up in the big city of Inverness. I married a girl from Stornoway and came to live here twenty odd years ago." He paused a beat. "We've been separated four years now, but I saw no reason to move away. One of my daughters lives down in Barras."

I can read subtext as well as the next bacherlorette. I replied in kind.

"I've never been married myself, and I've never put myself in the way of maternity."

He didn't get the joke, so I assumed he hadn't seen the show, *Mamma Mia.* "I suppose the major relationship in my life these days is with my job."

"I know how that can happen," he said, a little grimly, I thought. "Jock said you were, quote, a 'criminal investigative analyst.'"

"I've only just started that. I was a regular generic detective until recently."

"Thought you'd like a change, did you?"

"Something like that."

Detective Sergeant Morris is completely exonerated of using excessive force in this unfortunate tragedy. "*You killed my sister, you racist pig. I spit on you.*" *And she did, right across my mouth.*

Gillies was saying something.

"Needless to say, we no have any such thing as profilers here in Lewis, we're a mite short on serial killers, but from what I've heard, it's interesting work."

"I'm hoping that. When I was with the violent-crime squad, which is where you have to start, I might be stuck on the same case dragging on for two or even three years. With this work, so I'm told, there's nothing if not variety. Just when you think nobody can come up with any new way to kill themselves or somebody else, they do."

He grimaced. "Nothing like that happens here, thank God. Even with the summer tourist population, Stornoway is a small place. I know most of the people who live here, who's had a brush with the law, who's into drugs, teenagers mostly. We get virtually no violent crimes if you discount the occasional drunken brawl on the docks. Russian sailors usually with too much vodka in them. The perpetrators are usually lying right beside their victims. I don't get much chance to play Sherlock Holmes, and frankly I'm happy to keep it like that."

He didn't say it in any smug way, just matter of fact. The difference between small town and megacity.

"At least you get the satisfaction of seeing a case through to its conclusion. The downside of my job is I won't own a case any more. We're consultants. The local investigators still have to do the leg work, and the detectives aren't obliged to tell us what happened. Most of them do so out of courtesy, but they don't have to."

Neither of us asked why we'd gone into police work in the first place. Officers rarely talked about it seriously. But then neither do brain surgeons. *By the way, Doctor Medley-Brown, why did you decide to make a career of slicing through bone and flesh?* As for gynecologists, I don't want to go there.

As well as what I've already said about chaos and order, which was a private reason, I'd joined the police force because Paula's father was a cop and she wanted to be one too. We went to the academy at the same time. Until a few months ago, I'd had no regrets.

Sunrise DeLuca had been lying in her crib for two days. The room was freezing, because the windows were wide open and it was January. She was emaciated, wearing only a filthy diaper. She was blue with cold and exhaustion and so weak that I didn't know initially if she was alive or not. Her mother, Sondra, with an O, age about nineteen, was a crack addict and part-time prostitute, and had supposedly left her child with the next-door neighbour, another crack addict, who denied he knew anything about this assumed responsibility. They had both been there when I arrived on the scene, and it was he who said I had handled Sondra so roughly that she had a heart attack and died. The coroner said it was the crack that killed her. The DeLuca family, one sister and a demented mother, said I did it because I hated Native people.

I turned my attention to the scenery. The cloud-filled sky seemed vast, and the moor rolled away to gathering hills on my left and slate-grey strips of ocean on my right. The low-growing brush was a sombre taupe colour, with here and there slashes of coal-black soil where the peat had been cut out. Pockets of white wildflowers reminded me of snow patches, but the only flash of colour was the yellow of the wild gorse bushes that were scattered along the edge of the road.

"What happened to all the trees?" I asked Gillies, anxious to get away from my own thoughts. He seemed to enjoy the role of teacher.

"According to legend, an early Viking raider named Magnus Barelegs burned most of them down, and they wouldn't grow again no matter what. Some folks claim the fairies who dwell here underground refused to forgive Magnus. A less romantic interpretation is that the wind is salt-laden and the peat soil too acidic."

"Why was he called 'barelegs'?" I asked. "Were all the others 'trouser shanks'?"

"I don't know. Maybe he was vain about his muscular calves and wanted them to be visible."

"Hence the kilt?"

He just laughed. I had the feeling Gillies was one such possessor of shapely lower legs. He had removed his windbreaker, underneath which he was wearing the official short-sleeved white shirt with shoulder tabs, indicating his rank and number. His forearms could certainly be called muscular. All that knocking around with hockey sticks, I suppose.

Back to the scenery, which was beautiful but nowhere near as wild as I expected. A two-hour-plus drive from the megalopolis of Toronto and you could be having close encounters of the wild kind with bears, wolves, and moose. Not to sound superior, but this island was cultivated from stem to stern. However, I also sensed that I was looking at essentially the same landscape that had been there for hundreds of years. We drove on in silence for a while, and I continued to take in gulps of that fresh sea-tinted air. A sign in the two languages — English and Gaelic — thanked us for driving carefully through their village and we passed a gas station which seemed anachronistic at the edge of these moors. Gillies made a turn to the left. I remembered the map I had looked at.

"Aren't the Callanish Stones in this direction?"

He nodded. "They're further along."

So Joan was going to the monolith.

We continued on, not talking much except for my occasional exclamations about the cute black-faced sheep. I can't help it if sheep rarely appear in my life. Finally I settled back in my seat. Time to address the issue.

"I had only the briefest of conversations with Inspector Harris about the accident. Do you have any theories about what happened?"

"The road can be treacherous at night and it was raining heavily on Friday. It would have been easy to lose control of the car, especially for somebody not used to left-hand drive. As Jock told you, the passenger, Mrs. MacDonald, was thrown out and must have died instantly. There was no sign of blood in the car and nothing we could see in the vicinity, so we don't know if Mrs. Morris was injured or not."

"When was the accident discovered?"

"Not until six-thirty on Saturday morning. The constable from Barvas was on his way to the station when he saw it."

"Has the autopsy report come back yet?"

"Not so far."

"I understand from Harris that it's unlikely she's lying under a rock somewhere unconscious. Or that she's wandered into the sea and drowned."

He glanced over at me. His voice was kind. "I don't believe so. We've done a thorough search. She's no in the hospital here."

"All that's left then, is hiding out. Either with a concussion and possible injury, being tended to by a kindly but unsuspecting bed-and-breakfast landlady, or without — just hiding somewhere."

"That's not as likely as you might think. I told you we're a small island. We sent a constable door-to-door in the nearest villages, and nobody has seen her. There are a few one-family B & Bs round and about, and everybody talks." He adopted a heavy Scots accent. "'And hoo are yir guests, Mrs. MacLeod? I just got shut of an Englishman who would hev tried the patience of a saint. But noo, I have a bonnie lass from Germany. And yes, I will take that fillet for our supper, ye know how famished the incomers are for good fresh fish that hasn't been drinking in pison all its wee life.' Sorry, I didn't mean to be frivolous."

I excused him. "Joan could have got a lift somewhere. She certainly couldn't fly without ID, but maybe she's got to one of the ferries. I told Harris she had previously booked a B&B on Skye."

I was starting to feel as if I were with my old partner, Bill Matteo, chewing over the evidence, throwing out suggestions, worrying at the fabric of the case. It was calming.

"That is not totally impossible, but you may have noticed there aren't that many cars on the road. If one of the locals gave her a ride, by now we'd have heard of it. We did ring both the ferry captains sailing out of Stornoway and Tarbert, but nobody fitting her description was noticed on any of the ferries leaving the island. It's still early in the tourist season, so it's likely she would have been noticed. Besides we're back to the question of money. I can't imagine she was carrying enough loose change in her pockets to pay for a ferry ride. These days it costs an arm and a leg."

We came around a bend in the road and I saw a small herd of sheep with their lambs trotting across the moor parallel to the road. Two black-and-white border collies, tongues hanging out, heads held low in the typical border-collie fashion, were criss-crossing back and forth, keeping the flock moving. A tall man in a floppy tweed hat, matching jacket, and corduroy breeches was walking behind the dogs. He had a shepherd's crook in his hand. I thought I had gone through a time warp.

Suddenly one of the more adventurous or foolish members of the herd broke away and headed across the road, directly in front of the car. It was presumably intent on suicide or believed the grass was greener on the other side. Gillies jammed on the brakes and we skidded to a stop a few feet short of the sheep, which halted in the middle of the road, chewing its cud and regarding us impassively. Immediately, one of the dogs ran over. The sheep, or ram rather, turned, and the dog halted and went into a crouch. Dog and ram stared at each other, and the ram lowered its head and pawed the ground. The collie curled back his lip and showed a glistening set of teeth. The ram was unfazed and pawed again. First warning over, the dog, with one quick rush, jumped at the ram's head, giving it a smart nip on the nose. Then while he still had the advantage of surprise, he ran around and nipped the recalcitrant one in the rear. The ram conceded defeat, baaed loudly, and scampered off to join the rest of the herd, who were grazing indifferently at the side of the road, watched over by the second collie.

The shepherd whistled a signal, and while the dogs circled and got the sheep on the move, the man approached the car and bent into the window.

"*Feashgar mhah*, Gill."

"Good afternoon yourself. Close call that."

"Stupid creature. It's no the first time. He'll get himself killed one of these days."

The man was crouching down so he could see me better. I glimpsed blue eyes, a strong nose in a weather-tanned face.

"Good dog you've got there," I said.

Politely, Gillies indicated me. "Duncan, this is Miss Christine Morris. She's from Canada."

"Is she?" He jerked himself away from the window. "I'd better get a move on." And he strode off whistling to the dogs, who wheeled the sheep away from the road and across the moor.

Gillies put the car in gear and started off again.

"What's he got against Canada?" I asked.

"How do you mean?"

"He acted like you hit him with a shinty stick when you said where I was from."

"He did, didn't he? Don't take it personally, he must have been in a hurry."

"Who is he?"

"He's a local, an old-time crofter, grows some crops, raises a few sheep. Mostly gets himself a tidy living running his dogs for the tourists. In the high season, he'll do as many as three demonstrations a day."

"Border collies are supposed to be the most intelligent of the breeds."

"I suppose they are if you consider living only to work as a sign of intelligence, which is debatable . . . as we've said."

"Do you have a dog yourself?"

"No. I'd love one, but I'm at work all day and there's nobody else who could take care of him."

There it was, the last bit of information in his dossier.

Not that, given the circumstances, anything could come of it, but I was just the tiniest bit wistful. Paula accused me of being too independent and said I scared off prospective suitors. She was probably right, and it had been almost five years since my last lover had departed with hurt feelings, on his side more than mine, I have to admit. Secretly I found take-charge men attractive, as long as they weren't arrogant or patronizing. I think the sergeant's behaviour at the airport had got to me.

There was a beeping from the vicinity of Gillies's back pocket, and he fished out a cell phone and put it to his ear.

"Sergeant Gillies here."

I couldn't hear anything of the other side of the conversation, but he frowned and made a couple of hmm, hmm noises. I caught the involuntary glance over at me.

"Right. I'll go there at once." He disconnected.

"News?" I asked.

"Aye. We've had a call-in about a man over on the west shore. A local. His body was discovered in his house this morning. Cause of death at the moment is not known, but he's been dead for a couple of days it seems . . . " He paused, and I could see he was trying to find the right words, words that wouldn't be too alarming. "According to the report I just received, neighbours told the constable that they saw a hired car leaving the premises late Friday night."

"A car that fits the description of the one my mother was driving, I presume?"

"Yes. A red Vauxhall."

Before he could continue, he had to squeeze over to the left, just avoiding a head-on collision with a truck coming towards us. As the vehicle whipped past, I saw three black-and-white border collies, swaying like surfers, standing in the open back.

Gillies said something in Gaelic that didn't need translation and I waited for a moment for my adrenaline rush to subside.

"So we are to assume Joan was visiting a man, now dead, just before she was involved in a car accident and a fatality."

"Apparently so."

Oh great!

CHAPTER EIGHT

"**I** should go and check out what's happened. Do you feel all right about coming along?" Gillies asked me.

"Of course."

We were now driving by a cluster of small houses, most of them grey or dun-coloured, the colour of the moor. Here and there were what I assumed were the peat stacks, looking like large plops of dinosaur dung. A woman was pushing a stroller along the side of the road and waved to us as we passed. Gillies waved back.

"The constable from the village is at the house. He knew about the MacDonald accident, which is why he called in to headquarters when the neighbours spoke to him. The dead man's name is Tormod MacAulay. I've met him a few times myself. An older bloke. Good chap. I'd heard he was in poor health."

"Good," I said, knowing he'd understand what I meant.

"I'll still make a stop at the accident site. It's on the way."

The terrain was changing again, and rock-strewn low hills rose up to the left. The road snaked. On the right, fields, more rock than grass, swept down to the sea, which had turned slate grey. The sun had vanished and rain was spattering the windshield.

Gillies turned a bend, then slowed and pulled off the road onto the shoulder.

"There's the spot."

He pointed across from us, but I could see no signs of what had happened. A guardrail that followed the crest of the road was intact. Gillies reached into the back seat for his windbreaker and we both got out and crossed to the other side. The wind was blustery and I clutched the collar of my raincoat, bowing my head against the chill of the rain. I fancied the rock spirits were trying to drive me away like nesting birds dive-bombing approaching predators. There was a narrow verge at the edge of the road, and one step beyond that the hill fell off into a steep incline. Grey lichen-encrusted rocks broke through the ground, as sharp and vicious as the snouts of sharks. A small car crashing onto those rocks would have been shredded. The sea was about a quarter of a mile away and, in direct line from the site, was an inlet, the waves foaming white at the feet of the cliffs. It seemed too far away for anyone to have accidentally just fallen into it, but I did wonder if Joan — or rather, Joan's body — was drifting somewhere in that frigid water. I glanced around. Shards of glass were scattered among the rocks, but other than that there was little indication there had been an accident. The few low-growing bushes were sculpted by the constant winds into frozen motion. It was hard to tell if they had been flattened or not.

"Seen enough?"

The tip of Gillies's nose had turned red, and he had his hands thrust deep into his pockets.

"Yes, thanks. Let's get back into the car."

Once in, he turned on the heater.

"You can see how sharp a curve that is. She mustn't have been able to control the turn."

"I suppose there's no doubt about which direction she was coming from?"

"None. The angle of the car was conclusive. She was coming from the south."

He pulled back onto the road. I checked my watch, a deeply ingrained habit from being in the front line when it might be essential to pinpoint the time of an incident. Less than six minutes later, we were passing habitation again. Five minutes more and we turned right onto a narrow, unpaved road.

"The house is just along here," said Gillies. "Mr. and Mrs. MacLean live on that side." He waved acknowledgement to some invisible people. The front lace curtain twitched, but I didn't see them.

One hundred metres and the road dipped suddenly, then swerved sharply left, ending at a fence and wooden farm gate, which was open. The house stood alone in a rough, grassy field. A long, rutted driveway ran down to the front door, then made a loop in front. In the island formed by the loop was a flower garden, the pinks and yellows of the flowers a splash of colour in the sombre landscape. Directly in front of the house were two vehicles: a burgundy mini and behind it a marked white-and-blue police car.

"We might as well park here and walk down," said Gillies. "The ambulance hasn't arrived yet."

The house was typical of what I'd seen so far of island houses: small and compact, with sand-coloured stucco walls and a grey slate roof. The trim on two second-floor windows was painted a dull brown. As we approached, a uniformed officer stepped out of the side porch.

"Hello, Fraser," said Gillies.

"Afternoon, sir," said the constable, a young, thin-faced fellow — new to the force, I thought, from his "I've-seen-something-nasty" expression. He hardly glanced at me, but pointed to the inside of the house.

"I sent for Dr. MacBeth. He's upstairs. Mr. MacAulay's grandson and his fiancée are out in the rear garden. So is Lisa MacKenzie. She found the body about an hour ago. She worked for Mr. MacAulay."

"How is she doing?"

"She's bearing up considering, but young Andy is what I'd call very distressed."

The constable was another tongue chewer, and I could hardly understand him.

Gillies ushered me in ahead of him with a gallantry that was obviously second nature, but in this case I could have done without it. The stench from the decaying corpse was powerful. The windows were wide open, but the fresh air didn't stand a chance against the stink of a dead body.

CHAPTER NINE

The living room was drab, with too much dark wood trim and muted colour. A couch and matching armchair, upholstered in tartan, were grouped in front of the fireplace. The first impression was that the style hadn't changed since the early 1950s, although French doors had been created at the far end of the room and I could see through to a walled-in patio area. To my surprise, sitting there on an iron bench were the same couple we had recently encountered at the protest at the airport. Her candy-cane appearance was unmistakable. The man had his back to me. He was bent over, holding his head in his hands, and she was in close, her arm around his shoulders. Even from where I was, the sound of his noisy sobs was audible. They were protected by a striped awning, but a second woman, dressed in a yellow raincoat, was standing a few feet away at the stone wall of the patio. She was unmoving, seemingly oblivious to the drizzle, staring out towards the inlet. Her spiky brown hair was dyed a brilliant burgundy at the tips, and I guessed she'd have numerous piercings.

Constable Fraser had followed us over the threshold.

"You said Lisa MacKenzie was the one who found the body?" Gillies asked.

"Aye, sir. She has a key, and when she let herself in this morning, she discovered Mr. MacAulay in the upstairs bedroom. She telephoned Dr. MacBeth and he told her to call us, which she did."

"She didn't call the police first?" I added my two cents' worth. "I'd think that would be the first reaction for anybody finding a dead body."

Fraser was surprised. "Perhaps in America it is, but here most people know each other and what's going on. She knew Mr. MacAulay was Dr. MacBeth's patient."

This wasn't the time to explain that, even though we share the same northern part of the continent and, to the Scottish ear, sound completely alike, Canada and the United States are two distinct countries.

"When did the other two get here?" asked Gillies. "They were doing a protest at the airport not too long ago."

"They've been here about half an hour." The young constable swallowed hard. "I had to tell Andy his grandfather was dead. He's been crying ever since." He glanced at me. "His fiancée is from America."

"Does he live here?" I asked. "In the house, I mean."

"No, Ma'am. But he visits his granddad on a regular basis."

"We'll talk to them later. Don't let them leave just yet." Gillies looked at me. "Let's go and hear what the doctor has to say, shall we?"

He led the way up the stairs.

Like the first floor, the upper floor was dull in hue, and the landing was narrow and dark. A man, Dr. MacBeth, I assumed, emerged from the first room on the right. The force of his person-ality and appearance was like being hit by a gust of wind. I could almost feel my hair being blown back. The man was big. Not just tall, big. The impression of size was reinforced by the baggy tweed suit, full knickerbockers, and knee-high boots he was wearing. His grizzled mop of grey hair sprang off his head, and a full red beard jutted from his chin to mid-chest. He was sort of "Albert Schweitzer meets the Highlander."

"Ah, Sergeant. Took you long enough."

"Sorry, sir."

I could have sworn that even Gillies was intimidated, or maybe he'd learned how to deal with the doctor.

"Who's this?" asked MacBeth fixing on me.

"Detective Sergeant Christine Morris. She's from Canada. She's been attending a conference."

Fortunately, Dr. MacBeth accepted this scant explanation, but I had the impression that, if he chose to, we could have stood for a long time while he questioned me. He flapped his hand.

"He's in here."

He turned around and went back into the room. Gillies followed and this time didn't step aside to let me in first.

The room was tiny, and a double bed took up most of the space, leaving just enough room for a side table, a wardrobe, and an old-fashioned desk underneath the window.

Mr. MacAulay was lying on his back on the bed, his arms straight by his side. A yellow chequered coverlet was across his legs, and his position might have suggested a peaceful death, except that near his head, on his left, a towel was heavily stained with blood, as was his white T-shirt and blue terry-cloth dressing gown. It was hard to tell from what orifice the blood had flowed, because his skin was by now badly discoloured.

"What was the cause of death, Doctor?" Gillies asked.

"I'm attributing it to a pulmonary hemorrhage. Tormod had been suffering from advanced liver disease for a wee while now." For my benefit, although he didn't look at me, he added, "One of the side effects is that the veins of the esophagus swell and burst."

Gillies tuned right in. "Would death have been immediate? There was no call to emergency that we've recorded."

"I kenna say for certain, seeing as I wasna here, but the likelihood is that it was not a fast death. But he could quite possibly have been asleep when the hemorrhage started."

I interjected, probably foolishly. "But he would have woken up choking, wouldn't he? Was there any indication he tried to get to the telephone?"

MacBeth scowled. "The Lord was overseeing him, lassie, not me, so I don't know. Moreover the telephone set is downstairs, which he knew."

I was getting irked in my turn with Dr. MacBeth brandishing his claymore in my direction. And maybe in Scottish "lassie" was a common way to talk to women. To my ear, however, it sounded exactly like "little girl."

"So, he doesn't seem to have made the attempt and died on the bed as you found him."

"Precisely so."

I wasn't going to argue with the man but that made no sense to me. For one thing, the bed was close to the far wall and to get to the door, and presumably either to the bathroom or to the telephone, MacAulay would have been turning to the other side — to his right, which was not where the towel was or the spatter of blood on the sheet. When I was on the beat, I'd been called to an apartment where a woman had died in suspicious circumstances. It turned out she had choked to death on her own vomit after a three-day binge of Johnny Walker's cheapest. She was lying half off the couch, where she'd passed out, her head touching the ground, because the instinct to bend over and get rid of whatever was choking up the airwaves was a powerful one. Surely, Tormod MacAulay would have struggled against the red tide of blood surging up from his lungs to drown him.

"Was there blood anywhere else? The bathroom for instance?"

Dr. MacBeth stared at me. "I didna look. This isna Chicago, lass. It's no a gangland shooting. This man was a patient of mine and he died from natural causes."

He was being so preposterous, I didn't have much recourse. I was a visitor after all, and getting all huffy and challenging the man wasn't going to get me very far.

"When did you last see him, Doctor?" Gillies got in smoothly.

"About a month ago."

"What was the state of his health then?"

MacBeth wasn't budging an inch. "Bad. The only thing that was going to save him was a new liver, and you know how unlikely that was."

I couldn't tell if the doctor was so prehistoric he'd never heard of transplants or if he was referring to MacAulay's eligibility.

Gillies continued, which made things easier. "I take it there was no sign of trauma, Sir?"

"None."

"Will there be an autopsy?" I butted in.

Another scowl from the doctor. "There is no need to waste good taxpayers' money when the death is not unexpected."

"But it was sudden, wasn't it?"

I assumed the Scottish criminal code was the same as the Canadian, in which any unexpected or sudden death must be reported to the coroner.

I could see on his face that MacBeth was having a little war within. He couldn't bear to concede my point, but he was still a physician.

"I suppose you could say that. Although, I repeat, given his condition, this was always a possibility." He turned back to Gillies, dismissing me. "I'll sign the death certificate when I go downstairs. And unless the immediate family requests it, his mortal remains will be undisturbed and he will be buried intact."

So there, foreign lassie.

"Have the ambulance bring him to the morgue. Andy will be making funeral arrangements."

Again Gillies did something utterly wonderful.

"While I have you, Sir, I wonder if I might ask you a question on another matter. You just finished the post mortem on the accident victim, Mrs. Sarah MacDonald, didn't you?"

"Aye. All done with."

"I haven't had an opportunity to read your report yet. What were your conclusions?"

MacBeth snorted derisively. "What do you expect? Drunkness killed her. Sarah MacDonald was an alcoholic for years. She was, in common parlance, 'staggering drunk' — or 'completely pissed' as they say in America. Apparently she picked up some drinking companion at the hotel and they got hickey together."

"Did Mrs. MacDonald die from alcohol poisoning?" I asked.

"Of course not. The direct cause of death was the severance of the second cervical vertebrae when her car went over a cliff and smashed itself on the rocks. She was a foolish woman."

"Is that a description in common parlance or a medical opinion, Dr. MacBeth?"

"Eh?"

"Miss Morris is from Canada, Dr. MacBeth," interjected the sergeant. "She has a different kind of experience from us. I've told her, in this part of the world everybody knows everybody else."

"Quite so."

I couldn't resist the opportunity to push.

"I suppose there's no doubt that Mrs. MacDonald was the driver of the car? Given the nature of her injuries, I wonder if that is something you could determine"

He frowned. "That's more a question for the sergeant here than for me. All I know is she broke her bloody neck when she was flung out of the car." He addressed Gillies. "Have you found the other woman yet?"

"No, we haven't."

"If you ask me she's at the bottom of the sea. She'll wash up at the Butt one of these days. They usually do."

Of course he had no inkling of who I actually was, but the brutality of his words were like an assault. Gillies couldn't let it go any further.

"Actually, doctor, Miss Morris is here because the missing woman is her mother."

"What? I thought you said she was a police officer."

"I am. Both. The daughter of the missing woman and a police officer from Canada."

He stared at me, hardly abashed. "Well, I'm sorry for your loss."

This remark could not be pursued because there was a call from downstairs.

"The ambulance is here, Sir."

"Will you see to the removal, Gillies? I'll go on ahead to Stornoway."

"Yes, Sir."

The doctor paused in the doorway. "You should put a fresh steak on that eye," he said to Gillies.

A fresh steak! I'd expect him to bring out the leeches.

He left and Gillies touched my hand.

"Take a deep breath."

"I don't think so," I said ungraciously. "Not in here."

"Will you take care of Andy and his girl then? They might get upset seeing the body brought out. I'd better stay here."

"Okay." I paused. "Would you mind if I checked out the bathroom?"

"There's a toilet downstairs to the right of the front door."

"No, I meant this one. I'd like to see if there's any blood in there."

His expression was kind. "Why don't we both have a look round after they've all left. Set your mind at rest."

"Okay. Thanks."

I made my way downstairs, aware my legs were shaky.

CHAPTER TEN

I walked out to the patio. The rain had stopped and high, dry stone walls gave protection from the prevailing wind, so that the corner was pleasantly warm.

"Hello, everybody. Sergeant Gillies has asked me to let you know that the ambulance men will be removing Mr. MacAulay's body. They will take him to the morgue at Stornoway."

Andy MacAulay looked up, wiping his eyes with a handkerchief. "Thank you."

You can't fake the kind of distress he was experiencing, and my heart went out to him. His fiancée jerked her head in my direction. "Andy's had a dreadful shock. I hope you're not expecting him to say anything." I recognized the accent now — there was an American northeastern clip. His hand was locked in hers, and she had the fierce look of a woman who is ready to stand by her man no matter what: aggressive, ready to throw me out bodily if necessary.

She frowned. "Didn't we see you at the airport?"

"Yes, you did. My name is Morris. Christine Morris. I'm with the Canadian police force."

"Well this is Andy MacAulay, and I'm his fiancée, Coral-Lyn Pitchers. That's Coral as in reef — not Carol — and Pitchers as in baseball." She reeled it off as if I were officially taking notes. I had the impression she was accustomed to being interviewed, perhaps because of her involvement with the Lord's Day Observance Society. But I'd guess that even earlier than that, she'd had to divert lewd jokes from the male population. Her dress wasn't tight-fitting at all, but she was snugly belted at the waist, and she couldn't hide the size of her unusually ample breasts.

The other woman had turned from her sea watch and she came forward with her hand outstretched.

"Hallo to you, Miss Morris. I'm Lisa MacKenzie. I worked for Mr. MacAulay."

I was right about the piercings. She had a silver ring through her left eyebrow and several in each ear. She was older than I expected from her slim build and spiky hair, and was pale and drawn, but quite in control of herself.

"Can you tell me what happened?" I had no official right to ask her, of course, and I didn't know how the other two would react, but I could tell she needed to unburden herself of the experience of finding a decaying corpse.

"I have a key." She paused, and I caught the look that Coral-Lyn threw at her. So did Lisa, and her voice got an edge of defiance. "I am . . . that is, I was . . . employed by Mr. MacAulay. I do odd jobs, gardening, tidying, and so on. . . . Keep him company."

"Do you live here?"

She looked a little discomfited.

"He was kind enough to let me have the use of the spare room. I'm a student in Skye, so it was easier for me to stay two or three days at a time. Mostly on the weekends."

Suddenly, she stared at something over my shoulder and I guessed the ambulance men were bringing down MacAulay's body. Andy and Coral-Lyn didn't notice, since she was busy whispering comforting words into his ear.

I brought Lisa's attention back to me. "How soon after you came into the house, did you go upstairs?"

"Not right away. There was a dreadful smell, and I thought something had been left in the rubbish bin and gone rotten. I went into the kitchen to look, but the bin was empty. I threw open some of the windows." She bit her lip. "I realized the house was unnat-

urally quiet. Tormod always played his radio or sometimes the television, but I couldn't hear anything. I called out to him a few
times, but of course there was no answer."

She paused and I could see her remembering what happened
next. I nodded sympathetically.

"I went up to the bedroom."

Andy and his fiancée were both listening now.

"As soon as I opened the door and saw him on the bed, I knew
he was dead. I ran back downstairs and telephoned Dr. MacBeth.
Tormod's been ill for a little while, you see, and Dr. MacBeth was
his doctor."

"What did you do after that?"

"I telephoned Andy on his mobile phone and asked him to
come at once."

"We were still at the airport," said Coral-Lyn. "We knew
something was dreadfully wrong and we got here as fast as we
could. By the time we arrived, Constable Fraser was here."

"Dr. MacBeth told me to telephone the police," interrupted Lisa.

She was anxious to show Coral-Lyn she had done all the right
things, but I could sense the antagonism between them.

"Did you go upstairs?" I asked Andy, wanting to get an
answer out of him that wasn't monitored by his fiancée.

He shook his head. "The constable confirmed that Granda
was dead and recommended we come outside and wait until Dr.
MacBeth arrived. Coral-Lyn was feeling quite sick because of the
. . . because of the odour."

"I'm very smell-sensitive," interjected Coral-Lyn as if it were a
mark of virtue. She got the conversation back from Andy.

"We were completely devastated, of course. I mean, we
knew he wasn't in the best of health, but when Andy saw him
last, which was Thursday afternoon, he was quite well, wasn't
he, Honey?"

"Oh yes."

She touched Andy's head. "He's so upset because he usually
comes to visit Granda on Fridays, but he had a meeting that kept
him late at the church, so he couldn't come. He thinks that, if he

had been here, he might have been able to do something. Isn't that right, Honey?"

Andy nodded.

I gave that a respectful beat, then asked, "Did he say anything about expecting visitors the following day?"

"No, not at all."

Andy blinked, averted his eyes, and touched his finger to the bridge of his nose. Coral-Lyn kept her eyes fixed on me. "Why do you ask?"

"The nearest neighbours, Mr. and Mrs. MacLean, said they saw a car coming from the direction of the house on Friday night."

The door to the patio opened and Gillies came out.

"Your granddad has been moved to Stornoway, Andy."

Coral-Lyn jumped up. "We'd better get going then. We have a lot of arrangements to make. Come on, Darling. I'll drive us."

Andy got to his feet and she took his hand. He let himself be led out like a small boy.

As soon as the door closed behind them, Lisa said, "I don't know about you both, but I could stand a strong cup of tea. Shall I mash some, Gill?"

"Please."

"How about a drop of malt in it?"

"Great. We could do with it."

Actually, he looked fine, but I sat down on the iron bench, aware once again of his tact.

"I'll be back in a tick," said Lisa. She seemed revived at having something to do, and also, I guessed, because Andy and Coral-Lyn had left. It was my turn now to stare towards the grey sea.

If you ask me, she's at the bottom of the Atlantic.

I couldn't absorb the notion that my mother, after surviving all the years of turbulence and heavy drinking, might have died in a car accident.

Unexpectedly, a patch of blue sky had appeared overhead, and the capricious sun shone apologetically into the patio. In each corner was a large cement flowerpot, filled with yellow daisies and trailing ivy. Lisa's job, I assumed. I yawned, suddenly feeling very

sleepy. I could hear a bee buzzing near my leg, but it wasn't interested in me, only its hunt for nectar. I was sorely tempted to swing
my legs around, stretch out on the bench, and fall into blissful
unconsciousness. I glanced over at Gillies, who was watching me.

"You're exhausted. As soon as we've downed the tea, I'll drive
you to the hotel. There's not a lot more you can do here."

"Isn't there? I feel as if I should be doing something, though."

"This isn't exactly your case, Christine. We'll get to the bottom
of it, I promise."

I liked the way he said my name, and his tone was kind, not
the least dismissive. I leaned back against the hard iron bench and
closed my eyes. The sun was so soft and warm. I felt as if my face
was being caressed.

CHAPTER ELEVEN

In fact, the tea, which was very strong, British-style, woke me up. Lisa had added the whisky directly to the tea, which was probably a sacrilege, but it certainly gave it a nice kick. By the time I had downed the first cup, I was awake and raring to go. Lisa had disappeared while we had the tea, saying she needed to do some heavy work out in the front flower bed. Gillies didn't say much, once again taking his cue from me, which I appreciated. I just muttered banalities about the strength of the brew, the prettiness of the garden, the effect of the whisky.

"Do you want some more?" he asked, reaching for the teapot, which was underneath an embroidered tea cosy.

"No, thanks. That'll do me for the next week, I think."

He grinned. "If you stay with us for a wee while, your kidneys will get stronger."

"Or be wiped out completely."

"Aye, that too."

"I don't want to tread on any toes, or be intrusive, but I wonder if I could talk to Lisa."

"What do you mean, *talk*?"

"Talk the way I would with any witness to a . . . sudden death. There's a procedure we follow."

"I can't imagine any reason why not, if it's what you want to do. Frankly, I'd be interested to see you in action."

"Hey, come on. It's not anything you wouldn't do."

"Let's see then."

He got up and walked to the edge of the patio, leaned around the wall, and called, "Lisa. *Thig an-seo, tapadh leat.*"

I heard her call a response, also in Gaelic.

Gillies came back and sat down, and in a moment Lisa appeared, wiping her hands on the linen gardening apron she was wearing. There was a strong whiff of smoke around her, and I gathered she had been pulling on more than one kind of weed.

"You rang, Sir?"

"Miss Morris wants to ask you some questions. Is that all right by you?"

She shrugged. "Of course." She turned to me. "What do you want to know?"

The question was put politely enough, but she was wary, as if she were emotionally shifting to the balls of her feet like a boxer ready to handle whatever came his way. I didn't know why and didn't particularly care. Probably to do with the companion thing. She seemed young to be shacking up with a sick old man, but that wasn't any concern of mine. At least not at the moment.

"You heard me mention to Andy and his fiancée that Mr. and Mrs. MacLean apparently saw a car leaving the house on Friday night. Do you have any idea who that might have been?"

"No. Why do you ask?" she echoed Coral-Lyn's words.

Gillies helped me out. "It'd be interesting to talk to whoever it was came here, see how Tormod was."

She frowned. "I don't know what you're getting at. He was ill. Dr. MacBeth told him weeks ago there was a danger of him hemorrhaging."

"We're not really getting at anything, Lisa. You know how it is with police officers. We don't like unanswered questions, no matter what the case is."

She studied his face for a moment. "So you say, but there's something on your mind, I can tell. What the hell is it?"

Gillies looked over to me. "Your call, Christine."

Lisa hadn't sat down and she was between me and the sun. I shaded my eyes so I could see her better. She returned my gaze, her eyes a bit anxious but not abnormally so.

"The MacLeans said the car was a small red Vauxhall. There was a car accident not too far from here, which involved such a car. A rental. A woman was killed and the other woman . . . The other woman is somebody I know. We're trying to locate her."

"My God. Who was it, Gill? Tourists?"

"The woman who was killed was Sarah MacDonald."

"Sarah! What the hell happened?"

"The car went off the road at the Dail Beag turn. She was thrown out."

"Well, I regret to say I'm not surprised. Sarah's been in at least two accidents that I know of because she was inebriated. I'm amazed she still had her driver's licence. But still . . . the poor woman. Have you contacted Janice?"

"Yes, we tracked her down. She's on holiday in Tenerife, but she's getting here as soon as she can. Janice is Mrs. MacDonald's only daughter," he explained to me.

Lisa stared at me. "You said the other woman was somebody you knew."

"Yes, she lives in Canada. She was a visitor here."

"But she didn't die?"

"We actually don't know for certain. There was no sign of a second body at the crash site, and she seems to have disappeared."

"What does this have to do with Tormod?"

"Probably nothing, except that it would seem that their car was here on Friday night. Did he mention to you that Mrs. MacDonald was coming over? Or any other visitor?"

"No, he didn't. And I'm surprised she was here. She's an estate agent, and they had a tiff because he didn't list his house with her. Not at big thing, but she seemed to feel he owed her."

"I didn't know he was selling his house," said Gillies.

"Everybody wanted it kept quiet. You know how sensitive the crofters are about property changing hands, especially to incomers. In this case though, they'll probably be happy about it. Coral-Lyn's father has bought this place, and they're going to build a quote, religious centre, unquote here. Apparently, the intention is for it to be quite grand." She smiled a little. "At least as grand as you'll get with the wee kirk."

"I hadn't heard a word. When did all this happen?"

"Not more than a week ago. Tormod was going to rent a flat in Stornoway and move at the end of June. He didn't really want to leave this place, mind, but given his state of health, it seemed wise for him to be in town."

Abruptly, she flopped down into the other chair and ran her hand through her hair so that it spiked up even more. "I'm really sorry to hear about Sarah. She was a nice woman, especially when she was sober."

"Given what you've said then, it might have been a business matter that brought her out here?" I asked.

"Tormod didn't mention it."

"Would he have? Mentioned it, I mean?"

She bristled at my question. "What you're asking is did we have the kind of relationship where he'd share those things with me or was I just the gamekeeper?"

"I'm not asking if you were sleeping with him." I can play 'guess the literary reference' as well as the next English major. "My question was without subtext."

I must have passed a test of some sort, because she softened. "I told you I was his paid companion. Exactly that. No more and no less. I kept him company. He was lonely a lot of the time. He didn't make friends easily. He was divorced a long time ago, and his ex-wife lives in New Zealand with their daughter. His son, Andy's dad, died in 1999, and Andy was his only grandson. Since Miss Coral-Lyn came on the scene, he hasn't been around that much."

"As you were his companion then, he would share his day-to-day life with you. Who came over while you were away, that sort of thing."

"Yes. Exactly that sort of thing. Daily minutiae. But I haven't been here for two weeks, because I had exams and my nose was in my books."

"When did you last talk to him yourself?"

"Last Sunday. I rang him up. He didn't say anything then." Again she gave me a shrewd glance. "Is this missing woman in trouble with the law?"

"I'm not here officially if that's what you mean. However, she has apparently left the scene of an accident, which is an offence."

There was a silence. Gillies raised his eyebrows at me. I stood up, a bit stiff in the hips from the hard bench.

"Lisa, I'd like you to do something for me. You don't have to. As I said, I have no official role here whatsoever, but it would satisfy my curiosity."

She cocked her head slightly. "What?"

"I'd like to walk through the house with you, and I want you to look around as carefully as you can and tell me if there is anything at all that seems out of place. It doesn't matter how unimportant it might seem, just anything that isn't where you'd expect it to be, or on the other hand anything that is missing."

She grimaced. "Hey, I'm not that observant."

"You'll be surprised. You know the house well."

She was openly studying me now. "You're implying there's something shifty gone down. He was a sick old man; he died, as expected. End of story."

I had no alternative but to tell her. "I truly have no idea if something else has occurred, but I am anxious about a few things. The missing woman, the one involved in the accident, is my mother, although I'd appreciate it if you'd keep that under your hat for now."

She whistled through her teeth. "Did she know Tormod?"

"Not as far as I know. Did he ever mention a Joan Morris to you?"

"Never."

"Anyway, believe me, I'm not implying anything. It's just my training. To be useful, the kind of observation I'm asking you to make should happen right away."

She got to her feet. "All right, where do you want to start?"

"At the front door. No, I should say outside the front door. From the gate."

Gillies got up. "Do you want me to make notes?"

"Thanks."

Lisa said something to him in Gaelic, and he laughed. I hate it when people do that, as I suspected she was making a joke at my expense. Once again however, he showed himself the consummate gentleman.

"Lisa was teasing me. She said I'd make a good secretary."

"Oh really?"

I was sure she'd said more than that. She tapped my arm.

"You'll have to learn the Gaelic if you stay around here. It's our language."

"I think I'll have to out of sheer self-protection. Otherwise I'll get paranoid that people are laughing at *me*."

Gotcha. I headed for the door. "Let's start shall we?"

CHAPTER TWELVE

Nowadays, profilers have been glamourized too much for my taste. We've acquired an image as supersleuths, who can read invisible writing and come up with an astounding prediction about possible perpetrators. *Ha, Watson, you missed the yellow stains on the man's fingers and the crumbs of tobacco on his chest. We're looking for a heavy smoker who uses unfiltered cigarettes and probably has lung cancer.* The job, in fact, is more varied than the public thinks, because in Canada we don't have many serial killers. Some people think it's the inherent goodness of the Canadian character, which may be true, but it's also to do with the relatively small population. One of the areas of expertise a profiler is supposed to have is scene-of-crime analysis. However, we need front-line cops to feed us information. One of the things I was good at when I was with the detective division was the crime-scene inspection, which was what I was doing at the moment with Lisa. This usually happens before the clever dicks from forensics get in there, and really it's a variation of the "What's wrong with this picture?" question. A classic old chestnut, but one that still happens, is when a bad guy kills somebody, then tries to make it look as if the murder was committed by the proverbial "intruder." You'd be surprised how easy that is to detect. But you need somebody in that sort of inspection who has been in the place before — a spouse, a friend, a neighbour. I've walked into rooms that were so filthy and chaotic you'd swear an army of vandals had been ripping through, only to learn from the landlord that that's how the person had always lived. Once, I entered a small apartment in an upscale building on the waterfront where a man had been found dead from strangulation: plastic bag over his head, a cord wrapped tightly around his neck. The apartment was so denuded of anything but the most basic plain furniture that my first impression was that there had been a burglary of thorough proportions, and the man had been killed by the thieves. This turned out to be far from the case. The man was an ex-monk, who lived out his former vow of poverty, gave most of his considerable salary away to charity, and was into dangerous autoerotic practices. No burglar, no murder.

As a stranger on the scene, you really cannot always tell what is right or wrong with the picture. Basic rule: never make assumptions until you've got all the facts. Second basic rule: intuition is one of your most valuable tools. Third basic rule: intuition married to experience is the best partnership. Frankly, at the moment I was struggling with all three rules. This looked like an ordinary case of death by natural causes — that is, from disease that was known about beforehand. However, my intuition was beeping like a metal detector on a beach, although at the moment I couldn't say why. Joan fitted in here somewhere, but whether that was coincidence or a presage of very bad news, I didn't know. I should add, though, that one other thing you do have to watch out for if you are a police officer is an overactive imagination. Or to put it less charitably, it's all too easy to get jaded and suspect everything of having a criminal taint.

Gillies, Lisa, and I went outside and walked down the path to the gate. It was quiet out here except for the mewing of the gulls, which swooped around to see what was going on. The sun had made up its mind to stay out, and the freshness of the air was almost as heady as the single malt in my tea.

"What do you want me to do?" asked Lisa. She was trying to hold down some excitement, no doubt drug-induced.

"Take your time. Don't worry about whether you're right or not, just try to react without censoring yourself. I suggest you walk towards the house slowly and take note of whatever you see that seems out of place or changed from the last time you saw it."

She started towards the door, me a step behind, Gillies behind me.

Just before the threshold, she stopped.

"Do the flowers count?"

"What do you mean?"

She pointed at the right-hand flower bed. "I can't be certain, but I thought there were more mums than that." She stooped down. "Yes, see? Some of the stalks have been snapped off. I didn't do it when I was here last, because I wanted them to come up a bit more."

"Would Tormod have picked them?" I asked.

"He never has before. I think he considered it unmanly to care about flowers." She looked around some more and frowned.

"Yes?" I encouraged

"Oh sorry, nothing to do with this. I just noticed the rose bush by the house has given up the ghost. Too cold last winter. It's hard to grow roses over here."

"Let's go inside then, if you think there's nothing else."

She pointed to a lean-to attached to the side of the house.

"Do you want to see in the shed? He worked in there."

"Sure."

The door wasn't locked, and we went inside. The shed was larger than it first appeared and was the kind of workspace that would make sense to the worker and nobody else. To my eyes, it was a complete mess. Bits of wool and cloth were scattered all over the floor, odd-sized drawers were balanced precariously on various sets of shelves. Holes in the plank walls were patched with newspaper or masking tape. Fluff lay thick on every surface. The shed seemed to also serve as a storage area, and a few car parts and tractor tires had found their way into the corners. An older-model Suzuki motorcycle was standing just inside the door, and there were a couple of bicycles propped up against the wall. The big rusty metal loom itself stood in front of the only window at the far end of the shed.

"Tormod was a weaver by trade," said Lisa. She grinned slightly. "See that motor? He wasn't supposed to have it. His work goes to the mill and is advertised as 'made the traditional way,' but it's so hard on the legs to work those pedals that he couldn't do it. He installed this auxiliary motor and didn't tell anybody." She went closer to the loom. "Och! He's cut off the cloth. When I was here last he was working on a big commission for somebody on the mainland, but it wasn't close to being finished."

The severed strands of wool hung down dispiritedly from the stretchers.

Lisa shrugged. "Either that's something out of place or he got in more work than I would have thought and sent it off."

"What's your guess?"

"I don't know. He told me he had about three more weeks minimum, but some days he wasn't well enough to do a single row."

"Would it be anywhere else in the shed?" Gillies asked her.

She shook her head. "I don't think so. He always sent off the finished pieces right away. Those are discards over there."

There was a pile of colourful scraps nearby.

"Do you know who had commissioned the material?"

"No. He just said it was somebody from the mainland. Does it matter?"

Again the edge of impatience was in her voice.

I didn't answer. At this point I had no idea. I was just trolling for information.

"That's it then. I can't say any more."

We started to leave.

"Whose motorbike is that?" I asked.

"Mine. I park it in here."

"And Mr. MacAulay owned the bicycles?"

"One of them is Andy's. The clunker belonged to Tormod. He liked to bike when the wind wasn't too fierce. He gave up his car last year."

An expression of sorrow distorted her face for a moment, but she was determined not to give in to tears. She deliberately turned away from me, as if studying the scene again. I waited, as did Gillies.

"The place is such a mess, it's hard to know if anything is out of place or not. And I didn't come out here much. It was his domain."

There were some mugs sitting on the windowsill and an empty beer bottle. There was also a strong odour of stale cigarette smoke.

"Mr. MacAulay smoked, did he?"

"He wasn't supposed to, and he made out he'd quit, but I always suspected he was coming out to the shed when he got desperate."

Once again she was halted by her memories, but she shook them off.

"Let's go into the house then," I said.

Gillies led the way and opened the door for us. Lisa went in. I followed, then stood to one side while she looked around the living room. The smell of death was still bad.

"First impressions?" I prompted her.

"Looks the same as it usually does, although he did tidy up the newspaper, I see. He usually left it on the floor, no matter how much I ragged on him." She looked over to the kitchen. "And the kitchen's tidy. He's done all his dishes and put them away. Something he never does. He despised doing the dishes."

"Would you check to see if they've been put back in their right places?"

She went over to the cupboards that flanked the far wall of the kitchen and began opening the doors.

"It seems all right, although I wouldn't swear on a Bible. Cups aren't on the proper shelf, but they are in the right cupboard. But like I said, I was usually the putter-away, not him."

I followed her past the dividers that partitioned off the kitchen. The telephone was on the wall, the coils of the cord stretched to straightness, presumably so the receiver would reach the table. Pasted above the phone was a card with numbers on it. I saw the words DOCTOR and AMBULANCE.

"Nothing else I can see," said Lisa. "No, hold on a tick."

She walked over to the small white trash bin in the corner and lifted the lid. "I just remembered something." She reached into the bin and took out a bunch of yellow mums. They were still quite fresh. "Ha! I told you some of the flowers out front had been picked," she said, showing them to me.

"By the looks of it, somebody threw them away almost immediately."

"I wonder why. Maybe he picked them, then decided he didn't like them after all. He said flowers made him sneeze." She shrugged and dropped the flowers back into the bin. "It doesn't have to be significant, does it?"

Her excitement had evaporated, probably because of the memory of discovering the body. I didn't blame her, but I didn't want to stop now either.

"Let's keep going. Will you walk around the living room?"

She did so, me a few paces behind again so I could get my own impressions. Gillies didn't say anything, but I wondered what was going through his mind. What is driving this woman? He wasn't to know that what was propelling me wasn't just professional curiosity and the need to tie up loose ends. What was niggling away in the back of my mind was the persistent question: Given the contents of her suitcase, was Joan paying a visit to my own father? Hey, maybe there'd be a strip of DNA readout lying around somewhere.

Lisa halted in front of the dining-room table, which was bare of litter. A single blue glass vase stood on a tartan placemat.

"Same thing — tidier than usual. He always read the paper while he ate his lunch, but it never occurred to him to put it in the fireplace box when he'd finished."

"What's the date of the paper that's on the easy chair?"

Gillies took a look. "Last Wednesday."

"That fits. The *Gazette* only comes out once a week. He always walked into Carloway in the morning to get it."

She hesitated, watching me for guidance.

"Please go on."

"That vase shouldn't be on the table. It was kept in the back cupboard. He never used it."

"But he would have needed it if he'd got flowers." I phrased that as noncommittally as I could. Hey, in spring even the manly Scot might be moved by the rising sap to bring some flowers into the house. On the other hand, if his visitor had picked the flowers, it was a bit cheeky to take them from his own garden. Joan would do that, I was certain of it.

Lisa shrugged. "I suppose so." She went over to a glass-fronted cabinet that was adjacent to the door.

"Nothing has been moved in here that I can see." She opened the bottom door and peered inside. I could see one or two bottles of liquor. She straightened up. "Sorry again. I'm thick as a plank today. You said 'anything out of place,' and I was taking you literally. The bottle of Scotch is in here where it always is, but it's almost empty. I didn't really think about it when I poured you some, but now you've got me going. It was a full bottle when I was here last. I know because I brought it in for him."

"You don't think he drank it himself?"

"He wasn't allowed to any more. He kept it on hand just for visitors. It's a tradition in these parts that's as old as the rocks themselves. A wee dram for the road, right Gill?"

"A dram or two more often than not."

They smiled at each other, a smile that, intentionally or not, excluded me.

I pushed on. "Well, it does appear that Sarah MacDonald visited here on Friday evening. It looks like he served her some single malt. A lot of single malt."

"Maybe the other woman tossed back a few," said Lisa. "That's possible isn't it?"

I nodded. "Very possible."

"Do you want me to keep going?"

"Please."

She circled the room, making her mental tally. At the fireplace, she stopped and pointed at a framed photograph on the mantelpiece. Three men standing in front of a fluted organ, all of them in dark suits. There was no mistaking a young, beaming Andy MacAulay — or the family resemblance among the three men.

"That was Andy being accepted into the church. That's his dad, Iain, on the right, and Tormod's on the left."

At the other end of the mantelpiece was another photograph: an enlarged snapshot of Her Majesty the Queen, shaking hands with a beaming Tormod.

"The Queen came to Stornoway last year, and he was presented to her."

"He looks happy."

"He was. I took the picture, as a matter of fact. I tell you frankly, I didn't expect to be so impressed, but the Queen is still a pretty woman. Very sweet in fact."

We moved on. Lisa was a good witness. I could tell she didn't embellish anything or make up things to please me.

"Were any of the curtains drawn when you came in, by the way?"

She clicked her tongue against her teeth. "Yes. The living-room and kitchen curtains were closed. I opened all of them. Like I said, I had to let in some fresh air."

"Are you okay to tackle upstairs then?" I asked her.

"I suppose so."

"The sheet is still on the bed," added Gillies. "It's bloodstained."

"That won't bother me. I worked for three summers at the local old folks' home, and believe me, you develop a strong stomach for the sight and smell of bodily substances."

"Let's go then. Same instructions as before."

Our little trio made its way upstairs.

CHAPTER THIRTEEN

Gillies waited at the top of the stairs.

"Ready?" he asked.

Lisa nodded, and we went into the bedroom.

In spite of what she'd said previously, she flinched. The coverlet was folded back and the bloodstains were vivid on the sheet. The air was rank.

"First impressions?" I asked her.

"I'm sounding like I'm stuck in a groove, but I have to say the same thing. It's tidy, and Tormod was basically a mucky man. He always dropped his clothes on the floor as he took them off. He said he didn't see any point to putting them away when he was going to wear them the next day. They're not there."

"He was wearing a white T-shirt and grey jogging pants, with his dressing gown on top," said Gillies.

"That's it then. He hardly ever wore anything else these days. His pyjamas should be under his pillow." She went over to look and showed us a pair of folded, red striped flannel PJs. "Hold on . . . where are his books? He liked to read before he went to sleep, and he always had one or two novels on the go." She jerked open the drawer of the bedside table. "Aha. Here they are." She took out a couple of paperbacks. "He loved thrillers best. Especially the American ones. I wonder why he put them away? Did you do that, Gill?"

"I did not."

The only book on the table was a large Bible.

"Was that usually there?" I asked her.

"It was. He'd have what he called his sweet first, which was one of the novels, then he'd read something from the Bible before he went to sleep."

"He was a devout man, I take it?"

She looked at me with surprise. "Devout? More traditional, really. He grew up when everybody read the Bible daily, and it was a habit." She sighed. "Getting some people to move with the times on this island is as slow hard as scraping crotal off the rocks."

She didn't explain the simile, but I could guess what it meant.

"Will you check the wardrobe and the dresser?"

She opened the big, old-fashioned wardrobe and a waft of camphor floated out. The rack was packed with suits, all of them dark-coloured.

"He has hardly worn these lately. He stopped going to church months ago, because he didn't like having to explain how he was to people. He hated being sick and he said their sympathy weakened him." She closed the wardrobe door. "Nothing amiss in there." She did a quick check of the dresser with the same result.

I pointed at the desk underneath the window.

"Did you ever have occasion to go into his desk?"

"Once or twice, I suppose, for his glasses, when he didn't want to get up out of bed. Do you want me to look in there?" She went over to the desk and rolled back the top. "Hmn . . . nothing . . . Wait!" She picked up an envelope and peeked inside. "Shit! Cheeky bugger."

She held out two Polaroid photographs. They had been taken from the bedroom window, by the looks of it, and the photographer was focussing down into the side garden. The shots were of Lisa kneeling in the flower bed. She was wearing shorts and a skimpy halter top, and the position of the photographer meant he had a good view of her cleavage.

She peered at the pictures. "That was taken just two weeks ago when I was here last. It was hot that day, which is why I'm in my brevvies."

"I take it you didn't know he was photographing you?"

"I did not."

Her eyes met mine and she shrugged. "Some lads never give it up, do they?"

But I could see the anger. And the hurt. These photos were intended to be a secret.

"I suppose there's no doubt Mr. MacAulay was the person who took the pictures?"

"Who else would it be? There wasn't anybody else here that day."

Gillies had looked over my shoulder. He made no comment and she tore the photos in two and tossed them in the wastebasket.

"I don't suppose Andy will want these, and neither do I."

The desk was the kind that had a few cubbyholes at the back, and I saw a familiar British Airways envelope.

"Those must be airline tickets," I said, pointing. "Was he planning a trip?"

"Not that I know of. He was to move to Stornoway at the end of the month."

She looked inside the envelope, and I could see the shock on her face.

"That's ridiculous. It's a ticket to Houston, Texas, a week from now."

"May I see?"

She handed me the ticket.

"It's one way," I said. "He doesn't seem to have planned a return trip."

"That's crazy. He never breathed a word about going to America."

"The ticket was issued this past Thursday."

"Bugger that."

"Does he have family there?"

"None at all. Believe me, I know all his life history. His ex-wife and daughter live in New Zealand, but there's nobody in the States."

Suddenly she sat down on the wooden chair and put her head in her hands.

"I don't understand. We had a lot of plans for when he moved into his apartment. I was going to decorate it for him. Why wouldn't he tell me he was going on a trip? And why doesn't he have a return ticket?"

Another betrayal from Mr. MacAulay. Lisa had enjoyed the role of confidant.

She was crying. The choked-off cries of somebody who doesn't weep easily. Gillies put his hand lightly on her shoulder, fished out a white handkerchief from his pocket, and handed it to her. I moved away a little, waiting for her to regain her control. As I did so, I noticed a framed picture lying face down at the back of the desk. I took it out. It was a black-and-white studio portrait of a younger MacAulay and his family. He was wearing a formal suit, wide tie, and equally broad lapels, and his dark hair was thick, smoothed back from his face. The woman seated beside him, presumably his wife, was unsmiling. A long jawline and thin nose precluded any prettiness, and she hadn't helped herself by wearing a plain dowdy dress that was more appropriate to a Victorian servant girl. Each of them was holding a child. The boy on his lap was in short pants, wearing a Fair-Isle sweater, the girl, hair in careful ringlets, looked as if she were about to burst into tears. Nobody appeared happy, and the picture, shoved to the back of the desk, was testimony to the rancour of the breakup.

Lisa had wiped at her face and stuffed the handkerchief in her pocket. She spoke in Gaelic to Gillies, and I gathered she was speaking about the handkerchief. He smiled and nodded at her.

I showed her the photograph. "When did they get divorced?"

"Eons ago. More than forty years. She was a MacNeil and, according to my grandmother, the poor woman was considered one of the ugliest girls on the island. Tongues clacked when she got engaged to the handsome Tormod, who was a proper masher by all accounts." She grimaced. "When Iain appeared just six months after the wedding, the questions were answered. Everybody knew how Margaret had snagged him."

"And she's in New Zealand now?"

"She is. The divorce was quite a scandal at the time, because nobody whatsoever was divorcing on this island. She emigrated soon after, taking their daughter with her. She left Iain as if he were a piece of furniture she didn't want. Tormod said he never saw his daughter again after she went to New Zealand. Her mother wouldn't allow it. I'd better remind Andy to notify her. Although I don't know where the hell she is." Lisa indicated the little boy in the photograph. "That's Andy's father, Iain. He married Mary MacIver from Barra, but she didn't survive complications from childbirth. She passed away only two days after Andy was born. It was so tragic. I can still remember the funeral up at Back Church. Iain never remarried, and now he's passed on." She sniffed. "For what it's worth, I think not having a mom's the reason Andy hooked up with Coral-Lyn." She made a vague gesture with her hands to indicate big breasts. "I shouldn't gossip though. She's a good Christian soul. She works hard for the church, so I hear, and the two of them visited Tormod faithfully. Not on the weekend, of course."

"Church duties?" I asked disingenuously. I knew what she was getting at, but wanted her to say it.

"Partly that. More to do with me. Coral-Lyn didn't like the fact I live here."

"Right. As Mr. MacAulay's companion."

"Exactly." She sighed, and I could see her thinking about the small betrayal of his voyeurism. "Miss Pitchers is what I'd call 'intense,'" she went on. "Too much for me. Besides, all that Lord's Day Observance stuff is so yesterday. Who cares about preserving the Sabbath these days when the entire world needs preserving much more? Not working on Sundays isn't going to do it, believe me."

She gulped back a sob, but I knew it wasn't to do with any religious convictions. For all her "I'm a tough broad" attitude, Lisa was in a state of shock. I put my hand on her shoulder and she touched it briefly with her callused palm.

"Do you want to see the rest of this floor?"

"Yes, if you don't mind."

Her bedroom was across the hall, and we went there first. Given Lisa's rather determinedly teenaged appearance, I expected to see an unholy mess, but it wasn't that at all. There was a single bed covered with a beautiful plaid blanket, an armchair under the window, a set of bookshelves filled to overflowing, and a small student desk, neatly stacked with papers.

"Everything's as I left it." She stroked the blanket. "That's Tormod's work. He made it for me for Christmas."

"What are you studying?" I asked as we went out into the hall.

"Environmental issues. My specialization is oceanic conservation."

"That sounds suitable for a Hebridean girl."

She grinned.

Once again, Gillies was holding a door open for us, and she went into the bathroom while I stood at the threshold.

"It looks cleaner than usual, that's all. Maybe he was anticipating me coming in. We'd have big rows all the time about the mess. Me, I like things neat and tidy."

We moved back into the hall, and she stopped at the top of the stairs.

"I'm getting tired of this. Surely you don't want me to go on? We've seen everything."

"No, that's terrific. I appreciate your help."

She didn't say anything until we were downstairs, then, rather oddly, she addressed Gillies. "What's this all about Gill? Do you suspect a burglar or something?"

He passed it deftly on to me. "Miss Morris just wanted to satisfy herself that there was nothing untoward about Tormod's death."

That angered Lisa, who was already at the edge of frayed nerves. She rounded on me. "What the hell does that mean, untoward? Do you think somebody offed him?"

"I really don't know, Lisa. I told you, it's my job, and given the possible involvement of my own mother, I wanted to make sure Tormod died from natural causes."

"And are you sure?"

I stared at her for a moment.

"I wish I could say I was."

CHAPTER FOURTEEN

Lisa had left to go to the village store for some groceries. I thought she might be reluctant to stay in the house, but she said she had a lot of studying to do and this was her home as much as anywhere else. Before she went, she stripped the bed and put the sheets and coverlet into the washing machine. There was nothing I could do about that. This was not an official crime scene.

Gillies and I sat a bit longer in the kitchen drinking more fortified tea and talked over all possibilities. The most likely scenario was that MacAulay, against character, had tidied up his house because he was expecting visitors. All that told me was that the visitors were important — even important enough to possibly pick some mums, although I was still betting on Joan for that. The out-of-place cups, the newspaper, and the vase didn't say much. People moved things from one place to another without it meaning a damn thing. The hiding of the novels in his bedroom could also indicate a desire to impress. He was a Bible-reading man. Of course, that also suggested he was expecting his visitor to view the bedroom, and here the memory of the condoms in Joan's suitcase hung in the air. We didn't address it.

Several things niggled like a badly cut jigsaw puzzle. First, there were the whisky glasses. Unless they swigged from the bottle, the (at least) two women had downed several drinks, but the glasses were in the cupboard. Did Tormod's fit of tidiness extend to washing glasses after his visitors left? Second niggle: If he had gone up to bed as Dr. MacBeth insisted he had, why didn't he undress? Third big niggle: As I'd tried to say to the doctor, there was the side from which he'd hemorrhaged.

But if none of these niggles were the innocent variables of real life, what were they? And back we were again. But the picture slipped away like Jell-O on a spoon as soon as I tried to bite into it.

I hadn't mentioned to Gillies my interest in my sperm donor, but I was rapidly developing one possible story. This was a conservative religious community. Joan was only eighteen when I was born, and although from the beginning she called herself *Mrs. Morris*, I'd be very surprised if she'd had benefit of clergy. There was a good possibility that she got herself knocked up and fled to Canada. Was this a happy coupling or not? There was no way to know at the moment. She'd told me she wanted to lay some ghosts to rest. I just hoped she didn't create one.

Gillies pushed back his chair and began to gather the tea cups.

"Come on, let's get you to the hotel. I suggest you try to have a rest while I go to the station and see if there's any news. How about if I come over about eight and take you to dinner? There's a good wee restaurant near the hotel that specializes in Scotland's national dish."

"My God, not the famous haggis? I don't know if I'm up to eating sheep's intestines."

"That used to be Scotland's national dish. Now we're talking fresh-caught salmon with delicate herb seasoning and buttered potatoes. Tourist traps."

"Now you're talking. I'll just use the bathroom before we go . . . all that tea."

While he went to the sink, I trotted upstairs. I did have to use the facilities, but I was really interested in checking the bathroom. Before I washed my hands, I scrutinized the sink. Both it and the toilet bowl were scrupulously clean. If MacAulay had bled in the bathroom, there was no sign of it.

There was a medicine cabinet, but there was nothing in it except a flattened tube of shaving cream, toothpaste, and a toothbrush. No floss. There was a full bottle of prescription sleeping pills and the usual pharmaceutical paraphernalia you'd expect with a man in such ill health. Just as I was about the switch off the light, I saw a wicker laundry hamper tucked in beside the toilet. I looked inside. There was the usual pile of used T-shirts and underwear, but on top of the heap was a tea towel that had been saturated in blood.

Gillies smiled at me when I rejoined him downstairs. He had an infectious smile that softened the rather hard lines of his face, not to mention the ferocity of his black eye.

"And? How was the bathroom?"

"Clean as a whistle."

On the way to the car, I asked him for a favour.

"Could we stop and talk to the MacLeans?"

"I don't see why not. You're a visitor. We're not doing anything in an official capacity."

When we pulled into the driveway, both Mr. and Mrs. MacLean came out at once. They appeared to be in their seventies, and had matching soft white hair and tweed jackets. He was still chewing on his dinner.

"We saw the ambulance come. Puir Tormod. They've taken him away to Stornoway, I suppose."

"They have."

We were still in the car at this point, and Gillies leaned his head out of the window. "If it's not spoiling your dinner, would you mind if Miss Morris and I had a wee chat with you both?"

They nodded almost simultaneously. "Come on in," said Mr. MacLean. "We spoke to young Fraser, but I'm not sure how much he really understood. He was in shock, puir fellow."

Gillies came around and opened the car door for me while I was gathering up my purse. As we went in, he made introductions, but kept it to the fact that I was a police officer from Canada. The MacLeans were quite flustered by the excitement. Mr. MacLean asked me if I had met his cousin who had emigrated years ago and lived in Ontario — or was it Vancouver? No, I hadn't, I said. The odds were about five-million-to-one that our paths had crossed. But then you never knew.

They took us straight into the kitchen, which, like MacAulay's, hadn't changed since the 1950s. More tea was offered, which I declined, but which Gillies accepted. Finally we were sitting down around the Formica table.

"Could you just go over again what you told Constable Fraser? You saw a car leaving Mr. MacAulay's house on Friday night."

"Well now, let's see. Isobel and I had gone up to the community centre in Carloway. There's always a little *ceilidh* on Friday nights, and we enjoy going, don't we, Bel?"

"We do," said Mrs. MacLean, who was the less talkative. "It breaks the monotony."

"We must have left there about eleven o'clock, wouldn't you say, Bel?"

"Five past at the most. And I must tell you now, Tom had only had two glasses of beer. Isn't that so?"

"It is. I can't take the drink these days. More than two glasses and my prostate acts up fierce. So where was I? . . . Oh aye, we were jest approaching on our house. Look, why dinna I draw you a map? Bel, can you bring some paper and pencil?"

Mrs. MacLean got up promptly, as no doubt she had done all her married life when requests came from her husband. While we waited, Mr. MacLean took what appeared to be a single cigarette from his pocket and stuck it in his mouth.

"I'm trying to stop smoking, and these things are supposed to help you. They're menthol or some darned thing like that. Tastes like mothballs." He sucked in air from the plastic tube, which made a little whistling sound.

Bel placed a lined notepad in front of him and a stubby pencil. He quickly sketched out a double line that curved down to the bottom of the page.

"Here's Arnol, see? They've got a fine wee museum there of the old Blackhouses. Very worth seeing, isn't it, Sergeant?"

"Indeed."

"And here's Shawbost."

"We weren't anywhere near there, Tom," interjected his wife.

"I know that Bel, I'm just filling in some detail for the young lady so she can orientate herself." He tapped the paper. "This is the way you've come from Stornoway, see. You passed through Arnol and Shawbost. If you continued on the main road, you'd come to Carloway village." He drew an arrow off his double line. "Here's the turnoff to our house and Tormod's. We're on the right and Tormod's house is further down a wee way on the left." He made crosses on his map.

"She's already seen all that, Tom," interrupted Bel. "You don't need to go over it again. Just get on with what happened. If you don't, I will."

"Is it clear now?" he asked me.

"Quite clear, thank you."

"Aye, good. Well then, as I was saying, we were coming from the direction of Carloway and were almost at the turnoff when a car came roaring out of the side road and turned north right in front of us. It's a good thing I wasn't driving too fast."

"Tom's a careful driver," said Mrs. MacLean.

He grinned. "You have to be at my age. I had to brake sharp or I would have been up their boot."

I only half-understood this reference, but I didn't dare stop him now.

"That car just took off like a bat out of the Other Place."

"But you had a chance to see it was a red Vauxhall?"

"Yes, we did. My previous car was a Vauxhall, so I'm very familiar with them."

"Tom, could you tell who was in the car?" Gillies asked.

Mrs. MacLean couldn't hold back any longer. "There were two women. One was Sarah MacDonald, may she rest in the Lord. She died in that tragic accident, as you know."

"Did you actually see her when the car drove out in front of you?" I asked.

They both looked surprised, and Mrs. MacLean said, "We just told you we did."

Mr. MacLean waved his fake cigarette. "No, Bel, what the lady means is did we see her face? That's what you mean isn't it, Miss?"

I said yes, that was what I meant, and wondered if they could describe the other woman as well. I didn't add that it was dark and the only lights were car lights, which will make silhouettes of anybody who is driving in front of you. There was silence for a moment as they eyed each other and considered the question. Mr. MacLean sucked hard and made the whistling sound.

"My wife will have to speak for herself, but I would say that, no, I didn't get a good look at either person. I just assumed it had been Sarah because of what happened."

"We were right about the car though, weren't we," said Isobel quickly. They were starting to feel they'd failed as witnesses, which wasn't what I wanted at all.

"The car that crashed was a red Vauxhall," said Gillies.

"Mr. MacLean, do you know what time it was when you reached the turnoff and saw the car?" I asked.

"Oh, if we left the hall at five past eleven, we'd have been at the turnoff at twenty past. Right, Gill? Wouldn't you say it would take us fifteen minutes to get here from the *ceilidh*?"

"Yes, driving at normal speed, it'd take no more than that."

Mrs. MacLean regarded Gillies anxiously. "There's no funny business about Tormod's passing is there? He was not a well man."

"According to Dr. MacBeth, he died of natural causes, Tom. But as you probably know, the second person has disappeared, and we're just trying to pin down all the details."

She nodded. "That's what we said to Jamie Fraser. Deaths come in threes."

"I'm afraid I don't quite follow you, Mrs. MacLean."

She glanced over at me, but continued to talk to Gillies. I could feel that, in the meantime, her husband was scrutinizing me.

"When we saw the police car go by this afternoon, we thought we'd better go and see what was happening, in case Jamie wanted help. Young Lisa Mackenzie had arrived earlier. We heard her motorcycle. Dreadful thing that it is."

Her husband jumped in to finish the tale. "We walked down to the house, and Jamie said that Tormod had passed on. That's when Isobel said death comes in threes. First Sarah, then the visitor woman, now Tormod."

I felt Gillies's discomfort, but I was hardened now to any stab. "How did you hear about the car accident?" I asked.

"Bel's sister, Morag, rang us up this morning." He looked worried. "We always motor down to Harris on Saturdays to visit our daughter, and we didn't get back until after church. When we heard the news, we were actually talking about going to the police and telling them what we saw, weren't we, Bel?"

His wife nodded. "We were. Then we saw the police car and, well, we told you the rest. We mentioned to young Fraser we'd seen the two women leaving the house, and he said as how the other lady's body wasna found yet, so he'd better report what we said. He also asked us if we'd seen Tormod since Friday, but we hadn't, had we, Isobel?"

"We had not, being as how we were away at Harris. Besides, we might not have clapped eyes on him even if we were here. Tormod sometimes didn't come out for two, three days at a time if he wasn't feeling well. His grandson looked in on him most every day, so we didn't worry."

"According to Andy's fiancée, they didn't come over on the weekends," said Gillies.

"No, they didn't. Lisa was here then, and she and Coral-Lyn didn't get along." Isobel frowned. "People talked about Lisa and Tormod, but I say let them who are without sin throw the first stone."

I didn't quite know how to respond to that, so once again I nodded encouragingly. They had said their piece, however, and to press them might make them adapt their story. I wanted the freshness of the first telling. They sat quietly and watched me. Tom sucked energetically on his menthol tube.

"Is that it then?"

"It is, and thank you very much for talking to me."

We all shook hands. They asked if I was staying long and, if I was, to please come to tea and they'd show me pictures of Tom's cousin. I might have met him. You never know, stranger things have happened. Indeed, I said, and Gillies and I left.

"Well?" he asked. "What did you think?"

"It could have been any car and anybody in it."

He was quiet for a few moments, then he glanced over at me.

"I know that in a court of law what you say is true. But let's not abandon common sense. A red Vauxhall crashed not far down this same road late on Friday night. What other car would it be?"

He spoke nicely, but I felt reprimanded and that made me sharp. "Who knows?" I snapped. "We have no idea when the accident happened. Maybe there were other visitors. I'm just getting tired of all these ifs and maybes."

He reached over and briefly touched my hand. "You know what, I think the right word is tired. And by the way, we do know what time the accident happened. Sarah MacDonald was killed at precisely seventeen minutes past ten."

"What? Come on, how can you be that exact?"

"You may see us as a little backwater relying on primitive technology to solve our cases, but we have been able to determine the exact time of her death to the minute."

"Yeah? How did you do that?"

He chuckled. "Her watch was smashed on the rock. It had stopped at ten-seventeen."

"That proves nothing. She could have been wearing a broken watch all week. She hadn't gotten around to getting it fixed."

"You should have been a lawyer. They aren't interested in common sense. Would you wear a broken watch?"

"I concede the point, but then we have a major time discrepancy. How could she be dead at ten-seventeen, and the MacLeans see her driving away at eleven-fifteen?"

"They're dear folks, but would you consider them reliable witnesses?"

"I don't know them," I said. "It would be easy to confirm their statement though, if we talked to the other people at the *ceilidh*."

"Yes, it would. If this were a homicide investigation, I'd go and do just that. But it isn't. I know these people. They could have as easily sworn they left at midnight. Nobody was watching the time."

A rather thick silence dropped into the car and I said, "On the other hand, we don't know if Sarah's watch was accurate, do we? Unless it's a habit of the Lewishans to keep their clocks an hour late."

He laughed. "I'm sure some would do that, just to be perverse."

Tension evaporated.

"How about if I give you more history lessons while we drive, and then we can discuss the other stuff over dinner when you're rested?"

I stopped bristling and making a fool of myself. "That sounds like basic rule number three, or is it four? 'Never draw conclusions if you are so sleep deprived your eyes are falling out of your head.'"

"That's the one. Now, you expressed an interest in the Callanish Standing Stones. We didn't know they existed until . . . "

I did the best I could to concentrate on what he was saying, but I made the mistake of putting my head back and the next thing I knew we were driving into Stornoway.

CHAPTER FIFTEEN

My room at Duke's was square and old-fashioned without being charming. The orangey-red curtains framing the sash windows were heavy and probably dusty, the matching bedspread was a slippery synthetic material. However, the decorator had gone for the homey touch, and there were several framed needlepoint samplers on the walls. They all were pithy sayings, picked out in red and green threads. "*NICHT IS THE MITHER O' THOUGHTS,*" "*TOILIN'S THE HARD BIT–DYIN'S EASY,*" and my favourite, "*YER ONLY HERE A WEE WHILE SO BE NICE.*" I'd have to remember to say that to some of the brutal gang members I'd met. I shied away from composing a suitable aphorism to give to Sondra DeLuca's family. "*Do unto others as you would be done by,*" was one I'd like to share with them. I paused, realizing that one good thing that had come out of the Joan fiasco was that she had temporarily driven out my obsessive thoughts about little Sunrise and her mother.

I pushed up one of the windows and leaned out. I was facing onto a harbour slip, but the retaining wall hid all but the top masts of the fishing boats. Across the slip was a rare stand of trees, and behind that the castellated turrets of a castle, at the moment looking suitably impressive against an overcast sky. Even though I was a terrible sailor and would have become seasick on a waterbed, I loved looking at boats and sea-related objects. I watched the gulls swooping and screaming their sea cries, ferocious and beautiful, then I kicked off my shoes, plonked down on top of the shiny coverlet, and closed my eyes.

About an hour later, I woke up. For a moment I was completely disorientated, and it took me a few moments to realize where I was and why. The place was all right — even the travelling salesman aura of the Duke — and I actually was loving Lewis. But the reason I was here was not all right, and I felt myself dropping into a familiar state of mind, vaguely anxious, mostly helplessly angry. Only action lifted that mood, and I jumped up and went into the shower. Half an hour later, scrubbed, powdered, and lotioned, I felt better. By the time Gillies knocked on the door, I almost felt like the proverbial new woman. His appreciative smile confirmed that I had indeed risen from the dead.

Because it was Sunday, only hotels served meals, so we had no choice but to eat in the Duke's bar/restaurant, which was emphatically nautical in décor. Fishing nets studded with shells draped the walls, and there were at least two steering wheels and several brass-trimmed barometers. There was a similar plethora of framed needlepoint sayings. I liked the one hanging over the bar: "*NAE WORDS, NAE QUARREL.*" I had a vision of the bartenders pointing this out to obstreperous customers. Gillies was greeted by name by the waitress, who was about my age. I could tell by the way she eyed *me* up and down that she fancied *him*, but I couldn't decide if the feeling was reciprocated. She showed us to a table by the window, handed over the menus, smiled brightly at Gillies, and withdrew to the bar to pick up an order. A man and a woman who was hugely pregnant were behind the counter, both polishing wine glasses. The man called out a greeting, *Feashgar math*, which sounded like, Fesh-ga-ma.

Gillies replied, "Good evening, Colin. Any day now, Mairi?"

"Last Saturday was the due date." She patted her belly.

I opened up the menu, which had a photograph of a trawler on the front. "Are they the two who reported that Mrs. MacDonald and Joan were drinking heavily?"

"They are. Colin MacLeod is the manager. Mairi is Lisa MacKenzie's sister."

"I can't keep track of all these 'macs.'"

He laughed. "You're going to meet dozens of MacKenzies if you stay around here. And MacAulays and MacLeods. The real problem is that, for a long time on the islands, children were traditionally named after the immediate grandparent and, as you can imagine, we ended up with many identical names. To distinguish one from another, we use what we call by-names, or I suppose you'd say nicknames. For instance, to distinguish one Ann MacDonald from another, she might be called 'Anna Mhor,' which means 'Big Anna.' We also use names from their occupation, like 'Duncan Ciobair,' which is 'Duncan the Shepherd,' the man we met this afternoon. Sometimes a lad might get a nickname such as 'Shoes,' because he liked shoes when he was four years old, and it sticks with him for the rest of his life, even though nobody remembers the origin of the nickname. There's also patronymic and residential or local names. Shall I go on?"

"No, that's fine. I get the picture." I said trying not to do the "how quaint" thing, although I thought it was. "I guess you have to rely on people not changing that much. I mean, Big Anna had better not go to a Weight Watchers program or nobody will know who she is."

He laughed. "In fact, the 'big' didn't necessarily refer to her size but her place in the family."

"Are Mairi and Lisa related to the man we met on the road, Duncan the Shepherd?"

"They're his daughters. His wife, Anna, died about four years ago of cancer. Tragic really. Diagnosed in January and she was dead by April."

We were both silent for a moment each touched briefly by the cold finger of mortality. Then he checked out his menu.

"They don't have haggis, so you're off the hook."

He waved at the waitress, and she came over at once. She was wearing a plain white blouse and navy skirt, and there was a white sailor's cap perched on her head, the band of which read, "HMS *DUKE.*" Her nameplate read, "CATRIONA."

She and Gillies discussed the menu in Gaelic, and she managed to lean over and press her full bosom into his shoulder while she pointed out one of the choicer dishes.

"Catriona recommends the prawns," said Gillies. "They were brought in a couple of hours ago."

"They're like shrimps, right?"

"From away are you?" interjected the waitress.

"Canada."

"I almost emigrated there when I was in my twenties. From what I hear, it's a good thing I didn't."

I wondered what she was referring to, but decided against asking her. I put on a pleasant expression and said I'd take the prawns. Gillies did the same, and Catriona stuffed her notebook down the waistband of her tight skirt, gathered up the menus, and went to place the order.

"This is one of your regular haunts, I see." By now I have to admit I really was curious about Gillies.

"It's handy. I'm not a good cook and the food here is always fresh."

The conversation led easily into "places of interest" on the island, and we talked about that for a while. Then I said, "By the way, when is the funeral for Mrs. MacDonald?"

"Wednesday, I believe. They're waiting until her daughter gets here."

"Do you think I would offend anybody if I went to it?"

"I don't see why. Funerals are always well attended here. It would be appreciated."

Catriona dropped off a basket of bread. "Won't be long."

She seemed friendlier to me now she'd heard where I was from. Pity, I suppose.

"What are you going to do about your conference?" Gillies asked.

"The last session was scheduled for tomorrow, then I was planning to just hang around Edinburgh and take in the sights. But it doesn't make any sense to go back now, much as I'd like to. I guess this is going to be my holiday."

"If you feel like it, I can show you around the island tomorrow. It's not Edinburgh, but we're proud of it."

I must say I was pleased at the offer and said I did feel like it. See, I told you, Paula, I have a fantastic ability to concentrate.

All in all, in spite of the circumstances, it was a most pleasant evening. As promised, dinner was delicious. It might have been the sea air that was blowing in through the partly open window, but I was suddenly ravenous and, throwing delicacy aside, ate like a trucker. We got into a rather sober but sincere discussion of the difficulty of policing in the new age, and Gillies said again how glad he was that Lewis was maintaining its time warp and the crime rate was ridiculously low. I almost confided in him what had happened to me with the DeLucas, but it was still too raw a subject. Gillies appeared to be sincerely interested in my work, and I was happy to talk about it. He nursed a glass of wine through the meal, but it didn't seem to be an effort. I'm always on the alert for signs of a new man's drinking proclivities. I did my usual mineral water.

However, by ten o'clock, I pleaded to fatigue and the desire for an early night, and he escorted me to my door, shook hands — no kisses thank you — and left. I waited several minutes to give him time to leave the building, then I returned to the dining room. I felt a bit devious about this, because he had been such a great host, but I wanted to have a word with Mr. and Mrs. MacLeod, and I thought it would be better if I were on my own when I talked to them. Things had already got tense over at Tormod's house about me acting as if a crime had been committed.

There was only one couple remaining in the restaurant, lingering over their meal, but Catriona, the waitress who had almost been my countrywoman, was nowhere in sight. Colin was tidying up the other tables ready for breakfast.

"Hallo again. Did you forget something?" His tone wasn't particularly friendly.

"No, but I was wondering if I could have a word with you and Mairi."

"What about? Oh cheerie-bye, Mr. Plotnik. Mrs. Plotnik." He waved at the couple who had finally decided to leave. "I've got to set up for breakfast," he said to me.

"I'll help you. I waited tables when I was in university."

"Suit yourself. You can freshen up the flowers. Toss out the ones that are wilted, but try to stretch it."

He'd collected all the flower vases that were on the tables and put them on a tray. I took the seat at the table, while he began to put out cutlery. He was a stocky man, late thirties probably, with brown hair, short-cropped the way most Scottish men seemed to favour. I got the impression he'd be more at home on a fishing trawler than in a dining room talking nice to tourists. Maybe he'd been the influence behind all the sea treasures on the wall.

"I met your sister-in-law," I said, thinking I'd warm up to the subject I wanted to get to.

"So I understand. She was by here earlier on and told us all about what happened. Puir Tormod. But it was probably a quick death."

I didn't know about that, but I wasn't going into that now. I pulled some dead leaves from one of the white daisies. They'd last another day or two.

"She told you about me then?"

"Aye. She said you were a detective from Canada." He whipped off a soiled tablecloth and shook out a fresh one. "She said you were interested in the car accident that killed Sarah MacDonald. The driver hasn't been found. Is that what you want to talk to me about?"

I hoped Lisa hadn't told him about my relationship to Joan, but he didn't seem to know.

"As a matter of fact, yes. I have no official capacity, you understand, but the woman is . . . she is known to me, and I'm trying to find out exactly what happened."

He was putting cereal bowls on the table now. "Carry on, then."

"I understand you made a statement to the police that both women were drinking heavily on Friday night."

"If by 'a statement' you mean I told Gill what I saw, yes. But I didn't sign any paper or anything like that."

Once again, his tone verged on surly, and I wondered what had irked him. He was moving quickly and efficiently about the room, straightening the little pots of jam that were in the middle of each table.

"How many drinks did you serve them?"

"Och, I don't know. It was a busy night."

"Four? Five? What constitutes 'heavily'?"

He returned to my table and put the tidied flower vases on a tray, still without looking at me. "Sarah MacDonald had the capacity of a sailor, that one. Just last Tuesday she came in and tossed back six shots of single malt in less than two hours. Said she was celebrating. I was afraid we'd have to put her up for the night, even though she lives two streets away. But no, she got off on her own steam."

I heard the subtext. Not his fault if she left drunk.

"On Friday then, how many drinks did you serve her?" I repeated the question, because he'd avoided answering it.

He hesitated. "Myself, I wasn't the one at the bar. We had some tourists in, and boy they kept me busy." He waggled his hand to indicate that. Then he called out. "Hey, Mairi. Come over a sec."

His wife had come into the room from the kitchen. She was wearing a denim jumpsuit that was holding her belly like a sling. She waddled over to us, and Colin pulled out an extra chair so she could sit down.

"Miss Morris is asking about Friday night when Sarah MacDonald came into the bar with that other lady."

"Oh aye."

"She wants to know exactly how many drinks they had."

He underlined "exactly."

"I'll have to think about that. Two for certain up front when they came in. But you were serving them, weren't you?"

"No. I had the Russkies from the cruise ship."

"Are you sure?"

"'Course I am."

"Oh." They exchanged glances.

"Hold on," I said. "You, Mairi, know definitely that you served two single malts, but you don't know if they had more after that or not?"

"Of course they did," interjected Colin. "I saw Sarah when she stood up. She staggered. She had to lean on the other woman. They were sloshed all right. "

"But Mairi, you don't remember serving them more liquor?"

"It was crazy busy that night. I may have. I mean, I must have."

I was pressing them and making them uncomfortable. At least, Mairi looked uncomfortable. Colin was getting angry.

"Did you see if both of them were drinking or just Sarah?"

Mairi shrugged. "I can't say I was taking any notice. They were over there in that booth, by the door, all hugger-mugger. I thought Sarah was trying to close a real-estate deal. She's been in here before doing that."

She suddenly clasped her stomach. "Oops, the baby just turned and reminded me I have to use the loo." She got to her feet. "I heard that the post mortem showed Sarah was over the legal limit anyway."

"That's true, but they might have gone and visited somebody after they left here."

"Tormod MacAulay, according to what we heard," said Colin. You did, did you?

"Did you actually see the two women get into the car?"

"No, I told you. I had my hands full."

"Mairi, did you see them?"

She grinned with a hint of triumph. "I did. I had to go out to the back and get some more bitters. That's where the parking lot is. I saw them both get into the hired car."

"Was Mrs. MacDonald driving?"

"No, the other woman was."

"By the way, what did she look like this woman?"

Colin answered. "Blonde, bleached by the look of it, chubby. Older end of fifties. Shorter than me. She was wearing sunglasses the entire time. Either she has weak eyes or she thinks she's Elizabeth Taylor."

None of that description fitted Joan, but it was easy to dye your hair and put on weight. Dark glasses are surprisingly effective if you're trying to avoid recognition.

Colin picked up the tray of flower vases. "We've got to close up now."

I stood up. "Thank you for talking to me."

Mairi hurried off while Colin walked with me to the door. He paused. He was peering into my face and making no bones about the fact he didn't seem to like what he saw. Hey, he wasn't so attractive to look at either. There were lines of discontent around his mouth and forehead. Perhaps in a happier mood he'd have boyish good looks, but not at the moment.

"Lisa said you had her go through the house to see if anything was missing. What was that all about?"

"It wasn't to see if anything was missing exactly, just to see if anything was out of place. It's a common procedure if there's been a sudden death."

"Is it now? Well, it upset her to have to do that. She was good chums with Tormod."

I didn't know what to say to him, as he was blaming me and perhaps rightly so.

"She hasn't had an easy life," he continued. "And seeing as she's family, I'm protective of her interests."

"Naturally, you would be."

"Tongues wagged when she moved in with Tormod, but she wasn't involved with him except as a friend and employer."

He hovered for a moment, considering whether or not he would go any further. I waited.

"Tormod valued her. She told me he left her a bequest in his will. She didn't want him to, but he insisted." He started to fiddle with the small silver earring in his left ear. "When that is known, it'll be sure to start more gossip. And Miss hyphenated Coral-Lyn Pitchers isn't going to be too happy. But I know Lisa worked hard for the old man, and if he wanted to help her out, that's up to him, isn't it?"

"It certainly is."

Suddenly he looked up at the big ship's clock over the bar.

"I'd better lock up. It's way past ten. Breakfast's from 7:30 to 9:00. And I should warn you, we're prompt on the islands. Both ends — starting and finishing."

I honestly couldn't tell if his barely contained animosity was directed at me or was his general attitude to life.

He ushered me out, obviously not about to say anything else. I went up to my room and sat at the window for a while, watching the masts bob on the water. There was still light enough to read by, but the street was quiet. The Sabbath was being observed. I was definitely in another world.

CHAPTER SIXTEEN

That night I slept soundly for the first time in a long while, with only minimally anxious dreams. Daylight returned at four-thirty and slid through a gap in the curtains, but I pulled the sheet over my head and, amazingly, managed to sleep on until almost seven. A quick shower and then I went in search of a public telephone. I found one in a narrow hallway leading from the bar to the rear washrooms and the kitchen. I could hear the comforting sound of dishes clinking from the kitchen, and bacon smells wafted on the air, almost causing me to salivate.

I phoned Paula. We had been friends too long and through too many tough situations for me to hesitate about calling her, even though it was three in the morning Toronto time and I had to call collect. As always, she sounded alert and wide awake.

"Wow, kiddo. Bring me up to date. What's going on?"

I launched into my recital of events, but had managed only to tell her about Tormod MacAulay's death and the neighbours apparently identifying Joan's car leaving the house that night before Colin MacLeod came out of the kitchen, tray in hand.

"*Madainn mhath*, good morning," he said.

He continued into the dining room, but I was suddenly restricted in what I could say. At various times, on probably dozens of occasions, either Paula or I had been forced into cryptic conversations because somebody could overhear us. We'd developed a code.

"I can't hear you, please speak up." I said to Paula. "The connection is bad."

"Okay. The person you just said hello to?"

"Hmn, hmn. That's better."

"Do you think MacAulay was murdered?" Paula asked.

"Could be."

"Who would have?"

"It's hard to tell, really."

"Surely you don't think it was Joan?"

"Who knows?"

Colin came into the hall and made sign language to indicate there was a table waiting and was I hungry?

"Just a sec, Paula," I said and partially covered the mouthpiece. "Thanks, Colin. I'll be right there." I returned to the phone. "Sorry Paula, go on."

"Big ears, huh?" she remarked, laughing.

"Very. Anyway, I'm going to do a bit of touring today."

"Can you call me later from a private telephone? Not to mention at a slightly better time?"

"Sorry. But I'll try to do that. Phones aren't easy to come by."

"I'm tied up all tomorrow in meetings, but you can leave me a message at least. Are you all right, Chris?"

"As well as can be expected. The air's great here."

"Well, that's something."

"One of the local officers has offered to show me around the island."

"As a tourist?"

"Not entirely."

"Take care, Chris. This isn't an ordinary situation. I don't want you getting hurt."

"You're right. Anyway, get back to bed. I'll call again as soon as there are more developments."

"To hell with more developments. I want to know how you're doing."

"Okay, okay, stop fussing. I'm a big girl."

"That is not the point. Do I need to remind you that I care what happens?"

She sounded angry with me, but I didn't want to keep her on the phone any longer. Knowing Paula, she'd tell me what was on her mind.

We hung up and Colin, who had been waiting, ushered me through the door and led me over to the table by the window that I'd had last night.

"D'ye want the full Scottish breakfast?"

"Sure, why not?"

He poured me coffee from a carafe and disappeared into the kitchen. Two middle-aged couples came into the dining room at the same time. Both men were freshly shaved, with shiny chins and virtuous looks. The women were also dressed for action in pastel pantsuits and sensible running shoes. We all exchanged "Good mornings," "Lovely mornings," the way people do when they're on holiday and obliged to eat in close proximity to total strangers. I wasn't quite up to sharing life stories, but the others immediately began to find out where they were all from. One couple was German, one English. I put my head down and sipped at my coffee, which as I expected was depressingly weak. Ah, Tim Hortons, where are you when I need you?

Colin returned, carrying a plate of food, which he set down in front of me. Two fried eggs, fried tomatoes, fried bread, and one fat black sausage. There was a token gesture to health in a twist of orange, more peel than pulp.

He pointed. "That's a blood sausage. It's made here in town and it's very good. Try it."

"Thanks. I will."

"Anyway, I couldn't help but overhear you say you're going to do some touring today. Is Gill taking you?"

"Yes, he is."

"He's a great chap — for a police officer." This last was said with a grin meant to be disarming. "Did he say where he was going to take you first?"

"The Callanish Standing Stones, I believe."

"Good. They're a popular tourist site, although as far as I'm concerned, if you didn't know they were ancient you wouldn't be that impressed. Just a lot of grey stone pillars jumbled around."

The German man was waving his hand to get Colin's attention, but he still lingered.

"Sorry if I was a bit *crosta* last night. It's the old big-brother thing."

"That's okay. I'm sure Lisa is glad to have you looking after her like that."

He shrugged. "Maybe."

He looked as if he wanted to say more, but his guests were obviously in need of coffee. He left me to my breakfast. I started with the eggs, fresh, and then the tomatoes, soggy. If I ate one of these breakfasts every day, I'd soon have to be identified as "Big Chris." I was trying to get up my nerve to tackle the sausage when Gillies came in. He, too, was shiny of chin, and emanated a pleasant soapy smell and perky energy.

He grinned and walked over to me. "I came early. Hope you don't mind."

"Not at all. You've saved me from this bloody sausage that Colin is determined I eat. Have a seat." I pushed my plate over towards him. "Here. I didn't touch it."

"I actually ate already, but I'd never say no to blood sausages. They're made in town."

He took a piece of toast that was going cold and hard in the silver rack provided for that express purpose. I waited for a moment.

"Gill, if it's all right with you, I'd like to go to Sarah MacDonald's office. You know how it is, find out about the victim and you sometimes find out about the bad guy."

I was using criminal jargon again, but I couldn't help it.

He hesitated, then chomped down on the crisp toast. "I don't see why not, if it'll set your mind at rest. The office is just down from here."

Colin came out of the kitchen, greeted Gillies, commented on the sausage swap, then did a quick refill of everybody's coffee cup.

"Enjoy the Stones," he called as we left. "Callanish, not Rolling."

The Lewis Estate Agency where Sarah MacDonald had worked was a plain, square building with a dull façade of rat-grey brick. A rectangular display window held a few photographs of properties for sale. I had a quick glance before we went in, but didn't see the MacAulay cottage listed.

A bell like the kind you hear in an old-fashioned grocery store signalled our entrance. The office was long and narrow, with half a dozen movable partitions marking each agent's space. A mature woman was at the front desk. She was immaculately made up, with flaring red cheeks and clotted eyelashes. Her ash-blonde hair was teased into a stiff, high beehive that I had seen only in photos from the 1960s. When she saw Gillies, she yelped with excitement.

"Gill, rumour has it that Prince Willie is paying us a visit. Is it true?"

He dodged the question. "Where'd you hear that?"

"Morag Murray was down on the beach scraping crotal off the rocks. You know, for her dyes. A man appeared out of nowhere and asked for directions to the Blackhouse Village. Gave her quite a start, but she knew at once he was a secret-service man from the way he was acting. Ever so polite, but his eyes never stopped moving. He didn't want directions, he just wanted to know what she was doing. So are we right?"

"You know I couldn't tell you that. National security is involved."

The receptionist gave a little squeal. "So it is true. My grand-daughter's mad for that lad. She'll be over the moon. When's he coming?"

"Janice, I didn't confirm that."

She flapped her hand at him. "Don't worry, I won't mention you. Morag can winkle it out of Rosie anyway." She reached for her phone, thought better of it, and regrouped into her professional manner.

"What can I do for you then?" She looked pointedly at me, and Gillies responded.

"Oh, sorry. Janice MacIver, Detective-Sergeant Christine Morris. She's visiting from Canada."

"Nice to meet you."

"Likewise."

Janice wasn't a Scot, more Yorkshire.

"I'm just following up on the accident involving Sarah MacDonald," continued Gillies.

"My soul, what a shock that was. I was the one who got the call. I'm not usually in on Saturdays, but Andrea was off sick. Young Barry Irwin, the constable from Barvas, rang. He said Sarah was dead of a car accident. Well, right off I thought that was peculiar, because her car was in the parking lot. I noticed it because she'd taken Mark Faraday's spot, and I knew he'd hit the roof when he came in. I expected to see her in the office, but she wasn't here, and I just thought she'd gone out to get a coffee or something. I never in a million years thought I'd be hearing that she was dead." Janice paused to get her breath and pay a brief tribute to the departed. "Well, then young Barry said as how the car in the accident was a red Vauxhall, which was hired out by Arnol motors to a woman from Canada. Well, I knew right away who that was, and I told him. She'd come in here early Friday evening looking for Sarah. I told him as how I saw them later on, going into Duke's. I'd popped into the co-op to get some chops for dinner, and I saw them as I was coming out. Everybody's saying it was her driving the car and she's run off. Or drowned herself. Have you found her?"

"No, we haven't. We're just sort of backtracking Sarah's movements to see if we come up with anything helpful."

Both Gillies and I were perched on the edge of nearby desks at this point. We knew a garrulous witness when we found one. Let them ramble on, sift out the nuggets from the dust.

Janice smoothed back her hair, shifting it wholesale in the process. "Well, that woman came in here on Friday afternoon without a doubt. She was a blonde, rather plump, about my age.

Not a local. At first I thought she was from America, but she said no, she was a Canadian."

"Did she give a name?" he asked.

"No. I inquired, of course, but she just said, 'She doesn't know me.' She asked for Sarah particularly. I'm supposed to direct any clients to the agent on duty, but she wasn't interested. I had to call Sarah on her mobile phone and tell her to get over here."

"Did Mrs. MacDonald seem to know the woman?" I said, making my tone as casual as possible.

"I can't say. I was just packing up, you see. I leave on the dot of five. If I didn't, these agents would have me run ragged. I told the woman to have a seat and left."

"So you don't know why she was asking for Mrs. MacDonald?"

"I assume she was in the market for a property, but she didn't want to chat, I could tell that."

Janice reached in the drawer on her desk and took out a bundle of plastic-wrapped sheets of paper.

"I collect these myself, and I give them to clients to read while they wait. Makes them laugh."

I looked at the top sheet, which was a series of jokes headed, "CHILDREN SAY THE FUNNIEST THINGS."

"She just put them aside without even looking at them," said Janice. She was so indignant that for a moment I thought I'd better start reading, but I was saved by the sound of the door tinkling. A short, wide man came in. He saw Gillies and nodded a greeting.

"*Madainn mhath*, Gill. *Ciamar tha thu?*"

"Good morning, Mark. I'm good, thanks."

Mark beamed at me and stuck out his hand. He was dressed in brown pants and a tweed blazer that had probably been made locally years ago and, from the look of it, passed down from his ancestors. We shook hands.

"Mark Faraday, at your service. Looking ta buy a property are ye?"

"No, I'm afraid not."

His smile vanished. No point in wasting it on non-prospects.

He turned and addressed the receptionist in Gaelic. She replied in English.

"Your wife has rung twice already and says to phone the lawyer as soon as you get in. Coral-Lyn Pitchers rang half an hour ago. She wants you to get back to her right away. She left the number."

He took the slips of paper she handed him, grunted, crumpled one of them up, and dropped it in a nearby wastebasket. He went into one of the partitioned cubicles at the back of the room.

"He's going through a separation," said Janice in a conspiratorial voice, although I thought Faraday might be able to hear her. She tapped the side of her head. "It's shaking off a few slates if you ask me. So where were we?"

"I asked if Mrs. MacDonald had seemed to know her visitor, and you said you didn't see them greet each other."

"That's right. I wasn't present. I have to leave on . . . "

I'd been aware of Faraday talking in the background, but suddenly there was the sound of a receiver slamming down.

"Fuck! Fucking little sanctimonious bitch!"

Janice froze, and Gillies and I both turned to see what was happening. Faraday came hurtling down to the reception desk.

"Janice, did you know Tormod MacAulay dropped his clogs?"

"What?'

"He's dead. Gone."

She looked shocked. "When did that happen?"

"He was found in the house, yesterday. Now Miss Yankee Twinkle-toes says she doesn't want to go ahead with the sale of the property." He mimicked Coral-Lyn's nasal voice with a savage accuracy. "*Andy's too upset to go through that now. We've put everything on hold until the will is settled.*" Bullshit. Fucking bullshit. Lucille's got to her, you mark my words. As soon as the dust settles, she'll get that fucking listing."

Foolishly, Janice decided to take this moment to reprimand him. "I've asked you to watch your language in here. This isn't Glasgow. A client could come in."

Obviously, Janice considered Gillies's and my ears sufficiently hardened to swearing. I didn't exactly sympathize with Faraday, but Janice's self-righteous tone of voice and prim manner were the last thing he needed. She might as well have thrust a stick into a hornet's nest and waggled it around. I was almost afraid Faraday would grab her, and instinctively, I moved closer to the desk I noticed Gillies shifted too.

Faraday's face had turned red with rage. "I'll speak how the fuck I want. It's my deal we're talking about. Do you hear? It's my fucking deal that's in the fucking toilet."

Vocabulary has a tendency to become limited in moments of stress.

"Fuck it."

He shoved open the door and left. The air in the office swayed in his wake.

"I told you he was unstable," said Janice, but she looked shaken by the violence of the outburst. She reached in her drawer and took out a box of tissues. "Poor Tormod. Just when life was looking up for him."

CHAPTER SEVENTEEN

Janice didn't elaborate on her remark, and Gillies moved on and told her what we knew about MacAulay's death, omitting what the MacLeans had reported, although I thought she'd hear about that soon enough.

"Poor Andy. He was devoted to his granddad. And Lisa will take it hard too. Tormod was very fond of her, and she did look after him."

There was the slightest of emphasis on the "look after." Colin MacLeod was correct in his assessment of public opinion about his sister-in-law.

The telephone rang, and Janice answered it with a bright voice in spite of her upset.

"Good morning, Lewis Estate Agency. Yes, Lucille?... No, he's not here. I suggest you try the hotel. . . . .Yes, he is. . . . The MacAulay deal is on hold. . . . Yes, I just heard myself. Shocking isn't it? . . . Yes, Coral-Lyn rang him. . . . Yes, that's putting it mildly.... All right. I'll pass on the message."

She hung up. "That was Mark's wife. She laughed when I said he'd lost the deal." Janice shook her head. "I don't understand how married people can get to hate each other so much."

Gillies said, "Do you think we could talk a bit more about Sarah MacDonald? Are you up to it?"

"Oh yes. I'm all right. Your news was a shock is all."

She tucked the tissue up the cuff of her sleeve. Her heavy eyeliner had smudged, giving her "racoon eyes," but she was a woman ready to wreak vengeance.

"Sarah and Mark didn't get along at all. In fact, to be blunt, I'd say they hated each other. With all the uncertainties in the world, this is a very competitive business, as you can imagine. Those two undercut each other at the slightest opportunity." She averted her eyes, as people often do when they're about to say something they feel guilty about. "Not to speak ill of the dead, but Sarah MacDonald was her own worst enemy. She could have been good, but she messed things up. Missed appointments, things like that." A pause, another touch-up to the unruffled hair. "Too fond of her water of life: whisky," she added for my benefit.

"Did they clash over the Tormod MacAulay estate?" asked Gillies.

Janice smiled. "Yes and no. Mark got the listing originally, although for some reason Sarah thought she deserved it. She'd been engaged to Tormod's son many years ago, and it fell through, but she must have thought she was still in the family. Mark's had a few lean months since his wife dumped him. They were partners, and she compensated for his lack of polish, if I may put it that way. Now nobody wants to work with him. I was astonished when Tormod MacAulay gave him the listing on the property. To tell you the truth, I think he didn't know that Lucille was no longer in the picture. She was chummy with Coral-Lyn Pitchers. They go to the same church." She grinned, not able to suppress the touch of malice. "However, it's my belief that Sarah gazumped him."

I glanced over at Gillies for clarification.

"According to Scottish law, a real-estate negotiation isn't complete until what's called 'the concluding missives' are signed. In between the time of exchange of letters and so on, the buyer can be gazumped. That means that, if the seller receives a better offer, he can accept it without legal consequences. Did I get it right, Janice?"

"You did. Mind you, legal consequences or not, you make yourself very unpopular if you do that. But last Monday, Sarah came into the office like a cat who had an eye on a particularly fat canary. She didn't tell me what that bird was, but she dropped enough hints that I guessed."

"Did you write anything up for her?" I asked.

"No. That was why I suspected she was pulling a gazump. She usually got her pound of flesh out of me, but this day she said she'd type the offer herself. She had a long-distance call, which she took in the closing room, not at her desk. I had the impression she was working with a Norwegian group, and they always shell out big money."

"Let me get this straight then. Tormod MacAulay had already agreed to an offer to buy his property from Miss Pitchers's father, but he was quite within his legal rights to accept a better offer if one came along before what you called 'the concluding missives.' And you think Mrs. MacDonald brought such an offer?"

"That's correct. I'm positive she took it over to Tormod on Monday evening last. And, you should know, they had no legal obligation to inform Miss Pitchers that he'd changed his mind. She was in for a big shock. The deal was to close as of tomorrow. Anyway, that's all water under the bridge now. None of the offers can go through until the estate is settled. Mark was assuming Andy MacAulay would go ahead and sell as planned, with him as agent, but Andy's fiancée has other ideas, I gather."

Janice dabbed at the corner of her mouth and checked the tissue to see if she had lipstick on it.

"I think I need a little repairing." She stood up. "Is there anything else you want to know?"

"Do you mind if we have a look at Sarah's desk?"

"Doesn't bother me. She had the one on the right, just in front of Mark's."

Purse in hand, Janice sailed off to the washroom.

"Let's go," said Gillies, and we walked down to the cubicle that had belonged to Sarah.

The surface of her desk was tidy, with two trays marked, respectively, IN and OUT. The OUT tray was empty and IN had only a couple of sheets of paper in it which proved to be advertisements for properties listed by other agents. There was one framed photograph of a girl about seven or eight. I had the impression it had been taken a long time ago.

"Where's the daughter now?" I asked Gillies.

"She's married. She lives in the Midlands somewhere."

That was it for any clues as to Sarah's personality or current business affairs. Gillies opened the drawer, but there was nothing in it except typical office detritus, paper clips, a couple of pens, and a crumpled chocolate-bar wrapper.

"Was there a briefcase registered among Sarah's effects? I asked him.

"Not that I recall. She had a handbag, which was still in the car, but I'm pretty sure they didn't find a briefcase."

I pointed to Mark Faraday's cubicle, where a snazzy black-leather briefcase was leaning against the desk. "It's an agent's essential equipment. The badge of office. They all have them."

"Maybe it's in her flat."

"Joan came to see her in the office, not at home, which could suggest business. It sounds as if Sarah wasn't expecting her, but surely if you're an agent you come prepared to deal with clients."

"With briefcase and forms."

"Precisely."

"When we get back to the station, I'll look into it."

I grimaced at him. "You think I'm spinning cobwebs, don't you? That I'm finding a gunman behind every rock."

He shrugged. "I don't know if you are or not. It's frustrating not having much solid information."

"At least the gazumping thing gives us a possible explanation for Tormod MacAulay's sudden trip to Houston. If I'd accepted a better offer over my grandson's prospective father-in-law's, I'd get out of town, too."

Janice emerged from the washroom, tidied up and blooded for the battle.

"We're off then, Janice. Thanks for your help. By the way, do you know if Sarah usually carried a briefcase with her?"

Janice eased herself into the chair and carefully put her telephone wire over her head. "She always did. She had a new one. Snakeskin or some such silly thing. Garish, I thought, not really professional."

This from a woman whose cheeks and lips were as scarlet as any clown's.

I thought I'd been the only one to register Janice's remark about Tormod, but bless him, Gillies had too, and he went back to it.

"Why did you say things were looking up for Tormod?"

"Well he seemed so much better. I met him in the co-op, must have been on the Tuesday, and he was bright as a pin. He used the words himself about life looking up. Such a shame it wasn't true. The calm before the storm I suppose. I've heard that people often perk up right before they die."

The telephone rang and she wiggled her fingers at us as she answered it.

"Good morning, Lewis Estate Agency . . . "

We left in a flurry of silent goodbyes.

Outside, the sunshine had settled in for a while and, even back here, there was the tang of the sea on the breeze.

"Ready to be a tourist?"

"I am. Take me to the Stones. Callanish, not Rolling."

As we drove off, I realized I'd been relieved that Sarah MacDonald's daughter was an adult capable of taking care of herself. I didn't know what responsibility my own mother had in the fatal accident, but I was shouldering it the way I always had. I'd felt guilty when she skipped out of paying the rent on one of our numerous basement apartments, I'd squirmed when she told blatant lies in front of me to the creditors or the newest boyfriend. Later on, Paula, down to earth as ever, would get hold of me. "Repeat after me, '*My mother and I are two separate people. I cannot live her life for her. She is a grown-up woman.*' Come on, repeat . . . "

CHAPTER EIGHTEEN

The sunshine continued to hold as we crossed the Barvas moor. White masses of clouds filled the sky and the sunlight swept across the dun-coloured scrub and brown-black earth, warming and deepening. I felt as if I were entering a Rembrandt painting. When we'd got under way, I told Gillies about last night's conversation with Colin and Mairi MacLeod.

He grimaced. "I had a feeling you were going to go and chat them up."

I was embarrassed. "Sorry. I wasn't going behind your back. It's just that there I was on the spot, and it seemed natural to follow up."

He grunted, not totally buying that explanation. "What else?"

"Neither of them could really swear that the two women were drinking heavily. In fact, only two drinks were substantiated."

"Mairi told me Sarah was staggering, and the other woman, whom we're presuming was Joan, had to help her."

"There are lots of reasons people stagger. A stone on the ground, broken heels, emotions."

"Aye, that's true. But Sarah, at least, must have had a lot more to drink after she left the hotel. According to the post-mortem report, she was way over the legal blood-alcohol limit."

"Surely that confirms what Lisa said about Tormod's whisky being low in the bottle?"

"It does. It could be that Mrs. MacDonald took your mother out to see Tormod to celebrate her real-estate deal."

"Why?"

"I don't know. A new pal. Come and see my client and have a drink."

"Maybe."

"So they had too many drinks, left, and crashed the car. Tormod died that night — from a predictable hemorrhage. There's nothing sinister in that scenario."

Seeing his expression, I suddenly felt deflated. "For sure the case isn't nice and tidy so far, but that's real life, isn't it? It's only on television shows that everything is sewn up quickly in time for the final commercial."

He grinned at me. "We don't get those shows over here."

At the crossroads we turned left, as we had done before. We passed the crash site, but I resisted the impulse to ask Gillies to stop the car so we could get out and study it again. There was nothing to be gained from doing that, except more frustration.

The Callanish Standing Stones were about fifteen minutes further driving. Once again, the weather cooperated by dropping the sunshine, and grey clouds filled the sky, which was the perfect backdrop for viewing the ancient stones.

When I was in my second year of university, I'd done a tour of southern England, and had gone to see Stonehenge. By then there were barriers around the area to protect the ancient stones from the ravages of visitor wear and, worse, vandalism. However, not even the fences, nor the crowds of people with cameras, could detract from the magnificence of the site. I was expecting something similar from Callanish.

We parked the car and walked up a path clotted with sheep manure, which wound up to the top of the hill. On the slopes, ewes chewed the grass, their lambs at their side, and eyed us placidly as we went by. The stones themselves were situated at the plateau and I must admit that, on first viewing, like Colin MacLeod, I couldn't see what the fuss was all about. There were two dozen or so ash-grey stones, well-spaced from each other, and the height seemed to vary from chest level to double my height. Most of them were rough, elongated pillars, but some were wedges, like giant grave markers.

We stood for a moment at the edge of the field. The neat grey-brown Lewishan houses were behind us, keeping the stones in the realm of the homey and unglamorous.

"They're arranged roughly in the shape of a cross," said Gillies. "Nothing to do with Christianity, of course. They predate Christ by three thousand years. One of the theories is that they were used for some kind of astrological divination."

I noticed an elderly couple were standing in the centre, and the woman had placed her palm flat against the flank of one of the stones. I wondered if she was trying to soak up the ancient energy.

After a brief-but-intense attachment to the Catholic church, I had abandoned all religious institutions — one of the few areas of life where Joan and I had shared a similar point of view. She was firm in her convictions that the churches were man-made and had little to do with true spirituality. "Imagine killing somebody because they elevated a little piece of dry bread in the air." Surprising to me was how much she knew of religious history, and in our good moments together she would tell me stories of how the churches began and what they did to each other in the name of truth. Not for me, Winnie-the-Pooh or Spiderman. On a regular basis, she read passages from the Bible. "Only because this is your heritage and you should know these stories." She was right about that, and they stood me in good stead when I took an English degree at university. Later on, long after I'd run off and dived into my own life, she'd abandoned even that tie to traditional Christianity and embraced what I thought was whacky New Age stuff. A few years ago, she announced she was a "follower of the Wiccan way" — more popularly known as witchcraft — although I don't think she kept it up.

I still wondered if she'd come to Lewis to visit these ancient stones, met up with Sarah MacDonald, gone with her to visit her client, had an accident . . . all very innocent.

Frankly, I couldn't tell if the ancient stones were helping me put things in perspective or encouraging a state of denial.

The other couple left, and Gillies and I were alone. He didn't speak, giving me room to absorb the surroundings, which were actually impressing me more and more. Fields of closely cropped grass, sprinkled with dandelions, rolled away on all sides to gently rounded misty mountains in the distance. The clouds hung grey and sombre. The quiet of the place began to settle me down.

"Why don't you walk around a bit?" said Gillies. "If you go to the far side of the field, you can see clearly what is a sort of avenue to the centre. You can imagine a procession moving through the stones. It's my favourite view."

I did as he suggested, then walked slowly to the high, thinner stone at the centre, trying to tune in those ancient people. So many lives come and gone, a blink when measured against the age of the stones. I was beginning to feel decidedly insignificant, and I was most happy to be distracted by the sudden appearance of a border collie, who dashed towards me as if we were old friends. He had a stick in his mouth that he dropped peremptorily at my feet and demanded I throw for him. So much for profundity. I chucked the stick, and the dog chased it, got it, and brought it back, all at top speed.

Gillies came over. "He'll have you doing that all day."

"So I see."

I threw the stick yet again, but the dog stopped, stared into the distance, listening. Then, obeying some sound or command I couldn't hear, he dashed off as suddenly as he had appeared.

I was grabbed by a sudden vivid memory of arguing with Joan about whether or not we could get a dog. I wanted one so badly — a dog, any dog — but she was adamant, citing the smallness of the apartment, time, and so on. Then she said, "Besides, the only kind of dog worth having is a border collie, and we certainly don't have the proper place for one of those."

"What are you thinking?" Gillies asked. I had gone into a reverie.

"Just that I feel as if I have put a negative in the developing tray and, ever so slowly, the picture is emerging."

"That sounds intriguing. Do you want to stay a while longer

or would you like to have a coffee? You can tell me what's on your mind."

I opted for the coffee, and we went back down the hill to the parking lot where there was a restaurant and attached gift shop. This waitress also knew Gillies, and I was beginning to think he must eat out a lot. Once again, he introduced me as being from Canada. I received a smile and another *Failte*, which sounded like 'Fellcha,' and I now knew was the word for *welcome*. She didn't have any relatives in Canada.

We had coffee and scones, but the conversation was stilted, so I soon suggested we take a look at the gift shop. I bought a hand-crafted silver pendant for Paula and a cuddly lamb for my god-daughter, Chelsea, from the gift shop. I had one brief stab of memory, of a tiny skeletal child who'd never had a toy in her life.

Gillies was looking through the CD section, and he took down the disc of *Mamma Mia.*

"My eldest loves this show. I'll get it for her. Have you seen it?'

"Four times. It's wonderful."

We made our purchases and walked out to the car. I'm not sure if it was still the influence of the Callanish Stones, or just that I was feeling more comfortable with him than I remembered being with a man for a long time, but as we drove off, I found myself wanting to talk to him, *really* talk to him, I mean. "As you've probably noticed, Gill, my mother and I aren't what you would call 'close.' But it's funny that you should pick up that particular disc, because that is associated with one of my most pleasant memories of her . . . "

I stopped, suddenly unsure of myself, but he nodded encouragement. "I was in university, and I hadn't heard a word from her for several months. No letters, no calls. She said she'd been in a treatment centre. Did I mention she has been an alcoholic? Anyway, she called and invited me to see her new apartment and have dinner. I'm embarrassed to admit that I was pretty churlish, not complimenting her on the new place, which looked nice, or her new slim look. You know how omissions can be so ungenerous?"

"I know."

"I was about to leave, as I recall, when she asked if I'd like to hear the latest ABBA song. I didn't really, but I said I did. The song was "Does Your Mother Know?""

"That's my daughter's favourite. I think she identified with the words."

"Didn't we all? Anyway, Joan got to her feet and started into disco gyrations, which were all the rage at that time. She knew all the knee dips and hand rolls." I sang *"you're so young, and your feelings are driving you wild,"* and threw in a few hand gestures. Gillies laughed.

"I remember those."

"Keep driving, I'll do them for you. So we danced, my mother and I. When we stopped we were flushed and laughing, and I saw us both reflected in a mirror she'd hung by the window. Mother and daughter, same dark hair, same alive lively blue eyes."

I stopped talking. At this rate I was going to get all teary.

"That's a good memory," said Gill. "I've danced a Scottish reel at the school dance with my girls, but I don't think it was so much fun. John Travolta, I'm not."

I stared out of the window. Less than three months afterward, Joan had jumped off the wagon and crash-landed. She lost her job and the apartment and went back on welfare. I returned to university and spoke to her as infrequently as I could. But it was a good memory in my little box of treasures.

Gillies allowed me my thoughts for a while, then he said, "I'll just ring the station and see if I have any messages. . . . Rosie? Gill here. Got anything for me? . . . Okay. Let me write it down." He took out his notebook and juggled phone and book until I took the latter and indicated I'd be the scribe. "06732 . . . Mrs. Waring . . . Thanks, Rosie."

He hung up. "Why is that name familiar?"

"Mrs. Waring runs a B & B on Skye. She was the one who phoned me about my mother."

"She wants me to ring her."

He keyed in the number immediately. My anxiety came flooding back.

"Mrs. Waring? This is Sergeant Gillies here from Stornoway." He waited while the person on the other end of the line poured something out. He looked at me, frowning, and made an "I-don't-know-what-this-is" gesture. "No, I haven't yet been in contact with Mrs. Morris. . . . No, that wasn't me, Mrs. Waring. . . . You're sure he said Gillies? . . . Did he show you any identification? . . . I see, yes. Quite understandable. . . . He took the suitcase? . . . No, really, you haven't done anything wrong. . . . Can you tell me what the officer looked like?"

Gillies made motions to me to write down what he said. "Late middle-age, greying hair, tall, wearing a yellow mackintosh. And what time did he come? . . . About ten o'clock this morning. Did he come in a marked police car? . . . No? Could you tell me what kind of car he was driving then? . . . No, don't worry about it Mrs. Waring, there wasn't any reason for you to notice. . . . Green, not too new? Good that's something. Was he alone? . . . He was. You're sure of that? . . . No, please don't worry. . . . No, I'm sure it's just a miscommunication over here. We'll get to the bottom of this right away. . . . Yes, I will ring you back. Cheerie."

"What the hell was that all about?"

"She says a man came to collect Mrs. Morris's suitcase. He gave his name as Sergeant Gillies. He didn't offer any identification, but she was expecting somebody to come because you had warned her, so she didn't think twice about it. He said Mrs. Morris was fine and the matter had been cleared up. The only reason she called was to tell me she'd found one of your mother's earrings and wondered where should she send it on to."

"I assume there's no possibility that somebody from the station was sent over and she got the names confused?"

"Not a chance. Jock's left the case entirely in my hands."

"So who was it? How many middle-aged, greying, tall men with yellow raincoats do you know?"

"The description would fit a lot of men. Well, the good news is she must be alive."

"One would assume so. I mean, he could have found the address in her pocket as she lay dead and figured out there was loot to be had. Or, on the other hand, she could have told him all this with her dying breath and she could still be dead. However, the most likely scenario is that she's got some poor sucker to do her bidding."

The savagery of my words made him blink. He caught hold of my hand.

"There are several possibilities and we can go over each of them carefully and logically. Get in the car and we'll drive back to Stornoway. I'll have to report this to Jock anyway."

I realized I was shivering, although the car was quite warm.

"I'm going to operate on the assumption that this man is from Lewis. Do you agree with that?"

"He knew your name and rank, which would suggest a degree of familiarity, at the very least, with the police roster. He had Mrs. Waring's address and knew what to ask for, so he has obviously had some contact with my mother. What I've suspected all along is that she's met up with somebody. He's an accomplice. There's no reason to lie to Mrs. Waring otherwise."

"All right then, let's say he is from Lewis. One good thing about being on an island is that the entry and exit points aren't that hard to control. It sounds as if this man was driving his own car, which means he would have to take the ferry over to Skye. There are only two departure places. From Tarbert, which is down in Harris, or from Uist, even further south on the island. It's more logical that, if he's from here, he'd use the Tarbert ferry. Have a look in the glove compartment. There should be a schedule in there."

I scrabbled through a mess of flyers and found it. "According to this, the earliest ferry from Tarbert leaves at half past seven in the morning and arrives at Skye at five past nine."

"It would take him about three quarters of an hour to disembark and drive to Portree. We have an arrival time of ten o'clock, which is what Mrs. Waring said."

I pointed at the timetable. "And if he came right back, he'd have to leave on the two o'clock ferry, which arrives at Tarbert at three thirty-five." I checked my watch. "It's ten to. Can we get to the docks in time?"

"'Fraid not."

"Can you contact the captain? See if he's noticed a passenger of that description."

"We can do that. I'll have Rose ring him right now."

He was driving fast now, although the sense of urgency was emotional rather than practical. We weren't going to get to the mysterious man any sooner. However, I hadn't totally lost my sense of self-preservation and I undertook to key in the telephone number for him. Gillies relayed his request to Rosie. He disconnected.

"She should get back to us in a few minutes."

We drove on in silence. The threatened rain had started and was coming down heavily. He touched my hand, a gesture he seemed to use a lot.

"How are you doing?"

"I'm frustrated. It's the helplessness that I can't stand. You know, Gill, one of my last cases on the front line involved the disappearance of a little girl. She had vanished from the backyard where she was playing. We didn't find her for five days. She had been murdered by the apartment janitor, as it turned out. I was with the mother for a lot of the time. At first she couldn't sit still. She had to walk up and down the streets, searching. She did that over and over again. By the fifth day, she had become inert. People who saw her then thought she was callous, that she didn't care about her kid, but it wasn't that. She was driven to a standstill by the helplessness. Even though it was horrible when we finally found the child's body, it was also an intense relief."

I suddenly realized I was talking like somebody who cared. I reined in those particular feelings.

"Not that I truly believe my mother has come to harm, but I sure would like to know where she is."

His cell phone buzzed. "Gillies here! . . . Yes, Rosie. . . . Okay? . . . Nobody, huh? Thanks a lot."

"Rosie was able to contact the captain, and he says he has a sparse load and there isn't anybody that he can see who fits the description."

"Which means either the man is taking a different ferry or has stayed on Skye."

"I suppose so."

"And you can't get an officer down to the dock to check the passengers? No, don't answer. You already said you couldn't."

We made the turn onto the moor, which was now starting to seem like home. The rain and grey changed the look of it once again, and it didn't appear like a Rembrandt painting at all. It looked more like an etching by Gustave Doré. I sank down in the seat. Gillies turned on the car heater, but I felt as if I'd never get warm.

By the time we were on the fringes of Stornoway, I had got a good grip on my feelings and stuffed them down where they belonged. If she was really dead this time, so be it.

CHAPTER NINETEEN

"I'll go and make a report to Jock concerning these two calls. Do you want to come in?"

"No, I'll just head back to the hotel. It's your bailiwick and I know you'll let me know." We got out of the car and he came around to my side. For the first time since I'd met him, he looked unsure of himself.

"Can I buy you dinner tonight?" he asked.

"I'd love that, thanks."

He smiled with such undisguised pleasure that my stomach gave a lurch. The smallest of lurches. After all, I'm not a teenager who's going to fall for a guy she met a day ago. Right?

We agreed he'd come to the hotel about seven o'clock, but we'd try out a different restaurant. Wonderful man that he was, he had an umbrella in the car, which he insisted I borrow. I left him and walked off in the direction of the hotel. Then on the next block I spotted Lisa MacKenzie going into one of the stores along the harbourfront. An opportunity not to be missed.

I quickened my pace. The store was called Salman's Ladies Wear, and Lisa was still inside. She was standing in front of a mirror and studying the effect of a long black skirt and matching black-velvet jacket. She was wearing a shocking pink, fluorescent T-shirt, so the total effect was interestingly funky. I pushed open the door and went in, shaking off the water from the umbrella. A young woman wearing a hijab came from behind the counter.

"*Feasgar math*, good afternoon. May I help you?" Her skin was dark, her accent pure Scots.

"I'm just looking, thanks."

Lisa turned around when she heard my voice.

"Hello. . . . Sorry, I don't remember your name."

"That's understandable. You were in a state of shock. I'm Christine Morris."

She grimaced at my comment, then faced the mirror again. "What do you think? I need to be respectable for the funeral. Will I do?"

"The skirt and jacket are very respectable."

She laughed. "Are you saying you don't like my T-shirt?" She held it away from her chest so I could read the printed slogan. "*Gaels never do it on the Sabbath.*"

"Are you coming to Tormod's funeral?" she asked.

"Well, I'm not sure about Mr. MacAulay's, but I was planning to attend the one for Mrs. MacDonald."

"Then you will need a hat. You kenna go to church without a hat and expect not to be noticed. Sairi, show her some Sunday bonnets."

"Over here, Miss."

Sairi indicated the corner of the shop, where there were several shelves piled with women's hats.

"Try this one."

She handed me a brown felt cloche with a wisp of veiling. I put it on and immediately my face gained ten years.

"Ugh."

Lisa grinned. "I don't think so. Your hair is too dark for a brown hat. What about that one on the top shelf, the blue straw with the wider brim."

Sairi took it down and I put it on. They both stood back and studied me critically.

"Much better. That brings out the blue of your eyes."

"You don't think it's too colourful for a funeral?"

"No, you're not kin. And your raincoat is suitably sober. Do you have a skirt?"

"No."

"Never mind then. You're from away. They'll forgive you." She addressed the clerk. "Sairi , I'm going to take these clothes." She slipped off the jacket. "And I'll wear my white blouse," she said to me. "I'll look like an off-duty waitress, but I won't offend anybody."

I smiled at her. "I have the impression it wouldn't bother you too much if you did. Offend somebody, I mean."

"That's not really true. I'm always on probation in this town, and I'll no give the old ladies, of both sexes, the satisfaction of having me to tear apart with their finger sandwiches." She adopted a high-pitched, squeaky voice. "*And did you see her hair, Mary? It's against Nature. The Lord niver made anybody with that unnatural a tint, as I live and breathe.*"

Sairi returned. "Will ye be buying the bonnet then, Miss?" she asked me.

"Yes, I will, thank you."

She beamed at me and went off to make up the sale slip.

"Are you free to go for a coffee or tea?" I asked Lisa.

"As long as we can go to the hotel. My sister is likely to drop her pup any minute and I'd like to check in on her."

"Perfect."

I'd actually hoped for somewhere more private, but I'd take what I was given. Lisa had the same skittish air I'd been aware of yesterday, as if she'd run off at any minute. She also had the shiny eyes of somebody who'd been recently toking up.

We got our purchases. My hat seemed scandalously expensive, as I didn't expect to wear it again.

"What did you get up to today?" Lisa asked me when we were outside. We huddled together under the umbrella.

"Gill took me to see the Callanish Stones. We were going to visit the Blackhouse Village but we . . . ran out of time."

She flashed me an angry look. "Of course, it's completely ridiculous that those old houses are now set up as a tourist site. Not that long ago, the villagers were despised by the rest of the world. The trouble is most of you people don't look past the smoke. You cluck your teeth with delicious sympathy, '*poor things*,' but you don't understand that lack of material goods isn't what counts. Those villagers had a strong community, which is far more valuable than hot and cold running water and showers."

Miss MacKenzie was certainly mercurial in her moods. The chatty, friendly woman in the store had suddenly changed face. She had a good point, of course, but I'm not fond of being lectured at, and every hair on the back of my neck stands up if I hear the words, "*you people*." Two more steps and you're saying "*racist pig*."

I bit back my own angry retort. "Museums keep us enlightened, though. I believe in knowing our history."

"'Our' in the universal sense, I presume? You're no a Scot."

"Hey, that's no fault of mine, is it? And you know what? I'm fed up with people who exclude anybody else who didn't happen to be born in a certain place on the globe, or isn't a certain skin colour, or gender. As if we have any say in the matter."

Lisa glanced at me, took in my irritation, and her own expression changed.

"I'm sorry. You're quite right. I'm being a total bitch. It's a sore point with me — tourism and the culture."

At that moment we were about to cross the road. There were more cars on the street than yesterday, but it was not what I'd call busy. However, a familiar, maroon-coloured mini drove through the amber light and turned the corner so quickly that we were both forced to jump back. The car stopped beside us and the driver rolled down the window, letting out a blast of Gospel music playing at top volume. Coral-Lyn Pitchers was giving us a white-toothed smile. Andy MacAulay was in the passenger seat, looking, if possible, even more woebegone than he had yesterday.

"Good afternoon, Miss Morris. What a nice surprise. And you're with Lisa too. Mr. MacAulay's funeral is tomorrow, and I would like to invite you both to the service."

I could hardly hear what she was saying above the rocking rendition of "We Will Gather at the River." She turned down the volume.

"It will be at the Carloway church, and Andy will be the presenter. Won't you, Honey?"

Andy nodded on cue.

"It's at two o'clock," she continued. "Lisa can tell you how to get there, can't you, Lisa?"

I don't think I'd ever been exactly *invited* like that to a funeral.

Lisa bent over to look into the car. "How are you doing, Andy?"

"He's bearing up," answered Coral-Lyn. "Aren't you, Honey?"

"I'm sorry you've lost your voice," said Lisa without changing her tone. "The shock I suppose."

I rather admired Lisa's nerve, but her comment was cruel. Andy tried to act as if she'd made a joke, but he looked ashamed.

"No, I'm all right, thanks."

"I should offer you my congratulations, Lisa," said Coral-Lyn.

"For what?"

Their car was blocking the turn, and the driver of a van that had come up tooted his horn impatiently. Coral-Lyn waved at him, pleasantly. Then she turned back to Lisa.

"You haven't talked to Douglas yet? I thought you would have by now."

"No."

"Let me be the first to tell you the good news then. Grandfather MacAulay has made you his sole beneficiary."

"What! That's not true."

"Oh it is. It means you inherit the entire property. Isn't that splendid? I know how hard you worked on it."

Her tone too was sweet as maple syrup, but Lisa flinched. Andy laced his fingers together in a praying gesture. There was another, louder, toot from the van behind them, but Coral-Lyn wasn't fazed.

"As you know, Granddad Tormod had already agreed to sell the land to my father so we can build a place to celebrate the workings of the church. I hope that you will honour his wishes. Our offer, which is a generous one, still stands."

This time the van driver leaned on his horn. He couldn't be denied and Coral-Lyn shifted into drive gear.

"We'll be in touch with you as soon as the funeral duties are completed."

"LADY, WILL YOU MOVE THAT EFFING CAR OUT OF THE WAY!!"

Another wave.

"People have no patience these days, do they?" she said to me. "I'll see you tomorrow then?"

"Yes . . . thank you."

I couldn't help the "thank you." She leaned over and upped the volume on the tape player, then drove off slowly, the van right on her rear bumper.

Lisa was pale with anger and, ignoring me and the umbrella, she practically dived across the road, not looking, and barely missed being hit by a lean bicyclist. Gaelic swear words on both sides, delivered on the move. Lisa seemed to have completely forgotten my invitation to coffee, and she was hustling off along the street as fast as she could manage on the awkward platform shoes she was wearing. It was easy for me with my sensible Nike running shoes to catch up with her.

"Lisa! Wait up."

She waved angrily in the direction of the road. "Did you see that bloody bike almost run me down?"

This wasn't a time to debate the responsibility of jaywalkers versus Lance Armstrong look-alikes.

I just kept beside her, trying to shield her from the rain, although she was impervious to it.

"That's quite a bit of news you just received."

"Aye. And you heard the Madonna. She had to get the needle in, didn't she? Oh, as if I give a shit what she thinks. What they all think. Tormod and I were good chums most of the time. Silly fool would try to get in bit of tickle now and then, but it wasn't serious. More of a joke between us."

She seemed to have overlooked the cleavage photos. We were at another stoplight, and I placed my hand on her arm until the light turned green.

"I assume being made a sole beneficiary was a surprise to you."

"Of course it was. Tormod kept saying he'd leave me a bequest, but I didn't expect the whole kit and caboodle. Bloody fool. He wouldn't accept that he was dying. He probably thought I'd get what was left after he'd sold the property and squandered the profits living the good life until a ripe old age."

Suddenly, she stopped and stared ahead. "I will sell the effing house and the land, you can bet on it, but I'll no sell to that woman. I'm going to see if some dirty old Norwegian wants it for a snog shop. She wouldn't like that one bit. Poor bloody Andy. Did you see him? He's finally given her both his balls. She's had one of them for a long time, but now she's got two. Oh god. Oh god."

We were at the hotel now, and she shoved open the front door and went in. I followed.

CHAPTER TWENTY

Lisa headed across the deserted foyer to the dining room and bar. The door was locked, and she impatiently rattled the door knob and rapped on the glass pane. Mairi appeared on the other side and unlocked the door.

It didn't matter that they spoke to each other in Gaelic. The age-old conflict that resurrected itself before my eyes didn't need trans-lating. Mairi, the older sister, the sensible one; Lisa, the wild one, who didn't have the right social graces and always got her way. The German couple I'd seen the night before appeared at the top of the stairs on their way out for a spot of sightseeing. Mairi stepped back.

"Come in here."

We went in and Lisa immediately headed for the bar, saying over her shoulder. "I need a whisky. D'you want one, Chris?"

I didn't have a chance to answer, because Mairi set off after her sister.

"You are not going to drink at this time of day."

Lisa took down a bottle of Scotch whisky from the shelf behind the counter, but Mairi was right behind her and she snatched at it. Lisa held on and they both released a torrent of Gaelic words. I was still at the door, pinned down by social niceties. However, in a phys-ical struggle between a nine-months-pregnant woman and a younger, stronger gardener, there was no contest. They had got themselves ludicrously wedged in the narrow space behind the counter. I went over to help.

"Let go, Lisa, this isn't safe. Your sister is pregnant."

"In case you hadn't noticed," said Mairi.

Lisa's eyes met mine. Her pupils were dilated and there was a fleck of spit at the corner of her mouth. Abruptly, she released her hold on the neck of the bottle, but the movement caught Mairi off-balance and the bottle slipped out of her hand and smashed on the floor. The sweet, sharp smell of whisky stung my nostrils. Mairi yelped and bent over to see what was happening to her shin. A sliver of glass had bounced up and cut her. Nothing serious, but there was trickle of blood. She snapped at her sister, and I knew she'd said the time-honoured, "Now look what you've done."

"Oh shit," said Lisa.

Mairi straightened up and gasped. "Ow!" She pressed her hands against her stomach. There was real pain in her voice.

"It's nothing. I'll get you a plaster," said Lisa, still in angry-little-sister mode.

"Ow!" Mairi glared back. "That was a contraction, idiot. My labour's started," This was in English. She needed a witness.

She moved out from behind the counter and, suddenly, water gushed from between her legs, as if she had lost control of her bladder.

"What the . . . " She stared down at the puddle of fluid that had formed at her feet. "Oh no!

Seeing what was happening brought Lisa back into adulthood. "Oh God. Mairs, your water's broke."

Mairi rolled her eyes impatiently. "Brilliant. Good observation."

"Where's Colin?"

"I don't know, he went out a couple of hours ago."

"And he didn't think to mention where he was going, of course."

This wasn't the time to be sidetracked about the ongoing delinquency of Mr. MacLeod.

"We'd better get you some help right away," I said. "Do you want me to call an ambulance?"

"She's planned to have a home birth," said Lisa.

"Let's get hold of your midwife, then. Can you make it upstairs?"

Mairi shook her head. "I think I'm going to be sick." And she was, heaving convulsively all over the floor.

"I'll get a cloth," said Lisa as she rushed back to the bar for a dishcloth.

"Soak it in cold water," I told her, and I grabbed a couple of table napkins from a nearby table and held them to Mairi's mouth. I got her into a chair.

Lisa raced back with the cold cloth.

"Put it on the back of her neck."

Mairi was alternately leaning forward to spit out bile and straining back in the chair for relief from her labour cramps.

"Lisa, go and phone the midwife! Tell her to get here right away!"

Lisa bolted.

"You might be more comfortable walking," I said to Mairi and, when she nodded, I helped her to her feet. She clutched my arm and we began a decidedly un-Austen-like walk around the room.

"Are you sure you don't want to go to the hospital?"

"No. I'll hang in. We've planned for a home birth. I was looking forward to it." She gave a wry smile. "Please God, though, I don't want to deliver in the bloody bar." Another contraction seized her and she bent over, pulling me with her. "Ow, ow."

Lisa came flying back into the room. "Gillian's on her way. I phoned Norman to see if Colin was there, but he hasn't seen him. He said he'll call around."

Mairi started into another "Ow" that transmuted into a long drawn-out howl. She was gripping my hand so hard it hurt.

"Let's get her jeans off," I said to Lisa. "The baby might come soon. Can you get a clean tablecloth we can put on the floor?"

"Thank goodness you know what you're doing."

I did not share her confidence. As cops, we all had fundamental emergency training, but the one time I'd had first-hand experience of a delivery assist, the baby died. I wasn't going to make that mistake again.

I got Mairi to lie down on the tablecloth, and Lisa managed to remove her jeans and underwear. Mairi was finding it impossible to keep still and thrashed from side to side, groaning.

However, the answer to all our prayers came hurrying into the room. Gillian, the midwife. She was on the stocky side, middle-aged and grey-haired, the kind of sensible, brisk woman who immediately inspires confidence.

"Little wretch couldn't wait, eh?" she came over to Mairi. "When did you have your last contraction?"

"Now," said Mairi, and I saw the ripple down her stomach and she did her "ow, ow, ow" cry again.

The midwife crouched down beside her. "I doubt you want the bairn to make his entrance in here. Let's get you on your feet and up to the bedroom. Wrap the cloth around her. All right Mairi, stand up, then Lisa will get you under one arm and I'll get the other. Fast as you can make it. When a contraction comes we'll stop, but I do want to get you upstairs. Perhaps you can open the door for us," she said to me.

Mairi leaned her head on her sister's shoulder and the little procession proceeded upstairs. I let them go; I was the stranger here. I went back into the dining room. At the least I could clean up for them.

I located a bucket and mop and a bottle of disinfectant and set to work. The mingled stench of vomit and liquor was depressing-ly familiar, as was my task of cleaning up the mess. Joan had gone through a particularly bad period when I was fourteen, just before I went to live with the Jacksons. Most days I'd come home from school and find her passed out on the couch. There was invariably cleanup to do. I wrapped the broken shards of glass in some news-paper and dumped them in the wastebasket.

As I said, I'd had experience with an impromptu delivery once before — and it wasn't a good one. I was a young constable on the night beat in Toronto. We received a call that a woman was acting strangely down in Nathan Phillips Square, which was in front of the city hall. It was deep winter, and we found the woman pacing up and down, making grunting sounds. I tried to talk to her but no luck. She was both stoned and mentally challenged and she ignored me. A small crowd of late-night skaters gawked at her.

"I pissed myself," she kept repeating. "I pissed myself."

I've never forgotten that image of her large, wide face as she stared in bewilderment at what was flowing down her fat legs. It was late, almost the end of my shift, and I was tired and irritable.

"What's your name? Where d'you live?"

No coherent answers, only louder cries. "Come on, we'll take you home," I said, and I tried to get her into the cruiser, where at least we could talk in relative comfort. She resisted violently and my partner, Joe Csonka, got out of the car and came over to help me. That really set her off, and she swung at him. I grabbed her arm, pulled it behind her back, and snapped on the cuffs, forcing her to the ground. It was only then I realized she was in the last stages of pregnancy. She was so bundled up in a stained winter parka that it wasn't at all obvious. Somebody in the crowd guffawed. There's always one. We radioed for an ambulance, but they took a long time to get there while I did what I could to comfort the woman. Finally, the paramedics arrived, brusque and unsympathetic. Even as they were loading her into the ambulance, one of them was tugging off her pants. When I followed up on the case a couple of days later, I found out the infant had died from birth complications. Probably nothing to do with the rough struggle, but I had been troubled by the memory many times. The baby had not been born into love and the mother received no tenderness.

After my cleanup, the bar area had a pleasant, tarry smell from the disinfectant. Other than the stirring of painful memories, it hadn't bothered me to wipe up the barf. I'd been a front-line cop for seventeen years and, if you are going to survive at that, you have to get used to every known variation of bodily fluid. I'd even been able to assess what Mairi had had for lunch. Automatic response. You never knew when you'd be called on to make a report on what had been emitted.

I was stowing away the mop when Lisa came in.

"I thought I'd come and clean up the mess."

"I did it already."

"You did! Oh my God, thanks a lot."

"You're welcome. I was glad to make myself useful. I'd have boiled water if needed. How's Mairi doing?"

"She's all right. After all the urgency, she isn't even fully dilated. The baby might not come for another couple of hours."

"Did Colin arrive?"

Lisa looked away. "No. We can't locate him." She grimaced at me. "I could cheerfully wring his neck. He's a selfish twerp as far as I'm concerned, but she would marry him, wouldn't she?"

Her feelings didn't jibe with Colin's expressed fondness towards his sister-in-law.

"You'd think he'd know enough to stay in close touch with Mairi at the stage she is," I said, girls in agreement.

"Ha! The Hebridean men are in the dark ages when it comes to these matters," she scoffed, her tone full of experience. "Babies are the women's realm. The men stay out of it until it's over."

"Colin was responsible for creating the baby just as much as Mairi, though."

I get self-righteous about this issue.

Lisa frowned at me. "Dream on. That's true in theory, but you can't expect a man to have the same feelings as a woman when all he's done is shot his load for twenty seconds and she's the one who's carried a living creature in her guts for nine months."

Anatomical inaccuracy aside, Lisa had a point, and one that had been made many times before. As an officer, I'd had my fill of trying to get young stallions to claim the results of their two-minute flings.

She took a package of cigarettes out of her back pocket. "Do you mind?"

"Hey, it's your place."

She lit up and dragged hungrily on the cigarette. "This is my last one. I promised Mairi I'd quit." She ran her free hand through her hair. "I wanted to apologize for that little scene earlier. It was embarrassing. Truth is I'm on the wagon, and Mairi can't let go of being Big Sister."

"You've had trouble with alcohol, I take it?"

"You could put it that way. Trouble — yes, I've definitely had trouble. Another way of putting it is that I've been a drunk most of my adult life."

More lung-filling drags. She looked so wretched, I felt a rush of sympathy for her. I liked Lisa, brat that she was.

"Are you in a program now?"

"No. I just decided to quit. When Mairi got pregnant, actually. I want to be a sober aunt, set a good example and all that." She waved the cigarette in the air. "Same goes for this."

"Hey, I believe in the importance of role models."

Her eyes met mine. "Do you have nieces and nephews yourself?"

"No. I'm an only child. But I do have a goddaughter."

"I bet you'll be a good role model to her."

"Thanks. I hope so."

With vigour, she stubbed out her cigarette. "Goodbye forever, ciggies. I'd better get back to the momma."

"Let me know what happens, will you? I'll be out for dinner, but then I'm here."

She wrinkled her eyes at me. "Another date with Sergeant Gillies?"

"I don't know about a date, but we're going out for dinner together."

"Did he ask you?"

"Er, yes."

"That's a date then. He must be interested in you. I haven't known Gill to go on a date for two years. Anyway, have a nice time. See you. 'Bye."

She left and I quivered around for a bit. A date! What the hell was I going to do with that? A date with a very attractive man who just happened to live several time zones away. Wasn't that just my luck?

CHAPTER TWENTY-ONE

Gill and I went for dinner to a hotel just up from the Duke. The carpet was a riot of overblown roses, the upholstery on the stiff chairs was a completely different pattern of lush vegetation, and the heavy drapes were vigorously floral. All of the wood was the colour of malt vinegar. In the background, a tape was playing bagpipe music. As a visitor, I found it charmingly authentic. The waitress was a woman of advanced years, who acted as if she'd rather be at home with her feet up. It was like being waited on by your grandmother, and I had to resist the impulse to jump up and help her with the tray. I might have, except I thought she wouldn't like it. The food was unmemorable, except for the odd fact that they served toast (cold and crisp) instead of dinner rolls. I tried to wash that down with a half-pint of dark British ale, which as far as I was concerned could have been a meal in itself.

There was no news in the search for Joan. All the ferry captains had been contacted, but with no result. The description was so general, it wasn't that helpful. Gill told me that Jock was considering bringing in a tracking dog from Inverness, but he had to wait until they knew for sure if the Royal Prince was coming. If he was, they'd need the dogs for bomb detection.

"A higher priority, I'm sure," I said. I wasn't resentful about that. I understood the decisions that had to be made with limited resources. "Is the lad really coming?"

"It's a last-minute choice between us and St. Andrews. Because of the girlfriend there'll be a media frenzy if word gets out, so we're trying to keep it quiet." He shrugged. "You met Janice. Doing that successfully is rather like carrying water in a sieve. If he does come here, his intention is to play golf down in Harris — weather permitting — have dinner at Scarista House, then come back to Stornoway and fly to Edinburgh."

"Why would he come all the way over here?"

Gillies shrugged. "I suppose he thinks it'll be nice and private. You'd be surprised at how many people still think of the Hebrides as untamed wilderness. And of course, the tourist board plays it up like that."

I had been one of those people until I came here, so I didn't pursue the matter.

In turn, I related the afternoon's birthing crisis. This led into the inevitable inquiry, "Did you ever want to have kids?" Standard answer, "I wasn't in the right place at the right time." I might have elaborated if I'd been talking with a woman, but not with a man I'd just met and whom I was finding far too attractive. Maybe it was sympathetic hormones released by Mairi's pregnancy.

I steered the conversation around to his two daughters. Both of them were going in for law: the older one was already articling, the younger one was in her second year at Edinburgh law school. He said they intended to set up a practice together. I liked the way he talked about them. He seemed proud of them for themselves not just because they reflected well on him. I also liked the way his skin and eyes had a healthy glow to them. I liked the way he smelled of soap. I especially liked the way he didn't drink too much. And that's quite a list for a short acquaintance.

And that was that. Ten o'clock and time to return to the hotel. A hug at my door this time, a rather protracted hug. Very nice, but I was too old for the "handshake and bedshake" scenario, and I went into my room alone. Let's not be stupid here. So all in all, a great evening.

Contrary to the sense of "any minute now," the infant had-n't made an appearance by the time Gill had come to pick me up for dinner, but when I returned, the hotel was quiet. I considered going to Mairi's apartment, but I didn't want to intrude.

After a bit of restless tossing around, I fell asleep, but just after midnight I was awakened by a soft tapping at the door.

"Chris. It's me, Lisa."

I slipped on my robe and opened the door.

"It's late, I know, but I thought you deserved to see her after what happened." Lisa was standing there with the baby in her arms. She pulled back the blanket so I could see the tiny red squashed face, almost obscured by a pale yellow toque.

"She's two hours old. Here, do you want to hold her?"

I didn't get a chance to answer and she passed over the bundle, surprisingly light and warm.

"Does she have a name yet?"

"Anna, after our mother."

"And the birth went well? Mairi is all right?"

"She is fine. Apparently it was a totally normal delivery, but she's asleep at the moment. I stole the baby to come and show you."

"She's very cute. How does Colin feel about his new daughter? He has come back hasn't he?"

"About an hour ago, when it was all over. Gillian told him it was a girl, and you know what he said, the yobbo?"

"Nothing good, I gather."

"His words were, 'A girl! *What a piss off!*'"

Little Anna stirred and made soft smacking noises with her puckered mouth. Lisa rocked her. "Uh, uh, she'll be wanting her momma's boobie. I'd better get back."

"Thanks for bringing her."

Lisa was glowing with aunly pride. She kissed the sleeping baby on the cheek.

"Ye're going ta break their hearts are ye no, ma wee bonny babe?"

Colin said his sister-in-law had had a hard life, and I gathered from the intensity of her Miss Havisham remark that the opposite sex was a big factor in her difficulties.

She glanced at me over the top of the baby's head. "When you hear the expression, 'the miracle of birth' you don't really know what that means until you've actually been present at one, do you?"

"My best friend asked me to be birth coach to my now-god-child. It was one of the best experiences of my life."

"Was her husband there?"

"He was. While Paula went into the final stages of labour, he and I stood on either side of the hospital bed, calling out, PUSH! PUSH! for all the world as if we were rowing coaches. She said it helped though."

Lisa laughed. "Well I've never done the deed, and even though it was all so bloody marvellous, after watching what my sister went through, I don't think I will. Being an aunt is good enough for me, thank you very much."

We both stared down at little Anna, who was getting fitful, waving one of her tiny fists in random movements.

"That's it. Make your demands known," said Lisa.

I could see this girl child was going to get quite a feminist education.

"I'll be away then. See you tomorrow at the funeral." For a moment she looked sad. "Tormod would have liked to see the baby. He took an interest in Mairi's pregnancy. Not like her ass-hole husband."

Lisa took the infant's hand and waved it at me. "*Feasgar math.* Good night."

I imitated her as best I could. "Feshga ma."

"That was very good. We'll get you speaking the Gaelic in next to no time."

She left and I walked over to the window.

Lisa had used the expression "the miracle of birth," and her delight in the baby was apparent. I was overwhelmed by the memory of what we'd all kept euphemistically calling "the incident."

Little Anna had been so light in my arms because she was a newborn. When I'd picked up Sunny DeLuca, she was also light, but in her case it was because she had been starved. Sondra's apartment was on the second floor of a dilapidated building near Parliament and Queen streets. We'd got an anonymous call that a baby had been crying non-stop, and the caller, a woman, thought there was nobody with it. Usually, Children's Aid is called immediately, but this afternoon, there was a heavy snowfall and the worker was stuck on the Don Valley. I went to investigate and was there before anybody else, including the beat constable. It was about three o'clock in the afternoon. I had to bang hard on the door before a young woman finally answered.

"Good afternoon, Sondra here. Sondra with an O." She was clearly stoned and grinned at me in a befuddled way. I told her why I was there and she looked bewildered. "Sunny crying? She never does that; she's such a good baby."

"Can I see her?" She made a grand gesture to usher me in that almost made her lose her balance. I stepped into one room. Even with the windows open, the room stank as if the toilet was blocked and had overflowed. This turned out to be true, but Sondra hadn't reported it because she was so out of it she hadn't noticed. Besides, she was hardly home. Her child didn't have the luxury of getting out, and she was in her crib in the corner of the room. A man, who was the neighbour by the name of Anton Longboat, and who may have been Sunny's father, was sprawled on the sagging couch watching a tiny television set. He didn't speak to me at all and hardly seemed to notice I was there. I asked to see the child.

"Be my guest," said Sondra. "She's sleeping." She wasn't. She was just lying there in her own excrement in the filthy crib. I must have made some exclamation, although I don't remember doing that, and her enormous dark eyes looked into mine. She was physically alive, but the life of her soul had been extinguished a long time ago and would probably never return. I reached for my cell phone and started to dial 911.

"We've got to get this child to the hospital at once."

Sondra came over to the crib. "Why? She's fine. She just needs a little tittie, don't you, Hon?" She tugged at her T-shirt to expose her breast. She was staggering, and as she went to pick up the baby, she almost toppled into the crib on top of her. I grabbed her arm.

"Where are the child's clothes? She's going to the hospital."

Sondra scowled at me. "That hurt." Her T-shirt was still pulled up and her flaccid breast was hanging over her bra. "She'll be all right," she said, and made another attempt to pick up the baby. She managed to lift her and the sodden diaper slipped off. The rash covering the thin buttocks was like a burn, raw and oozing. Sunny let out a wail, but she was so weak it was like listening to a kitten mew. "Oh, fuck you then," said Sondra, and she dropped her roughly back into the crib.

I could feel my own anger hot up my back and I knew I had lost all objectivity. "I'm asking you once more where the baby's clothes are?"

Sondra suddenly turned nasty. "She doesn't have any clothes. She doesn't need any. We don't get out much."

"Did you leave her alone for the last two nights?"

"She was all right. A girl has to have fun sometimes. I can't stay home all the time."

"She's going to the hospital."

I suppose my contempt was unmistakable. Sondra yelled at me, "No she's not, she's mine," and suddenly, without warning, she flew at me, hands like claws ready to scratch whatever she could reach. I grabbed her by the wrists, but she struggled violently. I tried to get her arm pinned behind her back, but she was fighting too hard. I managed to get my leg behind her knees and she fell to the floor, me on top of her. There were a couple more violent upheavals, then suddenly she lay still. I thought she was playing dead, ready to attack again as soon as I relaxed, it's a common trick, but as I moved cautiously away I saw that she had stopped breathing.

After that things moved at warp speed. Fortunately, the paramedics had answered my first call promptly and they were at the door even as I realized what had happened. They couldn't revive *her. The boyfriend sat and stared. There had to be an inquiry, of course, by the Special Investigations Unit, and I was temporarily suspended from duty. The inquest revealed a damaged heart from constant intake of alcohol and drugs. Sondra DeLuca could have had a heart attack at any time. However, the boyfriend was aboriginal, Sunny was probably mixed race, and suddenly we were into another ball game entirely. He said I had handled her roughly, thought I might even have hit her. There were no bruises on her body to substantiate this accusation, so it was dismissed. I was completely exonerated of misconduct, but I knew how angry I'd been. How much I had wanted to hurt the self-involved wretch who was Sondra DeLuca. It had nothing to do with race, but there were many people who didn't believe that. I was literally spat on, yelled at, and generally the target of a corrosive hatred I could do nothing about. Sunny was immediately put into the care of the Children's Aid, but I had seen the look in her eyes, and I wept for her many times in the solitude of my own room. I had to undergo compulsory sessions with the police shrink, which was probably a good thing, although I doubt I was an easy subject. Not surprisingly, Sondra herself had been the object of terrible neglect and her life had been a miserable one, but I realized I hardly cared, and with that knowledge, I decided to resign.*

All my pals tried to talk me out of it, but I'd had it up to the eyeballs with policing. It was Paula who, yet again, came forward as the saviour who in some ways knew me better than I knew myself. She had been with the OPP special services branch for two years, and she loved the work. "You can't throw the baby out with the bathwater, pun intended. You're a cop. Come and join me. You've got the experience and the brains and you don't have to look at the likes of Sondra with an O ever again." So I applied, got the job, and had been there exactly one week when Jim suggested this conference.

I didn't go back to sleep, and daylight came again at four-thirty. At five I got out of bed, took a long shower, then sat at the window again, watching the rest of the world slowly wake up.

CHAPTER TWENTY-TWO

At seven-thirty, I went downstairs to the dining room. A sign on the serving table said "PLEASE HELP YOURSELF. BABY BORN LAST NIGHT." I was definitely not in the mood for polite conversation with other guests, so I poured some coffee, took a muffin from the basket, and was leaving to go back upstairs when Gill walked in.

"Chris. So glad I caught you."

His expression was serious, and my stomach did the usual lurch.

"Any news?"

"Not about your mother, I'm afraid, but there's something I want to show you. I'd like your professional opinion." He glanced around. "Do you mind if we go to your room?"

"Of course. Grab a coffee and muffin."

He followed me upstairs while I tried to remember if I'd left any unmentionables strewn around.

Whew. I hadn't.

The room wasn't exactly luxuriously furnished and there was only one chair and the bed to sit on. I took the chair.

"So what's up?"

He had a briefcase with him, and he opened it and took out an envelope and a piece of paper, both of them enclosed in plastic sheets.

"This letter was waiting for me at the station." The envelope was addressed to him, printed by hand. The letter, also printed, on a single sheet of paper, read as follows:

MESSAGE TO SERGEANT GILLIES: THIS IS A WARNING. YOU MUST STOP THE WHITE DOGS. THEY ARE GETTING OUT OF CONTROL AND WILL CAUSE TROUBLE ON ALL OF US. THEY INTEND TO ACT WHEN THE ROYAL PERSONAGE COMES TO LEWIS. YOU KNOW WHO THEY ARE. YOU MUST STOP THEM!

"Can I take it out of the sheet?"

"Of course."

I removed the piece of paper, holding it by the corner, and studied it and sniffed it. Then I did the same with the envelope. There was nothing discernible to the human nose, anyway.

"It was on the windshield of the police van that was in the parking lot. One of the constables handed it to me when I arrived this morning."

"You must have a high profile in Stornoway, Sergeant Gillies."

He smiled. "I've never thought so until now. Inspector Harris is the one who gets all the press."

"I wonder why it wasn't addressed to him."

"No idea. What do you deduce from the thing, Madam Sherlock?"

"Hey, we're talking two lectures here, not a lifelong study."

"That's more than I've got."

The printing was neat — there was no sign of a psychotic mind at work. There was no blood, semen, or excrement smeared over the page. However, I didn't have much doubt that the warning should be taken very seriously indeed.

"Who are the White Dogs? Not canine, I assume?"

"They're a fringe group that popped up about two years ago, claiming to be Gaelic separatists. They say they want all absentee landlords kicked out and that the Gaelic language and culture should be exclusive throughout the Hebrides. They want the Islands to be self-governing."

"My God, sounds like some of the reactionaries we have in Quebec. We've already had an expensive referendum about it. Separatism was defeated."

"The group doesn't speak for everybody, of course, and what they propose is ridiculously impractical."

That sounded familiar too.

"Are they a violent group?"

"Not in the usual sense of the word. They use embarrassment and so-called shock tactics. Last year, when the Queen visited Stornoway, a group of about five men in traditional kilts were standing with the crowd just outside the town hall. As she came out, they turned and lifted the kilts. Underneath they were mother naked. Then they hung their placards on their rear ends. 'Don't screw us any more' was the gist of it."

"Did she see them?"

"I don't think so. By the merest good luck, a little lassie from the school stepped forward from the opposite direction to hand her some flowers. The constables hustled the men out of the way."

"How did the locals feel about that?"

"Most of them thought it was outrageously bad-mannered. We're a polite bunch, and the majority of islanders are very pro-royal. There was another incident last year. A minor aristo who owns a lot of land here came for a visit to meet his tenants. He received a package, and inside was a long-dead and stinky hedgehog and a card saying, '*We were here first. Get out or die.*'"

"That's a much more threatening tone."

"It is. And the man turned right around and went home. We weren't even sure if the group responsible was the local animal-activist group, who were upset about the culling of the hedgehogs on Uist, or if it was the White Dog gang."

"Why the name?"

"There's a legend on the island that the ghost of a white collie will appear to give warning when the land is threatened. Apparently the collie really did exist decades ago and was responsible for numerous heroic acts, rescuing sheep or unconscious shepherds. People swear they've seen it running across the moor when the night is dark and the moon is on the wane."

He reached into the briefcase again and pulled out a folder. "I brought these newspaper clippings to show you. This has been since January."

There were four, and each incident they described occurred about a month apart. Several of the greens at the golf course had been chopped up. A note was sent to the *Gazette*. "*This seems to be the only thing the landlords care about. We have been hacked around ourselves.*" The second incident was a dump of fish offal on the front door of the council office. "*Your performance stinks. Get out.*"

Both of the other incidents involved smelly refuse being smeared around public buildings. One of them was Sarah MacDonald's real-estate office. The reason given for targeting it was that it was dealing with incomers, and therefore actively destroying the local culture.

"Do you know who they are?" I asked Gill.

"We got the five men involved in flashing Her Majesty, but they were pretty closed-mouthed. They said they were acting alone, no organization or secret society. When the other incidents happened we questioned them, but they all had alibis."

"But you think there might be more of them."

"Exactly. That one there with the dumping of the offal in front of the city hall, it happened in the middle of the night, but a tourist with a toothache, who was sitting by the harbour, says he thought the driver of the truck was a woman."

"So you would describe them more as a nuisance fringe than anything else?"

"That depends, doesn't it, on whether or not you're at the receiving end. The real-estate office had to close down while the entrance was cleaned up." He sighed. "In this day and age of bombs and assassinations, I suppose what they do is small potatoes, but frankly, it pisses me off. I'm one of those who find it outrageously bad-mannered."

There was an official police report sheet in the folder, with mug shots of the five flashers and their vital statistics. All were men under thirty, the thug age. One was scowling into the camera, even though I'm sure he'd been told to keep his face straight. He had long, wiry black hair and a bushy beard. His height was given as six foot six inches, age twenty-seven and his name was Black John Matthews.

"Is that his legal name?"

"I don't know if it's on his birth certificate, but that's what he answers to."

"Any priors?"

"A string of drunk and disorderly. Minor assault charges. He's been up on something or other since he was a lad. In my opinion, he doesn't have an honest principle in his body. He'd follow any group that offered him the chance to kick in a few windows."

"The others?"

"Nothing. Upright citizens. That one, Murray, was a school-teacher. Currently out of work. The other three do odd jobs around Stornoway. Murray's the one who'd be the thinker."

I replaced the originals in the plastic and picked up the copies.

"Okay. I'll deal with the content in a minute. Some of this is obvious. The printing is neat and the lines are straight across the page. The punctuation is sophisticated. A colon correctly placed after 'GILLIES.' An exclamation point after 'THEM.' No crossing out. There are no grammatical errors unless you count, 'will cause trouble ON all of us.' Which isn't quite English."

"It's a Gaelic construction. We say things like, 'the cold is on you,' or 'the Gaelic is on you.' Don't ask me why."

"We can assume then that the writer's first language is Gaelic. Not a huge help, considering where we are, but something. The words 'THE ROYAL PERSONAGE' are odd. Almost a joke. Certainly old-fashioned and very formal."

"Maybe they didn't know exactly who was coming? We don't always know ourselves until the last minute. The security thinks it's safer that way. Do you think it's a man or a woman?"

"A guess? I'd say a woman. Neat printing, polite language. But either way, this is definitely an educated person, maybe older generation, although the expression Royal Personage could be deliberately misleading. This is not an 'official' warning. Typically a group spokesman would be more aggressive. 'If the prince comes here, there'll be trouble, we're warning you,' or 'We're giving you fair warning,' something like that. The writer says, 'they' as opposed to 'us.' She hasn't identified with the group, although 'THEY ARE GETTING OUT OF CONTROL' is an interesting choice of words and suggests ongoing familiarity. She doesn't say 'THEY *ARE* OUT OF CONTROL.' There is urgency in the repetition of 'YOU MUST STOP THEM,' with the exclamation point, and the underlining of 'YOU KNOW WHO THEY ARE.' If you look at the other side of the paper, you can see how heavy the underline was."

"I noticed you sniffed at the paper. Looking for essence of rosewater?"

"Don't knock the power of the olfactory organ. We had a series of hate letters come to the station a couple of years back. There was a faint-but-distinct odour of disinfectant to all of them. We all went around sniffing and smelling to identify it and finally we traced it to a germicidal hand soap. Our forensic shrink suggested we were looking for some guy with the Lady MacBeth complex. In other words, he washed his hands several times a day because he felt so guilty, probably about excessive masturbation."

"I hate to imagine how you went about the questioning on that one."

"There was a maintenance guy who fitted the profile. Raw, clean hands and all. He had a grudge against the entire station because he thought we discriminated against him. He wasn't Black, by the way. He was an American."

Gillies was gazing at me with exaggerated admiration. "Och. I'll bet you were the one who identified the smell."

"Good guess. I hope that's not based on your perception of the length of my nose."

He laughed. "Not at all. You have a perfect nose. Not too long nor too short."

He wasn't joking. I rustled the piece of paper.

"I don't think there's much else I can say except that it would be worth checking up on the bare-assed five. So far they've stayed with scatological pranks, but the implication is that something much more serious could occur. How do you think the possibility of a royal visit was leaked, by the way?"

"You heard Janice MacIver. Somebody puts two and two together when they see increased security, then one of the constables tells his girl, who tells her friend, and it's off like a brush fire."

"Janice mentioned Rosie. Is she one of your support staff?"

"She is. I'll have a word with her. Your point being that the White Dogs need to have access to the information if they're going to do anything?"

"Exactly."

He gathered up the papers. "I really appreciate this, Chris. I'll be off now to have a word with Jock and send someone to chat up the lads. I'll come back about a quarter past one and drive you over to Tormod's funeral."

"Do you have time?"

"I do. Besides it's part of my job."

I didn't quite get what he meant by that, but he was in a hurry now. I walked with him to the ancient elevator, hoping he wouldn't have any trouble with the royal visit, but rather happy I'd been able to show off my stuff. It had quite chased my blues away for the time being.

CHAPTER TWENTY-THREE

Gill arrived punctually and dressed in a smart civvy suit of grey pinstripe with a discreet blue tie. We exchanged compliments, he about my hat, me about the tie. His black eye was much less noticeable, and I commented on it.

"Did you put a steak on it?"

"No, actually I used a couple of leeches."

"What!"

"It's true. I know it sounds horrible, but the little buggers really work. They suck out all the congealed blood."

"Oh, my gawd. I think I'll stick with Polysporin."

On the drive over, he told me that he'd sent out a constable to talk to the flashing five. Murray was laid up with a broken ankle, so he was out of commission. The other three were sufficiently intimidated by a friendly warning, but they hadn't been able to find Black John, which concerned him.

"Let's hope we get passed over in favour of St. Andrews."

The Na Gearrannan church was on a hill, just past the turnoff to Tormod's house and, as we drove into the village, I could see people were making their way there, walking in small groups, men in front, women following behind. They were all in sober clothes, the woman mostly in black coats and skirts, the men in suits.

Gill parked the car and we went over to the church, where a young man ushered us in and told us to take a pew near the rear. The church was almost full, people speaking softly to each other, all of them in their Sunday best. All of the women were behatted and I was glad Lisa had warned me. I took a quick glance around. Although I didn't really expect Joan to show up, you never knew.

On the rack in front of us were two black hymnals, and the pew itself was unpadded and so straight as to be uncomfortable. The church was quite large and austere. There was not a stained window to be seen, nor a cross or statue, nor the embroidered altar cloths that I was used to. In fact, there wasn't an altar as such, just a raised pulpit reached by two curving stairs. A low partition separated this part of the church from the rest of the congregation, and sitting in front of it were half a dozen men, one of them Andy MacAulay. Coral-Lyn was in the closest pew, and the coffin, covered by a white linen cloth, was on a low platform at the end of the aisle.

"Who are those men?" I whispered to Gillies.

"They're all the church elders. They run things."

A door at the rear opened and a tall man with the white dog collar of a minister, swept out and began to mount the stairs to the pulpit. At the same time, Lisa scurried in from the rear of the church. She was the model of decorum in her long black skirt and jacket. The skirt had a slit that was thigh-high but, hey, it was a skirt nonetheless. But she couldn't resist the thumb to the nose in her choice of hat. It was a red straw, and the wide brim was encircled with large, black-silk roses. It was a gorgeous hat that screamed for attention, and she certainly got a lot of it as she walked briskly down the aisle, her stiletto heels clicking on the hard wooden floor. A woman seated in the pew across from Coral-Lyn slid over so that Lisa could get in.

The minister was boyishly handsome, fortyish. Gill must have noticed my expression. "John Murdoch is our most eligible bachelor," he said softly.

Before I could comment on that, Murdoch spoke.

"Let us pray."

I expected the usual shuffle and creak of people dropping to their knees, but nobody moved. They didn't even lower their heads, as far as I could tell. Reverend Murdoch had a lilting voice which sounded almost Welsh to me and, in spite of my distractibility, I found him captivating. He used as a text the story of the raising of Lazarus, and although I'd heard it before, the human drama suddenly became alive, not fossilized as a "Biblical story." "As a man, Jesus grieved for Lazarus who was his friend. He wept." It was an appropriate text for a funeral and the minister then went on to talk more personally about Tormod MacAulay, who had been an elder in the church. The Reverend had obviously known Tormod well, so his words seemed real, not just the empty platitudes I'd heard at so many of the funerals I'd attended, at which the dead person was a complete stranger to the minister conducting the service. According to what this minister said, Tormod had been an active man all his life until his illness, a man of warmth and humour. This was not the time to talk about his betrayal of his grandson and his sleazy exploitation of his employee, even if the Reverend knew about them. I've no doubt the other elements of his character were true, too.

From where I was sitting, I had a good view of Coral-Lyn, whose eyes were fixed on her fiancée. He had his head down and periodically wiped away tears. The intensity of her desire to go to him was palpable, almost more predatory than supportive, and I wondered what it would be like to be the recipient of that kind of feeling.

Andy stood up, faced the congregation, and led us in singing two Psalms unaccompanied, ragged but vigorous. There was another parting prayer, and the service was over. The men who had been seated in front of the partition stood up and filed to each side of the coffin. They grasped its handles, hoisted it aloft, and slowly walked down the aisle. One pew at a time, the rest of us followed them out.

Outside the church, we stood for a moment, me wishing I had purchased gloves as well as a hat. So much for spring weather. It was freezing here. We watched the ushers loading the coffin into the hearse. Coral-Lyn was with her man, and when he got into the car, she jumped in after him.

"Got to give Miss Cheerio credit for that."

Lisa MacKenzie had come up behind me.

"Give her credit for what?" I asked.

"Traditionally, women don't go to the graveside. That's for the men. The lassies are back at the house making the funereal baked meats and sandwiches."

I glanced around and realized that most of the group now drifting away from the church were women. In his parting words, the minister had invited everybody to take refreshments at the boarding house where Andy lived, and that's where they seemed to be heading.

While Lisa and I were talking, Gill had stepped aside, and I could see him huddled over his cell phone. He was frowning and he glanced over at me. My heart did a little jump. Some news.

He disconnected and came over to us.

"Good afternoon, Lisa. Great bonnet you've got on."

"What's up?" I asked.

"I've got to get back to the station. Follow-up to that situation we were talking about. It will be occurring. No more news for you, sorry. I won't be able to go to the house."

"That's okay."

"If you're concerned about getting Christine back to Stornoway, I can take her," interjected Lisa.

"On your motorcycle?" Gill's voice was incredulous.

"Yes! It's safe. And she's no a wuss, are you, Christine?"

I didn't know how she could determine that on such short acquaintance. I am a coward about some things, and riding on the back of a motorcycle at the mercy of an unknown driver is one of them. On the other hand, if I took her up on the offer, I'd be able to stay for the post-funeral wake.

"Thanks, Lisa. Motorbike it is, if you promise not to speed."

She laughed. "I'm so conservative, you'd never know me."

I thought I'd keep an eye on what she was inhaling, just in case.

"I'll call you later on," said Gill.

He walked off to his car. Everybody else had pretty much left by now and a fine rain was starting to fall.

"Come on, let's get going. Our hats will be ruined." said Lisa. "You look good in yours, by the way."

"And you."

She laughed. "I thought I needed a wee bit of colour."

The house where the funeral reception was to be held was a beige pebble-stuccoed cottage with fresh green paint on the trim and a narrow, tidy garden. A tall, middle-aged woman was standing at the door greeting arrivals.

"Good morning, Penelope," said Lisa. "I'd like you to meet Miss Christine Morris, who is visiting us from Canada. Chris, this is Miss Barbara Stewart."

Miss Stewart beamed at me and shook my hand vigorously. She was a well-fleshed woman with springy grey hair and a tanned healthy-looking skin. She was wearing a patterned navy dress with a single row of pearls at the throat.

"Canada! We must have a chat. I have relatives who live in Canada."

I was saved by another woman who came into the yard behind us, and Miss Stewart reached out to her.

"Murdina. Come on in."

Lisa and I moved on into the small entrance hall, which was largely taken up with a decent-sized freezer, at the moment draped with a crocheted black cover. The bathroom was directly in front of us, door ajar to reveal pristine towels and gleaming fixtures. There was a hall to the left, which I assumed led to the bedrooms. Three or four people were standing in the hall with plates of refreshments in their hands, and they looked at us with friendly curiosity. I expected that at any minute somebody would come over and ask if I happened to have met their uncle Joe who lived in Manitoba. The living room was directly to the right and jammed with chattering women. As we hovered on the threshold, one of them turned around and greeted us. She was tall and weather-browned and was also wearing a dark-patterned summer dress, although hers was maroon-coloured, not navy. For a moment, I was startled that Miss Stewart had metamorphosed herself ahead of us into the room, and I actually glanced over my shoulder to check it out. The woman chuckled.

"I know that look. No, you're not losing your mind. I'm Penelope. You met my twin sister, Barbara, at the door."

You'd have fooled me. Lisa started to make introductions again, but it was hard to hear above the noise. Penelope smiled at me. "Give me your coats. Do you want to keep your hats?

Lisa did. I relinquished mine happily.

"Do have a look at the memorial we put together for Tormod," Penelope said, indicating something at the other side of the room, and then she moved on to serve the rest of the crowd.

"Hang on," said Lisa, and she took my hand and pushed into the crowd with lots of "excuse me's," me following in her wake like a baby pilot fish.

The mantelpiece had been set up as the memorial site, and there was a narrow oasis of space around it. A large framed photograph was on a plant stand in the middle of the hearth, where the fire would be. Several photographs of different sizes were on the mantelshelf and on two smaller tables.

Sitting tucked into the corner beside the hearth was a diminutive, white-haired woman, and she smiled a greeting.

"*Matainn mhah, Lisa. Ciamar a tha thu?*"

"Very well, thank you, Mrs. MacNeil. And you?"

I couldn't understand what she replied, but I gathered she was in excellent health.

"You should have a look at the photographs," she said. "Barbara and Penelope asked around for pictures of Tormod, and they put the best up there. It's a good history of him."

She got stiffly to her feet and joined us in front of the set-up. The central photograph was in an ornate silver frame. Tormod was in a formal brown suit. I could see the backdrop was the high podium of the church we had just come from.

"He had just been made an elder of the church," said Mrs. MacNeil. "He was very conscientious, I must say. Never missed a service until this past year when he got ill."

Her voice was sad.

"That's him when he was about six months old." She pointed to the picture on the left. A chubby baby was seated on the floor, curly hair, big eyes.

"Aww," said Lisa.

"He was a bonny boy and he remained so all of his life." Mrs MacNeil smiled. "Quite a masher as we used to call him in my day."

The next photograph was of an adolescent Tormod, flanked on either side by two lanky girls in identical print dresses.

"Are those the Misses Stewart?" I asked.

"Yes, indeed. Tormod's mother's sister married James Stewart, and Penelope and Barbara are their daughters."

Lisa pointed to the next picture. "Oh my, they don't look too happy do they?"

It was Tormod on his wedding day. A handsome young man, his bride younger and not at all pretty. No white gown and flowers here. He was in his Sunday-best suit, she in a tailored two-piece. They were smiling for the camera, but their pose was stiff, their arms by their sides, not even linked.

Mrs. MacNeil puckered her lips. "That was an unfortunate marriage. Chalk and cheese don't mix."

"But they *had* to get married, didn't they? Margaret had a bun in the oven."

I felt irritated with Lisa. She'd better grow out of the need to shock before too long. She merely sounded crude, and Mrs. MacNeil was a sweet woman. However, she was Lisa's match.

"I presume you mean that Peggy had conceived prior to her marriage date. Yes, that did seem to be the case, but that's not a good reason for not making a marriage work. I do believe she could have made him a good wife if he had accepted the circumstances."

In other words, Tormod felt tricked and trapped into marriage and never forgave her.

I might have passed right over the next photograph, because it had been enlarged from a smaller print, so it was a bit fuzzy. However, Mrs. MacNeil had adopted the role of moral guardian.

"No matter what, they had two beautiful children." She indicated the photograph.

Tormod was sitting on a bench. On his left was a boy of about five or six, on his right, leaning away from him, a girl, probably about three years of age. She was smiling, and she had her head comfortably against the arm of a young girl seated next to her. This girl was just on the edge of puberty, skinny, with wavy, dark hair that fell to her shoulders. She was squinting into the sun and grinning cheerfully at something off-camera. I grabbed the picture from the shelf so I could look at it more closely.

"Who are these children, Mrs MacNeil?"

"Those are Tormod's two bairns. Iain has passed on now, far too young, but that's for God to say, not us. The little girl is his daughter, named Peggy after her mother. And she's gone far away, too. Not passed on you understand, but her mother took her out of the country when she was but a lassie, and she hasna seen her homeland since." She shook her head in sorrow.

"Mrs. MacNeil, who is the other girl sitting beside Peggy?"

She peered more closely at the photograph, while Lisa looked over her shoulder.

"That would be Shona MacAulay."

"MacAulay? She was related?"

"She was. She was Tormod's cousin. She was much younger, of course. His father was William MacAulay, the eldest son of William MacAulay of Carloway. Shona's father was Norman, who was the third-eldest in the family. The second child was a daughter, Sarah. She married a MacNeil, and it was her first born, Alexander, who was my husband. I myself was a MacLeod before my marriage."

I was drowning in a sea of genealogy.

"Excuse me, Mrs. MacNeil. Could we get back to this girl for a minute? Do you know what happened to her?"

"It's dreadful isn't it. And they look so happy, don't they?"

"What was dreadful, Mrs. MacNeil?"

"All three of them are now gone from us."

"Including her?"

"Yes. Poor Shona. She was so full of life and mischief."

"What's the matter?" Lisa asked, staring at me.

I shrugged. "Nothing."

The photograph had been taken about fifty years ago, but the slightly tilted smile was the tipoff. That and the dark, straight eyebrows. As far as I was concerned, I was looking at a picture of my mother, Joan Morris.

CHAPTER TWENTY-FOUR

At that moment, Lisa redeemed herself in my eyes.

"I've never heard of Shona MacAulay. What's the story, Mary?" she asked.

Mrs. MacNeil sat down again with a sigh of relief. She seemed happy to gossip to us, but suddenly, Barbara or Penelope appeared with a tray, on which sat cups of tea, already milked and probably sugared.

"Cuppas for everybody?"

Lisa refused, but Mrs. MacNeil and I took one. I waited as patiently as I could.

The initial sips over, she said. "Where was I?"

"You were going to tell us what happened to Shona MacAulay."

"She went to Canada and ran off with a Red Indian when she was barely eighteen. She died somewhere in the wilderness. Such a tragic waste."

"She died? How?"

"Nobody really knows, my dear. All we heard was that she had passed away very soon after she arrived. One of those colonial illnesses, probably." She didn't give me time to ascertain exactly what a "colonial illness" might be. "You see, the problem was she and Annie didn't get along." Another drink of tea. "Annie Stewart became her stepmother. She was a sister of

James Stewart, who was the father of Barbara and Penelope, by the way. His wife, Barbara Morrison, was Tormod's aunt."

She glanced at me over her teacup, as if to see if I was following all of this. I wasn't.

"What did her and Annie Stewart not getting along have to do with dying in the wilderness?" Lisa's tone was more polite than truly interested. She had no idea I was seething with frustration. However, with somebody like Mrs. MacNeil, you could not hurry them nor lead them. I tried to calm down.

"Ach, there wasn't a direct connection as such, but if Shona hadn't been sent away to boarding school on the mainland, she wouldn't have gone back there to work when she left school and she wouldn't have gone off to Canada like that."

There was a logic in there somewhere.

"Mrs. MacNeil, could we backtrack for a moment?" I interjected. "You said Annie Stewart was Shona's stepmother?"

"That's right. Annie had a good heart, but she just wasn't used to children. She took care of her parents until they both died suddenly of the influenza. I suppose Annie was . . . oh, she must have been thirty at the time. I know that doesn't sound old these days, but it was considered so then. She had no doubt resigned herself to spinsterhood. She had never had a sweetheart, by all accounts, but she was comely enough to attract Norman MacAulay, who up and married her not more than a year after his first wife died. That was Kirsteen Morrison from Barva. She was only forty-four when she passed away." She lowered her voice. "It was cancer. Took her off within six months."

I tut-tutted. Lisa shifted restlessly, then took off her hat and fluffed up her hair.

"Lovely hat dear, so colourful."

"Thank you, Mary."

"Shall I go on? This must be boring old history to you and mean nothing at all to Miss Morris."

"Please continue," I said. "It's quite fascinating."

Lisa threw me a sceptical look.

"The problem was that Annie didn't know what to do with

Shona, who was just a wee girl. She'd been born when her mother thought she'd done with child-bearing, so she was the baby of the family and everybody indulged her. Then her mammy died and her pappa brought home another wife. I imagine she resented having to mind a new mother. Which is only natural, isn't it?"

We agreed.

"So . . . as I was saying. When Shona started to grow into a young woman, things got much worse with Annie. They fought constantly, by all accounts. Norman tried to discipline the girl, but it did no good." She sighed. "Poor mite. He was very severe, everybody knew it. He was used to raising boys, you see, not a wee lass. Finally, when she was but fourteen, Shona was packed off to a boarding school on the mainland. Which they could ill afford, by the way. At the same time, right out of the blue, Annie, who had seemed to be as barren as a board, poor woman, found she was expecting. After her own bairn came, she had even less time for Shona, who hardly came home at all. When the lassie could legally leave school, she did, but she stayed on the mainland and found some kind of work." Again she lowered her voice to whisper the unmentionable. "She got in with a bad crowd. Wild parties and drinking, that sort of thing. She was only just eighteen when the news came that she'd run off to Canada. Then we heard she had taken up with a Red Indian and was living in the wilderness. And that was where she died, may she rest in peace."

"Did they bring her back here to be buried?"

Mrs. MacNeill shook her head. "The family decided against it. Annie was not at all well. She suffered from terrible nervous states. Norman didn't want to leave her alone. They decided to leave things as they were. I presume the Red Indian man took care of the funeral. If they do that kind of thing, that is."

She finished off her cup of tea. My tea was cold by now.

"Norman just asked for prayers in the church. There wasn't anything more formal than that. Some might say they were cold-hearted. I was expecting my second, so I was preoccupied with my own affairs, but it all seemed very odd and unnatural."

I took the photograph again, suddenly full of doubt.

"Was there another daughter beside Shona, a twin even?"

"No, not at all. Just the wee one of Annie's. Her half-sister, I suppose you'd call her. Penny and Barbara are the only twins we've had in the village." Mrs. MacNeil dabbed at her mouth daintily and continued as if there had not been an interruption. "They were a private family, those MacAulays. Not Tormod's side nor my mother-in-law, who was as welcoming a woman as you might wish to find. But for some reason, Norman was a sour sort of fellow. He lacked humour, and he was very strict with his children. It got far worse after he lost both of his wives and his daughter. He withdrew into himself. Nowadays, I imagine he'd be called depressed and he'd get some help, but then we just accepted that was who he was. Private. His boys turned out the same way. Thank goodness they've all married good-hearted women who've managed to soften them up. Norman's gone now. He died of tuberculosis in 1979. I did mention Annie passed away as well, didn't I?"

"I know about that, but Christine probably doesn't," said Lisa.

"Poor woman died of a tumour when her girl was only eight. She'd doted on her own bairn, but it must have been a cold hearth for the child after that. Poor Sarah. She had a difficult life. She had one chance of happiness. She and young Iain MacAulay fell in love with each other. I've never seen her as happy as she was when she told me they were going to get engaged, but it all came to naught. Apparently, Tormod was quite opposed to the match, although Sarah was a sweet girl in those days. Iain gave in and went off to Perth. The next thing we knew he was married. Sarah was heartbroken. I've heard tell that sometimes it's the reason people turn to the bottle for comfort. Which she did in this case." Suddenly she looked flustered. "Not to speak ill of the dead mind you, but it was common knowledge."

I'd been in the middle of trying to down some of the cold tea. I almost choked.

"Hold on. Am I getting this right? Sarah MacAulay is one and the same as Sarah MacDonald?"

"Yes, my dear. MacDonald was her married name."

CHAPTER TWENTY-FIVE

I needed to go somewhere and think, so I did what women have
done for decades. I fled to the bathroom. I washed my hands with
the highly perfumed pink soap and regarded my own reflection in the
mirror. If I were a stranger meeting me for the first time, I'd think
"What a stressed out woman she is." Worry lines seemed to have
suddenly etched themselves between my eyebrows, and there were
dark shadows underneath my eyes. I concentrated on washing my
hands. It was one thing to look at an old photograph, say in a school
yearbook, and pick out so-and-so when they were sixteen. You knew
who you were looking for. It was different to come across a picture
and think you recognized somebody from fifty years ago. Was Shona
MacAulay truly one and the same person as Joan Morris, my moth
er? You can't really fake your own death. There are too many legal
ities to deal with. Did the family really believe she was dead? Given
what Mrs. MacNeil had said, especially with regards to the lack of a
proper funeral, I was more inclined to think they put about that story
because Joan/Shona was in some kind of disgrace. To disown her was
a kind of death. If that was the case, she had gone along with it. And
it would certainly explain why she had never wanted to talk about
her family, why she'd told me her parents were dead.

I dried off my hands on the pristine pink towel. I felt as if I
had stepped through the gate at platform nine-and-three-quarters

and I was into the true world where I belonged and had always yearned to be. I might have discovered relatives I never knew I had. If Sarah MacDonald was Joan's half-sister, she was my aunt. She had a daughter who would be my cousin. And there were brothers, Mrs. MacNeil had said. Uncles for me. More cousins. I was almost literally dizzy with the notion. My God, some of them might even be here, and if Tormod MacAulay was Joan's cousin, he was my second cousin. I was trying to work out how the Stewart twins were related when there was a discreet tapping on the door.

"Anybody in there?"

"Be right out," I glanced in the mirror again, and pushed at my hair, which was starting to frizz in the damp air. My eyes were much brighter now.

A man was waiting outside. We exchanged the polite smiles of two people passing on the threshold of the toilet, then he halted.

"Hello again."

He looked familiar, but I couldn't place him immediately. He smiled and helped me out.

"Duncan MacKenzie here. We met on Sunday on the moor. You probably don't recognize me in my good clothes."

It was the shepherd who had reacted so strongly to hearing I was from Canada. And it was true what he said. He was in a dark-blue suit with a white shirt and maroon tie, and I hadn't recognized him out of context of the moor and his border collies.

"Yes, of course." I was about to move on when I remembered. "Congratulations on becoming a grandfather. I've seen the baby, and she is quite adorable."

"I'm going over this afternoon to see Mairi. I hear you came to the rescue."

"Not exactly. She seemed to be going into labour and I helped until the midwife arrived, which wasn't long afterward."

"Well, according to Mairi, you were brilliant."

An older woman with a cane had come up and was standing near. "Are you . . . are you . . . ?"

She indicated the washroom.

"Go ahead," said MacKenzie. He stepped back to allow her entrance. I started to shuffle off. I wanted to get back to Mary MacNeil and ask some more questions. Duncan followed me.

"Have you seen Lisa?" he asked.

"Yes, we came together. She was over there."

The gorgeous scarlet hat was clearly visible in the midst of the blacks and navies of the other women. He frowned. "That's my Lisa for you." She turned at that moment, saw him, and waved a greeting.

I was easing my way through the crush at this point, and he was close behind. I could only assume his bathroom call had not been an urgent one. When we reached Lisa, she moved forward as if to embrace him, but his disapproval was palpable and she stopped herself.

"Hello, Dad." She tilted her head. "How'd you like my hat?"

He shrugged. "I suppose it's better than a bike helmet."

"I was considering that, but it's a bit cumbersome."

Lisa's tone was deliberately flippant, but I thought she was hurt by his disapproval. Mary MacNeil rescued all of us from an awkward moment.

"*Maitain mhah, a* Duncan." She said something else, and he replied in kind and gave her a friendly handshake, the contrast marked between that and his greeting to his daughter.

"Excuse me, I've got to go to the loo," said Lisa and she moved away. Ah, that useful bathroom.

I took the opportunity to look at the photograph once again. En route from the bathroom I'd been grabbed by doubt, but when I studied the picture again, I was absolutely sure. I became aware that Duncan and Mrs. MacNeil's conversation had tapered off, and they were regarding me with interest.

"I've been inundating Miss Morris with family histories, "said Mary. "You remember Annie Stewart, don't you, Duncan? And that branch of the MacAulays? They knew so much tragedy, poor folks. You were quite daft on Shona, as I recall."

MacKenzie would never be good at poker. His face turned scarlet. "That was a long time ago, Mary."

"You knew her, did you?" I asked.

"I'm from this village. We all knew each other."

"Mrs. MacNeil told me she died somewhere in Canada when she was only eighteen."

"Aye."

"A rather mysterious death, by the sound of it. Do you know where she went?"

"I do not."

I waited a moment, but it was obvious he wasn't going to be any more forthcoming. I turned back to Mary.

"Whereabouts did the MacAulay family live?"

She didn't seem to find my curiosity strange, thank goodness. "When she was born they were still in the black houses up near the coast. They've been turned into a tourist site now, more's the pity. I used to visit my cousin Peigi, who lived in the next house up, and it's now a youth hostel. And the MacLeods' house is a fancy self-catering cottage. I just can't get over it. Time just sweeps you away before you know it."

"Have you been to see Na Gerranan, Black House Village, yet?" Duncan asked me.

"No, I haven't."

"I tell you what," said MacKenzie. "I'll take you up to Na Gerrannan right now and you can have a look around. This is pretty much finished."

As far as I could tell, there was no lessening of the crush of people and the level of noise was even higher.

"The men haven't got back from the gravesite yet," said Mary.

"I can run you back to Stornoway after," continued MacKenzie. "I'm going in to see my daughter anyway."

"Thanks, but I was going to get a ride with Lisa."

"On her bike?"

"Yes."

"You wouldn't get me on that thing if you paid me. She goes much too fast."

"She promised me she'd ride carefully."

"Careful isn't a word that Lisa is familiar with." He said it jokingly, but I knew he meant it. The subject of the conversation was back in the room and she had a plate in her hand, which she thrust into the middle of our little group.

"Here you are. Barbara's homemade oatcakes and crowdie. Christine, you must try them. Crowdie is rather like cottage cheese but a thousand times richer. And delicious on oatcakes."

I did and she was right. Duncan swallowed his quickly.

"Lisa, I understand you were going to give Miss Morris a ride on the bike, but I'm going in to see Mairi and the new babe, so I can give her a lift."

"Okay. Is that all right with you, Christine?"

Frankly, I was rather relieved not to be on the back of her motorcycle, but I would certainly have preferred her company.

"Your father is going to take her up to the Black House Village to show her where the MacAulays used to live," added Mrs. MacNeil.

I hadn't accepted his offer and wasn't sure I was going to.

"Do you want to come with us?" I asked Lisa. I was hoping for a buffer. There was something about the shepherd that was making me uneasy.

"I won't this time, thanks. I'll stay and help Penelope and Barbara with the cleaning up."

"Shall we go then?" asked Duncan.

I took another quick assessment. He was sixtyish, fit and trim from shepherding, I presumed. There was no weird sexual energy emanating from him as far as I could tell, but he seemed awfully keen to get me out of here. The thought struck me that he might want to talk about Shona. I said my goodbyes, recovered my coat and hat, and followed him to his car.

He didn't speak at all, but we hadn't gone far when I realized two things. One, we had just passed the sign that pointed to the Black House Village, and two, he exactly fitted the description of the man Mrs. Waring said had pretended to be a police officer and who had picked up Joan's suitcase. What the hell! Was I being abducted? I looked out the window. We were travelling at a normal speed but trying to jump out would be foolhardy.

"Didn't we just pass the turnoff to the Black House Village?"

He nodded. "There's a smaller one at Arnol. It hasn't been converted into swanky cottages, so I thought it would give you a more authentic picture. And it's on the way."

Okay. But he was bloody tense, I could feel it. We were heading along the road towards the scene of the accident, and along this stretch of road there were no houses, the only life, placid sheep cropping the grass.

"Do you know somebody by the name of Joan Morris?" I asked, deciding action was better than not.

"Can't say I do."

I was watching his hands on the steering wheel, and I saw the tightening of his grip. Almost as good as a polygraph test. He was lying.

"She was involved in an accident right near here. Mrs. Sarah MacDonald was her passenger, and they went off the road."

"Terrible thing, that."

I turned my head to look at him, while he stared straight ahead. "Joan Morris is my mother. That's why I'm here."

"Is that so?" His tone was without inflection. He knew that already. His complete lack of surprise was unnatural. My heart was starting to beat faster, and I casually moved my hand to the seatbelt release. We rounded the bend where the car had crashed, but he didn't slow down or comment and continued on. Then, less than five hundred metres on, he slowed and made a sharp turn onto a narrow, unpaved road. A big wooden sign said, MACKENZIE'S COLLIES. There was a picture of a border collie facing a sheep.

"Where are we going?"

"I just have to stop at my house and pick up a present for the baby. I almost forgot. Won't take a minute."

The road dipped down towards the sea. I could see the roof and chimney of a house nestled at the tip of an inlet. There were no other houses in sight. I released the seat belt, holding it at the ready.

"Do you like music?" he asked suddenly

"Excuse me?"

We made another turn onto a long driveway. A dozen sheep were penned on the right, and on the left was an empty enclosure.

"I bet you like ABBA. I bet you grew up dancing to their music."

I can't tell you how bizarre this conversation sounded. MacKenzie was speaking in such an odd way, tense and jerky. He pulled up in front of the house. I let go of the belt, opened the door, and jumped out of the car. I was on the verge of throwing all civility to the wind and making a run for it, when he leaned over and said, "Does your mother know?"

I gaped.

"That's the name of the song. 'Does Your Mother Know?' I bet you danced to that. Am I right?"

CHAPTER TWENTY-SIX

MacKenzie was staring at me.

"Am I right?" he said again. "One of your favourite songs, isn't it?"

"Where is she?" I asked. "Is she still alive?"

He nodded, looking less crazed. "She's inside. She asked me to get you."

The front door of the house opened and four border collies spilled out, bounding over to meet us with tails wagging. A plump woman in dark glasses with bleached-blonde hair came to the doorway. She was wearing jeans and a sweater that sported an image of a border collie on the front. A tartan scarf was wrapped around her lower face as if she were suffering from a toothache. She gave a tentative wave. It was Joan, and I wouldn't have known her. I was flooded with feelings so tumultuous I could hardly breathe: relief, rapidly followed by anger. Fury, to be precise.

"Let's go in," said MacKenzie.

We had to push aside the exuberant dogs, who then peeled off and went to explore some essential thing. Joan retreated inside the house while Duncan ushered me in. I registered a hazy impression of a modern bungalow, white walls and light-coloured furniture, a smell of damp dogs.

Joan was standing with her back to me, looking out of the far window in a way that reminded me of Lisa staring out at the sea at Tormod's cottage.

"Hi, Joan," I said, and she turned around. Now I could see what she had been trying to hide. The scarf had dropped and the left side of her face was swollen and a livid bruise splotched her jaw. Her bottom lip was split.

"I understand you had a car accident." I knew my voice was thick with sarcasm, barely containing my anger, and she flinched away from it.

"I wasn't drinking, Chris. I know I wasn't drinking."

Duncan was right behind me.

"She was knocked unconscious. She banged up her leg, too. Show her."

Obediently, Joan rolled up the bottom of her jeans and revealed her shin, which had an angry-looking lump and a long, ugly bruise the colour of ink.

I gave the injury an insultingly brief glance. "You do know that the police are looking for you, don't you? Your passenger died. You disappeared. Not good choices, Joan, not good."

We stared at each other in the old familiar way, like two fighters trying to find the right balance so we could parry the next blow. I could see the flash of anger on her face, too. MacKenzie pulled out a dining-room chair and perched on the edge.

"I'll explain everything in a minute," said Joan, "but I'm just glad to see you, Chris. I couldn't believe it when Duncan told me he'd met you on the moor. What a shock. How did they get hold of you?"

"The usual way. Your ID was still in the car and the police found my number as next of kin. I was actually attending a conference in Edinburgh."

"Really! Then you were quite close. This side of the pond anyway."

"That's right."

"Well, thanks for coming." She glanced at me timorously. "You must have been worried." She seemed almost afraid to say that, in case I hadn't cared.

I didn't answer. She touched her bruised chin cautiously. "I was lucky."

Duncan had been watching us with the concentration of a referee. "Tell you what. Why don't I make us all a nice cuppa? Christine, come and sit at the table."

He pulled out a second chair with a gallant gesture, which irritated the hell out of me. I was sick of pretending this was all business as usual, a happy reunion between a mother and daughter. However, I couldn't refuse without being a complete boor. I sat down.

He chuckled. "You must have wondered what was happening when I was driving here. You looked like you thought I was kidnapping you."

"It did cross my mind."

"I wasn't sure how you'd react," said Joan. "whether you'd come or . . . send for the police or what. So I told Duncan to offer to show you the village or something like that and then to give you a sort of code so you'd know it was really me he was bringing you to. I thought that song was a good one. Only you and me'd know about that dancing."

That wasn't the only reason she'd chosen the ABBA song. She could have used anything, the name of the first hair salon she worked in, where I'd go to wait for her after school; any of the early places we'd lived in together when I was young. She had brought in the song because it was one of the few times we had felt happy together. I'm sure she hoped this would soften me up. Joan was a mistress of manipulation.

Duncan got to his feet and headed for the kitchen.

"I'll be right back."

There was a serving opening between kitchen and dining room, and I could see him as he started to make tea. He was alert to everything going on this side of the wall. Joan sat down in one of the easy chairs in front of the fireplace. She was obviously stiff and sore.

"Well, here I am, as requested," I said. "And you still haven't told me what happened."

There was a lively fire burning in the grate, and she said something, but she was addressing the flames.

"I didn't hear what you said."

She faced me and her eyes were filling with tears.

"Oh, Chris. I wish I could, but I don't remember. That's why I needed you to come."

CHAPTER TWENTY-SEVEN

"Here we go. Warm us up."

MacKenzie emerged from the kitchen, carrying a large tray with teapot, cups, and a plate of cakes. He put it on the table.

"Chris would probably prefer coffee," said Joan.

"You should have told me," said MacKenzie.

"No, no, tea is fine, really."

There was another weighty silence while he did the tea dispensing. He addressed my mother.

"Shona? Would you like a bannock?"

That answered one question. She was indeed the girl in the photo. Joan gave a little apologetic smile.

"Chris isn't used to anybody calling me Shona. That used to be my name," she added.

"Really? Shona MacAulay, I presume, whom I was told not more than an hour ago had run off in the wilderness with a Red Indian, never to be heard from again. You reincarnated as Joan Morris — I take it for reasons that I don't know of, but which you are surely going to tell me."

She winced, but she'd also come to the end of her patience. Same old pattern: me being deliberately provocative until she finally lost her temper and we screamed at each other.

She banged her fist on the arm of the chair and set off yelling.

"Cut it out! You just want your pound of fucking flesh don't you. Well, fuck off. Who needs you, you toffee-nosed little shit? Just fuck off. I'm your mother for Jesus' sake. I'm your fucking mother, and you just don't give a toss, do you?"

I'd heard these words many times before so the term "toffee-nosed" wasn't new to me. However, I was aware that an accent had returned. She must have worked hard to eradicate it. Now she was sounding quite Scottish, long e's in "shit" for example. I don't know if I would have jumped in and started retaliating with finely honed insults. I'd like to think I wouldn't have . . . that I'd outgrown that phase. However, I never had the opportunity. Her anger was spent as quickly as it had flared up and she dropped into painful sobs, deep and choking, unlike any drunken wailing I'd heard from her before. Duncan ran over to her and took her in his arms. She leaned her head on his chest and he stroked her hair, whispering to her in Gaelic.

My God, he loves her. I was still sitting at the table with my teacup in my hand, and I felt like Regan and Goneril rolled into one. I got up and went over to her. Tears and mucous were dampening Duncan's nice jacket and I fished a tissue out of my pocket and stuffed it under her cheek.

"I'm sorry. You've obviously had a bad time. I do really want to hear what happened."

It took her a while to stop crying, and Duncan stayed with her, not looking at me. I knew he was furious with me for acting like such a callous bitch, but who the hell was he to judge anyway? What did he know?

Finally, she quieted down. I couldn't get over his tenderness.

"All right now?"

"I'm fine."

She looked terrible, her eyes red and swollen and her cheeks blotchy. Funny thing was, I had never seen her so soft and vulnerable. Probably not since we had danced together.

I made myself useful by bringing over the cup of tea, which she accepted with a shaky smile.

"I just don't know where to start."

"As Humpty Dumpty said to Alice, 'Start at the beginning and go on to the end.'"

For a moment, she glanced at me warily, as if I was making fun of her, something I'd been guilty of more than once before. I helped her out.

"I guess I have to rewrite my résumé about where I came from."

"What do you mean?" a sharp tone in her voice.

"You always said you were from Down East, but that isn't true, is it? You were born here on the island of Lewis. You grew up here."

A small grin. "You could say that's out East."

She was not admitting to the outright lies she told me, but I didn't want to get into that now.

"Why did your family let everybody believe you had died? And I take it you didn't abscond with an aboriginal Canadian?"

Again tears suddenly flooded her eyes, and I had to wait while she mopped up. Duncan was crouched beside her, and he took her hand.

"Norman MacAulay was a self-righteous son-of-a-bitch, that's why," he said.

"It's such a long and complicated story, Chris, I think I'd better save it for later. Let's just say they thought I had disgraced them." She shrugged and I saw the vestiges of that old teenage defiance. "Two can play that game. I got a job as a nanny with the Cohens. You remember them don't you, Chris? We lived with them until you were four years old. They were very nice. They were in Scotland on holiday and, luckily, they needed a nanny for their wee ones. I just went with them when they returned to Canada."

"And you never had contact with your family again?"

"I wrote them to say I had decided to settle in Canada. . . . I said some silly thing about going to live on an Indian reserve. My father wrote back and said that I was dead to him and he never wanted to see me again."

"What did you do that was so terrible?"

She swallowed some of the tea and shrugged. "As far as he was concerned everything I did was bad. Me, the lost, perpetual sinner."

I still thought disinheriting your daughter was pretty drastic, but I let it ride for now.

"A woman at the wake, Mary MacNeil, told me you have older brothers. Did they know where you were?"

"Probably. But they and my father were like peas in a pod. I never heard from any of them."

She almost dropped her cup at this point because another burst of anguished crying tore out of her. This time both Duncan and I soothed her.

"Did you know she was in Canada?" I asked him over her head.

"Yes, I knew. She wrote to me."

"Why didn't you tell everybody the truth? How could you go along with such an atrocious lie?"

"I begged him not to tell, Chris. What was the point? At that time, I had no intention of ever returning to the island." She sat up a bit and gave another wry grin "I'd show them! I was going to make good, become rich and famous, and then I'd come back. Like Lazarus brought back from the dead." Then she looked into my eyes, and the depth of sorrow I saw pierced me to the core. "But it never happened. I truly fucked up my life."

"It's not too late," I jumped in.

The look of despair vanished, covered over by a mask of false cheer.

"No, it's not, is it? Which is why I came back to Lewis. I told you I had been seeing a wonderful therapist, didn't I?"

I nodded. I wasn't about to repeat my jeering remarks about psycho-banging.

"Charlene was the one who suggested I had to face my demons and get some closure before I could move on with my life. So here I am." There was some other expression in her eyes now, more angry than sad. "But as usual, I seem to have fucked up my chances. Oh God! Chris, I need your help like never before." Her agitation was such that she had to stand up, and she began to pace. "Oh God, oh God." She swivelled around and stood in front of me. "I was telling the gospel truth when I said just now that I don't remember what happened in the accident. I didn't even know there had been a car crash until Sunday morning when somebody rang Duncan. And people were saying the Canadian woman was the driver . . . "

"Weren't you?"

She clasped her hands, her eyes never leaving my face. "I truly don't know. I have a big blank in my mind. I remember getting into the car with Sarah, then nothing until I woke up in Duncan's bed on Saturday morning."

"I slept in the guest room," said MacKenzie hastily. As if it mattered to me.

"How did you explain the fact that you were battered and bruised? Surely you had to say something?"

Duncan was about to jump in and answer for her, but he stopped. I knew he was waiting to hear what story she would give first.

"You tell her, Dunc. I hardly remember."

He scowled at me yet again. "She said she had come over from her B&B in Skye, but her car stalled a ways from here. She decided to walk along the cliffs, slipped, and cracked her head."

"You were walking along the cliffs in the middle of the night in the rain?"

She shrugged. "I grew up doing that."

I didn't like that answer at all with its myriad implications, but I turned to MacKenzie. "Why didn't you go and get her car on Saturday?"

He was getting truly exasperated now, but I didn't care. "Because, Miss Sherlock, my car was dead as a doornail. Shona needed tending to, so that's what I did. I thought the car would wait. Do you want to get out and have a look to see if I'm telling the truth?"

Joan put her hand on his arm to calm him. "It's all right, Dunc. She's just asking."

Back to her. "Correct me if I'm wrong, but again according to Mrs. MacNeil, Sarah MacDonald was originally Sarah MacAulay, and she was your half-sister?"

She blinked and her hand flew to her bruised jaw. "Yes. She belonged to my stepmother."

Abruptly, she turned and went to the window. I could see her shoulders were shaking as she struggled for control. MacKenzie followed her and offered the comforting arm again. She availed herself of it while I waited. Finally, I said.

"In what way do you want me to help you?"

He answered for her. "Shona told me about your work. She's very proud of you, Christine. She says you've dealt with cases like this before." His tone and expression made it clear that he thought the pride was a tribute to Joan's generosity of heart and not much to do with my ability.

"What specifically are you referring to?" I asked her.

"You told me a few years ago that you'd been on a course with the FBI in the States somewhere. There's a way to help people get back their memories of what happened when they've been traumatized."

"You mean by the use of hypnosis?"

"Yes, that's what it was. Please, Chris. I want you to hypnotize me."

CHAPTER TWENTY-EIGHT

I was demurring like crazy with facial expressions and gestures —
as if to say "I can't hypnotize . . . you can't do . . . it's not a magic
trick," etc. — when Duncan interrupted me.

"Och, you're not giving your mother a chance. She's desperate
here. You could help her if you wanted to."

I resented his interference.

"I am obviously not making myself clear. Hypnosis is a useful
tool, and sometimes buried memories can be retrieved, but more
often than not, they are permanently lost. The brain has wiped
them out."

"But that bodyguard of Princess Di's who was in the crash, he
got his memory back didn't he? He remembered seeing a member
of the paparazzi forcing them over."

"No. As a matter of fact, Trevor Rees-Jones is a good example
of what I'm talking about. And he wasn't her bodyguard, by the
way. He was employed by Dodi Fayed. In spite of numerous sessions with a psychiatrist, Rees-Jones remembered getting into the
car as they were driving off, but that is all. Nothing else. And that
is the most common scenario." Yes, I know I sounded pompous,
but it was the truth. "Besides which, I'm not a psychiatrist. I took
one course four years ago. I've never practised the technique on
anyone since then."

Joan looked exactly like somebody who'd been turned down for a job she desperately needed. "I have faith in you, Chris. I know how you are. You were always top of the class, but you never believed you were smart. I'm sure it will all come back to you when you start."

"Faith in me, by either of us, is not the point. I might be utterly brilliant. The new Mesmer, but memory recovery through hypnosis isn't usually effective when there has been physical trauma."

I might as well have saved my breath. She had on her stubborn look.

"We can at least give it a try."

"No harm in that," said MacKenzie, throwing in his two cents' worth. I could have throttled him.

Oh God.

"But you're my . . . I don't know how objective I can be."

Her lips tightened. "For Lord's sake, Chris, I'm not asking you to give me a gynic exam. I just want you to put me into a trance and help me get my memory back. Besides, there's lots of times I've seen you act pretty detached where I'm concerned."

That was another minefield I wasn't about to walk through.

She tried again. "Please Chris. I need to know. I've got to clear my name."

"I see. And you're thinking that if you do the hypnosis with me, a police officer, you can bring whatever is said into a court of law? Well, I'm telling you right now, anything revealed in a hypnotic trance is not admissible evidence. It won't do you a damn bit of good if you tell me you weren't even in the bloody car."

"I thought you couldn't help but tell the truth when you were hypnotized."

"That's another common myth. People who lie in their daily lives are quite capable of lying even when they are in a trance. Besides which, the unconscious works in the same way dreams do. If you had a dream that you shot Kennedy, you wouldn't go and confess. Same thing. People say things when they're under hypnosis that aren't necessarily true. They're coming from the fantasy part of the mind."

"I don't understand what you're saying, Chris, but that's nothing new, is it? And I don't like the implication that I'm just trying to produce an alibi. That's not why I want you to do this for me."

Duncan interjected again. "She wasn't drunk when she came here and she wasn't drinking at the hotel. She's gone straight. But poor Sarah MacDonald was killed and Shona would like for her own conscience's sake to remember what happened. Wouldn't you feel the same way?"

I ignored him and focused on Joan. "But what if you discover you *were* the cause of the accident? And you walked away. What are you going to do if that's the case?"

"I'll turn myself in."

"You could be charged with vehicular homicide. You could go to jail."

"And not pass GO. Christine and I used to play Monopoly by the hour," she explained to Duncan. "She'd always put up such a fuss about going to jail. I think that's why she became a policewoman. Remember that, Pet?"

I nodded, not trusting myself to reply. The endearment that had, once upon a time, melted my heart, felt like a drop of acid. And she knew perfectly well how much Paula's dad being a police officer had influenced me. Realizing she wasn't getting a response, Joan returned to the issue.

"Let's put it this way. I have to go to the police sooner or later, but I'm going to be in a better position if I know what happened myself. Doesn't that make sense?"

"There's more than just the car crash. You and Mrs. MacDonald were identified as leaving the house of Tormod MacAulay that night. He's a relative, I understand. I presume you know he died?"

She averted her eyes quickly. "Yes, Duncan's daughter rang here."

"You did go there, didn't you? Was he still alive when you left?"

Duncan exploded at me. "She just said she doesn't remember anything. And how do you know she was there?"

"There are witnesses."

"Why are you hounding her like this?"

"Because if I'm going to help her, I need to pin down some of the facts."

Yes, my voice was raised too, and he had to force himself into some kind of control, spluttering indignantly.

It took a few moments for us all to calm down. Joan was looking so vulnerable I felt like a shit and toned down my voice.

"Let's backtrack a little. You said you can recall getting into the car with Sarah MacDonald. Do you remember where you were heading and why?"

She jumped away from that question like a spooked cat, but she nodded her head. "I do recall that we were on our way to visit Mr. MacAulay. Sarah was a real-estate agent. She had some business with him."

"Did she know you were her half-sister, by the way? She would have been pretty young when you disappeared, but I can only assume you sought her out to have some kind of reunion."

Joan was looking more and more like a cornered rabbit. "Christine, please! I know you're upset about all this, and I will tell you the whole story, I promise, but I can't do it now."

"Your mother's had a very bad time. You need to go easy on her," this was from Duncan, of course, who was building up a head of steam again.

"Okay. You, Joan, want me to help you find out the truth concerning that car accident, and I think one piece of truth deserves another. I was in MacAulay's house after his body was found, and something didn't sit right with me."

I could see the sudden flush of colour in her face but she didn't speak, didn't have a chance. MacKenzie leaped in.

"Lisa told me about you making her go through the house like it was a murder scene. Bloody irresponsible, I call it. Tormod was a very sick man. He wasn't expected to live out the summer. All these insinuations are malicious, if you ask me."

"First off, I wasn't making any insinuations. Second, I didn't make your daughter do anything. I asked her to help me, and she agreed to do so."

"Help you with what? Who are you making out to be a criminal?"

Before I had a chance to shout back at him, which I was on the verge of doing, Joan got off the couch and went over to him. She bent close and began to speak in Gaelic.

"It's rude to speak in a foreign language when there's somebody in the room who doesn't understand you." I knew I was getting loud again.

She hesitated, then nodded. "I apologize. I was only asking him to calm down. You've had a shock, and we're all suffering from frayed nerves."

She sat down and took MacKenzie by the hand, holding on tightly the way women do when they expect to receive bad news and are bracing themselves.

"You've got something on your mind, Chris. And we can't go any further until we clear the air."

"All right. This is what I'm thinking. I saw that photograph of you with Tormod and his children. You were about twelve or thirteen—"

"Thirteen."

"Okay. He was quite a lady's man, as I understand it. In other words, a sleazeball. I'm thinking that he sexually interfered with you and that you came back here to confront him." She stared at me in horror. I ploughed on. "Perhaps things got out of hand, I don't know. You would be furious with the man and rightfully so. Sexual molestation causes dreadful psychic wounds."

Duncan gaped at me. "It sounds as if you think your own mother *murdered* Tormod MacAulay."

Put like that it sounded ridiculous, but I was already so far out on a limb I couldn't come back.

"All I'm doing is trying to get to some truth for once in my life."

"But *murder*! You are out of your mind, woman. He's been properly buried, and there's no police investigation called for."

Again Joan laid a restraining hand on his arm. "Chris is a police officer, don't forget. She's trained to be suspicious of everything."

"Well this takes the cake. Her own mother!"

I was tempted to yell out at him that the majority of murderers have relatives, mothers, fathers, a spouse, and quite often children. Having a blood relative doesn't mean you never commit a crime.

I addressed Joan. "To put it bluntly, did Tormod MacAulay molest you when you were a child?"

She actually smiled briefly. "No, he didn't. Never. Not once. I swear that's the truth."

"So you didn't come back here to confront him?"

"No. Nothing like that."

"Why then, after all these years? What are these bloody demons you're hell bent on exorcising?"

"I . . . I had several reasons for returning."

I caught the quick squeeze she gave to MacKenzie's hand. He was involved for certain, but surely he didn't fall into the category of "demon," as in exorcising thereof.

"But come on, Christine," Joan continued. "You haven't spit it all out yet. I can tell. What else have you been thinking about me and Tormod?"

Now I was the one feeling cornered. I could deflect the question, deny it, which was a kind of lie or, as she said, "spit it out." I spat.

"Was he my father?"

I don't know what I expected really. A tearful acknowledgement, a tearful denial? Neither. She stiffened, stared at me for a moment, then answered calmly.

"No, he wasn't, Chris. And I swear that is the truth as well."

I believed her, but I'd also seen the fleeting expression of fear and the glance of surprise from MacKenzie. I wasn't the only one who had questions, it seemed.

Joan smiled slightly. "Well then, is that all? You thought Tormod had diddled me and you were the result."

"Something like that. It's not unheard of."

"You can put your mind at rest on that score then. I didn't hate Tormod MacAulay because he'd had his way with me."

"How did you feel about him?"

"It was a long time ago. I can hardly remember."

That comment made me hot with anger. "That's strange. I can remember how I felt about everybody I've ever known. I might not be able to tell you what Mr. and Mrs. Cohen looked like, but I can say for sure that I liked them."

"Are you asking me if I liked Tormod? Well, I didn't. Open your ears, Christine. I *did not like him*. Got that? And that's all I'm going to say about it. It's all in the past."

Lies if ever I smelled lies, but shaking her wasn't going to get the truth, so I just sat back defeated.

She stood up and said in a gratingly cheerful voice.

"Now we've cleared the air, are you going to put me into hypnosis or not?"

"The air is not cleared, Joan. It still smells."

Duncan practically eviscerated me with a look. "Cut it out. Don't speak to your mother like that."

"It's all right, Duncan. I know my daughter. She just needs a little time. Isn't that right Chris?"

"Yes! No . . . Oh hell, it doesn't matter."

"I tell you what, why don't Duncan and I go into the kitchen and give you a bit of space. Say, five minutes?"

That was so ridiculous, I actually laughed. I stood up.

"I'm going to go outside and commune with the sheep. It may be longer than five minutes."

"Of course." Joan was using her reasonable voice, which she did when she wanted something. I headed for the door. Joan called after me.

"Whatever comes of this, Chris, I will take full responsibility."

Ha! That would be a first, I thought.

CHAPTER TWENTY-NINE

I returned in about half an hour. The sheep had been indifferent, but the softness of the air and the quiet of the fields had worked on me. I walked back in and said I would do it.

It was obvious from his expression that MacKenzie's faith in the essential goodness of humanity had been grievously shaken by my lack of filial loyalty. However, Joan had enough lightness for all of us. She positively sparkled.

"Oh, I knew you would. Thank you, Chris. What do we do first?"

"The session will have to be taped. Do you have a tape recorder and blank tapes?" I asked Duncan.

"Aye. Will you be needing notepaper as well?"

"Yes."

He went off at the trot and disappeared through a back door that I presumed led to the bedrooms.

"I don't know what I'd do without him," said Joan in a conspiratorial tone. "What do you think of him, Chris?"

As Yogi Berra said, this was "déjà vu all over again." *What do you think of Joe, Pet? Of Tony? Of Clark?*

"He seems better than a lot of them."

She chose to take it straight. "Oh, he is. He's the best."

And I'm betting he's the reason for the sexy lingerie, not to mention the condoms. The return of the prodigal daughter to the arms of her childhood sweetheart.

"What do you want me to do?" she asked.

"First off, make sure your bladder is emptied. I don't want you to have to go to the bathroom in mid-session."

"Och. I'll go right now."

She passed Duncan as he came back with the tape recorder. They smiled at each other. Both of them in their sixties, he in good shape, she overweight and bruised and battered, but there was no hiding that glow of sexually satisfied love.

"Here you go. Where do you want me to put it?"

"She'll have to lie down on the couch, so I'll sit to one side and it can be on the floor between us. Is there a microphone?"

"Yes." He grinned at me. He was thawing a little. "I go in for the local singing competitions, and it's good to record yourself."

"Did you ever win one?"

"Placed second last year. I'm hoping for better this time. Oh, sorry, about paper, all I could find was my accounting book. Will it do?"

He handed me a blue bound book which had a hard cover.

"Great, thanks." I was trying for politeness at least.

Joan came back. "I'm ready."

"Okay. Go and lie on the couch, feet uncrossed, hands by your sides. I'll sit in the chair."

"What about me?" asked Duncan. "Do you want me to leave?"

"No, it's better if we have a witness to the authenticity of the tape."

"I thought you said it couldn't be used as evidence?"

"It can't, but it might be considered an investigative tool."

Joan lay on the couch and, without being asked, he covered her with a blue mohair blanket.

"Mr. MacKenzie, I'd rather you sat at the table," I said. "And please don't move or, of course, talk"

"No, Ma'am." He made a mocking salute.

So much for my being nice to the guy. He couldn't stand me, that was clear.

"Will you feel inhibited by having Mr. MacKenzie present?" I asked Joan.

"I'm sure he'd prefer you to call him 'Duncan.' Wouldn't you, Dunc?"

"If it makes her feel better to call me Mr. MacKenzie, it's no matter to me."

Okay. And it did make me feel better. The formality was propping up my pretence that I was actually working.

"To get back to your question," said Joan. "I'm happy to have Dunc here, but we are only going to deal with the accident, aren't we? You're not going to go into anything else, are you?"

"No, but you can't always control what comes up."

She raised her head. "I thought you said I could."

Once again, I held tight to my patience. "You can and you can't. We won't know what you're thinking or remembering unless you tell us, but you yourself might experience things you didn't expect."

She was starting to seem doubtful, and I wondered what she so much wanted to avoid. Could be her entire sordid history, of course, if she wanted to impress the latest boyfriend.

"Do you want to go on with this or not?"

She lay back on the couch. "I have to."

Her voice was full of emotion, and I could see how close to the edge she was. I leaned in a little. No smell of liquor. I wanted to make sure she hadn't taken a fast nip of something while she was out of the room.

I lifted the microphone. "Testing, one, two, three." I hit the playback button. Fine.

"All right, let's start."

I pressed RECORD.

Although few people nowadays think a hypnotist has to have a Svengali-like personality and deep-set burning eyes, there are still common misconceptions. The truth is you simply cannot be hypnotized against your will, but some people are more hypnotizable than others. It has a lot to do with fear of losing control. When we were practising with each other at Quantico, I could only allow myself to go to a certain level of trance. Not for me the imperviousness to a pin prick, which a few — not many I can tell you — experienced. I just went into a pleasantly relaxed state and never lost awareness of my surroundings. I was considered one of the control freaks.

A fairly resonant voice and calm manner were assets when taking somebody into a trance. I didn't know how much calm I was going to project, but I sat down and tried to resonate. Joan opened her eyes, startled. Too loud. I tempered my volume and we were off and running. It wasn't quite as difficult as I'd thought it would be, because I had in fact done dozens of practice sessions and, like riding a bike, the familiar patter came back immediately.

"Breathe deeply and exhale completely. Every muscle, every nerve relaxes."

I went through each muscle group from bottom to top, repeating the command to relax. Calf muscles relax, thighs relax, and so on. After about ten minutes, Joan's breathing had deepened considerably and she was entering into a light trance. Taking a person down into a deeper trance usually is done by counting in a slow and measured way to a plateau, like taking a boat down a series of canal locks.

By the time I reached fifty I thought she had gone down pretty deep.

"I'm going to touch your hand with the tip of my pen. If you feel the touch, just raise your forefinger on that hand. You do not have to speak."

I pressed the pen into the back of her hand, hard enough to leave a blue ink mark. She didn't stir. I pushed a little harder, no response. She was hypnotized.

I glanced over at Duncan, who was literally on the edge of his seat.

"Now, Joan. In a moment I am going to ask you to speak, but this will not disturb your state of relaxation. At any time you feel uncomfortable, you can tell me and we will end the session. Okay so far? You can just raise your finger again if the answer is, 'yes.'"

She did so and I continued. "I'm going to take you back to this past Friday evening. Just say whatever comes to you. Don't worry about whether or not it is true or what it means. You will have to talk, but it won't disturb your relaxed state. Deep breath again. Good. Now, can you tell me where you are?"

She was slow to answer, licking her lips. "I am outside the hotel in the parking lot." Her voice was low and breathy, as if talking were an effort, a typical trance voice.

"Is there anybody with you?"

"Yes, Sarah."

"Why are you meeting her?"

Her eyelids flickered, and I was afraid I'd been too directive. "Always keep your questions neutral," the instructor's Yankee twang leaped into my brain.

"Continue to relax, breathing deeply."

She quieted again.

"What are you and Sarah doing?" I asked. That was a better way to put it.

"We're going to see Tormod." Joan sighed. "Poor Sarah. The truth was such a shock. I'm thinking we should wait, maybe go tomorrow. I haven't even seen him myself yet. But she won't. She says we've got to go at once. She's had too much to drink as well, but if I don't go with her, she'll go herself. "

"What is the truth that shocked her so much?"

Damn. Another mistake. Too hot a question. She licked her lips and moved her head so sharply, eyelids fluttering, I was afraid I'd blown the whole session. I slowed down, reinforced the trance again, and waited.

"Go on, Joan. Just say what you're doing."

"We're in the car?"

"Who's driving?"

"I am. She wants me to drive faster, but I can't. She wants to know everything, but she's crying so much, she doesn't hear half of what I'm saying. . . . I can't believe I'm on the moor again. . . ." Another twist of her head and her breathing got more shallow. She began to speak to some unseen person. Her voice and even her face changed and she acted like a young kid. "If you make me do that, I'll run away. No, I won't. *Chan eil e tha mo maithir. Chan eil . . .*" the last words were pushed from her with so much energy she might as well have been shouting.

I glanced over at my shoulder at Duncan for a translation and he mouthed. "*You're not my mother.*" Joan must have dropped into an age regression, and I gathered the anger was directed at the wicked stepmother. It's quite usual for subjects in a hypnotic trance to shift time frames and revert to a previous age. Joan was still twitching and restless, muttering words in Gaelic.

I returned to the patter. "Continue to breathe deeply, relaxing completely. Breathing in . . . and out . . . in . . . and out . . . "

It worked, and she started to calm down. I repeated a few more *ins* and *outs*, then I thought we were ready to go on.

"Joan, we are going to stay with the immediate present. Focus on being in the car with Sarah. It is Friday. You and Sarah are going to see Tormod MacAulay. Tell me what happens when you get there. What do you see?"

A little smile appeared at the corner of her lips. "The house hasn't changed a bit after all this time, except he's got a flower garden in the front. I want to give him some flowers like I used to, so I pick some from his own garden. Sarah is banging on the door. . . . Oh poor Tormod, oh what a shock. He looks so ill. He doesn't even know it's me at first. Sarah wants to burst out at him on the spot, but I make her come inside. '*Alo a Thormoid, ciamar tha thu?*' Then he realizes it's me and he starts to cry. Just as if he was a girl. He wants to hug me, but I don't want to. . . . I make us all sit down at the table. Sarah starts yelling at him at once. She won't even let him talk, but he feels bad too. 'Oh no, look at what you've done. You'd better get a cloth. Stop it, you're being a brat. Uh, uh, somebody's come in. 'Who is it, Uncle? . . . Sarah give him a chance.' Oh poor Tormod. His skin is so yellow. I didn't know. 'No, Sarah, you've had enough . . . " There was a choked-back sob at this point, and tears began spilling from beneath her eyelids. "I'm so sorry."

Suddenly, she fell into another severe crying jag, and she opened her eyes and sat up. The trance state was shredded like paper.

I handed her some tissues and waited until she had calmed down. Duncan, not sure of what to do, was hovering behind me.

"I think that's all we can do at the moment, Joan."

She looked at me in alarm. "But we didn't finish. I still don't know what happened."

"You came out of the trance. Something about the memory was too upsetting for you. We never got past you being at Tormod's. Do you remember what you said?"

She nodded and wiped her face. "I do. At one point I know I was telling her she wasn't my mother. Which she wasn't, the bitch. My brothers sided with my father, too afraid of him probably, and Annie couldn't have wrapped her tongue around a good word for me if you'd roasted her on a spit. I used to mind Tormod's bairns for him whenever I could. His house was like a raft in the middle of an icy sea."

It was my turn to flinch. I'd once said that to her about why I wanted to live with the Jacksons, and I wondered if she was using those words deliberately. She gave no indication, however, and I assumed she'd just incorporated the expression unconsciously.

"Was Tormod's wife good to you as well?"

A quick blink. "She didn't like him to pay attention to anybody else."

"But you were his relative, a member of the family."

"Even worse. She thought our side despised her for trapping him. And they did. She had a face like the back of a bus, and he could have been in the pictures he was so handsome."

I wanted to get her back to the recent visit to Tormod, but just then we heard somebody calling from outside in the yard.

"Yoo-hoo? Anybody home?"

Duncan jumped to his feet. "God, it's almost two. I've got some customers from the sound of it. The sheep-dog demonstration," he added for my benefit.

I turned back to my mother. "You look done in. I told you it sometimes needed more than one session. Why don't you have a rest and we can pick up again in an hour if you want to. We've got it on tape if we need to go back to it."

"Okay. I am a bit knackered."

I was curious as hell about the weird exchange she had report-ed between Tormod and Sarah MacDonald, but I knew we'd gone as far as we could for now.

"Do you want to come and watch the demonstration?" Duncan asked me.

"Sure."

Joan lay back on the couch, and this time I was the one who covered her over. As I bent down, she touched my face so tenta-tively, in case I rejected her, that my stomach went into a knot. I gave her a quick peck on the forehead.

"Yer a brave wee lassie," I said. Hey, maybe we hadn't totally mended the bridges, but we were getting the pontoons in place.

CHAPTER THIRTY

Duncan grabbed his crook and tweed hat and went outside to greet his customers. The dogs were making a racket, barking excitedly because they knew it was playtime. Joan had already closed her eyes.

I followed him outside. There were two cars in the parking lot and he was directing the two sets of families to the risers at the side of the fenced field. The dozen sheep in the opposite pen were huddled together, heads up. They didn't look as keen on the game as the dogs did. Duncan waved at me to join the other spectators, and I climbed up the riser and took my place next to a young boy who was wearing a Toronto Blue Jays baseball cap. Before I could determine if we were fellow Canadians, Duncan walked into the field and stood in front of us. He was carrying a battery-operated megaphone. This was a well-organized business. The men in each group had passed him some money, and I wondered how much and if he could live on it. The four dogs were milling around his feet, heads low, making quick, agitated circling movements.

Duncan raised the megaphone to his mouth. "Good afternoon, ladies and gentlemen, boys and girls. Good afternoon and welcome, or, as we say in the islands, *feasgar mhah agus failte.* Our demonstration today will last about forty minutes. I have a small gift and souvenir shop in the barn over there, which you are welcome to visit afterwards. Let me introduce the collies."

He waved his hand at the dogs, who all simultaneously dropped to the ground and lay watching him.

"First is my oldest, seven-year-old Nic." The smallest of the four dogs trotted forward and did a bow.

A smattering of applause.

"Next at five years is Luna. She's named for her habit of baying at the moon."

She lifted her head and howled.

"Third is Mac. He's also five. He's my only male, and he's shy. The girls intimidate him."

Mac slunk forward, close to the ground, then dropped and buried his muzzle in his paws.

More laughter this time.

"Finally, my young, green dog, Mocu, which means 'my dog.' In Gaelic."

At a subtle signal, Mocu raced from her position, barking madly, and made a big circle around Duncan. He pretended to be having trouble getting her under control, until finally she flopped to the ground and rolled on her back, paws in the air. That trick seemed to have won over the spectators.

"Usually in shows involving animals, you are asked not to make noise or take pictures, but here that is not the case. The dogs wouldn't notice if you started up a rock concert. A collie's ability to concentrate on his task is legendary. They are considered the most intelligent of the dog breeds. I'd say that is debatable. What is so smart about living to work?"

My own ability to concentrate was seriously impaired. I was swirling with thoughts and feelings about what had just happened with Joan. It seemed to me she had answered one question — about my relationship to Tormod MacAulay — if she were to be believed, and left me with a dozen others. She'd offered, as yet, no explanation as to what Sarah MacDonald was so incensed about and what Tormod had to make up. I was puzzled about the discrepancy between her remark, "I didn't like Tormod," and her speaking about his house as a refuge. Once more, removed from the sight of her vulnerability, I was returning to a familiar state of exasperation.

There was a roar of laughter from the spectators, and clapping. I'd tuned out on some trick that the dogs had performed. I watched. Duncan had them lying close together side by side. He called out the name of one of the dogs and it got up, turned, and jumped over the other three, and lay down at the end of the row. Then they all rolled over in unison so that the next dog was ready to be introduced.

Mocu got to her feet, did her jumps over the other dogs, then turned around and jumped back again. As she did so, each dog raised its head and snapped its teeth in supposed annoyance. Very clever. Duncan gave the command again, and she jumped once more, but this time, at the end of the line, she dived into place like a runner getting to second base. It was funny. The spectators loved it.

"That rocks," said my young neighbour.

"It certainly does," I agreed.

The next dog was Mac, and his trick was to run in and out of the other sitting dogs, serpentine fashion. He did that up and down, then they all did a synchronized rollover.

"Take a bow," said Duncan, and all of the dogs got to their feet and did a lovely bow.

"That was to show you that collies aren't just obsessed by sheep. They love to learn tricks, and if you have one of these dogs, you have to give them a job to do or they get very bored and will get into trouble. They were bred to work hard and long, and shep herds relied on them. They had to be able to think for themselves, because often they are out of sight of the shepherd and rely on his whistled commands or their own instincts."

He held up a wedge-shaped piece of plastic. "This is a mouth whistle, and I use it because the sound carries further." He popped it into his mouth to give a demonstration. As one, the four dogs pricked up their ears and stared at him. He pointed at the penned sheep in the other field. "I'm going to send the dogs to fetch the sheep into this field. You'll notice one of the sheep has a red clip on its ear. That is the one we will separate out. A shepherd often has to separate the sheep, a ewe from her lamb or a sheep that he wants to look over. The dogs are essential for this. It would take a man all day to do it on his own. Sheep follow each other and they are timid but sometimes, especially in lambing time, the ewes get quite fierce and they will try to defy the dogs. That's why a really good herding dog must be calm. There's no barking or nipping allowed, but they have to be in charge. They cannot back down, even when a big ram is defying them. It's all in what we call the eye. That intense stare that you've no doubt seen in the pictures. There's nothing quite like it."

"Cool," said my Blue Jays boy. "Would the ram kill the dog, do you think?" he asked me.

His accent wasn't Canadian after all. More London, East End.

His sister, older, bigger, and wiser, heard this question. "Don't be so thick. Course it wouldn't. The dog has teeth, don't it? The sheep don't."

I felt like saying, "Well they do have teeth, actually, Miss Know-it-all," but I knew what she meant. The mother of the family was beside her, and she smiled anxiously at me, afraid her children might be showing her up. The father, who had on a plaid cap that looked new, ignored all of this. The children were the wife's province unless they needed a good slap or a bawling out.

Duncan was now walking to the end of the field; he opened the gate, and the dogs, still in circling mode, ran through and across the driveway to the opposite gate, where they lined up staring at the sheep, which were nibbling at grass at the far end. Suddenly he gave a signal, and all four dogs leaped over the fence and raced off towards the sheep; midway there, they peeled off into pairs. Alarmed now, the sheep lifted their heads and started to trot away from the closest dogs, which were Nic and Mocu.

Again, my mind wandered. So I knew who had picked the flowers, but I still didn't know why they'd ended up in the garbage bin and who had cleaned up. Or why. I was also trying to understand Joan's feelings. She seemed so grief-stricken, not just shocked and upset as you might expect.

Mocu had now slipped around the sheep, while Mac and Luna dropped to the ground, ready to stop them moving in that direction. The dogs were working together in a way that was obviously instinctual. There were no power plays or one-upmanship going on, just complete cooperation and mutual support. Wouldn't that be nice to have going in the United Nations?

The sheep were now making an erratic path towards the gate, with all of the dogs alternately running behind them, then dropping to the ground, never once taking their eyes off the sheep. Duncan was using his whistle to direct them. As they came closer, he opened the gate, and the sheep, bleating loudly, poured through. The dogs were panting. He'd said that the oldest and most experienced dog was Nic, and I could see how good she was — quiet, steady. Mocu was still too excitable and got too close to the sheep, causing them to make a little bolt for it.

I assumed that we'd have to go to the police station and report in. I didn't know what they'd do — if she'd be charged on the spot or not. I would guess they'd let her go home until there was a hearing.

Another collective gasp from the humans as the herd moved easily across the driveway into the second field where we were watching. More whistles from Duncan, and Luna moved softly down the middle. Two sheep separated out from the flock. One of them had the red ear-clip. The three other dogs were keeping the rest of the herd together. Another whistle and Luna ran between her two sheep and circled back to the red ear-clip. The other one trotted back to the herd. Now it was just Luna and one sheep, and she dodged from side to side, walking in the typical border-collie semi-crouch. Duncan opened the gate of the small pen, holding out his crook to keep the sheep from moving away, and Luna sent it in. He closed the gate and everybody clapped, me included. The remaining three dogs sent the rest of the flock away up the field, then with a whistle command, they came racing back to Duncan's side, looking I must say, very pleased with themselves.

He lined them up again to take another bow.

"That's it. That's our show. Thank you for coming. *Tapadh leibh.* I'll meet you at the barn. There's a toilet right next to it."

The father of my East Enders stood up. "Lesgo."

"Aw, Dad, can't we 'av a look at the shop?"

"No. We've spent enuff on junk already today."

"They have some lovely things," I said.

Yes, I hadn't a clue if the things in the shop were lovely or not, but hey, I had the blood of the islands in my veins, didn't I?

"See, Dad? The lady sez they 'ave some cool stuff."

I had on my sweetest smile, and he gave in. "Awright, but no junk and no more than two quid."

Off they went, and I clambered down from the riser. Duncan had gone ahead to the shop. The other group was already getting into their car, so this didn't look like a good day for sales. I hoped the Londoners would be more expansive when they got in the shop. The dogs were hanging around at the door, letting themselves be petted, although it was definitely "noblesse oblige."

I headed back to the house, wondering if Joan would be ready for another session. I hadn't done too badly, all things considered. Funny how things stick in your mind. I didn't know she 'd been aware of my marks at school. She'd never said anything before. My mind flitted back to the prospect of discovering blood relatives. I was beginning to feel like Miranda. "O brave new world." But then, of course, Prospero's comment is a little on the cynical side. "'Tis new to thee."

CHAPTER THIRTY-ONE

Joan was sitting up on the couch when I went back into the house. She looked tired and hurt and as if she'd spent the last several minutes staring into space, seeing things that were almost unbearable.

"How're you doing?" I asked her, cheery-voiced.

"Everything hurts," she said, and I understood she didn't mean just her bruises.

"We don't have to continue if you don't want to."

She leaned back on the couch and studied me. "Tell me, Chris, I'm curious. If I said I didn't want to go to the police, what would you do? Would you report me yourself?"

I didn't like the question, because I'd been asking myself that very thing — and I didn't have an answer.

"That's a moot point, surely. You said you were going to come into Stornoway this afternoon. It's far better that you go voluntarily than that they find you."

"I suppose you're right about that."

I hadn't answered her question, but she didn't press it. I thought she wanted to hold onto this fragile truce as much as I did.

The door opened with a puff of cool air and Duncan came in.

"Ha. The lady is awake."

She smiled at him. "I don't know if I went to sleep. How was the demonstration?"

"Ach. Bunch of skinflints. I sold one Mars bar, a packet of chewing gum, and a postcard. That won't pay for Mocu's dog food for a day."

"The dogs were awesome. That must take hours and hours of training," I said, definitely on the warmer side now. The dogs had done that.

"It does, but with collies, the instinct to herd is so strong, you can almost just put them out there and they know what to do." He hung his cap and crook on the pegs behind the door. "Are we going to continue with the sleep stuff?"

"That's up to Joan."

"You never call her 'Mother' or 'Mom,' I've noticed. How come? Is that a North American thing?"

Joan rescued me. "She's always called me Joan, since she was a kid. I don't mind. I rather like it."

He frowned. "Well if Mairi or Lisa turned around and addressed me as Duncan, I'd give them a cuff. It sounds disrespectful to me."

"It's an age thing," I said. "I'm a big grown-up now."

Joan interjected. "Come on then, grown-up person, let's get going before I lose my nerve."

The tension had got as thick as island crowdie, but not nearly as nice. We took up our positions again. Joan lay down on the couch and I started my patter. She took longer this time to go into a trance, probably because the last experience had caused her grief. Finally, I thought she was ready. I did the pen prick again, got no response, and switched on the tape recorder, which I'd already cued up.

"Joan, we are going back to Tormod's house now. But this time, you will be able to see the events that occurred there with more distance. As if you were watching a movie. You are aware of everything, but you are an observer. Can you go back there, Joan? Raise your finger if you are there again and understand what I am saying."

She lifted her forefinger and sighed deeply. We were back in the combat zone.

"Just start off by telling me where everybody is sitting. Where are you?"

"I am at the table in the kitchen."

"Where is Tormod?"

"He is at the table, too. He is on my right."

"And Sarah?"

"She is walking up and down in the living room."

"What are all of you talking about?"

I sensed Duncan move, and I frowned a warning.

Joan's soft whisper continued. "He is telling her he will make it up to her. He won't go to America. He'll give her all the money. She won't listen, not her. She's too drunk to listen." Her voice got stronger. "*What was he to do, Sarah? He had no choice. He couldn't allow you to continue on like that.*"

I could see she was getting upset again and quickly threw in some suggestions. She calmed down a bit.

"What is happening now?"

"Sarah says she's going to tell everybody about him. Uh-oh. She's got my purse. She's going to the car. I can't let her. She's been drinking. She's too upset. *Wait! Sarah wait!*" She stopped talking, watching some interior drama play itself out. Her eyelids were fluttering. This went on for several minutes but before I could prompt her again, she shouted, "She's driving too fast and it's raining. *Slow down Sarah! Slow down! Oh my god, watch out, there's a car coming.*"

I was afraid she'd come out of the trance but she didn't, although her body actually shuddered as she relived the impact of the car rolling. She didn't speak for several moments. Duncan was on his feet now, anxious, ready to intervene

"Joan, you are still an observer. You are watching but not involved. Go on. Just say what you see. What is happening now?"

"I can see Sarah. She's lying on top of the rocks. Her dress is up. I've got to get out and pull her dress down. Her head looks funny. It's touching her shoulder . . . " she moved her head restlessly against the cushion. "I've got to get help . . . "

I could see the trance state was lightening. I leaned forward to wipe away the leaking tears.

"She's had enough," Duncan whispered in my ear. I actually agreed, but I waved him back.

She was whispering painfully. "There's somebody else here. I can't make them understand . . . go to Sarah."

She tossed her head. I didn't want her to be jolted out of the trance again.

"Joan, I'm going to bring you out of the trance now. I will count to the number twenty-one and, as I do, you will feel lighter and lighter, and by the time I reach twenty-one you will be back completely in your everyday waking state and you will be able to remember everything you have said. You will remember everything."

I did my count and, at twenty-one, she opened her eyes and burst into heart-rending sobs.

Duncan rushed over. "It's all right, Shona. Hush, you're quite safe, hush."

He pressed her against his shoulder and rocked her. I wondered how much longer she could go through such emotional turmoil. Finally she calmed down, although a fearful tremor shook her body at regular intervals. Then she moved back from him, mopped her face, and looked at me.

"It worked. My memory's quite clear. I remember it all. I wasn't driving."

I kept the tape recorder running.

"Sarah took my keys and got into the car. I hardly had time to get into the passenger side and off she went. It was almost dark, and it was pouring with rain. She was going much too fast, but she wouldn't listen. We hadn't gone far, just to the bend near Dail Beag, when suddenly there was a car heading straight at us." Joan swallowed hard. "Sarah swerved, otherwise we'd have had a head-on collision, but we must have rolled, because the next thing I know is I'm lying on my side in the car. I must have blacked out then."

"You said there was somebody talking to you?"

"Yes, I'm positive there was."

"A man or a woman?"

"I can't tell. I have a vague memory that they were wearing a yellow mackintosh. I wanted them to look after Sarah. She was lying on the rocks."

She seized Duncan's hand and held tightly.

"Any sense of the time between the moment of losing consciousness and this person appearing?"

"Not really. I was cold, so it seemed a long time later, but I can't say for sure. I saw them walking over to Sarah, then I must have blacked out again, because when I came to, there wasn't anybody there and I was still half upside down. I released the seatbelt and I crawled out . . . "

"Why wouldn't the other bloody driver stop?" asked Duncan. "They must have bloody well known what had happened?"

"Maybe it was that driver I saw."

"If it was, they should be thrown in jail. They were the ones leaving the scene of an accident, not you."

There were more solicitous pats on both sides.

"Do you remember walking away from the car after you released the seatbelt?" I asked.

Joan averted her eyes. "That part is completely blank. But obviously I must have found my way here, and Duncan took care of me."

"What time did my mother show up on your doorstep?"

He shrugged. "Early. I don't recall exactly."

"Ballpark?"

"What?"

"She means approximately," said Joan helpfully. "It was starting to get light."

"About four-thirty then?"

"Yes, I suppose so. I didn't keep a record of it."

The crash site was only about ten minutes away by car. Joan anticipated me.

"I must have gone unconscious again."

"You're lucky you didn't die from hypothermia."

Duncan smiled at her. "You're a tough piece of mutton, aren't you?" He kissed her on the cheek.

I interrupted this sweet moment. "You must have been surprised to see her on your doorstep after so many years."

My voice couldn't have been more neutral, but he flushed. "She wrote to me that she was coming."

"I didn't want to give him too much of a shock," added Joan, all chirrupy.

Duncan looked over at me. "According to all this, Shona can't be held accountable in the least. First, she wasn't driving the bloody car and second, some criminal forced them off the road."

I nodded. I wasn't going to add that we hadn't really proved anything. Joan certainly seemed to be telling the truth, but as our instructor had warned us over and over, under hypnosis sometimes people "revealed" what they wanted to be true or had talked themselves into believing to be true. As I said, the session would never be considered admissible evidence.

Another shudder ran through her body. "At least I know I wasn't responsible for Sarah's death." A defiant glance at me. "And I know I wasn't drinking."

I leaned over and switched off the tape recorder.

Duncan stood up. "Maybe *you* weren't, but *I'm* about to. Christine, will you join me in a tot of *uisbeag*? I need it."

"No thanks. I'd better phone the police station."

"Are you going to talk to Gillies?" Duncan asked.

"Yes. He knows about the case."

"I'm a case, am I?" said Joan in a little flare-up of anger.

"Strictly speaking, yes. You are."

"Will I be put in jail?"

"That is highly unlikely. Sergeant Gillies will probably turn the case over to the Crown attorney or whatever the equivalent is here in the Hebrides. He'll be the one to decide what action to take."

"He's called the procurator fiscal," said Duncan.

I stood up. "If I can use your phone then, I'll call Gill right now. I have his number."

"It's over there." He indicated a black phone set on a side table, and they both watched me as I went over to place the call.

I wondered if Gill would be of the same opinion I was. Joan's story had as many holes in it as a piece of Swiss cheese, and was just as stinky.

CHAPTER THIRTY-TWO

It's not easy to have an argument with somebody who is pressed hip and thigh against you, especially when one of you is wearing a hat with a brim, but Joan and I were giving it a good try.

I'd phoned Gill to tell him what had happened and that we'd found her. He asked us to come in, which we were now doing, the three of us in the tiny front cab of Duncan's truck. I suppose I could have crouched in the open rear like one of the dogs, but I didn't think I could maintain that kind of balance. Besides, I had my church clothes on. So, front seat it was. I knew my mother was anxious about talking to Gill, but I would have felt like a hypocrite if I attempted to reassure her the way I did with other witnesses — "Just tell the truth in your own words about what happened." I had serious doubts that she was telling the truth. Correction: I thought the car accident had probably happened the way she said, but she was leaving out lots of other information, which is a kind of lie. I thought I'd try a little delicate probing. Sort of skilful investigative dentistry, looking for the soft spot, the nerve.

"Did Sarah take her briefcase with her when you went to see Tormod?"

She turned her head sharply, staring into my face. "Why do you ask?"

"There's been no sign of it. The receptionist says Sarah always had it with her when she went out on a business appointment."

Joan digested that for a moment. "Wasn't it in the car?"

"Not according to the police. They found just your purse and overnight bag."

She shrugged as best she could in the confined quarters. "I suppose she didn't have it with her then."

"Why was she so angry with Tormod?"

Joan managed a shrug. "I don't really know. She'd been drinking. It had something to do with business."

I allowed a little silence to develop and watched the road. The atmosphere inside the cramped space had grown decidedly icy as well.

"I don't understand why you're acting as if I'm one of your petty criminals," said Joan. So much for my skilful questioning.

"That's not what I'm doing. I was curious, that's all."

Oh boy. Who's exempt from the occasional fib?

"You always were," sniffed Joan.

More silence. Duncan was concentrating on driving, absenting himself from the discussion, although I expected him to jump to my mother's defence at any moment.

I tried to warm things up a little. "So, do I get to meet some long-lost relatives?"

If my question about the briefcase had annoyed her, this question compounded my transgression tenfold.

"Christine, I left this island when I was eighteen years old. My family disowned me. I have absolutely no intention of getting in touch with them in these circumstances. Why should I? They'll only gloat. There she is. The fuck-up, Shona. Hasn't changed a bit has she?"

Even through the thin nylon jacket she was wearing, I could feel heat flood her body. Maybe I simply absorbed her anger, I don't know. I was getting ticked off myself. Wow, that tenderness had vanished fast.

"Do you have any objection if I look them up for myself? After all, I gather I have three live uncles, not to mention several cousins. I'd like to meet them."

She couldn't comfortably turn her head to look at me, so she stared ahead, her jaw and mouth stiff with rage.

"Yes, I do object. Do you have absolutely no loyalty? How would you explain why you're here?" She did manage to shoot a glance at me. Her eyes were dark. "You, who profess to put such a premium on the truth."

Duncan intervened. "Look you two, this can wait. Christine, your mother has had a really bad time, and I think you should take that into account before you start getting into her life story."

He reached down and patted her on the knee. He said something to her in Gaelic and smiled into her eyes. Very sweet. I was about ready to tell him to stop the truck and let me out, but Joan took me by surprise. She patted *my* knee, and her voice was soft. And sincere.

"I'm sorry. I know how much you've always wanted to have a real family. Let me get my bearings and then we can talk about it some more. All right?"

It wasn't, but I nodded.

"Why don't we have a bit of music," said Duncan, and he snapped on the radio. The reception was poor and a scratchy sound emanated, which coalesced into some kind of pipe music, with a female voice singing plaintively over the top of the music.

"That's Jenna MacCleod from Inverness. She's considered my biggest competition."

It took me a moment to realize that he was referring to the singing contest, but it was a relief to change the subject.

Joan and I did not address each other directly the remainder of the drive. On one track of music, Duncan actually joined in and I had to admit, he had a good voice, excellent pitch and resonance. By the time he turned onto Church Street, the inside of the cab had thawed out sufficiently that we could scrape the frost off the windows.

Gillies was waiting for us in the outer lobby of the police station. "*Feasgar mhah*, Duncan. Afternoon, Christine, Mrs. Morris. I'm so glad you have come in."

He punched in the door code, whisked us through the glass doors, and led us down to the incident room we'd used before. A burly young constable watched us from the reception area, and I suddenly felt more keenly why Joan was so sensitive. His avid curiosity was like hot sunlight on scar tissue.

In the office, Gillies busied himself with chairs. "Mrs. Morris, why don't you sit here," he said, offering her a chair at the head of the table. Duncan took the seat to the right, leaving me the one at the opposite end.

"Would you like a cuppa?" Gill asked Joan.

"Yes, please," she answered in a small-girl sort of voice. I saw how frightened she was, and I remembered she was no stranger to the inside of police stations. She'd been charged more than once in the early years with being drunk and disorderly.

"I'll be right back," said Gillies.

Duncan, ever solicitous, had placed his hand over Joan's. After one quick glance around the room, she started to trace invisible figures of eight on the table. I too, glanced around. There was some writing on the chalkboard.

DEMO CONTROL. Constables MacIver and MacRae.

Gillies entered. "One of the women will bring us a pot. Now, why don't we just get right into the tape recording, because as I understand it, you've been able to recall what happened on the night of the accident."

On the telephone, I'd told him about the hypnosis session.

"It was quite remarkable really," said Joan. "I remembered vividly. Sarah was driving, and we were run off the road."

At that moment, there was a light tap on the door and a young woman came into the room carrying a large tray laden with tea paraphernalia. She put everything down on the side table. I did wonder if she got the fetch-and-carry jobs because she was low in rank or because she was female. I rather suspected in this station that it was the latter.

"This is Brenda Cullen," said Gillies. "She's our stenographer, and she's going to take down notes for me."

Ah, ah. The secretary still had the tea/coffee-making task.

Brenda smiled at us and went to the other side of the room and took a seat. She had a hardcover notebook with her, the kind that shorthand typists used to use, but I thought were now obsolete. Obviously not. Brenda took up her pencil and waited.

There was another delay while Gill got orders, poured tea, and offered round the plate of biscuits, which in the Hebrides seemed to accompany teapots like a horse accompanied a carriage. Joan was starting to look more comfortable. Gill was good at his job. Tea mostly consumed, Gill stood up.

"All right then, before you say any more, Mrs. Morris, let's play the tape, shall we?"

I handed him the tape and he inserted it into the machine. My voice came on, noting date, place, and time then, "Take a deep breath . . . "

He gave me an amused smile. And on it went. On this second hearing, I picked up more things. Joan's distress as she described the scene at Tormod's house was over the top. I hadn't believed her story about Sarah going to Tormod's on a business matter, but it was obvious that, whatever the argument was about, it was white hot. As we listened, I could see it was a struggle for Joan not to burst out crying again. She hid it by drinking more tea. When she described being in the car and the near-collision with the other car, I thought there was no doubt Joan had been in the passenger seat and Sarah MacDonald had been the one driving. But the mystery person who was checking her out was vague, and this part of the story was not as convincing. Not that Joan was lying, but whether the visitor was a fantasy or real was less sure.

I saw Gill making notes at this point. We went right through the conversation we'd had after she was out of the trance, then my voice recording that the tape was switched off, the time, and the date. Brenda's pencil stopped its rapid movements. In the ensuing silence, it seemed as we collectively let go of the breath we had been holding.

"My, that was most impressive. I'm sorry we had to upset you all over again, Mrs. Morris."

She nodded acknowledgement. "What happens now?"

"Brenda will type up the transcript of the tape and this interview, and then I'll have you come in and sign that it's all correct and so forth. Then I will pass it on to the procurator fiscal, and after that . . . it will be in his hands."

"So you're not going to arrest me?"

"No, I'm not. I want you to agree not to go anywhere without letting us know, but certainly you are free to leave. Where are you staying?"

"With me," said Duncan. "We're old friends."

"I gathered that," said Gillies. "And I assume you are the one who picked up Mrs. Morris's suitcase from the B & B?"

Duncan shifted uncomfortably. "Yes, that was me. She needed her things."

"You know that impersonating a police officer could be considered an offence."

"Come off it, Gill. It's me, Duncan MacKenzie, you're talking to. The woman asked me if I was Sergeant Gillies come to get the suitcase, and I sort of went along with her. It seemed easier that way. I didn't outright lie, for goodness' sake."

That wasn't how I'd heard it, but I knew how easy it was for these matters to get confused. Maybe it was the way he said. Impossible to prove, and Gillies for one didn't seem to think it worth bothering about.

"Well don't do it again, or I'll do turn and turn alike and go in the Seo Sinn instead of you. Then where'd you be?"

Duncan laughed out loud. "Thrown out of the competition, most like. You've got a voice like a corncrake."

We'd all forgotten about the stenographer in the corner, but she stood up.

"I'll start on this right away, shall I, Sergeant Gillies?"

"Thanks, Brenda."

"And thanks for bringing the tea," I added my two cents' worth for the feminist cause.

Duncan pushed back his chair. "If that's everything for now, I'm going to take Joan to see my new granddaughter, then we'll go out for supper, then back to my house."

"Before you go, I'll return your handbag and the overnight bag we got from the car."

"I hope everything's still in there," said Joan with such a suggestive expression that I almost choked on my cookie. Gill grinned back at her.

"It's all intact."

She turned to me. "Will you give me a ring tomorrow, Christine? You're not going to go back to Edinburgh right away, are you?"

"No, there's not much point. I might as well stay here until Saturday, then I'll have to fly back to Canada. What about you? How long were you planning to stay?"

"For a while longer. I took an open-ended ticket."

Prepared for any contingency, I see.

"Shall we go then?" said Gillies.

"Say 'hi' to little Anna for me," I said.

"Be right back," said Gill again. And they left me staring at the chalkboard.

CHAPTER THIRTY-THREE

Gill was indeed right back.

"You're very good at that hypnosis thing, Chris. I almost went into a trance myself, just listening to you."

That's not a result I'd particularly like to achieve with an attractive man.

"What do you think about what she said?" I asked him.

He hesitated.

"Listen, you won't offend me. As far as I'm concerned, there are still several unanswered questions. I'd be interested in your opinion."

"Okay. But you must admit, it's a bit odd to be talking about your mother like this, as if she's a case."

"Don't worry about it. Tell me what you think."

He picked up one of the pencils from the box and began to make doodles on a piece of paper.

"I'd rather you start. Are you concerned about who was driving the other car and where they are?"

"That actually wasn't uppermost on my mind but, yes, who were they? Are you going to pursue it?"

"Of course. Given what we've heard, the procurator will have to order some kind of investigation. What are the unanswered questions, if it's not that?"

"The first thing that leaped out was that huge time gap from the time we believe the accident happened, which we assume was about eleven-thirty, to the time she showed up on Duncan's door at four-thirty. If she'd been lying unconscious on the grass somewhere, surely she would have been in bad shape when she did arrive at Duncan's. He certainly acted as if she'd been out walking for half an hour, max. He made no attempt to get her medical attention."

He'd made a note on the paper. "Shall I deal with the questions one at a time?'

"Sure."

"Given she banged her head, it's quite likely she was in and out of consciousness. There are places to shelter among the rocks, and she grew up in the area, so she might know them instinctually. As for Duncan not rushing her off to the hospital, I'd classify that as an island characteristic that is a throwback to the time when you had to pay hefty fees to the doctor, who didn't necessarily know what he was doing, or else why was he practising here in the back of beyond."

"All right. We'll put that one in the grey area. Second unanswered question: Why was there such a scene at Tormod's that Sarah MacDonald ran out, threatening to 'tell everybody'? What was he promising to make up to her? Mrs. MacNeil told me that Sarah was engaged to Iain MacAulay when she was young and that Tormod disapproved of the match and broke it up. Is that what this is all about? But why now after so many years?"

Another note in his neat handwriting. "Maybe Tormod was doing another gazump right back at Sarah. Remember, the real-estate transaction still wasn't final. Perhaps he changed his mind and reverted to the original offer."

"I'll concede that as a possibility, but I'm puzzled as to why Joan would be so vague about it. Surely it would have been obvious what he was doing." I put on my best Scottish accent. "Och, Sarah me lass, I've gone changed me mind and I'm not selling the Swedes the property after all."

He laughed gratifyingly. "That was good. They weren't Swedes, by the way. Norwegians, I believe. Anyway, go on."

"She was extremely upset when she was reliving the scene at Tormod's house. You heard her. That is way out of proportion with what she said was going on."

"She did know him when she was a child. It's upsetting to see somebody years later when he's sick."

"True, but she never referred to that once. I thought her reaction was extreme."

"All right, I'll give you that. But if she wasn't upset to see him poorly, why was she crying like that?"

"An unanswered question."

"Next."

"We know who picked the flowers, but I'm still uneasy about this tidy-up that happened. Who did it?"

Gill raised an eyebrow. "Why not Tormod?"

"It doesn't feel right. His visitors have rushed out after a huge row, he's not a man to put things away, according to Lisa, and some things were out of place."

"I don't always put everything back in the usual place. My ex-wife used to complain about it all the time. 'How long have you lived in this house and you don't know where the pots go?' Maybe tidying up was his way of calming himself down."

"A woman maybe. Did you ever do something like that?"

"No. I'd chop wood."

"Okay. I'll put the Molly Maid issue in the grey area too. Joan referred to Tormod as 'Uncle,' but I assume that is a courtesy title."

"It is. Technically, Tormod and Joan were cousins, but he was a lot older and she would have called him 'Uncle.' By the way, Joan is the English equivalent of Shona."

"She hasn't explained yet why she chose the names she did, but in passing, Mrs. MacNeil mentioned a Morrison family. I'd bet Joan just abbreviated that."

A little doodle on the notepad. "I did wonder who came to the door? Remember she said, 'There's somebody at the door.'"

"A man from the village."

"What?"

"I took a course in Romantic poetry in university and, according to legend, Samuel Taylor Coleridge — who was in the middle of writing a brilliant poem, 'Kubla Khan,' while under the influence of a controlled substance — was interrupted by a knock on the door. A man from the village. He couldn't finish the poem."

"Ah, ah. I see you are a woman with an astonishing breadth of knowledge."

"How perceptive of you."

We both laughed, and I felt a little rush of happiness. We seemed so comfortable with each other in spite of the circumstances. I felt as if we'd known each other a long time, not just a handful of days.

"I'll have to assume the visitor was one of the neighbours, who wouldn't have had any reason to inform us because we have not been treating Tormod's death as a homicide." He put down the pencil. "Chris. Now *I* have a question. I think the issue of what happened at the accident is more or less settled. I believed your mother when she said Sarah was driving. We know she had an over-the-limit blood-alcohol reading, which would slow her reaction times. Joan walking away from the site is understandable, as is the temporary amnesia . . . "

"So what's your question?"

"Why are you so focused on what happened at MacAulay's house? We know he was very ill and could have hemorrhaged at any time and, according to Dr. MacBeth, that's what happened. There was no trauma to the body, no indication of foul play. Yet you're worrying at it like a terrier. Is this just a function of the overactive police profiler's mind at work or . . ."

"Or what?"

"Do you have some reason for wanting your mother to be in trouble?"

"No, of course not." But even to my ears my answer was too fast. *"I'm just a case, am I?"* I knew I didn't want her to be involved in any nefarious death, nor for her to be in trouble, but Gill was quite right. I couldn't let it go. This was a case, and the fact that my own flesh and blood was involved didn't stop me gnawing at it. I felt compelled — probably neurotically, I admit — to tie up loose ends.

"Anyway, you're right. What I came for seems to have been cleared up. She can't be accountable for vehicular homicide." I realized our official connection might be over. "Thank you for everything you've done. I do appreciate it."

"It's my job. I'm the family liaison officer."

"What does that mean, exactly?"

"I'm the one assigned to be a contact person with the family if there's a police matter. I talk to them, pass on information, and so forth. They don't have to deal with different officers all the time. It's much easier for all of us."

I absorbed that for a minute. I could hear Joan's voice. *I'm a case now, am I?* Were those dinners and hugs all part of the job?

My face must have been transparent, because he suddenly got up and came over to me, bending over the chair with his hands on the arms.

"Wipe those evil thoughts out of your head. I took you out because I liked your company."

He was so close I was in danger of seeing him cross-eyed, so I leaned back a little. He had brown eyes slightly flecked with gold. The shinty bruise was starting to turn yellow.

"The feeling is mutual."

I was aware of what Paula had said: "They think you're not interested in them and they get discouraged." Unfortunately, I was experiencing breathlessness, and the problem wasn't that I would appear indifferent but that, at any moment, I might throw myself on his bones.

Who knows what would have transpired next if the extension phone hadn't rung. Not a man from the village, but equally as disruptive. With a grimace, Gill went to answer it.

"Sergeant Gillies here. Will you speak up, Ma'am, I can hardly hear you . . . " Suddenly, he looked alarmed and signalled to me to hand him the notepaper. I did so, placing it on the desk and grabbing the pen for him.

"What are you referring to, Ma'am? . . . Will you please identify yourself? . . . Who are these people? . . . Ma'am? . . . Damn."

He replaced the receiver. The caller had obviously hung up. Quickly, Gill pressed the connecting button.

"Phil. That call that just came through. The woman didn't by any chance give her name did she? . . . No, eh? But she asked for me personally? Okay. Thanks, Phil." He disconnected. "That was warning message number two from our Royalist friend."

"Was it recorded?"

"No, we only do that for emergency calls."

"Quick. Write down everything you remember about the call. Sound of the voice, as exact words as possible. Don't embellish it at the moment. Write it line by line, with a space for your replies."

I moved away to be completely out of his orbit, and he did as I asked.

He finished and handed me the paper.

1. *I told you before they are out of control and you haven't brought them in yet.*
2. *You know, I told you before. We'll all be blamed if they pull it off.*
3. *No, I can't do that.*
4. *It's the White Dog group. They've lost it.*

I borrowed his pen and added what I recalled about his side of the conversation. I read it out loud.

"Hello, Sergeant Gillies here. *I told you before they are out of control and you haven't brought them in yet.* What are you referring to? *You know, I told you before. We'll all be blamed if they pull it off.* Will you identify yourself, Ma'am? *No, I can't do that.* What people do you mean? *It's the White Dog group. They've lost it.* Hang up. Damn."

"That's it, although I think she said, '*I already told you,*' not '*I told you before.*'"

I wrote in the change. "Did you recognize the voice?"

He grimaced. "She was speaking so low I could hardly hear her, and she had a heavy Lowland dialect that sounded phony to me. Shit. I hate this stuff."

"This woman is obviously somebody known to you. She addressed the other letter to you, she asks for you, she disguises her voice. Notice she said, '*We'll all be blamed.*' She might belong to a political group, and the White Dog crowd are a militant or fringe wing that she doesn't approve of. Do you have a list of known anti-Royalists?"

"We do keep track. The problem is it's a long list. I don't mean anti-Royalist but anti- anything. Anti-war, anti-landlord. You might think of us as a perverse bunch."

I studied the message as he'd written it out. "She says, *out of control*, then, *they've lost it*, which is ambiguous. Could be another way of saying the same thing, or they've lost the original purpose, which is the traditional development of every radical group in history, from suffragettes to IRA. Is it certain the Prince is coming here?"

"Oh yes. They've added a side trip on the way down to Harris. They're going to visit the Black House Village in Na Gearrannan. But it's still highly confidential. We'd like the laddie to have as much privacy as he'll ever get."

"Word does seem to have got out, though. Who'd leak it?"

He shrugged. "We've had several royal visits here. The people know how to read the signs like the collies watch the shepherds. A few well-dressed, polite men come ahead of time and hang out at the ferry watching visitors. Then a couple of sniffer dogs are flown in and walked around some building. A great local source of chat is to guess who's coming. Lots of the women keep track on all the activities of the family. 'Couldn't be the Princess Royal. She was here recently.' They'll zero in on which level of royalty it is within the hour. Also, some officers here have to know. They mention it to the wife, who bursts to tell it to her sister, and off you are."

"I noticed Tormod MacAulay had a photograph of himself shaking hands with the Queen. Was he a Royalist?"

"He was after her visit last year. He said she was a bonnie lass and knew more about weaving then any visitor he'd encountered."

"The common denominator of all these incidents attributed to the White Dog group is that they are public and some kind of metaphor, 'You stink,' 'We've been hacked like this.'"

"So, if this woman is warning us about another incident, we can expect something like that. Embarrassing, public, and symbolic."

"I hope so. I mean, I hope it's still at that level and not escalating into out-and-out violence."

He stood up.

"I'll go and talk to Jock."

"I would recommend you find out if there are any women around them, probably disgruntled. An ex-wife or girlfriend is a possibility, but that woman herself is politically active."

He nodded. I really wasn't saying anything he hadn't thought about himself, but I was confirming his ideas.

"Are you going back to the hotel?" he asked.

"I am. But before that, I'm going to rent a car."

He looked as if he were about to protest, but I stopped him. "You've got better things to do than be my chauffeur."

"I don't know how long it's going to take me to talk to these buggers, but can I call you, if it's not too late? We can go international and have Chinese food at the place next door. It's not bad."

"Sounds good to me."

We both hesitated, but the sexually charged moment when he leaned over me had gone. I hoped we'd get it back before too long.

CHAPTER THIRTY-FOUR

I squeezed into the tiny Peugot I'd rented at the local friendly car-hire. The man suggested I "give it a whirl" around the harbour parking lot to get used to it, and that turned out to be good advice. I hadn't driven a gearshift for years, and trying to deal with that with my left hand while getting accustomed to being on the wrong side of both car and road was challenging. I narrowly missed scraping the side of a van and moved too close to a pedestrian, almost giving her a heart attack. I crawled around for ten minutes or more before venturing out into the streets. Thank goodness Stornoway's idea of rush hour was five cars waiting at the light, so it was easy to get into the traffic flow.

I did a couple of big loops of the town, which confirmed my initial impression of a clean, sensible place with no tacky areas to compare with Orillia, and certainly absolutely nothing like Toronto, with its constant struggle against dirt. My palms were sweaty but I was starting to relax somewhat when a motorcycle zoomed across my path, causing me to stop so suddenly I stalled the car. While I grappled with a gear-grinding jolt to get me going again, the leather-clad driver started to wave at me with manic glee. It was Lisa MacKenzie and she was gesticulating in the general direction of the Duke, from which I surmised she wanted me to join her.

I'd had enough of road anxiety by then, so I turned into the harbour parking lot again and manoeuvred myself into a space. I got out and looked around for meters, but there wasn't one in sight, and I realized I hadn't even seen any on the streets. What! A town that didn't get an income from parking charges?

The Duke was in the next block over, and Lisa was waiting in the entrance.

"You'll get the hang of it eventually," she said with a grin. "I think you should try to go more than ten miles an hour though. It tends to slow down the traffic."

"I will, I will. Just give me time."

We went inside.

"I'm going up to see my brand-new niece. Do you want to come?"

"Sure. Love to."

I followed her up the stairs, through the door marked PRIVATE and into a narrow, dark hall.

"How did you like the black houses?"

"Oh . . . we never got there."

"What did you do then?"

"I watched the sheep-herding demonstration."

She laughed. "That's a crowd-pleaser. It's Dad's bread and butter." She looked over at me. "How's your investigation coming along? Any new news?"

I didn't have to answer beyond a vague shrug because we were at the apartment. Lisa swept open the door with sisterly unconcern for privacy.

"*Feasgar Mhah. Seo Lisa agus Christine.*"

Mairi was sitting in an armchair with the infant suckling at her breast. Her greeting to me was warm, but with a drop several degrees towards Lisa. She said something in Gaelic, the meaning of which was clear when Lisa ostentatiously returned to the door and knocked on it.

"If I didn't know better, I'd think my sister was born in a barn," Mairi commented to me.

"How's Anna?"

The baby had fallen asleep replete with milk, a tiny drop caught on her upper lip. Mairi gazed down at her. "She's latched on all right. She wants to feed non-stop though. I've no had time to even go to the loo."

'"Here, let me take her and you go pee," said Lisa.

"She's sleeping. Don't wake her up." Mairi handed over the baby.

"And I won't drop her either, relax. Don't hurry. Why don't you get in a shower?"

Mairi got to her feet stiffly and shuffled off in the direction of the narrow hall at the rear of the living room. Lisa started to rock back and forth gently, in that instinctive way all we women seem to have with a baby in our arms. She started to croon to the sleeping infant. She was singing in Gaelic, but something most peculiar happened. I understood what she was saying. Less than a week ago, I would have sworn on a Bible that I'd never heard Gaelic in my life. Now, some strange atavistic memory was starting to surface like artifacts that had gone down with a ship and were now floating upward.

Considerably agitated by this sensation, which I both liked and disliked, I resorted to my old training. Have a look around. Get impressions. Take mental notes. It didn't matter this wasn't a case, that mental activity had become second nature. The grey, dreary afternoon had settled in, and the lack of light didn't help the general appearance of the apartment. Two small windows faced out to the street, but the remainder of the rooms were located at the rear where Mairi had gone, which meant there wasn't much natural light. She hadn't switched on a lamp either. None of the furniture matched, and at the moment the room was messy with baby gear, including a large playpen that Anna wouldn't be needing for some months yet. As if picking up on my thoughts, Lisa flicked the light switch on.

"Bloody gloomy in here." She was doing a soft jog around the room, and she indicated the brightly coloured playpen. "Tormod gave her that. Too bad he didna get to see you, eh, *gle bheag Anna.*"

She'd said, "very small Anna." I was starting to spook myself out. Logically I could believe that Joan had said these words to me when I was "very small," and they had rested buried in my subconscious until now, but it was a strange sensation, rather like having another personality emerge, as in *The Three Faces of Eve*. I could only hope my buried Gaelic-speaking self was benign.

"Bugger!" Lisa had tripped over a dirty plate and beer bottle on the floor. "Ha. Colin leaves his spoor behind as usual." She looked angry. "You'd think the man'd make an effort to tidy up seeing as how his wife just had his baby." She shifted the infant to one arm and bent to pick up the plate.

"Here, I'll do that." I started to collect some of the other spoor, a half-filled mug of tea and a glass, and headed for the kitchen. The counter was covered with a mess of plates with partially eaten food on them, tea-stained mugs, and more empty beer bottles. Lisa joined me, still jiggling Anna.

"I almost forgot to tell you. You know you said to let you know if I discovered anything was missing from the house?"

I nodded, squeezing brilliant green dish soap into the pan.

"I slept over there last night, and I was so restless I decided to sort out some of Tormod's things. I know Miss Cheerio will want to get her mitts on anything worthwhile, but I thought I'd put in my dibs for anything of sentimental value. I knew she wouldn't want his paperbacks, so I went into the bedroom." She half-grinned at me. "You've got me wondering about everything. Well, I'm sure the cushion was gone from his chair. I didn't notice when we first looked around, because I mean, who looks for cushions? But I sat down to open up the drawer, and there was no cushion on the chair. It was one he wove himself when he was just learning, so it was old and ratty, but I can't imagine he'd throw it away. Those tweeds endure forever."

"Are you sure it was there when you were last in the bedroom?"

"I can't swear it, but I did read to him that last time, and I'm sure I would have noticed if it wasn't on the chair — the way I did this time when I sat down."

"Was the chair right beside the bed?"

"Usually it is, but this time it was over by the dresser." She jiggled little Anna in her arms. "Is it important, do you think?"

"Frankly, I don't know. Perhaps he spilled something and decided to chuck the cushion out."

"I looked in the outside dustbin. There was no sign of it."

The baby mewed and smacked her lips. Lisa gave her the tip of her little finger to suck. "Wow, what a grip."

We actually hadn't heard Mairi come back into the room.

"What are you two doing?"

"Cleaning up, what's it look like?"

"Lisa, for Lord's sake, Christine is our guest. She shouldn't be doing dishes."

"Please, I don't mind at all. You've got enough to deal with."

On cue, Anna opened up her mouth, the lack of teeth making it seem huge, and wailed the thin mewling of the newborn.

Mairi reached for her. "Surely she's no hungry again."

It seemed she was, and Mairi went back to her armchair, lifting her blouse as she did so. Lisa took a tea towel and began to dry the dishes, then opened the cupboard door, looking for a home for the mugs. She called over her shoulder to her sister.

"What do you want me to do with Colin's empties?"

"There's a carton under the sink. Put them in there."

Lisa opened the cupboard door revealing two twelve packs filled with empties. "There's no more room," she called to Mairi.

"Oh Lisa, for God's sake, give it a rest."

"You married him," Lisa muttered.

I continued to act with selective deafness to this rancour. A final whisk of the dish cloth and we were done.

"By the way, while we're on the subject of Tormod," Lisa said. "Mr. Douglas, his solicitor, rang me this morning. Apparently, Tormod left a message on his answer phone. He must have done that on Friday night after the office was closed. He said he wanted to add a codicil to his will."

"Really? What was the codicil?"

"According to Mr. Douglas, Tormod didn't specify. He just

wanted Mr. Douglas to give him an appointment as soon as possible to make it legal."

We had made our way back into the living room, and Mairi heard this remark.

"Make what legal?"

Lisa explained. Her sister frowned.

"Is that going to effect the terms of the will?"

"I don't see why. I did ask Mr. Douglas, and he told me Tormod would have had to put any such request in writing, even if he had said what he intended, which he didn't."

Mairi removed her nipple from the voracious infant's mouth and shifted her to the other breast, wincing as the baby latched on.

"Our Lisa is an heiress," she said to me.

Lisa snorted. "Hardly that, Mars."

"You'll get a good price for that house."

"I'm not going to sell it."

She'd obviously forgotten her vow to turn the property into a sex joint.

"Suit yourself."

"I will."

Being around these two was like experiencing a series of depth charges — under the water, but showing themselves by boats rocking violently. Lisa sat down across from her sister, watching the baby feeding. I took the other chair and watched, too. Where else are you going to look? Lisa addressed me.

"It seems that I have inherited Tormod's entire estate, house and all."

"So I gather."

"It's sort of complicated. Tormod made a will, oh, about a six months ago, after I'd come to work for him."

She cast a quick glance at her sister, ready to do battle if necessary. Mairi scrunched up her face, but it could have been the baby chomping down.

"Anyway, in that will, Andy got the house, I got five hundred pounds, and the church got another five. But then, Tormod made yet another will, only a few days ago, and made me his sole heir."

"I don't understand it," said Mairi. "Why would a man cut out his own flesh and blood?"

Lisa was working hard to keep her cool. She kept talking to me, but really she was explaining to her sister.

"I think I know what happened. Remember those airline tickets? He'd sold the house to Coral-Lyn's father, and I bet he then thought the money would just go into his bank account. He'd been asking all sorts of questions about medical treatments in America, especially liver transplants. I don't know if you know, but the medical system over there is private. If you can pay, you can get what you need."

I did know that was true, and it was a big bone of contention in Ontario with our universal free health services, which many people thought were inadequate. There were a lot of people with money who hoped it could buy them everything.

"You think that's why he was going to Texas?"

"Yes. I went on the Internet and did a search. There's a big hospital in Houston that does great work with his kind of illness. But you have to pay."

"What does this have to do with him changing his will over to you?" Mairi asked.

"If you hold on, I'm getting to that. I told you, Tormod wouldn't accept the fact that his days were numbered. I believe he thought he'd spend all that money on his treatment. Andy was taken care of by Shirley Temple, so he was all right. Me and the church could divide whatever was left in his account. He never thought it through. Mr. Douglas said he was his usual stubborn self. 'I'm not on my way out yet, Jim.' Quote, unquote. Unfortunately, the deal wasn't closed. The concluding missives or whatever they're called hadn't been exchanged. The house was technically still his when he died. Therefore, it comes to me." She chewed on a piece of skin at the side of her thumb. "Coral-Lyn will probably contest it, though."

Mairi looked as if she were about to say something, but she thought better of it.

"In which case, I'll just get what was in his savings account, which I know for a fact was negligible. It might not even be as much as the bequest. His house was the only thing he owned of value."

I thought this the moment for the truth.

"Lisa, did you know that Tormod had accepted a second offer on the house? Sarah MacDonald had done a gazump. He was selling to a group of Norwegians for a higher price."

She stared at me in astonishment. "That greedy bastard."

"Did that deal go through?" asked Mairi.

"No, it wasn't concluded either. The house still legally belongs to his heir. To Lisa."

"Lucky her."

Suddenly, Lisa got up and knelt down in front of Mairi, putting her hands on her knees.

"You and Anna can come and live with me. It'll be much better than this shit-hole. You don't want to raise her on top of a bar. The house has a great little garden. There's lots of room."

An expression of defeat crossed Mairi's face. "You forget I'm married. You might take marriage vows lightly, but I don't."

She might as well have slapped Lisa in the face. She jumped up. "Well, fuck you then."

"Oh that's nice language in front of your niece."

Not to mention my delicate ears, but they both seemed oblivious of my presence. That, or I was a good audience. They were speaking English.

"That remark wasn't called for. I told you, I'm not seeing him any more."

Mairi's despair at her own situation made her strike out, fierce as a cornered cat.

"Where were you then?"

"When? What are you talking about?"

"Last weekend, that's when." She raised her voice, mockingly. "'So sorry, Mairi, I can't come over till Sunday. I have so much studying to do.' Well, that's not what I was told when I rang the school. They said all your examinations were finished for the term."

Lisa stared at her, icy cold with anger. "So, I needed a break. I didn't want to work in the bar. You know how I feel about it."

"Where were you then?"

Lisa shrugged. "I just hung out at the school until Sunday."

"Really? If that's the case, why did they tell me you had signed out on Friday?"

"Oh, fuck you, Mairi."

And out she went, leaving Mairi and I and infant singed in the fire.

CHAPTER THIRTY-FIVE

"I apologize on behalf of my sister."

I had no answer to that and just made noncommittal gestures.

Mairi took Anna off her breast and laid her on her lap, bouncing her lightly. "I was the one keen to have a babe, not Colin, but nobody told me it would be like this. She won't leave me alone, and I haven't had more than two hours' sleep at a stretch for two days."

I was about to placate her with platitudes about how things would get easier, but her eyes were full of misery.

"I think you just need some help with practical things."

Wrong thing to say. She burst out in anger, "I was counting on my sister, but you'd as well hold the wind in your bonnet as get Lisa to commit to anything. You heard her. She should have been here on the weekend. I needed her. I wanted to get the apartment all ready. Look at it, it's a bloody pigsty. I had to serve in the bar."

Poor little Anna was getting a rougher bounce. Mairi wasn't through yet.

"Do you want to know the reason she wasn't here?"

"I, er . . ."

"I'll tell you. It's because she's been having an affair with a married man. Some big-shot politician from London. He's got three children, not to mention he's a lot older than she is. She swore to me it was over."

As a private citizen, this was more than I wanted to know. As a police officer with antennae quivering, I wanted to pursue it.

"Maybe she was telling the truth. She could have been anywhere."

"You don't know my sister. Lying is second nature to her. I don't think she even knows she's doing it half the time."

There was no answering that, but I certainly wondered about the implications, even if Mairi was speaking out of sibling anger. I decided it was time to get out of here, and even though I felt twinges of guilt at leaving Mairi alone, she assured me she was going to sleep and that Colin would be in soon. I went to my own room.

There was a piece of paper slipped underneath the door. A note from Gill.

"Sorry I won't be able to meet for dinner. I have to drive over to Ness to meet with some of the locals. They are up in arms about the proposed relocation of a convicted pedophile and I need to field it. I'll ring you later."

I was surprised that even in Lewis this hugely problematic issue was occurring. Does serving a sentence for your crime clean you of all sins? And perhaps more important, will you offend again? I was also disappointed about dinner, but cancelled appointments were par for the course with police officers. It wasn't surprising that cops tended to huddle together, and the marriages that survived the strain of the life were usually the ones where both spouses were working officers who understood the realities of the life. Firefighters had irregular hours, adrenaline rush alternating with the utter tedium, but they are the poster boys of an adoring public. My buddies on the other hand, often have to deal with such unreasoning hatred from the ignorant that it takes your breath away.

Why do it then? Why join the police? Because no matter what, even if it's never put into words, you believe in the power of order. Nothing can happen in a lawless state except more crime. No country can function without law and order; anarchy is the shark that devours the fish, especially the little fish. Oh sure, there are some laws that we think are stupid and we have to enforce them, and there are always guys (and a few gals) on the police force who are assholes and who like to throw their weight around, but mostly we know, even if it's never expressed in so many words, that without us, nothing could thrive. Go check out what Sir Thomas More had to say about that.

So that's my spiel, thoughts floating in the recesses of my mind while I decided what to do about dinner. The Duke didn't stretch to room service. You had to show up in the dining room or forget it. Frankly, I didn't fancy sitting down there and having to deal with Colin MacLeod. I was being hit with stabs of the lonelies, an unpleasant state that was no doubt intensified by the grey sky and chill rain that was promising to fall for forty days and forty nights. I looked out the window at the masts bobbing in the inlet. The street below was deserted except for one car that drove slowly by, the tires swishing on the wet road. I pressed closer to the window to see if I recognized the car, but I didn't. I wondered what Paula was up to. In her time it was one o'clock in the afternoon. I also allowed my thoughts to sniff at my mother, all cozied up with her new paramour.

That did it. Time to get out of this room. I hadn't changed out of what I had to think of as my funeral clothes, so I snapped open my suitcase, pulled out a wool sweater and my fleecy jogging pants, and changed my clothes. That done, I was warmer and in slightly better spirits. I'd noticed a pizza place just around the corner from the hotel, and the notion of gooey melted cheese was comforting. Pizza it was then. I could bring it back here and have a quiet evening at home. What fun!

The hotel had a stand of spare umbrellas for the guests, so I grabbed a tartan one and went to get my pizza. On the way, I passed by a café, currently almost empty of customers. However, sitting together near the window were Coral-Lyn Pitchers and the Reverend John Murdoch, Lewis's eligible bachelor. She was leaning across the table and he was leaning back in his chair away from her. Body language that was very revealing. I saw him nod in a sympathetic, pastoral, sort of way, but Coral-Lyn was obviously

agitated, gesticulating with her hands, and aiming all that intensity at Mr. Murdoch. I would have made a large wager on what she
was talking about and I didn't envy him. I couldn't hang around
outside the window, although I sort of wanted to, so I continued
on to the pizza shop.

There was a middle-aged, cheerful-looking woman behind the
counter, who was waiting patiently while three gangly teenaged
boys were trying to decide what toppings to get. Behind her, a wiry
dark-haired Asian man, the first I'd seen on the island, was stretch-
ing pizza dough on his hands, then tossing it around in the air.

"Hurry yourselves, lads. We'll be closed and in our beds before
you decide," said the woman.

The inside of the shop had a delicious smell to it and was
warm and cozy. No wonder it was obviously a favourite hangout
for the local teenagers. Another group of lads and lassies was sitting by the window devouring hot, high-cholesterol slices, the sta-
ple diet of youth.

The lads opted for pepperoni, bacon, and mushrooms. I dropped
the bacon but went for the same, and I watched them as they sloped
off to a table to wait for their order. To my eyes, the local Hebridean
teenagers were astonishingly wholesome. There was not a piercing in
sight, and the hair fashion for the girls was shoulder-length and
straight, with natural colours. The boys had short-cropped hair, and
ordinary non-jean pants. Two of them were still in school uniform,
which was a white shirt and a tie under a plain burgundy wool
sweater. I'd long ago passed the great generational divide, and I will-
ingly admit I found most of the North American teenagers that I
encountered lacking in manners or good taste. These kids had spo-
ken politely to the server and they were chatting to each other in normal voices, no shrieking and certainly no ubiquitous "f" word. How
refreshing. Perhaps if I'd asked them, I would have discovered they
all yearned to escape this sober island for the delights of tattoos,
body piercing, and ear-shattering music, as well as the availability of
controlled substances. For myself, I wanted them to remain in their
innocence as long as they could.

"Here, you go, Ma'am. Cheers."

My order seemed to have come up sooner than that of the lads, but the woman gave me a wink. Suddenly her expression changed. She was glaring at the kids behind me.

"Put out those fags this minute. Catriona MacRae, I'm going to tell your mother when I next see her. You too, Angus. Do you think I've gone blind? Put them out."

One of the boys and a girl had lit cigarettes and were drawing on them with self-conscious style. Sheepishly they complied. The woman shared a "what's-the-youth-of-today-coming-to" look. I grimaced, paid up, and left with my pizza.

Coral-Lyn and the minister had progressed to the coffee-or-tea stage. She was still the one talking, as far as I could see, and he had pushed his chair back a little further. As I passed, I saw her reach over and place her hand on top of his. There was something sexually predatory about the gesture. He seemed rather stunned by this move, and he left his hand where it was. I walked on. What was she up to and how had Andy managed to get out of her clutches for the evening?

The pizza turned out to be delicious, and I wolfed down two slices as soon as I got back to my room. The television had decided to show static, but I didn't feel like going in search of somebody to fix it, so I switched it off. What to do? There was no radio, and I'd come away in such a hurry that I hadn't brought anything to read with me except my notebook and handouts from the conference. I read through those for the next hour, finished, and still had a lot of time to spare. I could have started to write down what had happened since I'd "found" Joan, but it felt too hot still, like a burn that needed to cool down for a while. I had no idea where we'd go from here. Our relationship seemed to have undergone a seismic change, but I was almost afraid to count on that. It was a most peculiar feeling to know that I had blood relatives by the score in this very spot. I might even have already met some of them without knowing it, but I had to wait for Joan to lift the embargo before I pursued that angle. On the other hand, given what she'd said, maybe I also had an entire tribe of "red Indians" on my father's side that I had yet to meet.

Those thoughts were agitating, so I brought myself back to the usual source of mental stability, work. I took out a fresh piece of paper and wrote at the top: "*What Happened to Tormod MacAulay?*"

I was bugged by the unanswered questions in the case. Oh, that's another typical characteristic of police folk: we can't stand having a lot of questions but no answers. They become like mosquito bites on your back; you're always trying to get to that itch. Besides, tackling the whole situation in this way made me feel better, pushed the loneliness back into the cupboard.

There was no proof that MacAulay had died other than by natural causes, no forensic evidence (thank you Dr. MacBeth). But I did have the famous or infamous gut feeling that cops the world over swear by. There were, shall we say, small irregularities that bothered me.

QUESTION #1: *Why did Joan and Sarah go to see MacAulay, and why was Sarah so upset?*

I didn't buy what Joan had said about it being a business matter. There was no indication that Tormod had changed his mind about selling to the Norwegians and was reneging on his deal. The answer seemed pretty obvious to me.

Mrs. MacNeil had described Annie Stewart, Joan's stepmother, as being barren as a board throughout her marriage. Then, coinciding with Joan being sent off to boarding school, Annie conceives. Joan had made an interesting choice of words when she said, "*Sarah* belonged *to my stepmother.*" Parents raising their errant daughter's child as if it were their own was quite a common story. I'd bet my new hat this is what Annie MacAulay/Stewart had done. Even in such a close-knit community, you can get away with that kind of deception if you're determined enough, especially if the subject involved can conveniently be out of town. I'd say it was highly likely Sarah was Joan's child, conceived when she was a mere teenager. That would certainly account for her disgrace and her subsequent disavowal of her own family, described by Mrs. MacNeil as far too self-righteous. If that was the case, then who was Poppa? Come on, that's easy. Surely, it was Mr. Tormod MacAulay who would "make it up to her," meaning to Sarah, and who immediately after Sarah and Joan left, had phoned his lawyer to add a codicil to his will. I'd bet this was the "ghost" that Joan had to lay to rest. *Sarah, meet your real father. Tormod, meet your daughter.*

But still, Joan's feelings about all of this were obscure. She said, "No, I didn't like Tormod," but was adamant he hadn't molested her. But he must have. I did a quick calculation of numbers. When she went off to boarding school she was just fifteen, which would make him twenty-nine. Fourteen years difference wasn't a lot when you were both adults, but it was a huge gap when you were barely out of childhood. Not to mention, you called him "Uncle." She'd had me three and a half years later, when she was living in Canada. She'd only just arrived, mind you, and I could have been conceived before she left. However, gut feeling again, I believed her when she said Tormod wasn't the sperm donor and my biological father.

Which brought us right smack dab against the strange gap of those unaccounted-for hours. She said, "I didn't like Tormod." Was she being literal and did she mean "I didn't *like* him. I *hated* him?" I thought that the hypnosis session had brought back more than she was letting on. Had she returned to Tormod's house after the accident? Who knows . . . groggy from the bang on the head, all stirred up emotionally, had she killed him? If so, how? (Back to lack of evidence again.) Frankly, even though her evasions and half-truths were as numerous and as dodgy as Hebridean sheep, I didn't think so.

Question answered.

QUESTION #2: *Can we believe the accuracy of the time given by the MacLeans?*

If the time they gave was right, the car they saw couldn't have been Joan's. Who was it then?

No answer.

QUESTION #3: What happened after Joan and Sarah left? Who cleaned up? Why did they clean up?

Lisa said Tormod never tidied up after himself but, even if he did, surely he'd know where the glasses and plates lived, no matter what Gill said about genetic programming. And was this the kind of thing a man would do after going through the kind of scene Joan had described. Lisa said there were two things missing. One was the cushion from the bedroom chair. The other was a piece of woven fabric that she said should still have been on the loom. The fabric could have been sent somewhere, but surely not the cushion.

No answer.

QUESTION #4: Why was Andy's bicycle in the shed?

According to his fiancée, Andy visited his granddad every day except on the weekends. Didn't he need his bike to get around? As far as I know he didn't have a car. They seemed to use Coral-Lyn's rental. I hadn't noticed that the bike had a flat tire or anything like that, although I hadn't been paying close attention at that moment. Why was it left there, then? Usually you do that if you ride over one way and return by another means.

Possible answer: Andy had biked over to visit his grandfather as usual, and he was the person who had walked into the house....

Wait a minute.

I flipped to the verbatim notes I'd taken during Joan's hypnosis session. She didn't say "somebody has come to the door," she said "somebody has come in." Different. Even in this friendly, everybody-knows-everybody-else island, surely you knock on the door when you go visiting. Except for sisters, who feel free to walk in unannounced . . . and grandsons.

Which meant Andy had not told the truth when he said the last time he saw his uncle was on Thursday. Or rather, when Coral-Lyn had said that for him.

QUESTION #5: Why lie about it?

Answer could be trouble.

The real-estate shenanigans were vitally connected to Andy. As of last week, he thought the house was going to Miss Pitchers's daddy. What if he'd come back to the house that night after Sarah and Joan had flown off, and learned from Tormod that he'd been gazumped? He could have driven there, possibly with his fiancée, and it was their car that the MacLeans had seen.

Possible answer to the car sighting, but not to the bike in the shed and no answer at all to question number three and the identity of the tidy freak.

QUESTION #6: *Did Andy kill Tormod, thinking that, by the terms of the original will, he would get the house anyway?*

He couldn't have known that, in fact, Tormod had left his entire estate to Lisa.

Answer: highly unlikely.

Andy was truly grief-stricken when I saw him. I just couldn't see him as the murdering type. I know that, after the fact, there are always people saying about the worst murderers, "He was such a nice man." I don't buy that. Premeditated murders are never committed by nice people. The cracks always show somewhere. However, it was possible that, on hearing that he might not acquire the house, Andy had exploded in a fit of rage and killed his grandfather. But I doubted it. And neither could I see Coral-Lyn doing that. Besides, that question was totally hypothetical, without any forensic evidence. And there was no sign of obvious trauma to the body.

QUESTION #7: *How good a judge of character am I?*

Mairi declared that Lisa wasn't at her school that weekend as she'd said she was. And now she had inherited a property that could bring in money very useful to a struggling student.

I'd seen people lie during an interview so convincingly that I had to go back and recheck the videotape of the robbery, which was incontrovertible. But that was rare. When you're in this business, you get a very good nose for lies or evasions, which are the law-abiding citizen's form of lies. I believed Lisa had not arrived at the house until Sunday and was shocked by Tormod's death.

Her sister was probably right about her actual whereabouts. She was shacking up with her sugar daddy that weekend, and she wasn't telling the truth about that.

Answer: pretty good.

QUESTION #8: *Where is Sarah's briefcase?*

Janice had called her into the office at the request of a woman who could have been a prospective client. She'd bring her briefcase.

No answer.

QUESTION #9: *If it is true that Joan and Sarah were forced off the road, who was the driver of that car? Who apparently stood over Joan directly afterward?*

No answer.

I shoved aside the paper. If all of my speculation about Sarah MacDonald was the truth — and I was convinced it was — I had lost not an aunt, but a half-sister. A blood relative I hadn't known existed. I wondered what she had been like, other than a habitual drunk, that is. From the way the scene had played out, she must have been distraught at hearing Tormod was her natural father. No wonder he couldn't let her marry his son. Which suggested he knew the truth about her parentage. Did my grandfather and stepmother know? I suspected not. I was looking forward to hearing Joan's version of all this. I looked over my notes. It seemed to me there were still bits and pieces of the puzzle that weren't placed yet, but I felt much better, and I wasn't about to dash out now and satisfy my curiosity.

I got up and looked out of the window again. Hey, I was in the place of my ancestors. Some of them, anyway. Sondra and her sad story had started to recede from my mind. My boss had been more right than he knew when he said going to Edinburgh might be just what the doctor ordered.

CHAPTER THIRTY-SIX

That night I slept better than I had in months. I didn't wake up until seven, which was luxurious. I was eager to get going and dressed quickly and went down to breakfast. The gal at the reception desk handed me a note. She was a dark-haired lass, and I wondered if she might be on the cousin side. I grinned to myself. I was in danger of checking out the entire population of Stornoway at this rate.

She handed me a note from Gill, who had phoned to say he was busy today but would like to meet later for dinner. I was just as glad, because there were things I wanted to do on my own. I had a hurried breakfast, exchanged a few stilted words with the German couple, and escaped to my little toy car. Overnight, some kind of body-learning seemed to have taken place and, except for the occasional flinch when I felt I was drifting too far over to the right, I was more comfortable driving. I got myself out of Stornoway with only one missed turn and set off to Duncan's house.

I'd phoned ahead from the hotel to say I was coming, not wanting to risk finding Joan and him rolling around in bed together. Not to worry. By the time I arrived he was getting ready for the herding demonstration. Over a dozen people this time. The sun was teasing but there was no rain and it was warmer. The sheep were munching away placidly and the dogs were circling obsessively around Duncan.

I went into the house, ringing the bell first. Joan was in the kitchen washing up, but for a brief moment, I didn't recognize her. Her hair was back to being dark brown and the waves had reappeared.

She saw my surprise and patted her head self-consciously. "I went back to my own colour."

"Were you hoping blondes have more fun?" I asked.

She gave me a sharp look to see if I was getting at her, but I was deliberately bland. I knew why she'd dyed her hair.

"We all need a change from time to time."

She turned the tables on me by scrutinizing my own haircut. "You could do with a trim. And in my opinion, you'd look better with longer hair. It would balance out that jawline."

"I must have inherited it from my father . . . whoever he was."

The air went dead around her. "Don't start with me, Christine. I'm not up to it."

She did, in fact, look exhausted, and the bruises on her face were like dark shadows. Of course, I felt guilty at my jab.

"How are you feeling?" I asked.

"Okay. How're you?"

"Good."

"I hope they'll have settled the accident by the time you leave."

I saw on her face how much she wanted me to stay, because she was afraid.

"How did you feel after the interview with Gill yesterday?"

"I was relieved, really. Your officer friend was very nice. He put me at my ease." A pause to find the chink. "But that's his job isn't it? He's trained to appear sympathetic."

I nodded. "Yes, he's the family liaison officer."

Joan scrubbed at some more dishes and stacked them in the draining board. I took up a tea towel and started to dry. There were no wine glasses, I noticed. Just mugs, all with a border-collie design, and plates.

"It would help your case if we could find the person who was at the crash site. They could verify that you weren't driving."

She snorted. "They'll never come forward. It was their fault we went off the road."

"Don't forget Sarah had been drinking. That was a factor."

Joan slumped and concentrated on wiping off the counter. Tears had welled up in her eyes, and she tried to wipe them away with the end of her plaid scarf, which she was wearing again.

"How would we even find that other driver?"

"The police can put out a notice asking for anybody who saw a car on the road at that time to come forward."

She shrugged. "The road was deserted. Nobody was out."

The door opened and Duncan came in with one of the dogs.

"I'm leaving Nic inside. She's after limping again. Good crowd today." He took a look at Joan and immediately glared at me as if it were my fault. He asked her in Gaelic if she was all right, and she dragged up a smile for him, which elicited a quick peck on the cheek. It was all very chummy and familial. Then he breezed out again.

Nic ran to the window, rearing up on her hind legs to watch him. Joan clucked at her.

"Come on, Nicky. Come and have a bicky."

The dog got down, limped over to her, and sat down expectantly.

"That's my girl."

Joan was so comfortable in this kitchen. I'd never seen her quite like this. In spite of her fatigue, there was a relaxation in her face and body that I didn't remember seeing before. She caught my eye.

"I know we have a lot to talk about, Chris. And we will, I promise. Just give me a couple of days."

"That's fine. And in the meantime, I wondered how you would feel about some more exploring of what happened on Friday night."

"Using hypnosis you mean?"

"No, let's just talk, go over what you do remember. More might come back to you."

"Good. I don't want to do that trance thing again. It was too upsetting."

"Okay. Can we have a cup of coffee first?"

"I think he has some." She opened the cupboard doors. "We both drink tea. Yes, here we go . . . but it's instant and probably stale at that. You know how fussy you are."

"Tea will be fine then. I drink it black, remember?"

I was the visitor, the almost-stranger that she was accommodating.

Nic walked over to the door and lay down, her nose to the crack. I could hear Duncan's voice coming through the megaphone. While Joan filled the kettle, I went to the window to watch the dogs do their tricks. From here, Duncan cut a good figure. Tall and muscular, he was every inch the trusty shepherd with his crook and his tartan trousers and tweed hat. He wasn't the usual type Joan had gone for in the past. Those men were typically low-end guys with low-end jobs — and attitudes to match. Joan and Duncan had been childhood sweethearts, but I wondered how long nostalgia would sustain the present reality of what they had both grown into. And how long was the "new" Joan going to be around?

"Here you are." Joan put the teapot and a mug on the table and we sat down.

"I particularly wanted to go back to what you said about somebody coming to the house. If it was a neighbour, they may have seen you leave, and they could verify that Sarah was driving."

"You're talking as if you don't believe me."

"No, no, that's not true. I do believe you. But from the court's point of view, it would help to have a witness. Can you recall anything more? Do you think it was a man or a woman?"

"I didn't hear anything."

"Do you remember if they rang the bell?"

She shrugged. "I don't think so, but it's very vague."

Nic came back and flopped at Joan's feet. She reached down and began to twiddle with the dog's black fur.

"Do we need to go over this again? All I cared about was who was driving the bloody car, and now I know . . . thanks to you. I appreciate what you did, Chris. I am proud of you."

Another milestone, but I was uncomfortable with this overt maternal attitude. I moved on too quickly.

"We don't have to go over it all again if you don't want to, but it's a loose end that I'd like to tidy up."

Joan drank some of her tea, then put down the mug. "All right. But no hypnosis."

"I can't hypnotize you unless you are willing."

"What do you want me to do then?"

"I suggest you sit in the armchair, where you'll be more comfortable."

Still moving stiffly, she complied and sat down, pulling her scarf closer around her neck.

"Now close your eyes and take in a deep breath. And exhale. That's it. Do it again."

Her face settled into the lines and shape that always underlie our usual waking expressions. Joan's face wasn't mean-looking or angry. It was etched deep with sorrow. A face that had known much grief. Another surprise to me. Why hadn't I seen that before?

"All right? Comfortable? . . . Think back to the night of the accident again. Put yourself in MacAulay's living room. In your mind's eye, try to see where Tormod and Sarah are. . . . They're having some kind of row."

Joan opened her eyes, blue and sharp at the moment. "It wasn't a row. She was angry with him, but he wasn't mad at her. It takes two people to make a barney."

I couldn't resist asking, "Why was she angry?"

"I told you before, I don't know. Probably something to do with business."

"Had he decided not to sell the house to the Norwegians after all?"

"No, nothing like that."

"Her commission then?"

She looked away. "Probably."

Lie. I was disappointed, I had to admit. I would have liked it if she had come clean.

"Let's go on then. Why don't you close your eyes? It might be easier. You are interrupted by somebody outside. What does Tormod do?"

"He goes to talk to them."

"Does that person come into the room?"

"No, he stops them in the hall."

Got it! No doorbell, and somebody who felt free enough to walk in.

"How long is Tormod in the hall with this person?"

"Not long, a couple of minutes at the most."

"What do you do while he's out there?"

She sighed. "I got some tissues for Sarah to blow her nose."

"Was she crying?"

"Yes."

"Why was that?"

Joan opened her eyes again, but she stayed slouched down in the chair. "Drinkers cry easily . . . as you know all too well."

This last comment wasn't said defiantly, but with sad resignation — a woman who was coming to terms with her own past and not liking what she saw there. I felt a sudden and unexpected rush of feeling towards her.

"I'm glad you're going straight. Has it been hard?"

"It was at first. It's easier now."

I think I would have held on to this rare, rare moment of softness between us, but Nic suddenly jumped to her feet and ran to the window, barking. I heard applause coming from outside. Joan sat up.

"Sounds like they've finished. I promised Duncan I'd help in the gift shop. I'd better go." She paused. "Don't worry about all this, Chris. You've been a great help. If we don't find any witnesses, so be it. I know the truth now, and I'll just have to trust they'll believe me. Do you want to come and help me in the shop?"

"Another time. I'm going to drive around a bit. Catch this sun while I can."

"Come on back and have dinner with us then."

"I can't. Gill asked me to go for dinner with him."

"Did he?" she smiled. She wanted to say a lot more than that, but she didn't. I knew she didn't want to spoil the moment either, and comments about my dates were guaranteed to do so.

I followed her outside. The crowd of dog-watchers seemed more in the mood for buying than the last group I had seen, and they were all going in the direction of the barn. Duncan saw us and waved. With a light tap on my arm, Joan scurried off.

I walked back to my car. Next stop, Andy MacAulay's house.

CHAPTER THIRTY-SEVEN

One of the twins answered the door. I thought it might be Penelope but I wasn't sure. She was wearing a white summer dress patterned with bright yellow flowers. There were the pearls and matching earrings. I wondered what she had been doing before I called that she seemed so ready for company. Perhaps "at homes" were a way of life among the older generation of women on the island.

"Good morning. Is Andy in?"

"Oh dear me, he's not. He left for the church about half an hour ago."

Her sister appeared at her shoulder, in exactly the same dress, but with a navy cardigan. I wonder who made the decision of what they were going to wear every day, or if it was pure twin telepathy.

"Is there anything we can help you with? It's Miss Morris, isn't it? From Canada?"

"Yes, that's right. I just wanted to have a word with him."

They exchanged quick glances. "This might not be a good time, dear," said the orange twin.

"He's very upset today," added the navy twin.

"I'm sorry. I don't want to intrude."

"It's not just his grandda's passing that's upsetting him." She touched her right hand to her bosom and lowered her voice. "He's having love troubles."

"Really?"

"That's what he told us, didn't he Barbara?"

Ha. Navy twin was Penelope.

"Yes, indeed. He came home last night and said he and Coral-Lyn might not be getting married after all. We were so shocked because they seemed devoted to each other, didn't they, Penny? Well, we asked ever so kindly what had happened, and all he would say was that he was starting to think they were . . . what word did he use, Penny?"

"Incompatible. He said they were incompatible."

Curiouser and curiouser.

"He's gone over to the church, you said?"

"He did. He said he needed some guidance."

"Would you like to come inside and wait for him?" asked Barbara.

"No, no, thanks. I'd better be on my way. . . . Is he on his bike? Did he get it fixed?"

They looked equally puzzled. "It wasna broke, was it, Barbara?"

"It was not. It's a good solid bicycle, that one. He goes everywhere on it."

I hesitated, then smiled as pleasantly as I could, not really liking the George Smiley role I had put myself in. They were very nice women.

"It's such a pity he didna visit his grandda the night he died. He might have been able to get him to the hospital in time."

They nodded in unison. "Aye, 'tis indeed sad, that. He was intending to, but the Lord intervened and he got held up at the church elder meeting until late."

"He came back here did he?"

"Aye. We heard him come in about midnight. We were a bit surprised, because usually he bikes over to Shawbost on Fridays to visit his fiancée. She's renting a cottage up Shawbost way." They both looked discomfited at this statement. "After all, they were betrothed to each other," said Penelope. "And times have changed, haven't they?"

For a moment, I was puzzled by this remark. Then I realized she was referring to the implication that Andy and Coral-Lyn might be copulating without benefit of clergy.

"Perhaps it was an indication," added Barbara.

"Of?"

"Trouble in the nest. She must have picked him up at the church after his meeting, because I heard the car, and they were outside for quite a long time."

"Talking, probably," I said helpfully.

They both nodded in unison.

"I'll speak to him later," I said, not wanting to risk losing their good opinion by admitting I intended to track down Andy MacAulay, broken heart or no. I said goodbye and returned to the car. I drove down the hill towards the church, remembering just in time to keep to the left.

As I turned into the parking lot, without the distraction of many people milling around I had more opportunity to view the church. It was a tall, rectangular building with a smooth grey façade and straight, simple lines. There was no adornment, except for the long, narrow windows with arched lintels that pierced the sides and front. No stone angels or gargoyles peeked down from the roof. I saw now that it was a beautiful church with the elegance of utter simplicity, and the starkness I had reacted to yesterday wasn't that of poverty of spirit, but came more from the confidence of a religion that saw no need to gussy up.

The front doors were unlocked, and I pushed one open and went inside. Andy MacAulay was sitting in one of the front pews, his head bowed. I *might* have considered retreating, but he heard the sound of the door and he turned around at once, half-hoping, half-fearing who might be coming in. When he saw it was me, relief was predominant. I walked down the aisle, and he stood up to greet me.

"I apologize for disturbing you, Mr. MacAulay, but I wonder if I could have a word with you."

The polite smile vanished and he definitely looked nervous. "What about?"

"I am investigating the car accident that resulted in the death of Mrs. Sarah MacDonald."

"Why? I mean, why are you the one investigating it?"

"The other woman in the car is a Canadian."

"Have you found her?"

"Yes, we have."

"Is she all right?" His voice was tight with fear.

"Yes, she suffered only minor bruises."

He let out his breath, clasping his hands together and raising his eyes towards the high roof as if he were addressing God himself. "Thank the Lord. Oh, thank the Lord."

An intense reaction towards somebody I assumed was a total stranger to him.

"Is there somewhere we could go and talk for a minute or two?" I was uncomfortable having a secular discussion in a house of God.

He hesitated. "We can go into the meeting room, I suppose."

He stepped in front of me to lead the way, and I caught a whiff of his stale sweat. I followed him through the rear door, backstage to the offices. One door was closed and a simple plaque said "Reverend Murdoch." We went through the other door into a rather large room with folding chairs lined up in rows facing a podium. A notice board was at the side and I had a glimpse of dated notices, all in Gaelic. The room smelled faintly of antiseptic, and I saw that the linoleum floor was still damp from a recent cleaning.

He took one chair at the end of a row, which made it awkward for me. I took a chair in the row in front, turning it around to face him. In these close confines, his odour was far worse, easily overpowering the cleaning liquid. He hadn't shaved either, and that gave him such a haggard appearance, I felt sorry for him. I would have offered tea if I'd been able.

"So, where was the woman? How did you find her?" He asked.

"She'd made her way to the house of somebody she knew, not far from here."

He looked at me, wanting to ask who, but too afraid to show his hand. He rubbed his forefinger down his chin, testing the stubble.

"And she's not badly injured then?"

"The usual cuts and bruises you get when your car has rolled down the side of a hill. She did have amnesia for a while, but that has cleared up now." I let him digest that information for a moment. "Why I was interested in talking to you was because, just prior to the accident, the woman in question was at your grandfather's house with Mrs. MacDonald."

"Really? Friday night, you mean?"

"Yes. She says she went there at about nine o'clock. Then they both left about ten . . ."

I paused to give him time to react, but he had gone very still, listening to me like somebody sitting in the dark who needs to know if those sounds from the kitchen mean an intruder is in the house.

"She claims she was not driving, that Mrs. MacDonald was. As the accident resulted in a death, it would be helpful if we could find somebody to verify that."

He watched me, transfixed.

I continued. "The woman also says that Mr. MacAulay had a visitor that night while they were there. This person didn't stay more than a few minutes, but there is a possibility that they might have seen the car drive off and witnessed who was driving."

"Yes?" He stared at me, trying to keep his bottom lip from trembling; at the same time, he wasn't going to give me an inch if he could help it. To hell with it, I was losing patience.

"Andy, were you the one who came to the house that night?"

"Friday? No, of course not. I already told Gillies, I hadn't seen Grandda since Thursday. No, it wasn't me. No."

I threw out a line, baited. "Your landladies said you were intending to visit him, but you were late at the church."

"Right. That's right, I was."

"What time did your church meeting finish?"

"I don't know. I wasn't paying attention."

"Of course. Why would you? I understand you usually bicycle over to Shawbost to visit Miss Pitchers. Good for you. That's quite a distance."

"It's not so bad when you're fit."

"And in the rain, too. Friday was pretty miserable, I hear."

"I'm used to it."

I put on my best Columbo confused-bimbo expression. "Now, I'm a stranger here. Wouldn't you have had to go past the scene of the accident on your way to Shawbost?"

"I would not." The words leapt out of his mouth, loud and unconvincing. "What I mean is, yes. It is that road. But I didn't see the accident. It must have happened earlier . . . I mean later. Look here, I don't like answering all these questions. I'm not sure you have a right to be talking to me like this."

He was absolutely correct, of course, but some ugly suspicions were circling in my mind and I didn't care. After a while, too many people throwing evasions at you as if you were stupid was extremely irritating. I opened the trapdoor.

"Your bicycle was in Mr. MacAulay's shed on Sunday. When did you leave it there?"

He fell through. There was no way to escape it. "I don't know. Thursday. It must have been when I went over on Thursday."

"But you just said you went on your bike from here on Friday evening."

Fear made Andy suddenly bold. He had nice brown eyes that most of the time must have been soft as a cow's, but now they hardened in anger.

"I'm not going to answer any more questions. I haven't been charged with anything. You have no right."

He stood up and started to walk to the door. I darted after him and got in front, forcing him to stop. He'd have to shove me out of the way to get past.

"According to Ms. Morris, they were forced off the road by an oncoming car, just along the way from Dail Beag. The car was way over on their side of the road and, as they swerved to avoid it, they went over the cliff. The driver didn't stop to see what had happened."

He stared at me with an expression of utter horror on his face. This was the first time he had heard this.

"The car was a small, red one. Could have been a Nissan or a Ford."

Joan hadn't seen the car that clearly, but the MacLeans had. They'd seen in when it was leaving Tormod's house shortly after the accident. They thought it was a Vauxhall, but I knew it wasn't.

"Miss Pitchers drives a Nissan rental car, doesn't she?" A mute nod. "She must have been on her way to pick you up from the church. The Misses Stewarts said she dropped you off at your lodgings on Friday night. Quite late, about midnight. The timing fits. It was a wet night and visibility was bad, perhaps she didn't realize what she'd done. She likes to have her music up loud, I noticed."

Andy swivelled away from me and studied the notice board in front of him as if there were a message posted there that would save his own life. His shoulders were shaking and he thrust his fists deep into his pants pockets.

"Can you tell me what happened that night?" I asked in as soft a voice as I could. I touched him lightly on the elbow.

"No! You have no right!" he yelled. Then, shrugging me off, he bolted through the door and raced back into the church.

I was squeamish about questioning a suspect in a possible criminal act. I didn't want to charge down the aisle of a sacred place, either. And if I caught up with him, then what?

I ducked out the side door I'd seen next to the meeting room. I'd guessed correctly. Andy was unlocking his bicycle from the stand, and as I hurried over to my car, I saw him head out of the driveway and down the hill.

Cursing my clumsiness with the unfamiliar gears, I set off after him. But I didn't have to worry about losing him. Just as I turned out of the driveway, I saw a small Nissan was coming up the hill. Both the car and Andy stopped. He flung down his bicycle and got into the car, which did a tire hissing U-turn and roared off. I shifted into third gear and followed.

We must have been driving for ten minutes max, when I realized we were close to the accident site. I spotted the police tape fluttering ahead at the curve of the road. Coral-Lyn, whom I could see clearly now, suddenly pulled over to the side of the road, not quite stopping;

the passenger door flew open, and Andy started to get out. She did-n't give him a chance to step clear. The door swinging open, tires peeling as if she were in a juvenile drag race, she took off. Andy lost his balance and fell to the ground. The car swerved as she leaned over and closed the door, then she straightened up and the car disappeared around the bend in the road. Andy lay where he had fallen.

CHAPTER THIRTY-EIGHT

I pulled over into the passing place and got out. Andy was sitting up. The side of his face was scraped, but he seemed all right. He was moving anyway. As I approached, he gazed up at me in utter bewilderment, as if I had materialized out of the air. I crouched beside him.

"Are you okay? Can you stand up?"

"I don't know. I think I've broken my ankle." I helped him to his feet and he winced. He couldn't put any weight down — it was too painful. I checked his ankle; it had already ballooned out and was dangling at an unnatural angle.

"Here, put your arm around my shoulder. Let's get you to the car."

He managed to hop the few feet to the car. He was crying uncontrollably.

"I could have been killed. Oh, Lynnie, how could you?"

"Where's the best place to take you? There's a hospital in Stornoway, isn't there?"

He stopped and faced me. His breath was fierce this close to my face and his nose was wet with mucous.

"No! We've got to go after her. She's not in her right mind and who knows what she'll do?"

"Are you saying she's suicidal?"

"She could be. It won't be the first time. Please, Miss Morris, I'll be fine. You must go after her. She's heading for the Butt."

"If she's suicidal, we'd better get the police involved. Do you have a mobile phone?"

"No, I left it at home. Please, there isn't time. If we can catch her, I might be able to talk her into some sense."

By now, he'd hopped around the car and was getting into the passenger seat. I didn't have much choice. I got in and drove off. The Nissan was long out of sight.

"Just keep on this road. It'll take us there."

"How do you know where's she's headed?"

"She believes God will speak to her up there. She's done that before. I hadn't known her that long, and we were up there just walking on the cliffs. She suddenly decided that she had to trust in God and asked Him to reveal His will to her. She ran, literally ran, to the edge of the cliff and held out her arms as if she thought she could just fly over."

That didn't sound too promising.

"The wind is so strong up there sometimes," he went on, "I had to pull her away. She was so wild that day, I didn't know her."

"But nevertheless, you got engaged."

That was a bit insensitive of me, I admit, but I'd heard stories like his ad nauseum. *He/she was so sweet when we first met, they just had these off days.* Hey, put the light on and read the text, folks. These insane traits aren't going to vanish because you have so-called love stars in your eyes.

"She was so, er . . . " he turned quite red. "She is very warm-hearted. I thought she loved me. I've never had anybody love me like that before."

He wiped his face with the back of his sleeve. I wished I could offer him a tissue to mop up and blow into, but I didn't have anything. All this time, I was driving as fast as I could round the tight turns, as the road continued to wind around the foot of the hills. The sheep were scattered on the slopes and on the verge of the road. I hoped they'd stay out of my way. Then the road straightened out and we were driving through a village.

"Shall I stop and get somebody to phone the police?"

"No, please believe me. I'm the only one she'll listen to. Look! There she is."

I pushed down the accelerator, but I was already way over the speed limit, and it wouldn't do anybody any good if I rolled the car and killed us both. I tried to maintain a speed I could handle and still keep her in sight.

"Why is she in such a bad state?"

"She thinks she's lost everything she ever dreamed about."

"Which is?"

"Just everything. The house . . . me, I suppose . . . I told her I didn't think I could stay engaged."

Suddenly, he leaned forward and buried his face in his hands, sobbing. I could hardly hear what he was saying.

"I feel terrible. . . . What we did . . . . was very wrong."

It isn't easy racing along a narrow, unfamiliar road in a strange car with a young man crying his guts out right beside you. I didn't know if he was suicidal as well. I decided not to risk it, and I slowed down and pulled over onto the verge. He gasped at me.

"Why have you stopped? We must keep going. Please."

"Andy, we're not going anywhere at the moment. What are you saying? What did you do that was wrong?"

He was a sorry sight, red gravel burns on his cheek, tears and snot all over his face, and wide dilated pupils.

"It wasn't anything. . . . We just took her briefcase. I didn't want to, but Coral-Lyn said we had to . . . " More tears. Another story I'd heard before: abnegating responsibility. He looked frantically at the road. "She's almost out of sight. Please keep driving. I'll control myself, I promise I will. I wouldn't forgive myself if anything happened to her."

I didn't want to be left with that guilt either. "Andy, you've already handed me a pile of bullshit. If I think you're lying again or not telling the whole truth and nothing but the truth, you're on your own. You can walk to the Butt. I won't help you."

"I'll tell you, I promise. Please drive."

I shoved in the gear and, with a perceptible jolt and a little spit of dirt from the wheels, we started off again. I picked up speed and we saw the Nissan, further off but still visible.

"So, tell me what happened on Friday night. What really happened — no crap."

He groaned, but the floodgate was opened and he started to talk, almost gabbling he was so keen to tell all.

"I biked over to see Grandda about ten o'clock. I go every day, but I was late because we had a meeting at the church and we couldn't settle anything, so it ran late. We're trying to help one of the churches select a new minister — Oops, watch out!"

The warning was because the red and white postal van was hurtling towards us. He'd probably moved out to avoid a sheep. I leaned on my horn and the driver ducked back to his lane, giving me a cheery wave of the hand as he went by. More adrenaline rush.

"Carry on," I said to Andy, who seemed to have temporarily lost his train of thought.

"I almost didn't go because the weather was bad, but I didn't want to disappoint him. He liked company." Several sniffs at this point and another wipe with his sleeve. "I got there at . . . it must have been just before ten o'clock. I could hear voices even before I opened the front door. There was a car in front of the house, so I knew he had visitors. I walked in the way I always do. But I only got as far as the hall, because he heard me and came out of the living room right away. He looked really upset and he said he had company and he couldn't see me tonight. I asked him if anything was wrong, but he said, 'No, nothing is wrong.'" Andy paused, remembering. "Then he said something very strange . . . he said, 'It *has* been wrong, but it won't be any more.' I could hear a woman carrying on in the living room —"

"Carrying on how?"

"Crying. She sounded quite hysterical. I actually got a glimpse of her when he opened the door to go back in. It was Mrs. MacDonald, the estate agent. There was another woman I hadn't seen before, who was trying to calm her down. I didn't know what to do. Grandda was almost shoving me out of the door. So I walked to the shed where I'd left my bike and got through to Lynnie on my mobile." He pulled his sleeve over his hand and wiped his face off. "She told me to wait there, and she'd come over right away."

"Because of the estate agent?"

"That's right. It seemed odd that she was there, because Grandda had agreed to sell the cottage and the land to Lynnie's father. Mr. Pitchers wants to turn it into a centre for religious studies." He let out a hiccup. "Lynnie's father is a man of strong character. She has two older sisters who have married ministers, and her dad is so proud of them. . . . I think sometimes Lynnie has felt overlooked." He glanced over at me, offering the insight tentatively, as if this awareness of psychology was a foreign language. "When she and I met and when Grandda said he would sell Mr Pitchers his house, I think she felt as if she were going to join the charmed circle." He wiped again. "I do believe my position as a deacon of the church was a large part of my appeal."

His voice was dripping with self-pity, but I wasn't about to reassure him. His insight into his fiancée sounded accurate. Sometimes I think sibling rivalry is *the* most overlooked motivating factor in many major crimes. Think King Lear.

We had raced through another village, and now the houses were getting more spread out. The grey sea stretched to the horizon on the left.

"How much further is it?"

"About ten minutes. Can you drive faster?"

It had begun to rain again and the road was slick.

"No. We can see her. Go on with what you were saying."

"Lynnie was afraid our negotiations might be in jeopardy because the final papers weren't yet signed and you have to watch out in Scotland."

The infamous *gazump*.

"It was quite soon after I'd telephoned when Mrs. MacDonald came dashing out of the house. The other lady was right behind her. Mrs. MacDonald tried to get into the car and the other lady tried to stop her. The next thing I saw was Mrs. MacDonald had shoved her away and got into the car. The lady ran around to the passenger side and just managed to get in as Mrs. MacDonald drove off."

I couldn't help but let out a sigh myself. Vindication for Joan.

Andy rubbed at his shin. He was looking white around the gills, and I knew his ankle must be getting very painful.

"Anyway, I didn't know what to do. I stayed in the shed until Lynnie arrived shortly after. I told her what had happened, and we went in to see what was going on. Grandda was beside himself, and he looked dreadfully ill. He just burst out at us, 'I'm not selling the house any more. All plans are cancelled.' Lynnie asked him why, and he said, 'I've got to put things right.' If he said that once, he said it ten times. 'What things?' Lynnie asked. He just wouldn't say. Then he insisted we leave. There wasn't anything we could do." Andy's thoughts turned inward and I knew he was coming to the meat of the story. I concentrated on driving. One of the windshield wipers wasn't working properly and the windshield was smeared.

"We left. We had no choice. We were heading for Shawbost, where Lynnie is staying, but we hadn't gone too far when we saw the accident site. You know where it was . . . just before you get to the Dail Beag sign. I mightn't have noticed, because the car had rolled down the hill, but Lynnie saw it. So we stopped, of course. Mrs. MacDonald was lying across one of the rocks and it was obvious to anyone that she had broken her neck and she was dead. The other blonde lady was still in the car, pinned by her seatbelt. Lynnie went to see to her. She made me stay where I was."

His voice lowered as he bent his head, full of shame at the memory of his own cowardice. "I faint at the sight of blood, you see. She came back and said that both of the women were dead. She was sort of odd . . . almost exhilarated, actually. She had a briefcase in her hand, and she said we'd soon know what Grandda was up to." His face had turned even more red and his voice was strangled. "I wanted to ring the police right away, I really did, but Lynnie said, 'No. We can't help the women now.' She looked in the case and found papers that said that Grandda had . . . changed his mind, and was planning to sell the house to some Norwegians at a much better price." He glanced over at me. "You can do that here. Change your mind that is. We call it gazumping."

I nodded. "It's okay, you don't need to explain. I know what it means."

"I've never seen Lynnie so angry. She said she'd sue him, but that would be awful. Technically, Grandda hadn't done anything illegal, but Lynnie was so concerned about disappointing her father . . . "

He shuddered. I imagined her wrath had been fierce indeed. "She was angry with me too, because she said I was . . . I was being weak."

I thought she had probably used a less polite word, but I didn't press him. I got the picture.

"What could I have done though? It was up to Grandda."

I shrugged. Andy was the kind of guy who always hooked up with a domineering woman, then drove her crazy with his lack of spine. I was amazed he'd got up the nerve to break off with Coral-Lyn.

He rubbed at his neck. "I think she was a little hysterical. But she said it was obviously God's will that the religious centre be built. He'd led us to the papers and He would not tolerate any interference."

"Hey, that's a pretty high authority you've got there."

I won't go into how many people I've heard spout that sort of line. Including people on opposite sides of a war. Name any war.

We had a straight stretch of road ahead of us now, so I stepped on the gas. The Nissan had vanished from sight. Andy kept talking, fast and agitated.

"You can imagine how shocked I was when I heard that the other lady in the accident wasn't dead and that she had disappeared. What if she had been lying there injured and we could have saved her?"

"What indeed."

"But you said she's all right?"

"Yes. You must have felt awful when I told you Coral-Lyn probably caused the accident in the first place on her way to pick you up?"

"Oh, I did."

And from his expression, I gathered he'd probably wondered exactly what he'd got himself hooked up with. I was starting to suspect there was worse to come.

"So, after you checked out the accident, what did you do?"

"We turned around and drove back to my house."

"Did you stay together for the weekend?"

"No. She was too disappointed, in me . . . and Grandda. She left me at my lodgings, and I didn't see her until Saturday. But by then she was as nice as could be. She came and got me and we went to her house until Sunday." He shifted uncomfortably. "I did try to talk her into going to the police, but she said we were in God's hands and what would be, would be. She was very different, very sweet . . . "

Never mind God's hands, I'm sure Coral-Lyn had used something else to keep him in line.

"Did you talk to Tormod? Or go back there?"

"No, we tried his phone but nobody answered."

"Didn't you worry that he might have got ill?"

"Not really. I never spoke to him on weekends, and we thought that Lisa MacKenzie was with him. We decided to wait until Monday and then see what we could do. But then we got the call while we were demonstrating at the airport that Grandda had died. Lynnie insisted this was another message from God. She said nobody need ever know that he'd changed his mind about selling the house. I would inherit it and we could have the centre as we'd planned. She burned the papers that she found in Mrs. MacDonald's briefcase. She said it was better if we didn't say anything at all about being there on Friday. It would only complicate matters. I was so upset I wasn't thinking clearly, and I just went along with everything she said."

I'd gained on the Nissan and could see it now. It turned off the main road onto a side road.

"Is that the way?"

"Yes, please hurry."

I roared around the turn and up a bumpy gravel road. A sign said TO THE BUTT and, hardly more than two minutes later, I

saw the lighthouse and a small parking lot to the right of it. Coral-
Lyn had her head down on the dashboard in prayer position but
as soon as she saw us pulling in, she jumped out of her car, made
some frantic "leave me alone" gestures, and set off at the run up
the slope towards the cliffs. Andy scrambled out of my car but
despite all the best will in the world, he couldn't walk, and he
yelped with pain. He literally dropped to his hands and knees and
tried to crawl after her.

There wasn't another soul in the parking lot. "Try to get to the
lighthouse and get help," I ordered him.

I sprinted after Coral-Lyn. There was a flat grassy shelf at the
top of the cliffs and she was heading straight for the edge. I knew
that I didn't stand a chance of grabbing her, so I tacked off to the
left, running hard but trying to approach her obliquely.

At the edge of the cliff, she dropped into a half-crouch and scut-
tled out onto a narrow projection. There were sheer drops all around
her. At the tip, she turned around to face me and sat down, hugging
her knees. I immediately slowed to a walk. I was struggling for breath
and I tried to suck in air as deeply as I could. I too, went into a
crouch, and still approaching from the side, I stopped at the end of
the projectory. I squatted. I'd be able to move quickly if necessary,
although she was tantalizingly out of reach. In spite of the wind,
which was blowing fiercely, we could just about hear each other.

"You've come for me, haven't you?"

I didn't answer that. "Why don't you come back to the car and
we can talk properly."

She actually giggled. "What you mean is you're going to
arrest me."

"Why would I do that?'

"Because I killed Grandda, of course."

"Did you, Coral-Lyn? How did you do that?"

"He was a wicked man, you know, even if he was Andy's
grandda. We had made an arrangement, and he wasn't going to go
through with it."

"I heard about the centre for religious studies you are planning. It sounds like a very worthwhile project."

Yes, I was trying to keep her talking.

"It would have changed the life of the entire island. But he wouldn't listen to me."

She leaned her chin on her knees, and she looked about five years old. I couldn't risk taking my eyes off her, but I didn't get the sense anybody else was in the vicinity, which in this case was probably a good thing. Unless they had a lasso, she was unassailable.

"You went over to Tormod's house on Friday, did you, after you left Andy?"

My voice was as conversational as you can get when you're sitting on the edge of a high cliff being buffeted by wind.

"Yes, and it was a good thing I did. All of his wickedness was pouring out of his mouth. I could have left him, but I prayed for guidance and God said to help him," Like her posture, her voice, high and thin, was that of a child. "I felt so sorry for him, even though he'd been so very wicked. God said it was only kind to put him out of his misery. So I did. It didn't hurt him. He actually thanked me afterward when he was lying there. He looked so peaceful at last, and I knew he was grateful."

She smiled at me in an "aren't I a good girl" way that made my blood run cold.

"Did you use the pillow?"

"That's right."

Even trying to suffocate somebody as weak as Tormod probably was a needed determination and strength of conviction that no soft words of *it didn't hurt* could justify. She was a frightening woman.

She brushed at her coat in a matter-of-fact manner, then suddenly stood up and raised her arms sideward. "If God wants me, He will take me."

A fierce gust of wind caught her. She staggered, lost her balance, and with a shriek, she fell over backwards. There was nothing I could do. I dropped on my belly and scrabbled to the edge of the cliff, holding onto the sides as best I could. I was in time to see her hit the sea. Her coat billowed around her but, after a momentary thrashing with her arms, she didn't struggle. Either she was stunned by the impact or she was intent on death. A wave came and slammed her into the rocks, then pulled her out on the ebb, and then slammed her again.

CHAPTER THIRTY-NINE

It was more than four hours later before I could leave the scene. The cliff was too steep for the lighthouse attendants to climb down safely, and they had to send for a boat to come around the headland and collect the body, which was drifting out to sea. There was nothing we could do. Andy was distraught, and I sat with him while he sobbed and went over and over what had happened between them. He was consumed with guilt for going along with the deceptions of Friday night. I didn't tell him about Coral-Lyn confessing to the murder of his grandfather. That would have to come from the officer who would be in charge of the case. The local constable arrived, then reinforcements from Stornoway, because there started to be a buildup of onlookers. Gillies came with them and good old Dr. MacBeth, who immediately shot Andy full of tranquillizers and took him off somewhere. I was very glad to see Gill. The local constable was tense and inexperienced, and he seemed to be blaming me for precipitating the suicide.

"You chased her?" he'd asked in an incredulous tone of voice. I didn't need that. Would it have made a difference if I hadn't run after her? Rationally, I knew it wouldn't, but in the same way as Andy, I kept playing the last scene over and over again in my mind. What if I'd said something else? If I'd steered her away from talking about the murder? I poured all this out to Gill, who just let me talk it through, including my feeling that Coral-Lyn had created her own primitive justice and, in a weird way, I admired her for it. Together we checked the trunk of the Nissan and found, unwrapped, a green tweed cushion, heavily stained. There was a small possibility that Coral-Lyn was delusional and that Tormod had coughed blood into the pillow, but from what I'd seen in the bedroom, I accepted her version. She must have cleaned everything up in an attempt to erase all traces of her presence. An interesting mix of sanity and insanity. Gill impounded the car and said he'd have Tormod's body exhumed immediately. The forensic evidence would show conclusively what had happened.

Finally, it was all over. Coral-Lyn's body was recovered and the boat disappeared. The sea was rough, and they had a hard time getting out of the cove. The lighthouse attendants and the few tourists who had come to see the scenery started to move away, all of them subdued by the tragedy.

"What are you going to do now?" Gill asked me.

"I'm going to Duncan MacKenzie's." I thought I owed it to Joan to tell her what had transpired. She didn't know that a whisper of suspicion about her had fluttered across my mind, but I knew. And to tell the truth, I wanted to be with her.

The wind was pulling at my face. I was cold and dead tired — an aftermath of adrenaline outpouring. Gill pulled me close to him, and for a moment I was warm in his arms.

"I already know better than to tell you not to drive by yourself, but you've got my mobile number. Ring me later, will you?"

"Of course."

"Take care of yourself."

"*Tapadh leat,*" I answered in my best Gaelic.

He let go.

The drive back to Carloway was at a much saner speed. I had the windows wide open for a long time. I tuned the radio to a Gaelic station and distracted myself by trying to see if I understood what the announcer was saying. I didn't.

Finally, I turned into Duncan's farm and the dogs came racing over, barking. As soon as they recognized me, they each gave me a perfunctory tail wag, then ran off again to take care of business, which seemed to be hanging out in front of the barn. I pulled over into a parking space just as Duncan came out of the shop.

"Hi. Is Joan in the house?"

"She is not. She's gone for a walk over to the cove."

"How long will she be gone do you think?"

"She only just left. We heard about the American girl. What a terrible thing. Was it true you were there? Dorinda MacLeod rang us, but she'd heard it from Will MacIver, who helps out at the lighthouse, so we didn't know what was true and what was made up."

"I was there."

Something must have showed on my face, because his tone became less brusque.

"Aye. That must have been a terrible thing then, no mind ye're with the polis."

"It was." I got out of the car. "I'll take a walk myself. Which way to the cove?"

He pointed. "Take that footpath." He checked his wristwatch. "I'd come with you meself, but I've got to get my stock unpacked."

Thank God for that.

"You'll be after needing proper shoes. It's a decent hike."

I thrust out my foot. "Good, sturdy walking shoes, made to order."

"Aye. Your mother's still not quite herself. Take mind."

I didn't trust myself to say anything, so I just nodded and set off across the yard towards the gate. Nic, no longer limping, started after me.

"Can she come?"

"Aye. Just don't let her talk you into throwing sticks. I don't want her coming down lame again."

The rain had stopped, and even though the air was damp and on the chilly side, it was so fresh I was forced to take some deep breaths. With the border collie bounding ahead, I set off along the path, aware that Duncan was watching me — and aware of his disapproval.

The footpath wound up and around a hill that was dotted with clumps of dainty pink wildflowers. The ubiquitous sheep looked up warily at the sight of the dog, but Nic, knowing she was off-duty, ignored them and trotted ahead of me, like a normal dog, not a halfling. At the top of the hill, I paused. To the left, several low, humpbacked islands rose out of the slate-grey sea, and all along the curving headland to both right and left the waves crashed against the rocks in white spumes. The narrow footpath divided here, and I wouldn't have known which direction to go in, but Nic had bounded on ahead and was waiting for me. Left it was then.

Duncan had described it as "a decent walk," and that was one way to put it. After a good twenty minutes of clambering over rocky outcrops and dipping down and then up hills, I would have called it an "indecent" walk. Suddenly Nic halted and peered down over the cliff edge, wagging her tail enthusiastically. Then she jumped down and disappeared. We'd found Joan.

She was sitting on a rock at the bottom of a deep cleft. The sea surged in, then quieted down, splashed against the rocks, then withdrew. Joan was petting the dog and she looked up and saw me standing there. There was joy in her face that touched me straight in the heart.

I climbed down to join her, having to jump from rock to rock like an arthritic elk. When I got close to her, she called out.

"Are you all right, Chris? We heard what happened."

"Yes, I'm fine."

I didn't sit down, and she remained on the outcrop, hugging her knees.

"We heard Coral-Lyn Pitchers threw herself over the cliffs and that you'd tried to stop her."

"I guess that's it in a nutshell."

"You've always been a brave girl."

I'd never heard that from her before, and it was sweet to hear, even though I wasn't entirely sure it was true. She picked up a piece of driftwood and tossed it into the sea for Nic who gave an excited yelp and dived after it.

"Duncan said he doesn't want her chasing sticks."

She shrugged. "She's all right."

The dog climbed out, shook herself, showering me with cold water, and dropped the piece of wood at my feet, staring at it until the second it moved. I threw it out for her.

I squatted down on the rock. The thick moss was amazingly soft, and down here we were sheltered from the wind. Joan waved her hand in the direction of the sea.

"I used to come here all the time. You've never lived on an island, and Lake Ontario doesn't cut it." She was searching for words. "Here, the sea is always around you, so you never stop feeling its presence, and it's got moods, same as people have moods. Sometimes it acts all mad, as if doesn't give a shit whether you live or die; other times it's as gentle as a loving mother. Out there, past the cove, it's wild, but when I sat here on this selfsame rock, I used to believe I'd tamed it like you tame a wild creature. No matter how much it bucked and chafed against the walls of the cliffs, by the time it got to me, it was quiet and it couldn't hurt me. So we'd talk, the sea and me."

Beyond where we were, the sea stretched, restless and powerful out to the horizon. White caps topped the waves. Here in the cove, the edges of the rocks were worn smooth and round by the winds and as the sea surged through the opening, it was forced to quiet down, until near our feet it was splashing softly on the submerged rocks.

Joan took a quick glance at me to see how I was reacting. Seeing my expression reassured her and she visibly relaxed.

"When my stepmother ruled the roost, whenever I could, I'd run off and come here. I'd fix on one of the waves that was coming in and imagine that was my mammy out there, sitting on the foam like a mermaid. I'd watch while she rolled in, and then she'd come through the gap and eventually that wave would splash against my rock. I'd lean down so the spray would hit my face, and I'd pretend it was Mammy, licking me the way a bitch licks her pup. The salty taste was because she was crying for me."

She was silent and I waited for those memories to subside a little.

"Things must have rough for you. I don't know anything about it. You just gave me all those stories about having no family and your parents being dead." I reached over and touched her shoulder. "Joan, I'm not reproaching you or blaming you at the moment, but you can imagine I was taken aback when I saw that photo and Mrs. MacNeil told me the story. An entire family exists that I had no knowledge of. Sarah MacDonald isn't just a traffic-accident fatality, she is related to me by blood, one way or another."

Joan sighed. "I suppose you've figured it out, knowing you."

"She was your child, not your stepmother's?"

"She was." Her eyes teared up and she wiped at them with the end of the scarf.

"And Pappy was Tormod MacAulay?"

"You're a clever clogs, aren't you."

"That's why you came back here, wasn't it? To let both him and Sarah know about their relationship?"

"Clever again." She sat for a moment staring out at the sea swaying and surging along the foot of the cliffs outside the perimeter of the cove. I could hear sea birds crying overhead.

"So, after all these years, you decided to put things right . . . "

"Charlene calls it getting closure," she said primly.

"Right, closure. So you came home and you went out to see Tormod?"

Her sigh was heart-wrenching. "I did."

"What I don't understand though, is where you were in all of this? You were confronting the man who in many ways ruined your life. He'd taken advantage of you. He was a close relative, older, not to mention a married man. You must have hated him for what he did to you."

She swivelled her head and stared at me. Her eyes were shadowed with misery.

"Oh, Chris, you couldn't be more wrong. Tormod MacAulay was the love of my life."

CHAPTER FORTY

It was my turn to be shocked. I don't know what I'd expected, but there was no doubt that this time she was speaking
the truth.

"That's not what you said before." A lame remark, I must admit.

She actually gave me a little grin, almost mischievous. "I said
I didn't *like* him. You made an assumption."

"Oh cut it out, Joan. You were deliberately misleading me."

She flashed me a contrite look. "You're right, I was. I was too
upset. I just didn't want you to know how I felt."

I realized how much she had learned to protect herself from
me. That was not a good feeling.

"So what do you mean when you say he was the love of your
life? I thought that role was ascribed to Duncan."

She didn't miss the edge in my voice that I'm ashamed to say
slipped through. Hey, old grievances don't disappear overnight.
We'd gone through at least *three* major enthusiasms in my lifetime.

"Duncan and I were teenagers. You always think you're Romeo
and Juliet at that age."

Nic came back from stick-fetching and drenched me again.
Joan was about to throw another stick and I caught her hand.

"Will you stop that for a minute. I'm getting soaked, she looks
like she's limping again, and I want to talk seriously to you."

She actually looked afraid, and I tried to temper my irritation.

"I'm sorry, I didn't mean to get snippy with you, but it's maddening when you give me half-answers like this."

"All right, but let me tell it in my own way, will you? Don't correct my grammar every five minutes."

An exaggeration, but I winced.

"Okay. Go ahead. I'll listen. But I don't understand. You just said Tormod was the love of your life, but you had a child by him when you were, what? Fourteen?"

"Sarah was born two weeks before my fifteenth birthday." She sighed. "I never really knew her the way a mother knows a child, but I am so very sad that she is dead. I was hoping that we could at least become friends."

Nic had been waiting patiently, and she jumped up, came over to Joan, and started to nuzzle her hand. Joan buried her face in the dog's fur for a moment.

"I was one of those girls who blossom early into adolescence. Not like you. You were late. You might not think so now, but I was considered a pretty girl. Suddenly, it seemed to me, when I was hardly thirteen, all sorts of boys — and men for that matter — were looking at me differently." Joan smoothed the baggy raincoat over her knees. "Annie watched me like a hawk as soon as I started to bud and the lads were coming around. She soon twigged that I'd got preggies. 'Who did this to you? Who's the father?' I'll never forget that afternoon. She'd come into my room and she was quiet, almost sympathetic. I was scared to death. I knew what was happening to me and I was just a kid. So I told her . . . and did she sing a different tune. '*You wicked, wicked girl.*' Slap, slap. 'How could you try to drag this good man into your own disgrace.' She was related to Tormod by marriage, you see, and she couldn't bear to think of the shame this would bring on *her* family. I never mentioned his name again. I lied and said it was really some German lad who was working on the trawlers. Then she told my Pappy — not about Tormod, though — and he beat me with his belt until I was screaming so loud Annie had to stop him. I prayed I would miscarry after that, but no such luck. Remember, the attitude towards abortions was different from what it is nowadays. No local doctor would have performed one. So . . . I was locked in my room for two days —I'll tell you about that another time.

"They came up with a scheme. I was to be sent off to the mainland to one of the church-run homes for unwed mothers. . . . Oh Lord, defend me forever again against the righteous. . . . Annie would put it out that she was pregnant and then claim the child was hers. She'd been desperate for a bairn ever since they married. So that's what happened." Joan stuffed her fists under her raincoat, making it swell out. "She even took to padding her clothes so she would look pregnant. . . The baby was born and she came and got her, making up some story about going into labour while she was visiting me. The islanders aren't stupid. I don't know how many people she really fooled. Anyway, surprise, surprise, she took to Sarah as if she really was her own child, and I was pushed out even more.

"I came home one more time only. Nobody would talk to me — not my brothers, not my Pappy. And I couldn't stand watching that mean cow make such a fuss over the baby. My baby that I wasn't allowed to have anything to do with. I never went back, and when I could legally leave school, I did. I got a job in a hairdressing salon, sweeping the floor. Then I met the Cohens, accepted the position of a nanny, and the rest, as they say, is history.

"Did Tormod know you'd had his child?"

She hesitated. "I didn't tell him and he didn't ask."

"Naturally, then he wouldn't have to take responsibility."

I could feel myself getting all judgemental again, so I picked up the stick and threw it for Nic

"I didn't really want to tell him, anyway," she continued. "If the truth had come out, it would have ruined his life. He wouldn't have been able to stay on the island. Especially in those days, people wouldn't have tolerated him." She stroked the scarf so tenderly, I guessed it must have belonged to Tormod. Lisa had missed that one.

"So I was your second pregnancy without benefit of clergy. That must have really sent them off the deep end. I assume they did know, which was why you got disinherited and declared missing in Canada."

"That's right. You see, my Pappy hadn't wanted me in the first place. He was almost forty when I was born, and he was hard as nails and colder than the cod. He could just about tolerate the boys but, for whatever reason, he couldn't stand having a daughter. He thought all women were original Eves, ready to lead the pure man astray."

"He's right about that."

She grinned and we shared a bit of misanthropy together. "As far as Pappy was concerned, I was going to end up populating an entire island with bastard children."

"So you told him you had run off with a Red Indian?"

"I was dating a fellow who was part Cree, and he lived in Timmins — let's just say I elaborated." She cast another anxious glance at me to see if I was judging her. I kept my face neutral, although *the* question had popped into my mind. I let it ride for now. Joan took my hand in hers.

"You're cold. Do you want my gloves? I'm warm as toast."

"Thanks. I wouldn't mind."

She handed over her sheepskin gloves and they were indeed welcome. Even in this sheltered cove, I was beginning to get really cold. I needed my winter jacket and fur-lined boots. To heck with it being May.

"Back to Tormod. We seem to be avoiding the subject."

"It hurts," she said, but after a moment she continued. "Oh, Chris, he was so handsome and he could charm the pants off a parson, as we'd say. But most of all he was so kind to me. I must have been one of the most miserable kids you'd ever meet. By the time I was fourteen, I didn't know if I was going to survive. In spite of all the lads who were hanging around, I thought the loneliness would kill me, like the tuberculosis, which carried off so many young ones. Then that summer, Tormod's wife had to go and take care of her mother down in Benecula. They asked me if I would help mind his children for a few weeks. I'd done that before — you saw the snap of us together — so I went over. I hadn't seen him all winter, and I'd developed. I wasn't a skinny kid any more. He'd always been good to me, but this was different. He talked to me like an equal, made me laugh, made me think I was an attractive girl. I fell crazy in love with him. I was like somebody who'd been on a starvation diet and, all of a sudden, there's this banquet in front of me. He wasn't happy either. He'd never loved Margaret, and he certainly enjoyed female charms. How could he resist?"

No matter what she said, in my opinion, it was statutory rape, and my disapproval must have shown on my face.

"Chris, you have to understand, kids grew up faster on the island. He did fend me off a couple of times, but I was too determined. He was a human being. So we did the deed. Only three times, but that was enough. I got pregnant. And the rest I've just told you." She looked into my eyes. "Do you think I was such a bad girl?"

I smoothed away a strand of hair from her cheek. "Oh, Joan, I don't think that at all."

And I didn't. I was seeing something I'd never seen before. We both got a bit awkward with this dramatic shift in our relationship, and I got to my feet.

"Do you feel like walking a bit?" I asked her. "I'm getting stiff."

"Sure. As a matter of fact, I was going to suggest we go along to the village. That's where I was born and lived for a while, till we moved into Carloway. You want ancestors, I'll show you ancestors."

I helped her up and Nic came over, eager to go on a walk. Patches of blue sky were showing through the grey and an uncertain sun came out briefly. As we climbed back to the top of the cliff, a strong wind grabbed at us, and I was reminded of Coral-Lyn. I didn't know when I was going to tell Joan about Tormod's murder, but I had to trust there would be an appropriate time.

The path was narrow and we had to walk single file. Joan went on ahead of me which meant she was talking over her shoulder.

"I thought I owed it to Sarah to tell her the truth, but I'm not so sure now it was the right thing to do. When I told her Tormod was her natural father, she was livid. He had to put the kibosh on her relationship with his son because he suspected the truth, but she'd always thought it was because he didn't consider her good enough. Isn't it ironic that she'd fall for a MacAulay like I did. So they had a big barney. She was more than a little pie-eyed by this time. The rest of it you know." Joan faced me so she could talk more easily. "I'm sorry I didn't tell you this before, Chris." She turned away and pointed. "There used to be a ruined house just over this hill. It'll be sheltered and private. Let's go there." She left the path and crossed the cropped grass. "Good, it's still here."

In the lea of the hill were the remains of an old stone house. The roof was broken but the walls were intact. She pushed open the door and we went inside. The floor was carpeted with sheep droppings mostly, but there was a bench built into the wall along one side and there was a tartan shawl lying there.

"I thought so," Joan cried. "That's the shawl that Tormod gave me. He was working on it when we arrived, and I said I was cold. Nerves probably, but he gave it to me to keep warm. He hadn't finished it yet." I could see that the strands were unfinished at the ends. "After you did that sleeping thing with me, I started to have more bits of memories. I could remember walking away from the accident towards the cliffs. God knows how I did it really, but I must have ended up in here for a few hours." She put the shawl against her cheek. "There were some sheep in here as well, and they all kept me warm. It was a vile night, pissing rain and black as the peat." She shuddered. "I feel so bad about what happened, Chris. I was so dead set on telling the truth. Well you know, I'm wondering if sometimes it isn't better to leave things be. It was my truth after all that I was sticking their noses in. Maybe Sarah wouldn't have died the way she did if I hadn't got all that shit stirred up. And poor Tormod. He was so upset. It probably brought on the hemorrhage."

She looked so abysmally miserable that I decided it was time to tell her what had likely happened. I told it as gently as I could, but there is no way to blunt the brutality of a murder that involves people you know. She burst into tears, crying over and over, "Poor Tormod, poor Tormod." She was sitting on the bench at this point, and I held out my arms and she slid over to me and cried so desperately I thought she might not be able to stop. After a long time, we let go. She blew her nose into a tissue I'd found in my pocket, but she didn't move away from me.

"There's one more thing, Chris." She glanced over at me timidly. "It's about Duncan. He's a good man. I like him even more than I did when we were kids." Another blow into the tissue, so that her voice was muffled. "We did have what you'd call a fling when I was on the mainland, just before I left for Canada with the Cohens."

I stared at her in horror. "Oh God, Joan, don't tell me he's my natural father?"

She wiped her nose. "Well actually, Chris, he is."

CHAPTER FORTY-ONE

It was my turn to walk off and she had to trot after me. After all these years of longing to know who my biological father was, I was thrown off balance. Duncan MacKenzie! True, I hadn't known him very long, but he wasn't a man I had warmed to. Probably it would have been a shock whomever she'd named, but I wasn't in a rational frame of mind and all I could think of was "Why him?"

We walked for about twenty minutes, in which time I said exactly three words. "Does he know?" to which Joan replied, "No, he doesn't." Somewhere along the walk, Nic had gone back home.

"Do you still want to see the village?" Joan asked.

"Why not? As you say, I've always wanted ancestors. It's raining cats and dogs with ancestors now."

She smiled uneasily at this, but we went on.

We trudged across a rocky beach, up the path to a double gate. Ahead of us the slope was dotted with several low, grey stone houses, all of them with neatly thatched roofs. We pushed open the gate and followed a paved road through the centre of the village. Joan stopped in front of one of the houses. A hanging sign proclaimed it was the public toilet. A young fellow carrying a backpack almost as long as himself walked past us and ducked through the low door.

"Duncan warned me the village had been reconstructed," said Joan. "Our toilet was out in the back grass in summer and was a bucket in the byre in winter. Add some chickens, two or three dogs lying around, a cow tethered in the back, and the women coming and going to the shore with their heavy wash in a tub on their hips. It was never as quiet as this."

We walked on down the road, and she stopped again in front of one of the houses, which advertised itself as a self-catering unit. She was chattering at me over my own silence.

"The three MacLeod sisters lived here. They never married, even though they were all as lovely as daisies when they were young. Anna was a weaver and she designed her own patterns. She even won a prize for one of her rugs. It was a glass bowl and it sat in pride of place on her dresser. She'd let me take it down and look at it. I handled it as carefully as if it were as fragile as a new babe." Joan's face was wistful. "Nowadays, Anna would be considered an artist and she'd have a studio instead of a byre where the cow lived in winter. All three of them were middle-aged when I knew them, but I'd come here whenever I could and always be welcome. They made a pet of me at a time when I so needed to be fussed over. Christina would always make me a cuppa, even when I was young. She'd boil the water and the tea leaves together in a pot over the fire. It tasted of the peat smoke and was so strong almost nobody else could drink it."

I remembered how much Joan had liked her cup of tea in the mornings. When I hit my snobbish, critical adolescence, this was one more thing I held against her. All the other parents I knew drank coffee.

"Am I related to them?"

She managed to laugh. "Not directly. We have a lot of catching up to do, Chris. Like I said, I wanted to sever my roots completely when I left. Which was stupid and impossible anyway, but what can you do?"

What indeed.

We walked on and went into one of the black houses, which had been restored to a period in the 1950s and was crammed with furniture. The stone walls were lined by wood siding, painted a shiny beige, the linoleum on the floor was beige and brown. Nothing matched

"I think they've gathered together whatever they could find from lots of different people. That was Mrs. Duncan MacLeod's radio for sure. Her son brought it back from the mainland when we got electricity, and she was so proud of it. Oh my . . . " She halted in front of the dresser. "There are Auntie Peggie's best teacups. She'd bought them in London when she was with the herring boats. I don't know if she ever used them to drink out of."

There was a curtained bed tucked into the corner of the room, which was also the living room/kitchen. I could see that the only other room adjoining had two bunk-style beds, also with curtains.

"Most people had big families, and it was customary for unmarried sisters or brothers to stay living with the family. They were a healthy lot and most of the women lived into their nineties. Our house was about this size, but there was a little room off the kitchen, which I had. No bigger than a cupboard really." She shuddered. "I can't stand to think about it."

We walked out into a room that adjoined the entrance. It was unfurnished, more like a stable than a room.

Joan paused. "This is where the cow would be for the winter, and the chickens. I was good at milking." She pointed at an iron tub by the door. "Look at that! They've found a pee-tub. They weren't as common when I was a wee one as they were earlier, but every household had one."

The tub looked too big to serve as a chamber pot. "What were they exactly?"

She was happy to go on sharing her stories. "The weaving industry was crucial to the islands for a long time, and tweed became very popular, especially with the British. However, the sheared wool was oily, and before it could be woven into tweed it had to be cleaned. This was before you could get ammonia easily mind you, so they used urine to wash out the oil. The pee-tub was in every cottage." She held her nose. "It could get pretty strong back here when the tub filled up. We'd have a giggle about the fact that, on a humid day, the English la-di-das were likely to walk around in their tweeds exclaiming, '*Hm, dahling, smell that glorious heather!*' What they were actually smelling was human pee."

That broke my sulk, and we were laughing together when a young man ducked through the entrance. He was impressively clean cut, with short hair and a neat, unobtrusive, dark windbreaker and jeans. I would have pegged him as secret service immediately, even without the radio communicator in his ear with the strange growth-like curly cord down the back of his head.

"Good afternoon, I'm Simon Wilson. I'm with British security and I wonder if I could ask you a big favour, which is to leave off your tour for the moment and wait outside."

His accent was what I'd call posh British, and he was so polite, he was butter coated.

"What's wrong?" Joan asked.

"Nothing wrong at all, Ma'am. We just need to clear the area for security reasons."

"My god, a bomb?"

He smiled again. "No, Ma'am. Nothing like that."

"I believe the old homestead is about to be visited by Wills himself." I said to her.

She stared at me. "The prince?"

I nodded at the officer. "That's it isn't it?"

"We do have a royal party arriving."

Mr. Wilson's expression was friendly, but his eyes were ice. He'd had too much experience of the worst excesses of star-struck bystanders. He looked as if he were hoping we were too old for hysteria, and wouldn't suddenly lift our sweaters to display our breasts.

"Do you mind, Ma'am?" He indicated we should leave the house, and, rather excited, I must admit, I followed after him. Joan was behind me, also rather twittery. The royal lad had that effect. Outside, a couple of uniformed officers from the Northern Constabulary had appeared. Some tourists had been moved from the gift shop and were "standing back."

Then I saw two men walking up from the direction of the beach. Each was carrying an ordinary fisherman's pail with a closed lid.

One was Colin MacLeod, the other man was tall and thin, with a mane of dark hair almost to his shoulders, Black John in the flesh. At the same time as that registered on my brain, I saw two dark-blue sedans pull into the parking lot at the upper end of the village. Both had the royal-standard pennants flying from the front of the car.

Oh God. Colin was up to mischief. Both men were moving with far too much deliberation, and they were carrying the pails out rather carefully from their sides.

I grabbed Joan's arm. "Quick. Look at those men coming towards us. What do you think they're carrying?"

Responding to the urgency in my voice, but not understanding, she squinted at Colin and his pal.

"If I didn't know better, I'd say they were piss buckets, but I haven't seen them in years . . . "

The passengers were getting out of the sedans. First two bodyguards, then a tall young man with reddish-blond hair. He was casually dressed in jeans and a blue blazer. By any standard he was a handsome lad, but transferred excitement made the air around him shine. He gave a helping hand to his companion, a young woman who was also tall, with short, fair hair. I had an impression of easy grace from the young man and self-consciousness from the girl.

That was all I had time for. I stepped quickly over to Wilson, who had taken up his position in front of the cottage entrance.

"I'm a police officer from Canada. I'll show you ID later. Those two men at the gate are planning to do something. One of them is a known agitator. His name is Black John."

He didn't wait for a further explanation. He was an experienced officer and he observed the same thing I did. He started to walk forward to intercept Colin and his pals and spoke into his lapel. I went with him.

"They're planning to embarrass the prince. I think they've got urine in those buckets and they intend to throw it on him."

"Shit!" said Wilson, appropriately.

Colin had put down his bucket so he could unfasten the gate. The other man waited behind him. We were there now, and Wilson grabbed hold of the top bar.

"Excuse me, Sir, I can't let you through at the moment."

Over my shoulder, I could see the royal party was almost at the door of the black house. A little smattering of applause from the watching attendants and backpackers. William smiled and waved to them. Black John suddenly pushed on the gate, taking Wilson by surprise.

Colin seized his chance, grabbed his bucket, and was almost through the gap. I was hovering on the right of the secret service, and I shoved Colin back with my shoulder. He lost his balance and sat down, the bucket fell over and the lid came off, spilling stinking yellow urine all over his own pants. Black John tried to get past, but Wilson was too fast for him and pulled his hand through the bars so that he was jammed against the gate. Two of the uniformed officers saw what was happening and came running over.

"MacLeod, what the hell are you doing?"

Colin was too busy trying to wipe off his pants on the grass to answer, but Black John shouted out.

"Give us back our land. We won't tolerate cock-boys any longer."

Wilson spoke into his coat again. Immediately, one of the prince's bodyguards came out of the black house and ran over to us. The spectators watched curiously. An adventure indeed on a grey, ordinary day.

"What's happening?" asked the bodyguard. He was thirtyish and formidable.

"These two toerags were about to douse the prince with piss." Wilson had temporarily lost his cool.

He was still holding Black John jammed against the gate and had twisted his arm up painfully through the bar. He'd break the wrist if necessary.

"We'll ask you to come with us." The bodyguard never lost his polite, quiet voice, but I'd hardly ever heard a tone so chilling and powerful. In the meantime, I picked up the second bucket, which was now on our side of the gate, and carried it to the grass. To be safe, I emptied out the contents. Colin finally acknowledged me, but he didn't look embarrassed or ashamed. Just arrogant.

"We have a right to make a public protest. This is a democracy, isn't it?"

He was getting to his feet, but the uniformed officer, whom I realized was Constable Fraser, bent over him. He said something in Gaelic and Colin sat down again. A translation wasn't necessary.

"Everything under control?" asked the prince's bodyguard. A nod from Wilson and he hurried back to the black house.

I kept my eyes on Colin and his pal, as did Wilson and the constable. I heard more applause and gathered that the royal party had emerged. A quick glance over my shoulder and I saw the long-striding prince was walking back to his car. The girl was beside him. The second bodyguard gave a quick wave to Wilson. In a minute, they were all in the car and one of the black sedans drove out of the parking lot.

"Are you going to let us go?" demanded Colin. "If you're not, I want to know why we're being held."

"How about vandalism?" said Fraser. "You've spilled piss all over a public walkway, and that's an offence."

Joan had remained at the door of the black house, and she now came over to us. "What's going on?"

I stepped away from the gate. "Mr. MacLeod here was trying to perpetrate some public mischief."

She stared at him. "Colin MacLeod! You're Mairi MacKenzie's husband. Why aren't you home with your wee babe? Shame on you."

Hey Joan, way to tell it like it is!

Two more beefy constables arrived and they hustled the two men unceremoniously into their police van. Black John tried to shout out slogans to the spectators who were hanging around the cottage, but to my delight the onlookers, all of them ordinary middle-aged people and a few attendants from the shop, yelled back. 'Shame! Shame on you!"

Finally, the official cars left, except for Agent Wilson who stayed to thank me and to get my name and address in case of later charges against the protesters.

Joan and I started our walk back to Duncan's house.

If you were to ask me what had been the most unusual day I'd ever spent in my life to date, I'd say this was it.

EPILOGUE

I was relieved that Duncan was in the barn when we got back to the house.

"I might as well tell him now and get it over with," said Joan.

"Are you sure you want to? I've waited all this time. I can wait a few more hours."

She saw through that one and smiled at me. "I'm sure. This is going to be a happy occasion anyway, not like the other things."

I hoped she was right about that.

"Go and make a pot of tea," said Joan. "And you'd better take out the whisky. It's in the cupboard to the right of the sink."

She headed off to the barn, and I went inside. I was so nervous. And I didn't even like the guy. And I was sure he didn't like me.

Nic was in the kitchen, and she greeted me like an old stick-throwing friend should be greeted and immediately ran off and rummaged for a ball that was in a toy box by the door. She dropped it at my feet and stared at it.

I kicked it away for her. I didn't think Duncan and I resembled each other at all. Was Joan telling the truth? But I knew she was. My father wasn't Elvis or a randy Paul McCartney. He was a domineering shepherd, who was currently out there in the barn hearing the news that this rude woman from Canada was his very own daughter.

The kettle boiled and, as I went to make the tea, I saw a piece of notepaper on the counter.

"*Lisa rang to see how Christine is doing. Please phone when you can.*"

A stab of pleasure at that. Wow, I had a grown half-sister. I liked Lisa and Mairi, not to mention my little niece, Anna. Too bad I also had a brother-in-law who was a lout, but I'd have to deal with that. And I wasn't going to let on that Lisa had tried to turn him in, either, which I was almost positive she'd done, that she was the anonymous letter writer and caller. I guess I'd find out later what sort of involvement she'd had with the White Dog group.

I made the tea, dropping in an extra spoonful of leaves for Joan. I found the whisky bottle and poured myself a shot, but then put it aside. I didn't need a crutch. I'd been fantasizing about this meeting for years. I wanted to be completely sober. Yeah right! I picked up the shot glass and swallowed a gulp of whisky. It went down smooth as cream, then hit my stomach like hot chilli.

Nic got to chase her ball three more times before I looked out of window and saw Joan and Duncan crossing the yard. She had her arm around his waist, and he was walking with his head bent. He didn't look too happy. Funny thing was, from this angle I could see that we did resemble each other. I'd inherited his frame. Rather wide shoulders, straight torso, and long legs. We also walked the same way. I know that probably doesn't sound genetically valid, but it was true. He had a long stride and slightly pronated with his right leg, just the way I do.

I stepped away from the window so they wouldn't see me watching. The door opened. Joan came in first and Duncan behind her. He was as nervous as I was. Damn it, we were all nervous, except the dog, who went over to say hello as if she hadn't seen him for hours.

"So . . . " I started, and he spoke at the same time.

"Shona says . . . "

That made us laugh and eased the tension — a fraction.

"You could give each other a kiss and a hug," said Joan.

My dismay was reflected in his face.

"All in good time, Pet. We've got to get used to each other for a wee while."

"I suppose we could shake hands," I said. "Father, I presume."

He didn't get the joke and looked puzzled, but took me literally and held out his hand. I stepped forward, and we shook hands. His palm was rough and callused. Suddenly, he grabbed my hand in both of his, then pulled me to him and hugged me hard.

"My goodness, my goodness. What on earth am I going to say to the girls?"

I extricated myself, not wanting to admit to myself how much I'd liked that hug.

"You'd better call them right away," said Joan. "Mairi is going to need you. Ask her if she wants to come and stay with us for now. . . . I told him about the idiot, Colin," she added.

"Tea first. I've got to sit down and have a cuppa before my knees give way."

I was happy that he was so affected. We all sat down at the kitchen table, and Joan poured the tea. I could see she was intensely relieved that we were getting along.

"We've got a lot of catching up to do," said Duncan.

Suddenly, Nic erupted into loud barks as we heard a knock at the door. Duncan got up to answer it, and Gill came in.

"Allo to Duncan, allo to Joan. Chris, I was hoping you'd still be here. I've got something for you." He handed me an envelope.

There was an embossed initial in the corner that looked familiar, but I didn't immediately twig. I opened it. Inside was a seven-by-five photograph of a handsome young man with blond-red hair. The picture was signed, *William Wales. Thank you for your timely help.*

I shrieked like a smitten teenager.

"One of his aides told him what you'd done. He had them stop off at the local station with the picture. He's got good manners, that young lad has."

Suddenly and absurdly, I was choking on tears. I just couldn't help it, and believe me, I never cry.

"I don't understand," said Duncan. "What did he say?"

"Shh, it's not that, silly," said Joan in a most uncharacteristically motherly way. "She's had quite a day."

I was sitting between Joan and Duncan at the table, and they both leaned over and patted me. Duncan stroked my arm, rather as if I were one of the dogs.

I looked at him, through all the blubbering. "I'm not going to call you Dad, you know. So you can forget that."

Duncan grinned at me. "Here we often say Pappy."

"Maybe that."

Gillies, bless his heart, decided to await clarification and stayed where he was.

"I am going to refer to you as my daughter, no matter what you say," said Duncan.

"And so you should," chipped in Joan.

For some reason, that made me want to cry all over again, so I stood up instead.

"Hey, Pappy," I said over my shoulder. "Do you want a spot of *uisge beatha?*"

"Listen to her. She's got the Gaelic already."

I poured out shots for all of us, except Joan, who had some more tea.

"*Failte*," said Duncan, and he lifted his glass. "Welcome."

ACKNOWLEDGEMENTS

As always, I am grateful to the many people who generously shared their time and expertise with me. Detective-Sergeant Jim Smyth and Detective-Sergeant Ed Chafe answered my questions patiently and thoroughly about what it is like to be a forensic behavioural analyst in Ontario. Both Dr. Sharon Baltman and Dr. Albert Lyons gave me a quick course in pulmonary hypertension. The people I met on the Isle of Lewis completely lived up to their legendary reputation for hospitality. Our hostess, Christine Murray, was the best one could hope for. I can only describe Reverend Iain Campbell as a Renaissance man in a clerical collar. He was truly inspiring. Constable Philip MacRae spent time to initiate me into the workings of the Northern Constabulary, and Mike Ferris of MacDonald Real Estate did the same with the real-estate structures in the Hebrides. Thanks to Duncan Matheson and Dorinda and Calum MacKenzie and the dogs, who were our neighbours on the Isle of Lewis for all too brief a time.

Back in Toronto, Tony and Rena Cunningham made sure my Gaelic was on track. *Tapadh leibh.*